The S
The Back

By Stephen Romaine

The Book Cover

The cover illustration was created by artist Frederick Dielman, depicting the Abolition of Slavery Celebration in Washington, D.C., April 19, 1866. It first appeared in *Harpers Weekly*, Vol. 10, No. 489, May 12, 1866, Page 300.

Library of Congress, Public Domain.

Back of Book Illustration

A Postcard representation of the Van Lew mansion, Richmond, VA.

Virginia Commonwealth University Libraries, Public Domain.

"The First World War was a cruel and unnecessary war. The Civil War, with which it stands in comparison, was also certainly cruel, both in the suffering it inflicted on the participants and the anguish it caused to the bereaved at home. But it was not unnecessary."

John Keegan

Acknowledgements

Special thanks to Neal Fishman for his thoughtful suggestions and edits. Elisabeth Romaine for the additional editing of my many revisions, and her enduring patience. Randy Tatano provided insightful advice and formatting expertise for publishing the finished manuscript.

Extensive research was done for *Secret Army Behind Enemy Lines.* The bibliography in the appendix credits primary and secondary sources. A few books became pivotal for developing the fictionalized story. Elizabeth Varon's nonfiction, *Southern Lady, Yankee Spy: The True Story of Elizabeth Van Lew, a Union Agent in the Heart of the Confederacy,* is an authoritative source on the real Elizabeth Van Lew and her secret network of operatives. This was of great value in developing *Secret Army.* Although Van Lew's burned most of her papers, including correspondence she requested back from the U.S. Government in Washington, *A Yankee Spy in Richmond the Civil War Diary of "Crazy Bet" Van Lew,* edited by David Ryan, presents an intriguing composite view of the Richmond spy based on her own words from an occasional journal she secretly buried in her yard. Furgurson's, *Ashes of Glory: Richmond at War* provided detailed description of life in the Confederate Capital during the conflict.

The Confederate Dirty War by Jane Singer was also of great help. The book discloses the many planned efforts to commit large scale terrorist acts and insurrection in the North, secretly funded by the Secessionist Government in Richmond. The subtitle to Ms. Singer's book says it best: *Arson, Bombings, Assassination and Plots for Chemical and Germ Attacks on the Union.*

Michael and Jeff Shaara's Civil War trilogy, *God's and Generals, The Killer Angels,* and *The Last Full Measure,* set the bar for Civil War historical fiction. The way Jeff and his father Michael developed dialogue and story around seminal characters and Civil War battles in their books was a major influence.

Finally, thanks to Patrick Nolan, Villanova University, and Leo O'Connor, Fairfield University, who encouraged me to keep writing.

Author's Note:

Based in large part on real people and real events, the following story is a "connect the dots" historical fiction that postulates on the how and why certain outcomes of the Civil War may have been influenced, and in some cases significantly altered. The underlying plot assumes plausible hypotheticals based on extensive research that in some cases challenges consensus opinion. The storyline progresses with presentation of people and events based on the interpretation and conjecture of the author. Customs and mores were very different in the nineteenth century. Efforts were made to try not to make broad brush assumptions or stereotype groups of people, but instead highlight exceptional individuals who overcame adversity and hardship to help change the course of the war.

Acceptance of the language and dialects used in the United States in the mid-1800s has shifted in modern times. The dialogue in the story uses today's softer tones. However, the shift in the use of the language in no way serves to mitigate the egregious circumstances surrounding all aspects of American slavery, including laws that forbid the teaching of slaves to read and write. Speech patterns of the characters in the story vary primarily based on regional differences and access to education, not social class or ethnic background. In some cases, it might not be truly representative or completely accurate for the time. Despite the intentional barriers created to prevent slaves from reading and writing, some were secretly educated and others self-taught. Education became an important weapon against the tyranny of slavery.

The slaves and former slaves depicted in the story are referred to as African Americans. Yet at the time of the Civil War slaves were considered property, not American citizens with constitutionally protected rights. The appalling *Dred Scott* decision intensified the growing national divide on the subject of slavery when the Supreme Court essentially ruled that a slave, even one living on free soil, was still not an American. "The War Between the States," as it was often called, soon followed.

What happened as a result of the business of slave trading cannot be righted. But there were those, including a number of individuals within the Confederacy, who recognized much earlier than the general populace that the wrongs had to come to an end. A group of them, including Richmond elite, as well as from the working classes, banded together with slaves and former slaves to help defeat the Secessionist States, operating secretly behind enemy lines.

Introduction

Prevailing consensus suggests that covert intelligence activities during the Civil War were primitive at best on both sides. A southern belle living in Washington, D.C. may have helped influence the outcome for the Battle of Bull Run. Perhaps she heard information at a dinner party that was successfully passed on to Confederate General Beauregard. There may have been a few varying degrees of less than sophisticated spying beyond that, but certainly what little there was had little impact on the course of the war.

So goes general consensus, but what if this view is wrong? Much of the documents regarding espionage operations on both sides were destroyed – by Confederates when the war was lost, and by Union spies in Richmond who feared retribution from neighbors if their activities helping the North were ever exposed.

When Robert E. Lee decided to invade the North a second time, he swept west, using the Blue Ridge Mountains as a shield to disguise his early advance, and the bread basket of the Shenandoah Valley to reduce dependence on slow moving supply lines. How was it that the Union caught up and surprised him earlier than expected at Gettysburg? With the losses in Gettysburg and Vicksburg, the South knew they could no longer win a conventional war against the North. How did the North so successfully foil the numerous Confederate clandestine attempts to execute chemical and biological warfare against northern citizens? How did Grant take Richmond?

Secret Army Behind Enemy Lines underscores how two brave and intelligent women with no formal training in spy craft, as well as challenged by severely restrictive cultural and governmental constraints, create a highly effective clandestine network to help bring an end to one of the darkest periods in U.S. history.

Chapter 1: Richmond Burning

The city of Richmond was in a state of panic. Civil order was coming apart. Looters had spilled into the streets. It was April 2, 1865. To prevent resources falling into Federal hands, as the Confederate rear guard prepared to leave the city, they set fire to the tobacco warehouses and stockpiled munitions, setting off a cacophony of explosions. People in the street noticed that official papers in front of government offices were being burned.

An ill-advised city ordinance to destroy buildings containing alcohol further escalated the scale of destruction. Wind was kicking up, consuming more streets in the spreading flames. Almost all of the necessary elements appeared to be in place to assure the complete leveling of the downtown.

A final order came from the Confederate Secretary of the Navy to torch the James River Squadron. The fleet included several gun and torpedo boats, in addition to three ironclads, the *Richmond*, *Virginia II*, and the *Fredericksburg*. The late night shells and powder from these vessels set off a second round of blasts near Rocketts Landing, at the southeastern waterfront section of Richmond. Downtown residents could feel the ground tremble. It was as if the fleet had turned its guns on the already battered Confederate Capital.

Threats had been made in the past to burn the Van Lew mansion in the posh Church Hill section of Richmond. While Elizabeth Van Lew came from one of the city's exclusive upper class families, well regarded in the community, she herself had been suspected for most of the war of being a Unionist sympathizer, and perhaps also a Union spy.

Wayne Evans, a close friend and manager of the local dry goods store, and Daniel Gates, an African American servant of the Van Lew's, sat awake on the front porch for most of the night. At one point in the early evening

Wayne Evans joined Elizabeth in her back yard. There they had a full view of the downtown fires from the high ground of the Church Hill property on Grace Street. They could see the bursting shells lighting the sky.

Wayne said, "My store is already ruined. Not much will be left of the downtown when this is over."

"I am so sorry, Wayne. These very same men who pledged to defend us are now setting torch to our city," Elizabeth asserted, her voice cracking.

"Just awful. I'm thinking of moving west. Not sure you should stay here either, Elizabeth. All this built up resentment will not go away anytime soon. Do you think you and your mom will join your brother John Newton in Philadelphia?"

"This is our home. I will never leave Richmond. I think once this is all over John will probably want to come back here to stay."

The next day Elizabeth was up at five o'clock in the morning. Fires were still blazing. Clouds of smoke hung over the entire city. The smell from the burned buildings, gun powder and tobacco from the massive downtown warehouses set ablaze was stifling. Elizabeth could hardly stand it. She had no appetite.

Harriett Anne, the Van Lew cook, and Daniel's wife, told her that Daniel and Wayne had left earlier to help put out the downtown fires. She also shared with Elizabeth that some advance units of the Federal Army were now moving into Richmond. This was welcome news for Elizabeth who had waited eagerly for this day.

Elizabeth asked Harriett Anne if she could fetch Isaac, another servant. In the meantime, she brought out her American Flag, which she had hidden away, since receiving it as a present last Christmas. She asked Isaac to raise it up on the pole in the front yard that had been flagless since the secession of the Confederate States from the Union. The sun had just come up.

"You sure 'bout this, Miss Van Lew?" Isaac asked. "Lots of people 'round here ain't gonna like it."

He was the family coachman, and had been very protective of Elizabeth from the days he had taught her to ride horses. Isaac Drury had been with the Van Lew's the longest. He still had boyish good looks. Elizabeth noticed his calloused, weathered hands as he hoisted up the flag. If not for them and his graying hair, he could easily be mistaken for a much younger man.

A few passersby looked angry when they saw it. One old man yelled out a few crude taunts. It didn't faze Elizabeth, as she stood admiring the flag. Harriett Anne and Isaac stood next to her.

Isaac noticed her first. Mary Bowser, starting up the walkway from the street, carrying a sack with her belongings. She had been a slave housemaid with the Jefferson Davis family in their residence, the Confederate Executive Mansion.

"Hope you can put me up for a night or two," Mary called out.

"God bless you child," Elizabeth said as she hugged Mary.

Taking turns, the others did as well.

Continuing to stand close together, and in a much lower voice, Mary explained. "My husband, Wilson, has been scouting for the Union, but I don't know where. Not sure when he will be back. Our home is right in the thick of the fires. May not even make it."

"You know you are always welcome here, Mary," Elizabeth said.

"Glad you didn't decide to take the last train with the First Family," Isaac joked.

"They would have had to carry me kicking and screaming onto that train," Mary retorted.

"Chloe and I have your old room completely ready for you, Mary. You can stay as long as you like. So can Wilson."

"We might have some trouble here," Harriett Anne, said as she shifted her gaze toward the street.

Two disheveled men were passing through the front gate at the Grace Street entrance to the Van Lew property, just as Mary had done a few minutes earlier.

One of them noticed the flag, stopped and saluted. The other did the same.

"I don't think we need to worry," Mary whispered to Harriett Anne.

"Can we help you?" Elizabeth asked.

The first one said, "We were Union prisoners from Castle Thunder. Got out after the guards all left. My name is Clyde Benson, and this is Joel Higgins."

"I'm Elizabeth Van Lew, and this is Harriett Anne Gates, and Mary Bowser."

"Nice to meet you. Heard lots about you, Miss Van Lew," Higgins said.

"Castle Thunder. Conditions there were always terrible, can't imagine how bad it must have gotten lately," Elizabeth said.

"Really bad," the man named Benson said. "We had always been told that if we get out go to 2301 Grace Street."

"You came to the right place," Elizabeth said, smiling. "You can sleep here. We can also get you something to eat."

"That's very kind of you, ma'am. We only need a place to stay for one night. If you could put us up and don't mind. We're supposed to meet with a staff sergeant tomorrow who is going to help us out," Benson explained.

"We can put both of you up. Happy to help," Elizabeth added.

Harriett Anne spoke next. "Why don't I make some lemonade and prepare some fixins to eat?"

"Thanks Harriett Anne. I'll get Chloe to prepare another room. My brother was a little shorter than both of you, but I'm sure we can get you some clean clothes you can make do with. Come on in, we'll show you where you can get cleaned up."

"Thank you, ma'am," Higgins said.

Benson added, "Much obliged, Miss Van Lew."

The bulk of assigned Union forces began entering the outskirts of the city around eight o'clock. African Americans, and a few white folks, lined the streets cheering. The soldiers immediately went to work putting out the fires.

Another day or two passed. The former Castle Thunder prisoners had moved on. Friends from the spy network and other Union sympathizers continued to call on the Van Lew's, expressing their sense of joy and thankfulness. The fires had all been extinguished. The odor was still bad.

Federal soldiers were now working hard in cleaning things up, and repairing the infrastructure. They were taking down the vestiges of burned out buildings to avoid further accidents, clearing up the debris, and making communication and transportation operational again.

A Union colonel showed up in front of the Van Lew mansion with several men on horseback, along with a horse drawn cart filled with food, water containers and a sundry of supplies.

When Daniel, back to his normal duties, answered the door, the Colonel asked for Miss Van Lew. She came to the entrance immediately.

"Good morning, Miss Van Lew. Colonel Ely Parker. On orders from General Grant, I'm here to make sure that we take care of all your wants, providing the supplies you need. We took the liberty to bring a few things with us."

"I can see that," a still very surprised looking Elizabeth said. "Good morning, Colonel."

Elizabeth noticed the contingent of men behind the colonel, and the cart full to the brim.

"Colonel Parker, please step into our parlor and have a seat. We can talk there. Do you want to invite any of your men in as well?" Elizabeth asked.

"No ma'am. They can unload the cart while we speak."

He followed her into the house, passing the ornamental columns on both sides of the entrance to the main parlor. This was where Edgar Allan Poe had once recited *The Raven* for delighted guests, who were fascinated, and at the same time, visibly flustered by the suspenseful rendition. It seemed like a century ago.

Parker tried his best not to peer around, but couldn't help but observe the high gilt leaf ceiling hosting elegant imported chandeliers, the walls covered with brocaded silk, and the mantels of white marble. He had never seen anything quite like it before. Parker waited for Elizabeth to first take her seat on a rosewood sofa. He then sat on a high-backed chair close by.

After a few formalities and a brief exchange of additional small talk pleasantries, Colonel Parker stated, "I hope you do not mind our making some assumptions on what we brought without speaking to you first, but please do let me know whatever it is that you and your household may need."

"I think you and your men have already surpassed my expectations."

The soldiers were continuing to unload the truck, bringing things through the back kitchen door at the direction of Harriett Anne.

Colonel Parker informed Elizabeth that General Butler had put through a request to the War Department to grant permission for her brother, John Newton Van Lew, to return to Richmond from Philadelphia. John had fled, rather than fight for the Confederates. Parker gave her a handwritten note with his contact information.

"Please do not hesitate to reach to me personally, if there is anything that you need," the Colonel said as he left the house and rejoined his men.

It was all Elizabeth could do to contain her emotions.

When General Ulysses S. Grant arrived in Richmond, he barely stopped to talk or shake hands with city officials lining up to greet him. His first nonmilitary call was to the home of Elizabeth Van Lew. She was delighted to host the General. She first introduced him to Daniel Gates and Dolores Halsey, both of whom had played critical roles in helping Union prisoners escape, as well as spying on Confederate activities. She looked to introduce him to Mary Bowser as well, but she must have been preoccupied with something else at the time.

They had each asked Elizabeth not to reveal the extent of their clandestine activities within the spy network. For example, Mary did not want anyone else to know that it was she who had been the servant in the residence of the Confederate President, spying for the Union.

They were all concerned that there might be retribution, if word spread to the wrong people. Elizabeth tried to convince them that their secret would be safe with General Grant, but in the end, she respected their wishes.

When General Grant asked to have a word with her, Elizabeth invited him to sit with her on the front porch, sipping tea that Harriet Anne prepared. One of the many rare commodities not easily obtained in Richmond during the war.

She had read and heard the many disparaging remarks about Grant's demeanor and appearance. His alleged drinking problem, aloofness, unkempt beard, sloppy uniform, scoffed-up boots. Here he was, the head of the Union Army still fighting a war, sitting next to her and it was nothing like that. His copper brown beard covering most of his strong squared-off face was neatly trimmed. His uniform well-fitted and neatly pressed. His boots were clean and well-polished. She was intrigued by his piercing gray eyes that suggested alertness and intelligence. There also seemed to be a kind gentleness in the tone of his voice.

"I am very grateful things in Richmond now seem to be settling down and that your home and neighborhood, Miss Van Lew, were spared from the fires. Nice to see the skies clear again."

"First beautiful day we've had in a while and thankfully we can no longer see the black clouds of smoke that have engulfed most of our city up until now. Hopefully we can return to a sense of normalcy very soon."

Grant politely smiled and they both sipped their tea.

He guessed that she was in her mid to late 40s. She looked frail and tired. Not what he expected her to look like. This was the woman who had exhibited such strength and bravery during the Confederate occupation of Richmond.

Grant could see that she must have been an attractive southern belle in her youth. Did this woman from Richmond's exclusive upper class not receive marriage proposals? No arranged opportunities to wed an eligible, proper gentleman from society? Perhaps, Grant speculated, more likely that a streak of strong will and independence led to a conscious decision to stay single.

"The tea is very good," Grant mentioned as he took another sip.

"Your Colonel Parker provided the tea and many other provisions, as per your request. We were reduced to drinking hot water. Having tea again, especially this tasty, is most appreciated, General."

"Good, very good." Grant glanced up at the flag, the wind snapping it against the pole. "I'm also very happy to see the Red, White and Blue proudly displayed in your front yard."

"Hoisting it up to greet your troops as they marched into Richmond, gave us great satisfaction."

"I only wish we could have taken Richmond sooner. Can't imagine what it must have been like for you."

"I'm just glad that you and your soldiers are here now," Elizabeth responded. "I'm afraid the downtown fires have added to the difficulties in restoring any degree of normalcy in the short term."

Grant nodded. "That will take some time."

"Could have been a lot worse, General. If it had not been for your soldiers, going right to work when they arrived, putting out the spreading inferno, the whole city would be a map of smoldering ruins by now."

"We did what we could, and do appreciate your kind words." They both sipped at their tea as Grant continued, "Miss Van Lew, what you have done for the preservation of the Union is nothing short of extraordinary."

"Much of the credit goes to others, General, far braver than me. Many of them were slaves who had to endure exceedingly inhumane treatment and extreme hardship. They constantly put their lives in severe jeopardy to help the Union cause."

"I am aware of that. Soon they will all be free from the tyranny of slavery. God willing."

"Now that you have sent the enemy fleeing from its own self-proclaimed capital, I can enjoy raising this beautiful flag you had sent to me last Christmas, each and every day. This will always be one of my most cherished gifts."

"...And your gift to me was the intelligence I received. Often gathered from others, I know. But you, Miss Van Lew, have sent me the most valuable information received from Richmond during this war."

Chapter 2: Homecoming

FOUR YEARS EARLIER

In May, 1861, Varina Davis who was expecting their fourth child, joined her husband Jefferson in the new Confederate Capital of Richmond, Virginia, leaving Montgomery, Alabama, the temporary first capital behind. She was not thrilled to be thrust into the Richmond social life and conducting all the expected duties of a First Lady.

The Civil War was only a month old. Arkansas had just become the ninth state to secede from the Union, joining South Carolina, Mississippi, Florida, Alabama, Georgia, Louisiana, Texas and Virginia. North Carolina and Tennessee were expected to do the same shortly.

A convenient argument for leaving the Union was that the Federal government was attempting to trample on constitutionally granted state rights. Self-proclaimed state advocates objected to elected leaders in Washington interfering with the traditional "institutions" of the South.

It was the institution of slavery, often conveniently downplayed in this argument that was the underlying cause. The potential threat of granting freedom to slaves led to the massive hemorrhaging that tore the country apart.

There were approximately 4.5 million African Americans in the United States. Almost four million of those were slaves, primarily in the South, a few states in the Midwest, as well as in U.S. controlled territories. Virginia, although less dependent on an agrarian economy, had close to 500,000 slaves, making it the most populous slave state in the country. Richmond was the center of commerce for the slave trade where it was estimated that over 350,000 slaves were bought and sold from 1830 and into the Civil War.

In the more industrial North, opposition to slavery had continued to grow prior to the war. As the country expanded west, with new territories seeking statehood, how to determine whether they should be free or slave states became a primary national issue consuming the general public. Neither side wanted to lose in the balance of power as newly admitted states leaning one way or the other and permitted to self-determine, could one day help chart a new future direction for the entire country. Violent civil confrontations were breaking out in territories such as "Bleeding Kansas." The divided electorate demanded action from representatives in Washington, beyond their ongoing rhetorical speeches and fiery debate on the subject.

A series of Federal legislative compromises did little to appease either side on the question of slavery. Two subsequent events concerning slavery escalated regional tensions to the breaking point. The 1857 Dred Scott decision by the Supreme Court reaffirming that a slave was not free, even if residing in a free state, infuriated many northerners. This was followed two years later when the abolitionist activist John Brown unsuccessfully tried to storm an arsenal at Harpers Valley in western Virginia. He intended to arm slaves to stage a massive rebellion. Brown's action escalated concerns about future insurgencies throughout the southern slave states. Many northern abolitionists defended Brown's actions as morally acceptable. Southerners in general considered this response from their fellow citizens as reprehensible.

The 1860 election of Abraham Lincoln, a member of the newly formed Republican Party, became the final tipping point. The party was organized to oppose the expansion of slavery. Lincoln was considered a "moderate." He was personally against slavery but believed it was protected by the constitution. This didn't matter. Lincoln was a Republican.

Many southerners believed that if Republicans had their way, future new territories entering the Union would be forced to join as non-slave states. The South would eventually lose its ability to preserve slave ownership, critical to its agricultural industry and the region's economic prosperity. Pro-slavery advocates were convinced that Lincoln would work to continue to severely restrict slavery everywhere. By early February 1861, the first seven states seceded from the Union. All eyes were on the critically important State of Virginia.

Few believed Virginia would ever leave the Union. Although the slave trade was important to the local economy in areas such as harvesting tobacco, as prices declined, the market for tobacco became less profitable. While many within the state still owned slaves, with Virginia's emerging industrial growth in areas such as mining, ironworks manufacturing and the railroad, it seemed the state now had more in common with the Northeast than the Cotton Belt Region. As Virginia continued to develop more diversified industries, it had become more dependent on interstate commerce with Northern States.

The April 12, 1861 bombing of Fort Sumter in Charleston, South Carolina by Confederate forces changed everything. It was humiliating for the new Lincoln Administration when the Federal soldiers holding the fort had to evacuate. With the Confederates opening fire on a Federal Fort, there was no longer a way to avoid it. War was declared.

President Lincoln called for troops from all states to help put down the rebellion triggered by the attack at Fort Sumter. The Virginia State Legislature shocked the nation, including many of its own residents, when a few days after Lincoln's call to arms, it voted to secede. Virginians were already divided on the question of slavery. Leaving the Union further split the populace. Some Virginians opposed to slavery supported the decision to leave the Union. Those opposing secession included both abolitionists and others who were pro-slavery, united solely in their opposition to leaving the Union.

Despite previous marital difficulties, Jefferson Davis was glad to have his wife Varina join him in Richmond. A native of Mississippi, the President of the Confederate States was lonely. He regretted leaving his farm near Biloxi, so distant and dissimilar to where he now was living under a microscope. While he was committed to do all he could to ensure Confederate victory, Davis missed the plantation lifestyle he left behind.

So did Varina, who came to provide her husband comfort and much needed support. Jefferson Davis liked to delve into the details of things, which heightened his level of anxiety in the dual roles of presiding over the new government and prosecuting the war.

Tall, with an angular face and a distinctive short gray beard at the tip of his finely chiseled chin, Jefferson Davis was easily recognizable. Before joining the Confederacy, he had been a well-known and respected statesman. A former military commander, he served as a U.S. Senator and Secretary of War.

Davis had secretly hoped he would be asked to serve in a military leadership position for the newly formed government, versus named as President. To the despair of his generals, his presidential duty as commander-and-chief was already becoming an obsessive preoccupation. Davis often micromanaged their battle plans, escalating tensions and demonstrating a serious lack of trust in his generals.

Varina now being with him would make things more tolerable, helping to reduce his level of stress. Even with her high pedigree, and social graces, she was determined not to immerse herself into Richmond society. In her view, supporting her husband did not extend to that. She was turning down invitations to mix with city figures and their spouses. Illness related to her pregnancy became a convenient excuse. Her husband was constantly asked if there was something more to it than this, and he was running out of explanations.

Jefferson Davis eventually decided to intervene, and implored his wife to become more active in Richmond social activities and events. He saw it as an important aspect of lifting spirits of Richmond residents, as well as helping to raise local morale during difficult times. Varina reluctantly gave in.

Phoebe Reynolds was the reigning queen of Richmond society. She had recently formed a volunteer group of women to work together sewing Confederate uniforms for the new soldiers. In addition to recruiting proper ladies as volunteers in support of the war effort, she also enjoyed throwing extravagant galas and charity balls for Richmond's upper class.

Unfortunately for Phoebe, she was married to a husband who she usually had to browbeat to accompany her at the many events she often had a major hand in staging. For the elite women of Richmond, however, coveted invitations to Phoebe's social functions were almost always gladly accepted.

Eliza Van Lew, Elizabeth's mother, was a regular volunteer. With plenty of coaxing, Eliza persuaded her daughter to join the group. Elizabeth had missed the last get together, and suggested that her mother go without her again for the next one. Eliza decided to ratchet up the pressure.

"Elizabeth, it is not only that I enjoy your company. Your lack of attendance could easily be misinterpreted. I wish you would reconsider and come with me," Eliza said. "It really is not so bad."

"Please, mother, I'd rather not. Frankly I don't know how you can continue to do this yourself."

"What do you mean, my dear?"

"Pretending to support the Confederate government, when you are just as much against it and everything they represent, as I am."

"We don't want trouble, Elizabeth..."

"Trouble?" Elizabeth interjected. "We have nothing but trouble since this war was declared. All these poor misguided boys signing up to fight. We should instead be telling them to go home to their farms," Elizabeth said.

"That would do no good, whatsoever, and we both know it. Given the challenges we now face, it is extremely important that we, as a family, demonstrate we can be trusted. Especially, given that our family has northern roots."

"Yes, you have made yourself very clear on this subject, mother."

"By volunteering, we can hopefully deflect the scrutiny now being placed on so many families. Some of them are previously well-respected Richmond families, similar to ours."

"Father always said that I wasn't very good at bluffing when we played euchre."

"He did have a point there. Your father also said ladies were not meant to gamble. He was not simply talking about one of those Mississippi riverboats, either. But, bluffing when playing cards is not what we are talking about here..."

"Mother, what I am trying to say is that I can't hide my true feelings when it comes to helping the war effort. We are probably both better off if I don't go."

"Alright. It is entirely up to you, Elizabeth. I was simply hoping that you might consider accompanying me again."

Even with other less exclusive volunteer women's groups also forming to sew uniforms, it was becoming an impossible task to keep up as hundreds of boys were pouring into Richmond eager to enlist. A few of the new soldiers came to town already sporting makeshift rebel outfits. Still, there simply weren't enough uniforms to go around to fit the rest. Most recognized something else would eventually need to be done. Yet Phoebe rarely had any difficulty keeping her volunteers coming back to sew more. All except Elizabeth.

Arrangements had been made by Phoebe to use the auditorium in the downtown City Hall, a spacious room with dark granite walls and a high ceiling. The ladies sat around five tables waiting for Phoebe to distribute rolls of fabric and sewing material. Chatter on the latest local gossip filled the room.

Before Phoebe began to make the rounds, she demanded attention to announce that she would soon be organizing a luncheon for woman volunteers helping with sewing and other activities such as preparing meals, visiting hospitals and donating money.

"No need cajoling my darling husband into attending this one, or for any of you to do the same. It's ladies only," Phoebe joked as others laughed.

Phoebe couldn't stop bragging as she moved from table to table. This time, Varina Davis had accepted Phoebe's invitation to attend. She was still working out the date to accommodate the First Lady's schedule.

Sitting briefly at Eliza's table, Phoebe announced, "Naturally, all of you are invited."

Eliza asked Phoebe if she could invite Elizabeth.

"I suppose so," Phoebe responded, after pondering this unexpected request. "Elizabeth has helped in the past. On a few occasions."

Eliza couldn't wait to get back to the family home to tell her daughter.

"Mother, I understand why you think accepting these types of invitations is so important. I just find Phoebe and her friends to be intolerable. Surely, by now they must know how I feel about them. And why would I want to spend time around the wife of the Confederate President?"

"Bet, please. Just do it this one time for me."

Like the Van Lew's, the Reynolds family owned a beautiful mansion in the prestigious Church Hill section. Phoebe had gone to great lengths to make the luncheon an extravagant affair. As anyone who knew her would surmise, it was primarily to impress and ingratiate herself with the Confederate First Lady.

The 30 or so ladies invited for lunch were each escorted as they arrived by the family butler into an enormous drawing room. The butler was an older man whose entire family had been slaves to the Reynolds for several generations.

Elizabeth and her mother were among the last to arrive. Elizabeth had been in this room in the past. She immediately noticed how not much had changed. An enormous room, it was over furnished with ornate hand upholstered chairs and an embroidered dark Persian carpet. An oversized chandelier with extravagant bedded crystals that spun downward like a revolving staircase hung from the ceiling in the center of the room. The windows were covered with deep red velvet drapes. Family portraits in overbearing champagne gold frames covered the walls.

Her mother nudged her. "There she is," Eliza said, directing Elizabeth's attention to the other side of the room where invited guests were swarming around Varina Davis. "I met her once before at an official government event. She didn't seem to enjoy it then, and not doing so well to look thrilled to be here, either," Eliza added.

Varina Davis was taller than the other women around her. She was slender in frame. Not yet noticeably pregnant. Her skin was olive colored, a stark contrast from the powder pink skin tone of most of the socialites in attendance. She looked nothing like what Elizabeth had expected. Perhaps 8 to 10 years younger than she would have guessed. Even more surprising, Varina must have been close to 20 years younger than her husband Jefferson Davis, Elizabeth thought to herself.

A young African American girl carrying a silver tray with glasses of peach brandy stopped in front of the Van Lew's. Both women took a glass. Elizabeth whispered something to the girl which made her smile. The young girl bowed graciously and moved to another nearby group of women.

"Let's go and see if we can rescue her from the hordes," Eliza quipped as she looked across the room in the direction of the Confederate First Lady.

The circle parted for Eliza, with Elizabeth following in tow.

Turning her attention away from the other ladies standing beside her, Varina smiled warmly. "Hello Eliza, nice to see you again."

"Nice to see you as well, Varina. Pardon me for interrupting."

"Not at all," one of the other ladies said, while looking slightly annoyed.

"Varina, I would like to introduce you to my daughter, Elizabeth."

Varina extended her hand. As the women began to exchange greetings, Eliza asserted herself again. "I believe you have something in common with my daughter. You both were educated in the same town."

"Is that right?" Varina asked.

"I went to Quaker School in Philadelphia. Mother, please..."

"That is wonderful," Varina said. "The Quakers are fine educators and I respect them immensely."

Several of the women who were still standing nearby began to drift off to other parts of the room.

"Where were you schooled, Mrs. Davis?" Elizabeth inquired.

"Please call me Varina. I studied at Madame Deborah Grelaud's French School."

"I am familiar with it. An exceptional school. I once went to a recital there," Elizabeth said.

"Didn't you just love Philadelphia?"

"I absolutely did," Elizabeth replied.

Phoebe was the last to enter the room. Wearing an exquisite green wool brocade gown, with yellow threads, she surveyed the room and then sashayed her way over to where Varina Davis and the Van Lew women were standing, politely acknowledging her guests along the way.

Phoebe was an attractive southern belle, with raven black hair and green eyes matching the color of her gown, and accentuated by her blush complexion. Her face was shaped like a heart, with high round cheeks and a slightly pointed chin. Her full bosom looked as if ready to burst out of her stylish but slightly daring dress.

"Thank you so much for coming, Varina. Hello Eliza. Elizabeth."

"Hello Phoebe, what a beautiful gown," Varina commented.

"Well, thank you, Varina. I do apologize for not greeting you sooner. We had a slight challenge in the kitchen that I had to resolve."

"Very nice to see you, Phoebe, and thank you so much for the invitation," Varina said.

Phoebe continued to engage in conversation with Varina, as if the Van Lew's were not standing right there. Phoebe babbled on, clearly attempting to monopolize the attention of the First Lady. Elizabeth took her mother by the arm and escorted her into the center of the room where the largest group of ladies were standing, sipping their brandy.

When it was announced that lunch was ready, Phoebe led the way into the dining room. She began directing the various women guests where to sit.

"Varina, will sit up here, next to me," she announced.

"Certainly," Varina replied. "I do hope you will not mind terribly, and I definitely do not intend to offend anyone, but Elizabeth and I were having a splendid conversation. Would you mind if I sit next to you, Phoebe, on one side, and Elizabeth on the other?"

Phoebe stood tight jawed and looking stunned. She finally gathered herself to reply, "Of course we can manage that. Elizabeth, please come and sit over here next to Varina, on her left.

Elizabeth was completely taken by surprise. Her mother was delighted, but tried hard to keep her external composure in check.

The meal consisted of roasted lamb with port gravy, peas, and a potato casserole, served with sweet white wine. Dessert was a buttermilk pudding, followed by tea.

Varina was polite, engaging in conversation with the ladies on both sides. Her demeanor, however, was completely different when she spoke with Elizabeth. Her face was beaming as the two ladies shared stories about their education, Philadelphia, books, and travel. Varina also talked about living in Washington D.C., which she loved. They never talked about the war, although at one-point Varina said, "Such a shame women are not allowed to vote. Perhaps we wouldn't be in such a mess."

Elizabeth and her mother shared notes on the event along the short walk home. Most of the conversation was about the Confederate First Lady.

"I have to admit I liked her very much, which is so surprising," Elizabeth confided.

"Not so surprising for me," her mother replied. "She obviously liked you as well, and why not? Two strong, well educated, highly opinionated woman. Poor Phoebe, she may not invite you to any more events."

"That would be just fine. I must hand it to you, mother. Not only have you helped create the facade of our family being supportive of the new government in its illegal war against the Union. Thanks to you, we have cultivated a potentially invaluable relationship with the First Lady."

"I simply introduced you to her. You did the rest, my dear."

Elizabeth had always loved her mother, but she had no idea how strong she was until her father passed away. In deference to her father, her mother had always seemed to acquiesce. Elizabeth now suspected her mother got her way more often than she realized. She simply made her father think they were his ideas. With her dear father gone, her mother was much more open about her thoughts, and was now exerting her will on the family affairs. Open about everything, except freeing the family slaves.

While she was opposed to slavery, just like her father had been, Elizabeth's mother worried more about the impact on her son's business and being ostracized from the Richmond community. Failing to conform to accepted norms, Elizabeth was often told, could have a disastrous impact on the economic position of the family, and also present a legal jeopardy. It was the same argument that her father used to make.

Elizabeth still deeply mourned the death of her beloved father. She had loved and admired him, an astute businessman, a successful hardware merchant, and a respected member of Richmond society, but most of all, as a wonderful father.

Always kindhearted with family and close friends, he could also at times be stern, intractable with mixed company, leaving her mother perplexed, and very annoyed. His ancestors were new world Brahmin, colonial Dutch heritage. They helped build the communities where they settled.

Her father had loved Elizabeth as well, but her streak of independence and strong opinions she so often shared in mixed company confounded him. For years, she had been considered a desirable Southern belle with deep blue eyes, high cheekbones, obviously intelligent, and with a wonderful, yet sometimes mischievous, sense of humor. He had worried that her strong character would result in her falling out of the category of a suitable wife for the right established Southern gentleman.

John Van Lew, Senior, had come to Richmond as a young boy from Long Island, New York. In addition to building a successful business, he had immersed himself in Richmond civic affairs. Her mother, Eliza, hailed from Philadelphia, daughter of Hilary Baker, who had held the office of mayor. Philadelphia at the time still served as the Capitol of the United States, while the new Federal City was being constructed in the District of Columbia.

In 1787, before becoming Mayor, Hilary Baker had joined "The Pennsylvania Society for Promoting the Abolition of Slavery." Hilary Baker died in office. Attending to the sick, inflicted from a yellow fever epidemic, he himself had succumbed to the wretched sickness. Elizabeth wondered how her family, with a rich legacy of service to others, had become more concerned about social status than doing the right thing.

Over the years, neighbors took notice that none of the Van Lew's appeared to treat their slaves, harshly, neither verbally nor physically. Elizabeth, however, was well aware of the horrible abuses taking place around her. Some slave owners and traders were notorious for flogging what they considered their rightful personal property. Elizabeth had observed first-hand the cruel treatment of African Americans in her hometown.

If the lash didn't work, those proving to be incorrigible, continuing to resist, would be sent to Lumpkin Prison for slaves. Many at some point ended up there. Some never came out. They were crammed together and given limited rations. Small barred windows limited sunlight. There were no toilets. Instead, the inmates had to share buckets for excrement. The stench was unbearable. Slaves named it "Devil's Half Acre."

She remembered how one day as a little girl, Elizabeth and a friend decided to sneak into the back pew of a Slave Auction. The auction was being held on Cary Street, one of the oldest sections of Richmond. The street grid was original from 1737, when Richmond was founded. With multiple auction houses, this area was the most significant slave trading center of the United States. International slave trade was banned by U.S. law in 1807, but national slave trade was booming. With the invention of the cotton gin, demand for slaves to pick the crop had exploded in the deep south.

Richmond's Shockoe Bottom became the national gateway. Slave husbands, wives and children were often split apart, never to reunite. As countless numbers passed through, those considered most fit were shipped off to the cotton fields where a miserable, brutally inhuman existence of long hours, difficult outside labor in the burning sun. Often, the harshest possible treatment became their fate.

Almost exclusively white men filled the audience. In addition to the cotton growers who had travelled north, there were local tobacco planters, representatives from the Tredegar ironworks, the flour mill, and other occupations such as blacksmiths, private farmers and the railroad. They were gathered in a makeshift store front, not far from the Davenport Trading Company which also specialized in the slave trade. The room was filled with tightly arranged benches. Behind them was standing room only, where new arrivals continued to push through, attempting to occupy whatever little space was left.

She would never get out of her mind the sight of three young children, two boys and a young girl, tied and dragged onto the platform in the front of the room. One of the boys was defiant. He pulled back at the man who dragged them onto the stage. The man smacked the boy across the face, knocking him down. There were cruel cat calls.

"That's the only way to train 'em."

"Send him down to the cotton fields where he belongs."

Another about the girl. "With hips like that she could mother the whole world." This was followed by more jeers and fiendish sounding laughs.

A business associate of her father had tapped her shoulder and told her that if she and her friend didn't leave, he would tell her parents. She would never know what happened to the three children. This continued to haunt her.

At the Quaker School up north she later attended, her views on the slavery issue hardened further. So did spending time with her relatives in Philadelphia. By the time she came home to Richmond, she was now as much against slavery as her maternal grandfather had been.

Shortly after returning to Richmond, she took a family trip to White Sulphur Springs in the beautiful mountain country of western Virginia.

She befriended people on vacation from the Northeast who were also committed abolitionists. She enjoyed listening to the intense after dinner discussions, often under the stars. On one occasion when the subject of slavery broke out, Elizabeth joined in on the debate as a passionate advocate for ending slavery. She surprised her family, arguing passionately on the subject with family friends from the South taking the opposing pro-slavery view.

At one point, her father had called out, "Enough Bet. Time for you to retire for the evening."

Elizabeth had learned to hate every aspect of slavery. She also hated being told by her family that as horribly immoral as it was, nothing could be done. The argument "perhaps one day things could change," seemed incredibly disingenuous. Now, with a declared war to protect the southern established, "institutional" way of life, her family told Elizabeth it was even more dangerous to skirt convention, or express views that could be construed as subversive.

What continued to trouble Elizabeth were the 15 family slaves. At one point, shortly after her father's death, she had suggested to her mother, and her younger brother, John Newton Van Lew, who had taken over the father's hardware store, that they should consider freeing them but this had set off a nasty argument.

Her brother had reprimanded her, ending his soliloquy with a cutting rebuke, "We must respect father's wishes as he plainly stated in his will that we keep the family slaves, and lest we forget, he has not been gone from us that long." He announced that the discussion was settled for good. Her mother had agreed.

She promised herself she would try to do something to change the minds of John and her mother. As disappointing as it was for her, she knew she would need to try again, but not for a while.

Several weeks went by since Phoebe's luncheon. Elizabeth and her mother decided to go into town to do a little shopping. "We have to get you a more suitable dress for the next Phoebe's soiree," Eliza quipped as they left the house. Isaac brought them back and forth with the family carriage. Daniel greeted them at the carriageway entrance to help carry the items they had purchased.

They both noticed he was not his usual jovial self. Daniel was tall, formidable looking man who could be quite engaging when he wanted to be. With a smile, combined with his natural good looks and charm, he could melt an ice cap. Particularly when he was performing his butler duties, always dressed to the nines. No wonder Harriett Anne, his lovely wife, had fallen for him when she became the family cook, Elizabeth thought to herself.

"Everything alright?" Eliza asked Daniel.

"I'll tell you once you get settled in. Here, let me help you with that." He took one of the satchels Eliza was carrying and a bundle of clothes from Elizabeth.

They followed him into family mansion, placing the rest of their booty on the table in the kitchen where Daniel had assembled the other things. There were a pile of blouses for Elizabeth and yarn for Eliza's sewing. Also, a resupply of condiments in the satchel as requested by Harriett Anne.

Daniel turned to the ladies and said, "We have visitors sittin' in the library who insisted on seein' both of you. Hope you don't mind I told 'em to wait there."

"Why the library?" Eliza asked. "We generally reserve that room for family, and our invited guests. You know that, Daniel."

"Chloe was cleaning the foyer," Daniel answered.

"Who is it?" Elizabeth asked.

Before Daniel could respond, Eliza spoke next in a low tone, "I hope it is not that annoying local constable again, with one of his deputies. Always prying for information on our activities. They don't trust this family at all."

"No, not them, but one of them knows all 'bout this family. Better if you go see for yourself," Daniel said.

This made it even more puzzling. Eliza shook her head and frowned as she began to walk to the library. "All right, if Daniel is going to be so coy about it, let's you and I go find out what this is all about." She looked annoyed.

Eliza stopped in the hall, directly in front of the closed library door, waiting for Daniel and Elizabeth, still trailing behind. "I hope whomever it is isn't snooping around in our family library," Eliza whispered as the others caught up.

Also in a whisper, Elizabeth asked her mother, "Are you afraid these mystery guests may be in search of objectionable books in our cherished collection, mother? Like *Uncle Tom's Cabin?*"

The two ladies smiled at each other and then back at Daniel to assess any change in his countenance. He remained stoic.

Daniel's comments and lack of sharing any of the particulars in advance, concerning the mystery guests perplexed Elizabeth and Eliza. It was not like him.

Elizabeth shrugged her shoulders, and then suggested, "Well, mother, let's go see for ourselves."

Daniel passed in front of the ladies and swung the door open.

She stood erect as they entered the library. The cute, inquisitive little girl they fondly remembered was now a beautiful woman. Almost five foot, seven inches tall, she possessed an hourglass physique, even her poorly fitting navy-blue travel suit could hardly conceal. She had a high regal forehead and intelligent, chestnut brown eyes. They were warm, welcoming, but at the same time, one had the sense they didn't miss a thing.

Behind her was a handsome man, slightly taller than her. He was dressed in a brown Sunday suit. He stepped forward and bowed gracefully, clinging to his straw hat close to his chest.

"Mary Richards, you look so lovely. My, it is so wonderful to see you after all this time," exclaimed Eliza.

"I thought we would never see you again. When did you arrive?" Elizabeth asked, adding, "And who is this fine looking gentleman?"

They smothered Mary with hugs and kisses before she could answer the barrage of questions thrown her way.

Mary finally spoke. "My name is now Mary Bowser, and this is my husband, Wilson Bowser. He's a free man. We met in Philadelphia before I left for Liberia. We've been living with Wilson's family in Norfolk."

"We have so much to talk about. Please, let's all sit down," Elizabeth suggested.

Eliza spoke. "Would anyone like some coffee?"

Both Mary and Wilson nodded. "Thank you, ma'am," Wilson said.

"I'll tell Harriett Anne," Daniel declared, as he turned and left.

"You rascal, Daniel," Elizabeth called after him. Then turning to Mary, "Have you seen Chloe yet?" Elizabeth inquired. "I'm sure she will be thrilled."

"Oh yes, we were both crying our eyes out before you came. We're going to spend next Sunday together. She looked well. A little older of course, but still very much the way I remember her."

Elizabeth expression turned serious. "You know Mary, there is serious danger coming back to the South. What do you tell people when they ask about your background?"

"I tell them that I am a free negro, just like my husband."

Mary was born into slavery, the daughter of the Van Lew head housekeeper, Ella, who had passed away when Mary was only five years old. Ella was a victim of cholera. Elizabeth begged her father to keep Mary and promised that between Chloe Jenkins and herself, they would take care of Mary. In a short time, Elizabeth began to realize Mary was an exceptional child.

One evening when Mary was six years old, the Van Lew's had entertained dinner guests. After retiring to the drawing room, Elizabeth played the piano as the guests gathered around. They sang the words to an old Irish poem by Thomas Parnell, put to music by Philadelphian Francis Hopkinson, an original signer of the Declaration of Independence. Mary must have left her bed and managed to hide someplace close by to hear the music. Elizabeth was astounded when a few days later she heard Mary signing. She remembered the words to "My Days Have Been So Wonderous Free," reciting them perfectly after hearing it only once.

Elizabeth began to teach Mary to read and write. Before long, Mary could recite long passages from *Lessons for Children*. She could also recite catechism from the *Book of Prayer*, exactly as it was written, including the "Question and Answer" annotations.

When she was a young girl, Elizabeth's favorite book was *Swiss Family Robinson* by Johann Wyss. Her father had acquired the English version published in London. She herself had grown to love the book as a child for the adventure and its lessons on good behavior and self-reliance. Mary loved it as well. Not only could Mary read several paragraphs for the first time and retain it, she could describe vividly the illustrations in the book, including the "New Switzerland" map.

Elizabeth asked her to sketch what she remembered. Mary drew a picture that provided an outline of the land mass that could be laid almost perfectly across the original in the book. What was even more impressive was how Mary was able to fill in the detail. The sugar cane field, the bamboo forest, the marsh, and even Shark's Island, off the coast. All were symmetrically placed by Mary in close approximation to the map illustrations from the book.

One day Elizabeth brought Mary with her to St. John's Episcopal Church, the family place of worship. St. John's built in 1741, was considered to be Richmond's first public house of worship. It was made famous throughout the colonies when one of the nation's Founding Fathers, Patrick Henry, proclaimed from inside its walls:

> Is life so dear, or peace so sweet, as to be purchased at the price of chains and slavery? Forbid it, Almighty God! I know not what course others may take me, give me liberty, or give me death!

She had Mary recite lines of catechism for Reverend J.H. Morrison. He too found it remarkable. At first he was reluctant, but with intense coaxing from Elizabeth he agreed to baptize the young slave girl with the extraordinary gift in a private ceremony in his church. Slave children were usually baptized at the First African Baptist Church.

When Mary was older, Elizabeth told her mother she was going to Philadelphia to visit relatives and friends from school. She then added in a casual manner that she planned to take Mary with her to see if she could enroll her in the same Quaker School that she had attended.

"Bet, you must realize how this could turn out to be disastrous for young Mary. I don't think this is a good idea."

"As you know, mother, Mary is a very gifted young girl. Such a waste if she can't take full advantage of her capabilities, and receive a real education, living a more fulfilling life."

Her mother cautioned her, "I know she is extremely bright, but I'm not sure they will take her. Assuming they do, are you sure this would be the best thing for Mary? She will be all alone, and when she comes back here, it will be so much more difficult for her to accept things the way they are."

"As much as I care about her and will miss her, I don't want her to come back, mother."

Both Mary and Chloe were still thrilled by the possibility, even after Elizabeth tried to explain, as her mother insisted on, the many necessary adjustments and periods of loneliness Mary would no doubt encounter. The great adventure she might anticipate would not always be so great.

Mary was undeterred. Chloe helped the young girl pack her things. The Quaker school accepted her immediately. Before departing, Elizabeth strongly encouraged Mary to stay in the North as a free woman.

"I'll miss you terribly, Mary. We all will, but your life will be so much better than it ever could be here. I'm sure of that."

There were disturbing setbacks. Even in the northern "City of Brotherly Love," and the home of Elizabeth's maternal grandparents, she experienced racial bigotry, and on a few occasions had to escape inappropriate overtures from overly aggressive men who tried to take advantage. Still, she grew to love Philadelphia, as well as her school where she exceeded all expectations, impressing most of her teachers with her academic capabilities. She easily made friends with classmates.

Mary, like Elizabeth had a strong independent streak. Upon completion of school, she jumped at an opportunity where she could both teach and experience adventure. Instead of staying in the North, or returning home after completing her education in Philadelphia, she decided to go to Africa. She would go as a missionary to help the new settlers in Liberia.

The Republic of Liberia in Western Africa came about when an antislavery group known as the American Colonization Society began to establish settlements in the early 19th century. They believed the "Grain Coast" of West Africa could be a freer and more suitable environment for freed American slaves than continuing to live in the United States. The first wave of freed American slaves accompanied by members of the Society landed there in 1822. Proclaimed an independent republic in 1847, by 1860 it was estimated that close to 15,000 former slaves migrated to Liberia from the United States.

Mary explained to the Van Lew ladies that Wilson was working in a Philadelphia shipyard when they met. They married when she came back from Liberia, just before the war. They had moved back to Norfolk to be closer to his elderly mother, who recently passed away.

With the Union Blockade, there was little work left in Norfolk, loading or unloading ships. Wilson could only find part time jobs. He had just been offered a job by a family acquaintance down at Shockoe Slip in Richmond. Mary planned to teach singing for children at the First African Baptist Church. They found a place to live in the Shockoe area.

"I always knew at some point I would come back home."

"Lovely to see you, Mary. I just wish the circumstances were different. That we didn't have this terrible illicit war going on," Elizabeth said.

Elizabeth sipped her coffee and placed the cup and saucer back on the table. "This will be so nice, Mary, having you close by. I think fondly of the times we spent together. I am so looking forward to getting caught up on your adventures since you left, and spending time with you and Wilson."

"We do as well," Mary said. She turned to look at Wilson. They smiled and both nodded politely.

"Although, I do have to say, with so many slaves, and former slaves too, trying to flee the South, it's just like the Mary I remember to do the opposite. Mary, I sincerely hope you and Wilson don't live to regret coming back here."

Chapter 3: Contraband of War

The Van Lew Grace Street family mansion, three stories high, was built with gray stucco walls and trimmed with Scottish limestone. It sat on an extensive piece of property, taking up a full city block. Built in 1801, the residence had always stood out as one of the most elegant structures in town. When Elizabeth's father acquired it in 1836, he added a magnificent portico in the back of the mansion, elevated above the terraced garden. The Van Lew mansion commanded a fabulous vista of the James River.

The entire downstairs interior was equally impressive, with its Victorian architecture and lavish furnishings. Before the war, this home was where Richmond society often gathered and prominent out of town visitors were entertained. In addition to Edgar Allen Poe, Supreme Court Justice John Marshall and the world famous Swedish opera star Jenny Lind were among celebrity guests of the day hosted at regular Van Lew social events.

The Van Lew's had given the appearance of a family living in antebellum bliss. Now, at war over the issue of slavery, appearances were critical to keep out of jail. Richmond families of distinction were expected to have slaves, and status was often measured by the number they possessed. Releasing a slave would not only set dangerous precedent, it was against Virginia law.

Several outspoken residents criticizing the new Confederate regime had already been imprisoned, including friends of the Van Lew's. Assimilating to acceptable Richmond society to avoid being labeled a dissident was paramount. Despite their outward appearance of conformity, this created an undercurrent of ambivalence within the family.

Saturday morning, John and Elizabeth were sitting in the kitchen with Harriett Anne when Daniel joined them. The talk was mostly about the war.

"I'm guessing there may be fewer slaves trying to escape now," John commented. "More patrols, troops in the area guarding the borders. They'll surely want to make an example of any who tries to go North."

"You hear 'bout what happened at Fort Monroe?" Daniel asked.

John shook his head.

"No," an inquisitive looking Elizabeth responded. "I know the Fort is still in the hands of the Federal Government. Please, tell us, Daniel."

Before Daniel could speak, John spoke again. "I have heard that ships keep coming in filled with more soldier and supplies. 'Cause it's on the tip of the Hampton Roads, straight across from Norfolk. A good position for the Union to advance up the Peninsula to attack Richmond."

"That's right," Daniel said. "Guessin' because of that, the Confederates put a bunch of slaves to work. Wanted them to build a battery at Sewell Point. Tryin' to protect Norfolk from attack."

"I once picnicked there with our Norfolk cousins. Back in happier times," Elizabeth said. "You were too young back then to come along, John."

Daniel continued. "Well, one night, three slaves forced to work there, decided they had enough. They stole a skiff and rowed across to the Fort."

"I'm guessing Sewell Point must be almost 15 nautical miles straight across to Old Point Comfort," John pointed out.

"Yes, Mr. Van Lew, that's probably 'bout right."

"A long, dangerous boat ride where the James meets the Chesapeake and currents can be treacherous," John related.

"I suppose they decided their freedom was worth the risk," Elizabeth commented. "Did they make it to the fort, Daniel?"

"They did, ma'am. Then it got real interestin'. Soon after a young soldier in the Virginia Army rode out on his horse, all the way out around that big fishhook of land. Straight up to Fort Monroe, waving a white flag."

"Wanting his slaves back, I assume," John said.

"Yes, sir. Well, they belonged to somebody he reported to. Went there on orders."

"That shameful Fugitive Slave Act passed by the U.S. Congress," Elizabeth remarked, adding, "Runaway slaves who are caught, regardless of where, are supposed to be returned to their owner."

"Not only that. The Fugitive Slave Act stipulates that anyone helping slaves escape is breaking the law," John pointed out. He peered across the table at Elizabeth, and then back at Daniel.

"We call it the 'Bloodhound Act,' Daniel said. "Well, to tell you what happened next. This new Union general there, rode out himself to meet him. I heard he told the general the law was still on the books up North. Escaped slaves needed be returned. Even President Lincoln agreed with that, he told 'em."

Daniel paused for a second, looking to see how Elizabeth and John would react to what he was saying.

Breaking the momentary silence, Elizabeth asserted, "I truly believe President Lincoln when he says he is against slavery and maybe hopes one day it can be abolished, but for now he wants to try to bring the South back. Doesn't want to do anything that could make that impossible. Personally, I think we are beyond any hope of that." Looking at Daniel, she asked, "What happened next?"

Daniel, expressionless, nodded, before continuing. "I then heard the soldier asked the general what he intended to do. The general told him if Virginia believed they were a different country, he didn't feel any need to return 'em. He said he intended to keep 'em instead. That Virginia soldier got real mad."

Elizabeth couldn't help but smile. John did as well.

"He told the general, 'but you breakin' the law.' He says he had to return 'em to the rightful owner." This general, well then he said, leavin' the Union was breaking the law. Told him the Slave Act no longer applied. 'Cause Virginia ain't no longer part of the Union. He tells 'em, 'You are asking me to return what you think is property. Even if this were so, then they are not your property anymore. Spoils of war. Called it something else."

"Contraband," John commented.

"Yes sir, contraband, that's the word the general used," Daniel said, nodding as he began to grin.

"How did this soldier react?" Elizabeth asked.

Daniel had the undivided attention of both siblings and also his wife still seated at the table.

"He brought up Dred Scott. Says even the Supreme Court agreed slaves are always slaves. Makes no difference where they are, even if they escape to free territory. They needed to be returned to their rightful owner."

"Worse possible decision ever made by the high court," Chief Justice Roger Taney and the others should have been ashamed of themselves," Elizabeth passionately declared.

Her brother nodded. "Anything else happen after this, Daniel?"

"Well, yes. This general said, 'I don't have to return nothin' to my enemy. You Rebels stole land that belongs to the U.S. Government.' He then said, 'and I intend to get it back.' The soldier then rode off, steamin' mad."

"Who is this general?" Elizabeth asked.

"Pretty sure they said his name is Butler. General Butler. Just arrived to take over at the fort."

"Who told you about this argument between this General Butler and the Confederate soldier, Daniel?" John inquired.

"Slaves working for the Virginia Army heard a bunch of soldiers talkin'. One of them was this soldier I been talkin' about. He was very upset. Got yelled at when he couldn't get them back. He got real drunk talkin 'bout it to the others. Got more angry 'bout it as he kept fillin' his glass. That's what I was told."

"That is a pretty remarkable story," John commented. "This newly arrived general taking a stand like that."

"Reason I told you'll this, cause word spread fast among slaves. Now, a bunch of slaves are starting to sneak off to Fort Monroe. So many, the soldiers now pitchin' tents for them. Hear it's becomin' a city of tents around the fort."

"If they are caught trying to get there, and I'm sure some will be caught if not careful, they will make terrible examples of them," John noted.

Daniel was surprisingly firm and direct, saying, "Mr. Van Lew, you are probably right, and I think most know that. All I'm sayin' is that many more slaves are now escapin' to Fort Monroe. A couple were caught, and at least one drowned tryin' to cross over the river. But others are willin' to chance it. To be free."

Benjamin Butler was a Massachusetts lawyer before joining the army. He had been a pro-slavery Democrat, but was appalled by the secession.

A political appointed general with no formal military training, Butler had been in trouble with his commanding officers in the past for acts considered insubordinate. At first his legal argument that slaves were "contraband of war," and therefore did not need to be returned to the Confederates, was taken as another example of his out stepping his authority. He was making his own rules with no authority to do so.

With a groundswell of support from a very vocal group of uncompromising abolitionists, known as "Radical Republicans," Butler's position eventually became an accepted principle in the North. This also led to a continuing surge of runaways, willing to take life threatening risks to reach Fort Monroe. A few months later, close to 1,000 slaves had escaped there. New contraband camps began to spring up near other Union Army forts as well.

That evening when she was with her mother and brother, Elizabeth decided to approach the subject of freeing their slaves again. John immediately tried to cut her off.

"Now is definitely not the time, Bet. We had an agreement. Discussion on this is over."

"When is the right time, John? Given this new set of events, I think we need to reconsider. You heard what Daniel said this morning. We can no longer hide our heads in the sand. Please hear me out," retorted Elizabeth, as she looked back at her mother, who with a nod of approval indicated it was alright to continue.

Elizabeth felt strongly she could no longer go on accepting things as they were. This was a matter of conscience. If John won the argument again, Elizabeth decided she would leave. Head north, she imagined.

"Go on," John said, still shaking his head.

Elizabeth continued. "This is all about freedom and leaving the horrors of slavery behind. That's why so many are willing to risk escaping to Fort Monroe. What if any of the slaves who work for us decide they want to go? I don't think we should prevent them. We should explain the risks, but let them go if they want to try."

Eliza looked over at her son. "I think Bet has a point. I also think if they are willing to take the risk, we should not stand in their way. With this war dragging on, it might be the only chance they get to escape. Before they

clamp down and prevent others from escaping. The Confederates will surely keep working to make all border crossings, on land and sea, more secure
over time. In any case, I'd like to see if we can come to consensus on this, as
a family."

Her brother remained standing. Elizabeth was sitting perched on a favorite lounging chair, a neoclassic cream and gold rope trimmed seat. Her
mother sat across the room in a meticulously carved walnut chair.

Gathering his thoughts, John once again presented his unwavering position. "I think we would be responsible if they are killed trying to escape,
God forbid. If caught, they could get hung, even if we tried to intercede for
them. Things have gotten very bad. As Daniel told us, one of them already
drowned trying to get there. They should know that even if they do make it,
the Fort isn't prepared to take care of so many. They will be living in tents.
Probably in terrible conditions."

Elizabeth countered. "But they would be free. Maybe there is another
solution. Why don't we offer, should they choose to stay, to pay them for
their services? We can afford to do so. Give them the option, stay here and
work for a fee, not as slaves. Or if they still want to take their chances, they
can try to leave."

Before John could respond, Eliza spoke. "After all, while your father ex-
plicitly wrote in his will that we should never sell our slaves, there is nothing in it about giving them their freedom. They can leave, knowing the risk
of doing so, or if they decide to stay, Elizabeth is right, we can change the
arrangement so they are paid workers. The same for all, whether they are
house servants, work in John's store, or on the family farm," Eliza said. "If
they decide to leave, we could easily afford to pay for additional help. I
think paying them for their services will be a good incentive to stay, and potentially avoid the dangers in trying to escape."

"We can't just free them like we once could. The laws have changed."

Elizabeth thought for a while and then said, "No one needs to know
that we are paying them for their services. For those who decide to stay with
us, we pay them, but hold their money until they do decide to leave."

"Please, we must be realistic about this, Bet. Eventually word would
most surely get out. Whether by an accidental slip, or perhaps one of the
servants bragging to others. Then what happens when neighbors hear that

we have decided to free our slaves and pay them for their work? Surely they'd report us to the authorities." John was noticeably irritated. "They would argue we are setting a dangerous precedent."

"Perhaps a good precedent. Why should we care what the neighbors think? Also, if we hold their earnings for them and they are not in town throwing their money around, they are less likely to talk about it," Elizabeth added.

He stood up, walked over to the study door, and looked down the hall, before closing it. He did not notice, Daniel Gates, the family butler, in the middle of the darkened hall, who quickly slid behind a ceiling high cupboard. Now, with a diminished risk of being discovered, Daniel moved straight up to the hard oak door, placing his ear against it.

As John walked back to a seat near the edge of the wall length bookcase, he spoke out firmly, "We need to be sensible about this. Do you believe people on Church Hill have forgotten that our family is from up North? I doubt there would be any lenience in passing down judgment. We will be frowned up as social pariahs. Losing friends. My business. Yet, that's not the worst of it. We could all end up in jail."

"Illegal to free them if you accept this government as legitimate. I don't," Elizabeth ended up saying, "Regardless, it's immoral to hold them as slaves."

Eliza who had been sitting, listening, patiently said, "John, I think Elizabeth's idea has merit. I suggest we talk with them, give them the option, explaining the potential risks. They can leave, and while it may be the best chance they have to do so, there are dangers they need to know about. Or, they can continue to stay with us, but no longer as slaves, but as employees. They would have to agree to keep this secret. I believe they would. We keep up appearances, as if nothing has changed."

John laughed nervously. "You can't be serious, mother. Your imagination must be running wild. Do you think they could possibly keep this secret? All it would take is for one of them to mention it to another slave working somewhere else. Surely whoever hears about it will start asking why they aren't paid like our servants are. We not only run the risk of being exposed for disobeying the law. We could be accused of starting a new rebellion."

"I think you are being overly dramatic, John," Elizabeth commented.

"Dramatic or not, I say, let's try it." Eliza's tone was emphatic.

A complete reversal from her previous declaration. John Newton stormed out of the room. Elizabeth was stunned. She stood up from her chair, walked over to her mother, leaned downward and kissed her on the forehead. No words were spoken.

The next evening they gathered all of the family slaves in the parlor room. John did most of the talking and Elizabeth was impressed. He was convincing, not forced. John made it clear what they could expect if they chose to stay for a modest salary. This was a radical departure from the past arrangement.

He also told them that they would not be able to go around spending the dollars they would be paid, as it would arouse suspicion and place all of them, as well as the family in trouble. He suggested that the Van Lew's would hold their earnings until they decided to leave. They would then collect all of what was saved for them.

"You mean, we will get paid if we stay on?"

"We can leave when we want? Up to us?"

"You don't have to tell us your decision now," John explained. "Think about it. We can also talk it over in private if you like. With me, or my mother and sister, as well."

Most of them looked very pleased. A few looked confused. Only Daniel, followed by his wife, Harriett Anne the cook, and Isaac the coachman, announced immediately that they would stay. The others decided to think things over.

Elizabeth rose early the next morning and walked out to the garden. On most days, there would have been a spectacular view from this side of the house, looking across the stone carved piazza. On a clearer day, one could easily see much of the downtown, extending out to the James.

The garden surrounding Elizabeth, when in season, was exquisite. Even on this dreary afternoon it had its high points. The walls were draped in perennial plants. A few ornamental flowers were starting to bloom. The symmetric rows of the large vegetable section weeks away from it seasonal peak had started to fill in. As it began to drizzle, Elizabeth didn't seem to care.

She appeared not to notice Harriett Anne spying on her from the window, soon joined by Daniel. Both were perplexed, but did not say a word. Daniel turned away and disappeared, as Harriett Anne remained fixed in place at the window. Daniel reappeared with an umbrella.

"She looks like she wants to be left alone," Harriett Anne whispered.

"Yes, maybe so, but at least she won't get as wet. Be right back," Daniel mumbled as he strutted out the door.

Breaking from her apparent trance, Elizabeth finally noticed his approach as Daniel closed in. "Mr. Daniel Gates, very kind of you. You didn't really have to," she said.

"Miss Van Lew, you could catch the devil of a cold out here."

He opened the umbrella, leaning it over her. As Elizabeth began to reach to take the umbrella, Daniel pulled it slightly away and said, "Please Miss Van Lew, let me hold this for you. I have something I need to tell you. While we are alone."

"Very kind of you Daniel, but you could catch a frightening bad cold yourself while talking and trying to keep me dry at the same time. Let's move under the portico."

She stood up and began to walk back towards the ornate overhead structure, stretching out from the back of the house. Daniel followed, close behind, trying as best he could to provide her cover, without much success. They reached the portico, with its high, elevated roof supported by white columns providing shelter. Climbing the steep limestone staircase, they just barely made it to the covered portico in time as the rain began to pour. Wind swells were kicking up.

Daniel was soaked. Elizabeth was also wet, but she was now smiling back at Daniel.

"You are too kind, Daniel. I do very much appreciate your efforts."

"Miss Van Lew, you did not make it easy for me, trying to keep you dry. Much better here."

Daniel followed her, closing the umbrella as Elizabeth moved to the farthest edge of the deck. Daniel was now a few more paces behind. He abruptly stopped as Elizabeth turned.

"Miss Van Lew, please promise me you will never breathe a word of this to anyone. Ever."

"I promise Daniel."

"You know about the Underground Railroad."

"Yes, certainly. I think it is highly admirable."

"Well, that's why I need to stay."

Daniel confided that he helped slaves to escape. He explained how they instructed runaways to follow the North Star at night. The Underground worked to line up safe places for them to stay along the way.

"Sometime homes of nice white people. Like you, Miss Van Lew. Sometimes churches, slave quarters. They know it's safe when they see a quilt displayed correctly on the rail. If it's facin' inside out, they know it's not safe."

"This is so commendable, Daniel," but when do you have time? You're here almost always. How is it neither I, nor my family, was ever aware of this?"

"I don't work so much as a guide these days. I help mostly organizin' and plannin'. Do it mostly Sunday's, my day off. Several of us from the First African Baptist Church help out. Sometimes, when we are short of helpers, at night I sneak out and down the back staircase from our quarters upstairs. To help move 'em along. Pass on to the next station, as we call it. I always try to get back before dawn. Been lucky so far."

"I don't know quite what to say. I am most certainly amazed and think this is a most noble effort."

"The reason I bring this up, Miss Van Lew, I don't think too many of the help are interested in leavin' right now, but if they do, I can help them."

"Do they know about your involvement?"

"Yes ma'am. They do. I couldn't sneak in and out without them knowin'. Some of them have helped too. Once in a while."

"I do have a question for you, Miss Van Lew. If I do by chance decide to leave, you wouldn't pay me in Confederate graybacks, would you? Don't think they'd be accepted where I'd be goin'."

They both laughed.

"You almost did it again, Daniel. You had me assuming you were being serious."

"Shame on me, once again."

"Rest assured, Daniel, I don't think we plan on converting all of the Van Lew assets to Confederate currency. Graybacks? Is that what they are calling the new Confederate dollars?"

"I heard somebody in town call them that."

The next day Elizabeth awakened early. After taking the stairs, Daniel cornered her in the foyer. It was just the two of them.

"Morning, Daniel."

"Mornin', Miss Van Lew."

Daniel could see in her facial expression that something was bothering her. "Everything alright ma'am?"

"To be perfectly honest, I had some trouble sleeping last night. I got up and sat down at my desk. Thought I might write a letter to one of my dear friends in North Carolina, but I kept thinking about our conversation yesterday."

"If what I said was upsetting, and disturbed your sleepin', Miss Van Lew, I am very sorry."

"You didn't upset me, Daniel. On the contrary. Well, it is just that I want to help you in what you are doing."

"You already are, Miss Van Lew. Your family gave us our freedom. We are all overjoyed."

"I want to do more. Here is what I was thinking about. We don't have as many servants anymore, and as you know, Daniel, we have a couple empty rooms upstairs."

"Yes ma'am."

"What if we built a false wall in one of the empty rooms? You would have another safe place for runaways to stay while you make arrangements."

"Miss Van Lew. To be honest, I have used the upstairs slave quarters for this before. Please forgive me for never sayin' nothin'. Not often, I swear. Only when we didn't have anywhere else. Always just a day or two before we moved em' to another place."

"No need to apologize, Daniel, but I must say, you are full of surprises. I never suspected anything like this."

"I think your idea of a false wall is a good one. Just in case one day they come lookin'. I'll get Isaac to help me build it. There's a large cupboard upstairs not bein' used. We could push it in and use it to hide the entrance."

"You should know, Daniel. This is not why I couldn't sleep."

"No? Then what was it, Miss Van Lew?"

"I feel somewhat obligated to tell my family, but not sure about this. I'm pretty certain they would object. Especially after what was agreed to the other day. They may think this is going too far. But if I don't tell them, and they find out later, it would be much worse for all of us. I'm sure of that."

There was movement on the steps. They heard John Van Lew call out, "Mornin' Harriett Anne. No time for breakfast. Need to get to the store early today."

"Will you be home for dinner, Mr. Van Lew? I was planning to cook one of your favorite meals."

"Yes, I'll be there and I'll see you then. Have a wonderful day."

They heard the door close behind Elizabeth's brother. Daniel turned back to gaze at Elizabeth who still looked lost in her thoughts.

"Miss Van Lew, there may be another way to look at this. One of the reasons I never told you before. If I was caught sneakin' a runaway upstairs, you and your family could honestly say you knew nothin' about it. That would be true."

"With all my thinking this through last night that never occurred to me."

"May be better for them not to know, but of course, now, you do."

"Yes, and I was never a very good liar. Thank you, Daniel. This really helps. You just convinced me. Let's build that false wall when no one else in my family is home. In the meantime, let me know what it will cost for the materials you need."

"Yes, Miss Van Lew. Thank you."

Daniel started to leave.

"Before you go, Daniel. Don't you also worry that if you, or anyone of your Underground helpers is caught, they would torture you until you tell them everything you know? Destroying the whole operation?"

"That why, Miss Van Lew, we keep it broken up in station to station segments. We only supposed to know from the station we pick up a runaway to the station we deliver him, or her. To be honest, I know little more, 'cause of what I do, but they'd be hard pressed to get anything out of me. Believe me."

"I think I already know that, Daniel."

With the new false wall, Elizabeth encouraged Daniel to use the upstairs of the Van Lew mansion more often as a regular Underground Railroad station house. He agreed, but indicated that he would continue to keep it secret from her when it was being used. "Better for all of us this way," he said.

"I agree when it comes to my family, but for me who already know about what you are doing. Not sure I understand."

Daniel tried to explain. "I remember one time when a slave I knew, an older fella, never goin' to leave himself, was caught helpin' another slave from up river escape. The slave he was helpin' managed to get away, but not him. He was put in Lumpkin Prison for a few days, but then it was mostly left up to his owner to discipline him. They never suspected his owner was part of it too."

"Who was the owner?"

"Sorry, but I can't tell you, Miss Van Lew. Keepin' secrets is what makes the Underground Railroad work. I'm just sayin', there are other decent white folks like you who come to our aid when we need it most. Like I said, better for all of us that everyone knows only what they need to know. Please, don't take offense, Miss Van Lew, but the less you know, the less you have to worry 'bout not being a good liar. Like you said."

Elizabeth was smiling. "I see. You just might have something there, Daniel. You clearly have thought this through."

"Let's say they catch me, better they don't think you know 'bout it, or been helpin' with what I do. Also, keepin' you out of it makes it less likely that any of the runaways doesn't ever say anythin' about you, neither."

"Well, I do appreciate your being so concerned about me."

"I am, Miss Van Lew, but it could also help me. If, let's say, I do get caught one day, you just might be able to help me out of Lumpkin, too. But not if they think you knew what I was up to or, even worse. Figure you been helpin' us, too."

Over time with her constant prodding, Elizabeth would learn more about Daniel's overall responsibilities, but he would never divulge specific activities. He was playing a much larger part in orchestrating many of the Underground plans and strategies than she would ever have imagined. Recruiting volunteers, mapping the best routes based on the latest information passed by word of mouth, timelines, supporting activities, and arranging for provisions with help from the First African Baptist Church. Elizabeth was both fascinated and deeply moved.

One evening after supper, a month or so later, Daniel called out to Elizabeth and asked her to come up to the servant quarters on the upper floor.

As she rose to the top of the stairs, Elizabeth asked, "Do we have a guest staying with us this evening?"

"No ma'am, but if we did, we would have hid that person away first. Chloe has somethin' for you," Daniel answered.

She followed him to the housemaid Chloe's room. There, Harriett Anne and Chloe sat on the opposite corners of the bed. Chloe had something bulky on her knees, wrapped in old newspapers. She slid it off onto the bed and stood when Elizabeth entered. So did Harriett Anne.

Pointing down at the package, Chloe said, "This is somethin' for you, Miss Van Lew. Please, come open it, ma'am."

Elizabeth knelt by the bed and ripped the wrapping, exposing a vibrant colored quilt. The quilt had four patched panels. The top left hand panel depicted geese in flight, with a red barn and blue sky in the background. In the upper right panel was a sail boat. The bottom included a church steeple, a night skyline with an oversized moon and scattered stars in the left panel. In the remaining panel was the silhouette of a man, women and child holding hands.

"I don't know what to say. Simply exquisite."

"Chloe made it herself," Harriet Anne proudly shared.

"I see that," Elizabeth said. "Chloe Jenkins, you could be a very accomplished seamstress. I love this, it is so beautiful. But, why give it to me?"

"Miss Van Lew, we are all very grateful for what you have done for us and for helpin' Daniel with the Underground. Hasn't he told you, Miss Van Lew, about how we use quilts?" Chloe asked.

"I think I did mention once about how we try to help runaways find the next station house along the way," Daniel said.

"I remember," Elizabeth responded. "Follow the North Star. I recall something about using a quilt to signal if a hiding place along the way it is safe or not."

"Yes, ma'am." He picked up the quilt and continued, "When the quilt is folded across a porch rail or fence like this, with the bottom side out, it ain't safe. Not safe to go to the house until you see the front showin' the right way, like this." He flipped it around.

"Do you already have a quilt you've been using here?"

"Well, no ma'am. Not here. Like I said before, only a few times have we had guests stayin' with us here. Daniel answered.

Handing the quilt back to Daniel, Elizabeth said, "Why don't we use it at 2301 East Grace Street?"

"But this was meant as a present for you, Miss Van Lew," Chloe said.

"I am very appreciative, Chloe. This quilt is very beautiful, and I have no intention of ever giving it away permanently. Think of it as on loan. Why should we not put it to good use until present circumstances change? Getting it back when it is no longer needed. That will make it even more precious to me."

As Elizabeth descended the stairs, she realized Daniel was following close behind.

"Miss Van Lew. Somethin' else, if you don't mind. I do have a request."

"What is it, Daniel?"

"Seeing Mary again reminded me how you helped her when she was little. Her and Lucy's children. Learnin' them to read and write. Could you teach me and my wife Harriett Anne, too?"

"Daniel Gates, I'd be delighted."

Daniel said, "it just might be useful one day."

Surprisingly, only 3 of the 15 slaves left the Van Lew's, and none of the household help. Two from the farm and one from the hardware store. John was convinced he could get by in the store. His bigger problem was losing business due to the war. He didn't need more help. All the servants were excited and appreciative of getting compensated, even if they couldn't spend it right away.

Chapter 4: Cloaked in Secrecy

Soldiers in the regular army from Virginia, as well as other states electing to secede were forced to make difficult personal decisions. Should they remain faithful to the United States they had sworn to defend? What if they were asked to attack their own homeland? Should they continue to support the Federal Government, or should they resign from their command? Many southerners believed it was their higher duty to defend their family, friends and neighbors, preserving their way of life, with all that entailed, including the right to own slaves. Many U.S. soldiers concluded state rights and personal responsibility to protect against any outside infringement trumped allegiance to their country.

Robert E. Lee was one of those soldiers. Son of an American Revolutionary War hero, "White-Horse Harry," Lee was also married to the great granddaughter of George Washington. His classical appearance with strong facial features and well-proportioned torso accentuated by perfect posture conveyed the image of the mythical Virginian Cavalier. Shortly after Virginians voted to switch sides, he had resigned his military commission to join the Confederacy. He had been Lincoln's first choice to command the Union Army. A painful decision he claimed, but in the end loyalty to Virginia trumped his allegiance to the Federal Government. Instead, he accepted a position to help organize Virginia forces and advise the new Confederate President on war related matters. Like his Commander-in-Chief, Lee would have preferred a battlefield command.

With the prized addition of Virginia joining the Rebel states, the move of the capital to Richmond seemed like a prudent decision at the time. Robert E. Lee understood immediately that his home state with its industrial base, mixed allegiances, and proximity to Washington, would be a primary target for Federal assault. Many southerners believed the Yankees would not put up much of a fight and the war would end quickly with a Confederate victory. Lee thought differently. He believed the war would be a long, costly slog for both sides.

Jefferson Davis, who was originally against secession, was among those who shared the more common view, believing the war would end without a prolonged conflict reaching "proportions more gigantic." He was convinced the stakes were higher for the southerners, fighting to protect their native soil. The South did not need to defeat the Yankees. They simply needed the North to give up the fight. This could come from battle fatigue, for example, or rising antiwar sentiment from the populace. To defeat the secessionists, on the other hand, the Federalists would need to invade, capture, and hold Confederate territory.

It was also the belief of Jefferson Davis that the Confederates had some of the best generals, including several top West Point graduates. The most proficient battle tested field commanders, as well. By defecting from the Union Army to fight for the South, Davis was convinced these officers and field commanders gave the Confederates another crucial advantage – not only in training and experience, but they were knowledgeable about the personality of enemy commanders, and could anticipate strategy and tactics as these Union field generals took the offensive, launching attacks against the South. He was convinced the Confederates could rout the invading Unionists. However, this assumed a successful buildup of military forces and supporting infrastructure where none currently existed. Davis became consumed in all things related to this effort.

On paper, the Union seemed to hold considerable advantages over the Confederate States. There was a significantly higher population in the North, with approximately 21 million people, against less than 9 million in the South. Almost with 3.5 million of those who were slaves. The Union possessed 100,000 manufacturing plants versus 18,000 in the Confederate South. The Federals also held a 30-to-1 edge in arms manufacturing, and a 2-to-1 advantage in available manpower. In addition, the North had better highways and a much more powerful navy that could blockade southern ports of entry.

The Yankees had their own challenges. Northern ranks contained a higher proportion of men from urban areas, including immigrants from

Ireland and Germany. Southerners were better equipped to cope with rural conditions in battle, and many of the potential hazards to survival in the southern terrain. Calvary was still an important element in waging war, and the South had more proficient riders, most who owned their own horse – an early advantage, as long as replacements weren't needed. They also had a greater number of enlistees who were already adept at using firearms.

As spring turned to summer with temperatures swelling, green pastures already engulfed with large patches of brownish yellow, and the air intensely dry and thick, residents of Richmond did all they could to find some comfort from the punishing heat. Concerns about the weather, however, were secondary to the looming expectation that their city would soon be under attack. This disturbing, inescapable fear hung even heavier over the city.

Since the first shots were fired at Fort Sumter the previous April, there had been isolated skirmishes in places such as in the western part of Virginia, near the towns of Philippi and Bethel, for example. Local newspapers reported the Federals were amassing a large army just outside Washington, little more than 100 miles away from the new Confederate Capital. Citizens of Richmond braced themselves for the inevitable siege sure to come. Perhaps what felt like a subtropical heat wave was the only reason it had not happened already.

For the most part, Elizabeth continued to respect Daniel's wishes and kept her distance from his work for the Underground. There was one exception, when Daniel came to her and asked for help. A runaway named Zach who had struck his master.

"You know, Miss Van Lew, I wouldn't, be talkin' to you about this, unless I thought it might be the only way," Daniel explained.

With Elizabeth's concurrence, Daniel brought Zach down to the kitchen, early morning, and already sweltering heat was beginning to invade the downstairs of the Van Lew home. Both her mother and brother were out. He introduced Zach to Elizabeth. Zach had worked on a local farm. Elizabeth knew the family that owned the farm. She never liked the husband. She remembered he was mean to his wife in public.

"Nice to meet you ma'am. I'm so sorry for what I did. So sorry." Zach was visibly shaken.

"You have nothin' to be sorry or ashamed about, Zach. Tell Miss Van Lew what happened in your own words."

"He doesn't have to do that, Daniel. Only if he wants to tell me. Zach, please sit down here at the kitchen table. Can we get you something to eat or drink?"

"No, ma'am. Thank you."

"Go on, Zach." Daniel said encouragingly.

Zach tried to steady himself.

"I came into the barn. Saw him rip clothes off Becky, a little slave girl, maybe 12 years' old. That's all. Tried to pull him away but he resisted and told me to go away. I pushed him again, and had to punch him before he could punch me. He fell over. Think I knocked him out. I turned around and there was Becky lookin' scared as hell, oh excuse me, ma'am..."

"No apology necessary, but please I'd like you to continue," Elizabeth requested.

"Told her to get out of there as fast as she could and go to her mamma. I stood there lookin' down at him. He was still out. Didn't think anythin' else to do but run."

Daniel spoke next. "Thanks, Zach. Why don't you go on back upstairs. I'll be there shortly."

Harriett Anne had stepped into the kitchen. "Come with me first, Zach. I'll get you corn bread and some milk to take back up with ya."

"Do tell, Daniel. I am sure there is a good reason you wanted me to meet Zach and hear firsthand about his predicament."

"Yes, Miss Van Lew. I have an idea to help Zach escape up north, but I wanted to ask for your advice. Help too, if you agree."

"With the Underground Railroad?"

"That's just it. There are search parties combing the area and newly assigned Confederate pickets surroundin' the outskirts of the city. Guess they think the Yankees might be plannin' to attack Richmond real soon. Be very dangerous to try and move Zach right now. The way we usually do."

Daniel shared the scheme he had in mind.

"Zach is about the same height and build as Isaac. He's good with horses, too. He used to take a horse drawn wagon to bring farm goods in for the town market on a regular basis."

Isaac, as Daniel explained, was supposed to travel to Fredericksburg re-plenish supplies for John Van Lew's hardware store. A normal ride Isaac Drury did a few times a year to pick up additional hardware supplies. Isaac was scheduled to go in a couple of days. Zach could take the place of Isaac, wearing Isaac's hat and overcoat. Daniel could travel with him and bring the horse drawn wagon back along a different route.

"I would think this would be very dangerous. Wouldn't it be more like-ly that he would be caught this way?"

"Sometimes when they are out lookin' under every stone, it's best to pass right under their noses," Daniel responded.

There was one problem with the plan as Daniel explained to Elizabeth. It was against the law for slaves to travel without papers and with the Con-federacy, in a declared state of war, these regulations were strictly enforced. Severe penalties were being enforced for violators. In addition to wearing Isaac's hat and coat, Zach would need to use Isaac's papers.

"All we need is for you, Miss Van Lew, to write up travel papers for me," Daniel pointed out.

"A well thought out idea, Daniel, but there is another problem."

"Your brother, John."

Given it involves my brother's business and his business contacts in Fredericksburg, we really need to let him know about this one."

"You sure about this, Miss Van Lew?"

"No, I'm not, but Zach's story is very compelling. Let Zach tell it to my brother, too. He may not always appear to be, but deep down, John is a good man. My brother doesn't need to know about the room, or about any of the others. Just that you are trying to help a man falsely accused. John knows his owner like I do, and the kind of person he is."

After Zach told his story to John Newton, just as he had with Elizabeth, her brother asked to speak privately with Daniel.

"Poor Zach. Has himself in quite a bind. I believe him and would like to help, but not sure how we can. They are desperate to find the poor fellow. Make a lesson out of him for others."

Daniel presented his idea and then waited for John to respond, assum-ing the answer would probably be no.

John stared back at Daniel for a few seconds and then said, "Why did Zach come here?"

"Zach knows me from church. Told me he thought of goin' there first but figured it might get the minister and a bunch of other members of the church in trouble. Guess he decided to single me out first."

"I'm worried about getting my family in trouble. I'm sure you can understand this, Daniel. He can't stay here."

"I agree with that, Mr. Van Lew. Can't stay anywhere in town. Need to get him out."

"Must be some other place he could stay until things quiet done. He could try leaving when it safer."

"They ain't goin' to give up lookin for him. There's a reward for his capture. They been puttin' posters 'bout Zach up all over town. Make him sound real bad. You never know who might turn him in. When they do find him, and they will if he stays in Richmond, he may get lynched. No judge gonna believe his word over his master."

Sympathetic to Zach's predicament, John confided that he still thought Daniel's plan was "too risky and far-fetched." He again stated "there must be a safer place he can hide. "Some other way to get him out."

"Maybe, Mr. Van Lew. I have racked my brains but can't think of any. Not with search parties all 'round Richmond. He is good with horses like I said. Both Isaac and I will vouch for him. I'll be with him the whole time. Isaac will fill in for me around the house. You have my word, sir. I'll be real careful and make sure I bring your supplies back with the horses. Do my best to make sure all goes well."

"You must realize, Daniel, you would be putting yourself in great danger, too."

"I do."

"Sorry, Daniel, I feel bad for Zach, but too many things could go wrong."

Not surprised by John's answer, but still very disappointed, Daniel left the room to resume his duties around the house.

The next morning was a Saturday. Daniel was eating an early breakfast with his wife Harriett Anne in the kitchen when John entered the room.

His store was usually opened Saturdays, but John had decided to close it on this particular day.

"I have an idea."

Daniel was convinced the idea would be a polite way of suggesting again how Zach should hide someplace else.

"Yes, sir," Daniel said, preparing himself to hear out John's suggestion, whatever that might be.

Let's test this out first, and then I will decide."

"Sorry, Mr. Van Lew. I don't understand. Test what?"

"Go get Zach. I assume you have him tucked away in the servant quarters. Meet me and Isaac at the barn."

It became a dress rehearsal. Wearing Isaac's cap and overcoat, Zach took John Van Lew for a ride around the neighborhood. With Zach hunkered down over the reins, and his cap dipped over his forehead, John was surprised how easily Zach could pass for Isaac.

They rode by people he knew who said hello to him and also called out to Isaac. Zach played it perfectly, raising his left hand as a greeting but never looking up. His expertise as a driver was clearly evident.

As they pulled back into the Van Lew property, where Daniel and Isaac waited for them, John jumped off the carriage as Isaac took the reins from Zach.

Speaking directly to Daniel, John said, "I'm satisfied. Let's plan on Zach and you leaving Monday morning. In meantime, better get Zach back upstairs before one of the neighbors starts to wonder if Isaac Drury has a twin. After Isaac puts the horses away, the three of us should work out the rest of the plan."

As they walked back to the house, Zach questioned Daniel, "what changed his mind?"

"Don't know and figured better not to ask."

Later, when Daniel could speak privately with Elizabeth, he began by saying, "I don't know how you did it, but thank you..."

"Wasn't me. Mother overheard John and I talking last night. She told my brother how proud she was of him recently. Also, how terrible we would all feel if Zach was caught. It was her idea, taking the ride and testing Zach out."

"God bless her."

"Like I said, my brother is a good man. Just took a little more of a nudge from mother. John is a shrewd and tough businessman. Doesn't want anything to spoil the family business. Also is trying to be protective of mother and me. The way father was."

"Yes, I know this is true. Thinkin' maybe he also knows how terrible the two of you would make him feel if he didn't try and help Zach."

Elizabeth smiled. "Could be little of that, too."

The wagon was stopped a few times as Daniel anticipated. Two African Americans travelling by themselves was sure to attract attention. They checked the papers and inside the wagon cart, but each time they were allowed to keep going.

Daniel dropped Zach off at an Underground station house just outside Fredericksburg and then went to the supplier's warehouse. When the supplier asked about Isaac, Daniel explained he was taking his place as Isaac was sick. Zach would end up in Pennsylvania with an older brother who had escaped slavery years ago.

John was delighted when Daniel arrived in front of the store with the needed supplies. After unloading the cart, Daniel drove it back to the house where Elizabeth and Isaac greeted him at the barn. Elizabeth had just finished riding one of the horses.

"I hope you didn't forget to bring my clothes back with you, Daniel," Isaac yelled as Daniel entered the property.

"I have them all, Isaac," Daniel shouted back, as he lifted Isaac's coat in the air.

Before he could step off the carriage, Elizabeth said, "John knows."

Sorry ma'am? Daniel was confused. "Pardon me?"

"He has known about runaways hiding upstairs for some time. Long before the false room."

"Mr. Van Lew never mentioned anything about it. I don't understand."

"I suppose, just like you once explained to me, Daniel, John decided the less he knew, or pretended not to know, the better for all of us."

"He told me after he went upstairs to the servants quarters the other day and noticed the divided room with the fake wall."

"Never saw him go up there before. So what do we do now?"

"I think we carry on just as before. If my brother doesn't say anything to you, no need to change what you have been doing. No need to bring it up."

The first major battle of the Civil War, the Battle of First Manassas, as Southerners called it, was fought July 21, 1861. The North referred to it as the Battle of Bull Run; and run they did. At the time, many northerners believed the Union Army could cross the Potomac and easily push through, encountering little resistance, as it advanced all the way to Richmond.

At the height of the battle, both sides had comparable numbers of soldiers, around 30,000. Union forces suffered an estimated 2,600 causalities, including 480 killed, 1,000 wounded, and 1,200 missing. While the Confederate army was the presumptive winner, it too suffered significant losses. Over 2,000 causalities, 390 killed, 1,600 wounded, and over a dozen missing.

Over the past 10 years, Manassas had become an important railroad junction. Using it to their advantage, an additional 10,000 Confederate troops were transported by train from the Shenandoah Valley to Manassas in response to the Federal offensive. This was the first time in history trains played a critical role in troop movement to an active battlefield. This action proved decisive.

The confrontation quickly shifted to a Union rout and became known as the "Great Skedaddle." The untested rag tag Rebel soldiers sent the Union Army fleeing through the crowds of spectators who had assembled to show their support, as if it was a sporting event. It concluded as a fragmented, disorganized retreat, with panicked Union soldiers scattering away, ignoring their commanding officers.

The defeat on the battlefield could have been further exploited. As Union soldiers fled back to Washington, the exhausted Confederate troops failed to give chase. They very well might have advanced all the way to the Capitol, less than 40 miles away, meeting little resistance.

The battle helped incubate the legend of General Thomas J. "Stonewall" Jackson throughout the South. When another general told him early in the conflict that they were being beaten back, Jackson refused to budge, "standing like a stone wall." In the end, lead command General

P.G.T. Beauregard was lauded for defeating Union forces under General Irwin McDowell, a fellow classmate from West Point.

The war had a profound effect on Richmond. Manufacturing ammunition was replacing tobacco as the largest industry. Just as trains had played a critical role in the First Battle of Manassas, they were now helping to transport both the wounded, as well as Union prisoners to Richmond. Many homes were converted to makeshift hospitals.

Over 1,000 Union prisoners were brought to Richmond, many in railroad cattle cars. Some were paraded through the streets as onlookers jeered. Ligon's Tobacco Factory was converted to a provisional prison. Not much was done in the beginning to make these facilities capable of holding large numbers of prisoners, or to adequately secure them. Confederate leaders believed Richmond would only need to provide a temporary holding facility until they were transported further south, or exchanged for prisoners.

The Van Lew's were depressed when they heard the news. So was Daniel. As he confided in Elizabeth, "I heard those dang Confederates whipped the Union soldiers good. That true, Miss Van Lew?"

"I hate to say it, Daniel, but I'm afraid they did."

Elizabeth worked her family connections to arrange a meeting with Brigadier General John H. Winder to request privileges to visit enemy prisoners. Winder was the Inspector General of all Richmond camps, which included prisoners. Elizabeth assured her mother that if her request was granted, she would keep up the pretense of loyalty to the new government.

It was a mild, pleasant day. Elizabeth decided to walk to the General's Office, less than three miles away. General Winder was a distinguished looking, 60 plus in years, with silver gray hair. He had a strong, athletic build of a much younger man. He too was a graduate of West Point, who had served with distinction in the Mexican War. As was the case with the wife of Lincoln's family, Mary Todd and her half-brothers fighting for the Confederacy, the Winder family was divided over the war. General Winder had a son who was a soldier with the Confederates, and one who was a captain in the Union army.

"Brother against brother" became another gruesome aspect of the conflict. This most often occurred in families from states bordering the north-south divide. Maryland, home to the Winder family, or Kentucky, where the Todd's were from, were typical border states. Along with Delaware and Missouri, slavery was legal, but the border states never declared for secession from the Union.

Elizabeth came armed with a letter of introduction from an acquaintance, Confederate Treasury Secretary Christopher Memminger. In that letter, Memminger recommended that Winder should consider allowing her to meet with prisoners, but only officer prisoners. As Memminger had explained to her, "We don't want you exposed to the riff-raff from northern cities. General Winder will have the discretion to say no, or if he accepts, to terminate this privilege whenever he deems fit."

They began by talking about the Confederate victory at Manassas. Winder was polite and amiable. Elizabeth did her best to overwhelm the general with a charm offensive, complimenting him on his regal appearance and striking mane of silver hair. While he appeared flattered, the general still expressed reservations about granting the request, even if it was for officer prisoners only. He explained how she would see many unpleasant things, terrible injuries and men suffering from serious depression.

"I am aware of this, General. All the more reason why I am convinced by visiting with these men and providing even a small bit of comfort, it just might help lift their spirits. Even captive enemy soldiers deserve a little compassion. I'm sure you must agree with this."

There was an uncomfortable few moments of silence. Elizabeth waited for the general to speak first.

Finally, he said, "Alright Miss Van Lew. We will give it a try and see how it goes."

As she entered the gate on her way home, she saw Isaac walking up from the barn. Isaac had given up trying to convince her to avoid walking by herself through some of the downtown streets not suited for a lady of privilege. He noticed that she looked upset.

"Somethin' wrong, Miss Van Lew?" he asked, as he increased his pace to catch up with her. "Hope the General didn't say no."

"Hello, Isaac. He agreed to let me meet with prisoners, but only officer prisoners. No, not that..."

"Well that's good to hear, but what is it then, Miss Van Lew? Not feelin' well?"

"No. I mean, it's not that either. You caught me lost in my thoughts, Isaac. I supposed you could say, I'm not very comfortable doing certain things. Things I never would have dreamed of doing in the past."

"Oh? Sorry ma'am. You don't have to say nothin' more..."

"It's fine Isaac. Just that, well, to get access to visit the prisoners, I had to pretend as if I was a loyalist to the Confederate States. More disturbing, I found myself fawning to win the general's good graces."

"Flirting with him, Miss Van Lew?"

Elizabeth was startled. Before she could reply, Isaac laughed.

"Isaac. I'm never sure when you are kidding. No, of course not, but I'm not used to being deceitful like this. Made me feel very uncomfortable to say those things. I'm surprised the General couldn't see through my exaggerated flattery."

"Way I see it, nothin' wrong with what you did, ma'am. You could say the Underground Railroad was built on a rail of lies all these years. How else could they make it work?"

Elizabeth smiled. "You have something there, Isaac."

"I know I can say this to you, Miss Van Lew. The biggest lie I know 'bout is slavery. As if it's the normal way things should be. That's why we all gotta hope and pray the Yankees win this war. Do what we can to help, too. Just like you're doin', Miss Van Lew."

On her first visit to what was now called Libby Prison for Union Officers, Elizabeth brought some home baked goods that she helped Harriett Anne prepare. Daniel had provided a description of the newly converted prison. It was based on second hand information from slaves who were still owned by the former tobacco factory owner, but were now working on a loan arrangement for the prison.

The description was quite accurate, but seeing it, firsthand, was not the same. The stench was nauseating. The men were crammed together with hardly any space for themselves. Many looked unnaturally thin and weak.

Hundreds of them were crowded together in separate rooms, some as small as 40 by 100 feet on upper floors. Cots were reserved for the wounded and sick. Most of the men had to sleep on the bare floor of their rooms, in a spooning position. There was also no secure space outside the prison where they could get fresh air. Stifling hot in warm weather with little ventilation. Cold and dank the rest of the year.

Elizabeth was particularly upset seeing prisoners who were in obvious need of medical attention. One soldier they met with was a recent amputee. After removing his leg, he was sent back to the general holding cell. The man was in excruciating pain and badly needed additional medical attention. She managed to have him brought back to the makeshift hospital room.

For the next several weeks, Elizabeth would bring her mother and continue to visit with northern prisoners. They brought extra blankets that were in short supply. She asked her brother John to order a bulk shipment of bandages and lint through his store, also badly needed.

"Given what we see here for officers, I can't imagine what conditions are like in the prisons for the regular soldiers," Elizabeth whispered to her mother during one of their visits.

When she explained to Daniel one day about the conditions, he made a suggestion that was completely unexpected.

"I know a couple of the slaves on the inside. The guards they say are easy to bribe. They provide tobacco and liquor to prisoners willin' to pay. We just might be able to bribe them to help some prisoners escape."

"Really, you think so, Daniel? I'd be willing to provide some cash from my inheritance."

"Worth a try. We can use my connections through the Underground, but, just so you know, Miss Van Lew, we have to be even more careful today with so many soldiers protectin' Richmond and all those search parties lookin' for runaways. Seem to be everywhere."

"Yes, I understand, Daniel."

He continued. "Often times gettin' away depends on runaway slaves of color blending in with other people of color as they move north. A white man with a northern accent could easily stand out. He also might not be comfortable hunkering down with negroes in some of the hidin' places we use along the way."

"I don't think so. I suspect many are abolitionists. They were all fighting against an illegitimate government that wants to preserve slavery of their fellow human beings. A few, perhaps, may be uncomfortable at first. Out of ignorance. But, it's a path to freedom, and my guess they would be willing to do whatever is necessary."

"You do have a point there, Miss Van Lew. I've seen people do some amazin' things over the years for that."

"These prisoner soldiers, I'm sure, are more than willing to take the risk of getting caught, same as runaway slaves. Whatever they encounter has to be better than being stuck in that awful prison."

"I do hope you are right," Miss Van Lew.

The highest-ranking Union officer in each assigned room was designated as an advocate for the other prisoners, and more importantly from the Confederate view, to help keep order as per standard military conduct. Food rations were sparse. Pleading for better treatment changed very little.

Elizabeth always made a point of introducing herself to the ranking officer. They were generally very pleased to have her visit with the other men. During one of their visits, they met with a young good-looking officer. He was sitting up on the bare floor against a wall, reading a manual. He sprang to his feet as the women stopped in front of his bed area. The young man was boyish in both appearance and mannerism. He was gangling in his sudden movements, and seemed nervous.

"My name is Elizabeth Van Lew, and this is my mother, Eliza."

"Good day, ladies," he responded. Establishing eye contact with Elizabeth, he continued, "I know who you are, Miss Van Lew. I am Lieutenant Peter Jennings. Nice to meet both of you."

Jennings had sad eyes and appeared nervous. He asked if he could speak privately with Elizabeth.

"I'll go visit with some of the others," Eliza said as she moved away.

Another officer, noticing Elizabeth standing, pulled over one of the few empty stools in the room, smiled and walked away.

"Thanks, Tibbits," Jennings called after him as he sat back down on the floor.

They had as much privacy as they could get in a room filled with other prisoners. A few feet away were a group of high ranking officers playing cards. Another group of men were talking by the small barred window which cast a meager hint of light into the room. Another officer was napping a few feet away.

Looking around, making sure no one else was in ear shot, Jennings whispered to Elizabeth, "Miss Van Lew, I need your help."

"We visit here to do as much as we can for captured Union soldiers, but there is a limit to what we can do. May I ask, what kind of help do you need?"

"Help me get out of here, please, he mumbled under his breath." He sheepishly looked around to see if he could spot anyone who might have heard him.

"As I am sure, every other prisoner here would like to do as well," Elizabeth softly responded. She added, "What makes you think I can help?"

"I have heard about you. They don't let others come and go like they let you. They say you got some pull with the prison authorities."

Jennings looked around and noticed another stool recently vacated.

"One second," he asserted as he pulled himself up, scurrying quickly across the room to retrieve it. He snatched it away just before someone else was about to claim it. He placed it side by side to where Elizabeth was already seated, and squatted down next to her.

"I don't think you intended to do so, but you now have gained the attention of most in the room," Elizabeth noted.

"That's all right. As long as they can't hear us."

"You realize trying to escape would be very dangerous. Probably severe penalty too, if caught."

"I do know that," Jennings quickly blurted out a little too loudly.

Elizabeth gazed back at Jennings. She then said, "If you don't mind my asking, you seem very upset. Did something happen to make you feel this way?"

"Been happening for some time. Frankly, it's little embarrassing. A few of the Confederate guards got to calling me "Lamb Chop." I took a swing at one of them and was punished for it. They locked me up in a separate room for a few days. Fed me only bread and water."

"That is terrible."

"It got worse." Jennings pointed to a set of doors in the far side of the room. "See that closet over there? That's what we call the water closet. Got a sink with running water from the James River, and a trough used as a toilet.

The guards tell us we are lucky. One of the few buildings in the area with running water."

"One of the many amenities, I assume," Elizabeth sarcastically whispered.

For the first time Jennings cracked a smile before continuing. "About a week ago, one of those same guards found me in there alone. Grabbed me from behind. Said he was going to teach me a lesson. Luckily, I was able to push him away and get out."

"Did you tell Colonel Davies? Isn't he charged with helping the rest of you assigned to this room?"

"I did, but he said it was his word against mine, and as a prisoner my word wouldn't count for much. He said he believed me, but not much he could do. Didn't expect much from him. He thinks I am a hot head."

"Are you?" Elizabeth asked.

"No, at least don't think so. They keep pushing me to my limit," he responded, defensively, clenching his fist. He then added, "Some of the other prisoners started calling me the same names too. I can't stand it much longer."

"Well, I could talk to General Winder about his guards."

"Nah, don't bother. Doubt it would do any good. Could make things worse. If you can't help me, I'll figure something out on my own. Can't do this any longer."

"I'll be back in a few days. Give me a little time. No promises, but let me see."

Five days passed. Jennings was a wreck, fearful Elizabeth might not return. He was delighted when he finally spotted her enter his designated room with Eliza. He had been talking to another prisoner. Quickly ending the conversation, he approached her walking up with an awkward gait.

Elizabeth greeted him, loud enough so others could hear, "Lieutenant Jennings, so nice to see you again." She then whispered, "The prison warden has limited the number of my visits. Otherwise I would have come sooner. Let's just stand here and keep it very brief. Don't want to raise any suspicion."

"Yes, I understand," Jennings said.

Elizabeth waved to another prisoner she recognized. Continuing to whisper to Jennings, she said, "Stay here with mother. She will fill you in. I'm going over there." She walked over to the man who was now motioning for her to join him.

As Elizabeth walked away, Eliza began to speak in a very low voice a she pointed out the window. "You have a nice view here of the James River."

"Yes, ma'am. I'd rather be viewing it from the outside."

Eliza, unaffected, continued. "You can see the Kanahwa Canal and some of the loading docks in the distance." When she was sure no one else was paying attention, she changed the subject. "There is a slave who cleans the water closet. His name is Walter. You can trust him."

"Yes, I know who he is."

"When you see Walter enter the water closet, follow him there. He will explain everything. The plan is for Walter to help you slip out tomorrow night. When you are outside of the prison, there will be another negro man waiting for you at the northeast corner of Carey Street. He will be hiding in the shadows behind the warehouse across from the prison. He will take you to a safe place."

"I can't thank..."

"Please don't. There's my daughter. We can't stay any longer. Good day, Lieutenant."

That night Walter explained the plan. Jennings was impressed with his attention to detail and clear, concise directions. There was nothing that portrayed submissiveness in Walter's conversation or behavior. His eye contact was direct. Medium height, with a muscular torso, Jennings assumed this was a man who had endured unspeakable hardship. Much worse than he ever had. Walter, he decided, was unbreakable.

Just as Walter described, the next evening a guard came to the door of the holding room and then stepped aside for Walter to pass by. He came through the door with a push cart filled with buckets, brushes and towels. Jennings was waiting in the water closet as he was told to do. He watched Walter approach the closet through a small knot hole in the pinewood wall.

Several minutes passed. The guard was still at the door. Walter finished up in the water closet and rolled his cart toward the door. The guard held the door as Walter pushed his cart through the door of the prison room.

Pulling his cart down the hall, Walter turned the corner and approached a storage area.

When he heard "Ok, now" from Walter, Jennings threw the towels covering him aside, hopped off the cart and followed Walter down a back staircase. He started to panic and step back when he saw another guard at the foot of the stairs.

"Don't worry," Walter muttered. "He's here to help. A few dollars' worth of help..."

The guard held up his hand for them to stop. He stepped around a corner, came back and signaled for them to follow. He took them to a side door and unlocked it. No words were exchanged.

By the end of the next week, Daniel proudly told Elizabeth that Lieutenant Jennings who had stayed in the secret room in the Van Lew mansion had made it safely to Union territory, north of the state line.

There would be other isolated escapes. Elizabeth helped to fund several. So did other Unionists. In some instances, imprisoned officers who had successfully horded their own cash into the prison were also able to bribe guards to escape.

A minor skirmish between the North and South in Northern Virginia took place, October 1861. Based on a bad intelligence report and poor planning, Union forces were routed again at the Battle of Ball's Bluff. With approximately 1,700 soldiers committed to the battle for the North, they suffered over 400 causalities, and the Confederates took close to 500 prisoners.

The Confederates, with a comparable sized army, suffered less than 300 causalities, with only a few captured prisoners, making it another humiliating defeat for the North – small in terms of battle size, but politically devastating for the northern military command. Shortly after, Winfield Scott, "The Grand Old Man of the Army," would retire, and President Lincoln would name George McClellan his new commander for the Army of the Potomac.

Richmond's already overcrowded tobacco factories being used as prisons would have to absorb more Union soldiers and officers.

The Van Lew's were distressed when articles began to appear in Richmond newspapers criticizing a mother and daughter from Church Hill for visiting enemy prisoners.

The *Richmond Examiner* reported:

> Two ladies, mother and daughter, living on Church Hill, have lately attracted public notice by their assiduous attentions to the Yankee prisoners...these two women have been expending their opulent means in aiding and giving comfort to the miscreants who have invaded our sacred soil, bent on rapine and murder, the desolation of our homes and sacred places, and the ruin and dishonour of our families.

The *Richmond Enquirer* article was harsher and threatening in tone, as it described these "certain females of decidedly Northern and Abolition proclivities," and the potential consequences. Elizabeth read it aloud to her mother:

> The creatures, though specially alluded to, are not named. Were their names unveiled to the world, it would doubtless be found that they were Yankee off-shoots, who had succeeded by stinginess, double-dealing, and cuteness, to amass out of the credulity of Virginians a good, substantial pile of the root of all evil. If such people do not wish to be exposed and dealt with as alien enemies to the country, they would do well to cut stick while they can do so with safety to their worthless carcasses.

As she put down the newspaper, Elizabeth looked up at her mother and said, "If there is a silver lining, we won't have to worry about receiving anymore invitations to those ghastly Phoebe Reynolds social events."

Eliza, trying to make light of it herself responded, "No more sewing, hurrah." Yet she could not stop her true feelings from overwhelming her again. "Imagine printing this. Referring to us as a 'creatures', 'worthless carcasses', 'Yankee off-shoots'." Her voice was cracking and she was visibly upset.

"Well, Yankee off-shoots isn't so bad. After all, both you and father were from northern families. There is some truth to that," Elizabeth pointed out in a sarcastic tone, doing little to relieve her mother's distress.

Eliza suggested they should refrain from visits for a while. Elizabeth disagreed. With additional captured soldiers added to the already overcrowded prison, the visits were even more important than ever, she contended. They eventually compromised.

To help deflect criticism and suspicion of the family, Eliza would become even more involved in volunteer work to support the Confederate soldiers. Elizabeth would also occasionally participate with her mother, but she would continue her visits to Federal prisoners. Most of the time by herself.

With her trips to the prison, and the negative publicity it had generated, Elizabeth knew her activities were becoming more closely scrutinized by neighbors. She was still struggling, trying to come to terms with her new double life and the duplicity in behavior it entailed.

At one point when she and Daniel were alone she joked, "I could have benefited from formal training on this as opposed to all those unending school lectures on proper etiquette I had to sit through."

Elizabeth's next visit to Libby was shortly after new prisoners had arrived. One of the men she had become accustomed to meeting with greeted her with surprising news.

"We have a famous name in our midst," he said. Clarifying his statement, the prisoner noted, "Well, he is actually related to one. A famous Revolutionary War hero. Shares the same name. Paul Revere. Grandson of the Boston patriot himself."

Major Paul Joseph Revere suffered a leg wound injury at Ball's Bluff and was taken prisoner. He had been recently released from the hospital quarters, but was still recovering from his wound.

"Where is he?" Elizabeth asked.

"Over there," he responded, pointing to a man lying in his cot, apparently fast asleep.

"Thanks," she said. "I'll meet with a few others first. I'll check back later to see if Mr. Revere is awake and open to seeing visitors."

Later, he was sitting upright. Elizabeth approached him.

Standing to the side of the cot, Elizabeth said, "Major Revere, my name is Elizabeth Van Lew. A pleasure to meet you, sir."

He was a handsome man, with a long handlebar mustache. Instinctively, Revere started to get up, wincing as the pain from his leg spread.

"Please, don't try that."

Revere nodded. "Nice to meet you too. Are you a nurse?"

"No, I'm simply here to visit. I can get someone who is and can help you."

"Nah, I'm fine, thank you, Miss Van Lew. Very kind of you."

"I met several of your relatives, years ago at White Sulphur Springs."

"My cousins. Mother's side of the family. I can remember them talking about it. Very pleasurable resort, but a long trip from Boston."

"Yes, it would be. We had others from the Boston area that also made the long journey. Must have been 15 years ago, but I can remember Daniel Webster when he visited. As you might expect, when someone asked him about State's rights and the possibility of some of them breaking away, he made a passionate argument about preserving the Union. He got into an argument with several annoying secessionists."

"I would assume that would rouse a most passionate rebuke from 'The Great Orator,' God rest his soul."

"Sorry to admit, but I joined in on a few separate occasions myself, to rebuke the separatists."

"Well done, my good lady."

He looked over Elizabeth's shoulder, noticing a guard who entered the room and strolled close by. This caught Elizabeth's attention, as well. Lowering his voice, Revere added, "Secessionists are worse than annoying. All of them."

Elizabeth could hardly contain her glee.

"I am sure you get asked all the time about your famous grandfather," Elizabeth commented.

"That I do. He was a great man, although, he didn't do all he gets credit for these days. Not diminishing his brave actions, but the myth keeps growing. Especially after Mr. Longfellow wrote his poem about grandpa's *Midnight Ride*. There were other brave souls who also rode that night to warn about the British, all doing so at their own peril."

On subsequent trips to the prison, Elizabeth always made a point of spending some time with Major Revere. His injuries required a long healing process, and he was always most grateful for the visit. Elizabeth guessed he was about 30 years old, about 15 years younger than her. Elizabeth found him to be well read and most interesting. Revere was a graduate of Harvard.

He loved exploring, and shared some of his adventures prior to joining the army. This included a summer expedition around Moosehead Lake in Maine, the largest mountain lake in the eastern United States. He also led a camping trip in the Adirondack Mountains. Major Revere shared another story about an outing in Lake Superior that turned deadly. He argued with his friends who accompanied him against taking their boat out amid inclement weather, with high gusty winds and unusually high waves. Three in the party drowned. Revere saved himself, and one other friend.

"Changed me forever," Revere confided. "The loss of my close friends was devastating."

Elizabeth shared with the Major some of her deep convictions against the breakaway government and slavery. She talked about her connection to the network run by slaves and how it was used recently to help another prisoner escape.

"Perhaps if you were healthy enough..."

"If only, however, my leg would prevent me from making a go of it. At least for now."

He told her about a recent attempted escape that went badly.

"We know there has to be a snitch in our midst, providing information back to the guards. We must assume the walls have ears," Revere cautioned.

One night, Revere explained, prisoners had been taking turns trying to cut a hole to an exterior facing wall, behind a large trunk, used to store blankets. They were digging through with a stolen cutlery knife, along with a hammer and chisel, one of the men had successfully smuggled in. Made quite a bit of noise, and they had to be careful that there were no guards nearby. They knew, according to Revere, that the guards often slept instead of doing their rounds. Upon breaking through the wall, the plan was to then tie sheets together and slide down between guard rounds.

Revere recounted for Elizabeth how one early morning, without warning, three guards entered the prison room with a couple slaves carrying construction tools and materials. One of the guards went directly over to the trunk. He pulled out the stolen knife and tools underneath blankets. He then dragged the trunk away from the wall exposing the partially dug hole. The other guards grabbed two prisoners, one still resting, and the other standing by a window on the opposite side of the room.

The slaves immediately went to work repairing the wall. As the guards pulled the two men along to the door, the other guard held up the tools. Revere recounted how he hollered, "Next time any of you Yankees try something like that, somebody's going get themselves strung up by the thumbs."

"What happened to the prisoners they pulled out?" Elizabeth asked.

"They were placed in a closed off room in the basement. Dirt floor wet after rain. Dank and miserable, I've been told. They were there for over a week. To this day, we don't know who squealed on them."

On her next trip to Libby Prison, Elizabeth, with the help of Isaac and Daniel, brought close to a dozen books. Some were historical; others were a combination of popular and classic novels. They were to be distributed based on what they thought various prisoners would find most enjoyable, recalling conversation from previous visits.

A guard was appointed to look through and check the books, prior to passing them out. His job was to make sure they weren't promoting anti-Confederate propaganda, or to catch anything that appeared to present abolitionist sentiments. Or, cut out sections of pages to hide weapons or digging tools small enough to hide in the books. This had happened once before. He gave each a cursory glance, before giving the pile back.

She waited until the very end of their book distribution mission to bring a specially selected gift to Major Revere. His leg was feeling a little better, and he had completed walking a few laps around the room earlier in the day.

He couldn't believe it when Elizabeth handed him the beat-up leather-bound book. It was Volume I, *Journals of the Expedition,* recounting the adventures of Lewis and Clark.

As Revere flipped the pages, Elizabeth explained, "This belonged to my father. I can only lend it to you, however, if you don't mind."

"Mind? Not at all Miss Van Lew, I would insist on returning it to you. This is a treasure that belongs to your family. I will take good care of it, and make sure I give it back, before I go anywhere. Not that I have any near term plans."

They both laughed. Others nearby looked over.

Major Revere continued, shaking his head. "I don't know quite what to say. This is extraordinary," he added as he continued to page through the printed journals.

"Like you, my father was from the northeast. He also loved to explore when he was young and single."

Looking at the copyright page, Revere noted, "This is a first edition, published in 1814."

"Yes, in Philadelphia, where my mother's family was from. Through her connections, father acquired one of the first copies, a few years before I was born."

Revere had stopped scrolling and placed his finger on a section, near the midsection of the book, and began to read aloud:

> The hills and river cliffs which we passed today exhibit a most romantic appearance. The bluffs of the river rise to the high of from 2 to 300 feet and in most places nearly perpendicular...the soft sand cliffs worn into a thousand grotesque figures...with the help of a little imagination are made to represent the elegant ranges of lofty freestone buildings...columns of various sculptures both grooved and plain...

Weeks passed before she was allowed to return. When Elizabeth went next to visit prisoners, Major Revere was no longer there. When she inquired about it, she was told by one of the officers that he was one of 14 taken away to separate jail cells in another facility. Another officer approached her.

Handing her the Lewis & Clark's journals, he said, "The Major wanted to make sure you got this back."

She immediately went to General Winder's office for explanation.

The General tried to explain. "President Lincoln continues to refuse to recognize the Confederacy as a legitimate separate government. He considered the actions of those fighting for the Confederacy, especially privateers, as treasonous insurrection. He has threatened to execute 14 privateers captured from the schooner, *CSS Savannah*."

"I don't quite understand, General Winder. What does this have to do with Union prisoners of war?" a perplexed Elizabeth inquired.

"Our President Davis decided to retaliate. "Any eye for an eye," as Shakespeare put it.

"Why Major Revere?" Elizabeth asked, obviously furious about the life threatening decision.

"I was ordered to pick them by lottery. Simply a case of bad luck for the Major."

When Elizabeth tried to respond, he talked over, saying, "Sorry, Miss Van Lew, it is completely out of my hands."

Realizing the hopelessness of arguing, she checked her anger and changed subjects. "Before I leave, General, I heard when I was waiting outside your office that one of your clerks resigned."

"Yes. Unfortunately, we have a much smaller pool to choose from with so many men fighting as soldiers. Taking longer than I would have liked."

"I know of someone looking for work who was an administrator at Tredegar Ironworks before the war. He lost his job when he got hurt. He's fine now, but too old to fight. Still wants to do his part for the Confederacy. His name is Erasmus Ross."

"Well, thank you Miss Van Lew. Kind of you to mention this. If you don't mind, before you leave, please leave contact information for Mr. Ross with my Secretary, Mr. Bates."

What Elizabeth didn't tell the General was that Ross came from a Unionist family; as much against the separation of states from the U.S. as the Van Lew's. His cousin, Franklin Stearns, a friend of the Van Lew family, had been imprisoned by the Confederate government for expressing his anti-war sentiments in public.

When Elizabeth got home, she realized there was something tucked away in the returned Lewis and Clark book. There was a letter that appeared to be sealed with candle wax, with a Boston addressed envelope.

There was also an attached note, clipped to the letter in the middle of the book.

To whom it may concern:

This envelope contains a very personal note to my wife and family in Boston. Unfortunately, they have blocked us from exchanging regular mail. If there is any way you can help get this through to my beloved family, I would be eternally grateful.

Yours Truly,

Major Paul Joseph Revere

Elizabeth asked an obliging Daniel to use his clandestine network to transport the letter north. She then penned a note to President Lincoln, knowing full well that even if Daniel's chain of connections could successfully pass her note through enemy lines and get it delivered to directly to the White House, odds were low he would ever personally read it. Still, she addressed it to the President, pleading for leniency for the southern privateers. Elizabeth argued it was necessary to save the unfortunate Union prisoners chosen by lot, and destined to receive the same sentence if the convicted privateers were executed.

"I'll do my best," Daniel promised. "The Underground has connections in Washington. We have some that go up past Boston, too."

She was not alone writing to the beleaguered Union President. Many from the North did as well. Begging for clemency for the crew of the *Savannah* to save Union lives, was a prevailing theme of letters to the White House at this time. These included families of some of the hostage Union prisoners.

Whether Van Lew's letter or any of the others reached the President directly and influenced his position was not clear. However, a prisoner exchange was eventually negotiated. Lieutenant Paul Joseph Revere, along with the other selected officers, was swapped for Confederate prisoners. Revere rejoined his regiment.

Shortly after Elizabeth received the good news, Isaac, the Van Lew coachman, presented Elizabeth with a gift while she was sitting alone at the kitchen table, finishing breakfast. It was a hotplate she could use to bring warm pies and other specialties to the prisoners at Libby.

"This belonged to my mother who used it to visit my father in jail. Once a white woman accused him of spittin' in the street. She said, he did it right in front of her," Isaac noted.

Picking up and holding the hotplate, she said, "Thank you, Isaac. This will come in handy. I never knew that about your father. How awful."

"A very special hotplate. Let me show you something." He reached out his hands and took back the hotplate from Elizabeth. "It has a false bottom," he added as he slid open a curved metal plate at the bottom.

"I love this. No one would ever notice the false bottom."

Harriett Anne and Daniel were now standing behind Isaac. "You can use it to pass notes to prisoners," Harriett Anne said, approvingly.

Elizabeth quickly asserted, "Or money, to help bribe prison guards. I can't thank you enough, Isaac, but tell me, what happened with your father?"

"My mother used it to pass a small knife to my dad. He was able to chip a big enough hole in the jail cell wall, under his cot. He managed to get out. We never saw him again."

Chapter 5: An Anonymous Source

There was no intelligence organization in the United States before the Civil War. During the Revolutionary War, George Washington created a spy network. He was the first and last commander-in-chief to do so. Washington proved himself to be a skilled military intelligence manager, often referred to as "America's First Spymaster." By the early nineteenth century, espionage was regarded as an "unsavory" activity, considered unnecessary for the new nation protected by two oceans and content not to meddle in European imperialistic squabbles.

The Confederates invested heavily in spying activities, with agents in Washington, including "secessionist clerks" who carried on their U.S. governmental duties after the war began. Spies engaged in clandestine activities and passed sensitive information to the other side. Rumors persisted, for example, that a Southern Belle living in Washington had tipped off Beauregard prior to Manassas.

Some Confederate agents worked with Northern Democrats sympathetic to the South, known as "Copperheads." Combining forces, they worked to try and convince influential Northerners to give up the fight. In some cases, they worked to incite violence. Southern spies scouted Union troop movements. Others were dispatched to France and England where the Confederates were attempting to influence leaders to recognize the breakaway southern states and encourage these European powers to enter the war on the side of the Confederacy.

As the Union intelligence chief appointed by Lincoln, Allan Pinkerton was now advising General George McClellan on Confederate troop strength. Pinkerton was credited with uncovering a plot to kill Lincoln on his trip to Washington to be inaugurated. His performance with McClellan, however, was questionable. The overly cautious behavior of McClellan, ongoing drilling, fortifying defenses around Washington, versus aggressively pursuing the enemy, was most certainly compounded by Pinkerton's consistent miscalculations. Pinkerton's primary source of information came from interrogating Confederate prisoners. He was off many times by a multiplier as high as two to three, versus actual Confederate numbers.

Pinkerton was determined to create a spy network in Richmond. Rather than looking to recruit Unionists already placed within Richmond society, he decided to try to embed northern "plants" within the city. He often relied on employees from his former detective business, with limited success. Where he did begin to have success was when he started to interrogate runaway slaves. On a few occasions he convinced runaways to return to the South as spies.

One of his most successful spies was Timothy Webster. A former detective employee of Pinkerton, he had arrived in Richmond in late 1861. Webster posed as a secessionist courier, who also traded in contraband. He gained the trust of the Secretary of War Judah Benjamin. Thinking he could take advantage of Webster's courier activities, Benjamin gave him secret correspondence to deliver to his Confederate agents in the North. This proved invaluable in identifying spies and gaining enemy intelligence. After Union officials read the letters, they were resealed and delivered to the agents, so they wouldn't suspect that they were compromised.

Like Webster, other Pinkerton spies in Richmond had to travel on their own, back and forth from the North to share intelligence. Sometimes information arrived too late to be useful. There was also additional risk with each trip that their cover could be blown. On a trip back to Richmond in early 1862, Webster became ill with inflammatory rheumatism. He was laid up in the Richmond Monument Hotel. Pinkerton sent a woman spy, Hattie Lawton, to pose as his wife and help nurse him back to health. He also sent a former slave turned spy, John Scobell.

Pinkerton then seriously miscalculated. He sent two more spies to check on Webster, and report back on his condition. The two additional spies were already being tracked by Confederate counteragents. They were arrested, along with Hattie Lawton. John Scobell, playing his part perfectly, was never suspected. The Confederate who took the rest of the spies, including Webster, into custody let Scobell go.

He was never even questioned. Scobell spent some time with his wife, who was a freed slave working in Richmond as a cook for an influential Confederate family. She continued to be one of his primary sources for information gathering. Scobell then travelled back to Washington without incident to brief Pinkerton.

Pinkerton's man, Timothy Webster, was convicted of spying and sentenced to hang. He had been Pinkerton's most effective agent. Efforts by the U.S. government to have his sentence commuted were ignored. Webster's final request was to be executed by firing squad, not hung at the gallows like a common criminal. His request was denied.

His wife, Charlotte Webster, traveled to Richmond to comfort him and stay close by. Elizabeth went to see the distraught woman who asked her to accompany her to the execution. The hanging would take place at the old Richmond fairgrounds. About 200 people turned out for the occasion. They witnessed a horrific event.

Webster gave what was believed to be his last words, expressing his wish that "The Union might be preserved." The rope slipped as the trap door sprung and Timothy Webster fell to the ground in pain. As the executioners re-rigged the scaffold, and tied the rope a second time on his neck, Webster said, "I suffer a double death."

Webster's wife bawled and started to totter. Before losing control of her legs, Elizabeth reached over and pulled her in by the waist. She continued crying, buried in Elizabeth's shoulders. Elizabeth felt awful for Webster and his grief stricken widow. She was also appalled how this had been turned into a spectator event. Obviously designed to send a message that this could happen to anyone caught spying.

Immediately following the hanging, Elizabeth asked the Confederate authorities if Webster's widow could stay at the Van Lew mansion. Her request was denied.

Timothy Webster was the first U.S. spy to be hanged since Nathan Hale, back in the Revolutionary War. His hanging was broadly publicized throughout the South. Not only for the general readership, but as a deterrent for other would be spies. In the case of Van Lew, it had an opposite effect. She was more determined than ever to work against the rebel government.

Days later Elizabeth was reading in the Van Lew library. It was a pleasant early afternoon, with the curtains rolled back to maximize the sunlight filling the room. The door to the library was partially open. Daniel poked his head in, tapping lightly on the open door.

He said "Excuse me, ma'am, Wilson Bowser is here. I asked him to come. Has some information to share."

"Come in. Hello Wilson, nice to see you. How's your beautiful bride?"

"Doing well, ma'am. I have gotten some information Mary thought best to get to you right away."

"Please have a seat, you as well, Daniel."

The two men stepped into the room. Daniel sat. Wilson remained standing.

"Thank you, Miss Van Lew. My clothes are dirty. I'd rather stand."

"Please...," Elizabeth pointed to the seat next to her. Wilson reluctantly acquiesced.

"Wilson, tell Miss Van Lew what you told me."

"Yes, my cousin works in the old Gosport Shipyard in Norfolk. Where they've been building a new iron-clad ship."

"Please, go on," Elizabeth said.

"Well, the Confederates been using the Dismal Swamp Canal for some time to move supplies back and forth from Norfolk to North Carolina. My cousin tells me they think there is too much risk launching a new ironclad from Norfolk straight out into the Chesapeake Bay. With the blockade the Union Navy would surely spot it right away and could easily destroy it. Instead, they plan to use the canal to send it out from Albemarle Sound. He said they plan to do it pretty soon."

"This could prove to be very useful information. Thank you, Wilson."

"Well, Mary and I talked about it and agreed. If anyone could get it to the right people, it's probably the two people sitting right here. But Mary reminded me to make sure and tell you if you do decide to do something with this, to please be careful. Especially with what recently happened to Mr. Webster."

"Yes, Wilson, we all need to be very careful these days. It's critical, however, that we do what we can to get this into the hands of the right people. What they did to poor Timothy Webster makes me more angry than scared."

Elizabeth penned an anonymous letter with the additional details Wilson was able to provide. She then asked Daniel if he could use his connections to get the information to General Butler at Fort Monroe.

"I'll do my best, Miss Van Lew."

"I know you will, Daniel."

When one of his assistants first brought the anonymous letter to him, General Butler asked to see the person who delivered it. He was told it came from a runaway slave who had passed it to a sentry when he first arrived at Fort Monroe. It was almost a year ago he had declared slaves "contraband of war."

That spontaneous response created a firestorm on both sides of the Mason Dixon. After initial criticism in his chain of command for exceeding his authority, Congress and the Lincoln administration eventually ratified Butler's consequential decision into law, naming it the "Confiscation Act." It stipulated that the Federal Government could seize property, including slaves, from the rebellious Confederates.

The famous African American orator and abolitionist, Frederick Douglass, called the Act a "moral bombshell" for the Confederacy. A self-educated escaped slave who became a recognized northern statesman, he had previously been critical of Lincoln's moderate approach on the essential question of slavery.

Slave owners in the South were shocked as the numbers of runaways increased dramatically; incorrectly assuming they would always remain loyal to their masters. Confederate leaders worried about the impact to the military where tens of thousands of slaves provided non-combat labor. They worked as ditch diggers, railroad repair workers, teamsters, cooks, medical workers, body servants, building fortifications, and in many war related menial jobs. The continued depletion in the ranks of slaves, used and abused as resources to provide critical non-combat roles, was negatively impacting the capability of the South to conduct traditional war activities.

Finding the man who brought the anonymous letter would be difficult in the encampment. Hundreds of runaway slaves were now encamped at the only fort in the upper south not to have fallen to the Confederates.

Ironically, Fort Monroe, originally built by slaves, was referred to as "Freedom Fortress" by those who had already escaped, and those who still yearned to do so. One of them had brought this latest information across enemy lines to the fort.

Finally, after a frantic search, a young man fitting the description of the newly arrived runaway was brought to the guard who had passed the note up his chain of command.

"That's him," he assured the soldiers.

"Please don't send me back."

The two soldiers looked at each other and laughed.

"Send you back?" You don't have to worry 'bout that," the soldier closest to him said.

"What's your name?" The other soldiers asked.

"Percy."

"Well Percy, today is your lucky day. General Butler wants to see you."

They met in a private room within the Engineering Quarters Building, next to the parade grounds. It was where an increasing number of tents were constantly being pitched to accommodate the influx of escaped slaves.

"Have a seat sir," the General instructed, after shaking Percy's hand from across an office desk.

Percy sat shaking his head. Not only did this paunchy short man with droopy inset eyes not look like what he thought a general should look like. General Butler didn't much act like what he would have expected, either.

"What's the matter?" Butler asked.

"General, well, you called me 'sir,' you shook my hand," Percy answered. "Not used to bein' treated like that."

"Just common courtesy. Hopefully you will begin to experience much more of that, along with some basic human kindness from here on. Where did you come from, Percy?"

"From Richmond, General. I was a slave at the Haxall Flour Mill."

"I see, and how did you get here?"

"Spent a couple nights in homes along the way. Where they hide slaves like me tryin' to run away. Once I left Williamsburg, I walked. Stayed off the main roads 'til I got to the fort."

"You did well, Percy." Changing the subject, Butler held up the letter and said, I understand you brought this with you, addressed to me."

"Yes," sir, Percy said, gripping both sides of his chair and nervously shifting his balance. "Had it sewed into the inside of my shirt so no one would spot it."

"Who gave this to you, son?"

"Another slave helpin' me escape."

"Can you tell me his name?"

"I can't, General. Sorry, never told me. We not supposed to ask, neither."

"Is there anything more you can tell me about this letter. Who wrote it, or where it came from?"

"All I know is someone from Richmond wrote it. That's all I was told."

"If you take a little time and think about it. Is it possible, just maybe, you might remember something else?"

Percy sat still for a few moments. His head was raised, looking out the window. He could see the Old Point Comfort Light House on the narrow tip of land surrounded by the Chesapeake.

Finally breaking his silence, Percy responded. "I am very sorry, General. Nothin' else I can think of."

"Well, still, I must say, the information in this letter is very helpful, Percy. Thank you for your bringing it to us. Also, for your bravery doing so."

"You're welcome, General. Thank you."

"Percy, are you hungry?"

"Well, yes. I could use somethin' to eat. Supposed to serve us food later, but I can always eat."

"Louis, could you come in here, please?" Butler called out, summoning one of his staff assistants waiting patiently outside the office door.

"Yes, sir," Louis said as he stepped into the entrance to the room and leaned his arm against the half opened door, pushing it further back.

"Bring Percy to the quartermaster. Make sure he takes good care of him. Tell him I said he should start by making sure Percy gets a good supper."

As the two men left, the general looked back down and reread the letter. He then asked for his secretary to come in and close the door behind him.

"I want you to draft a communication to Allan Pinkerton for me. Ask him if he can assign one of his spies to help figure out who sent this letter. Tell him we have reason to believe it came from a Union sympathizer in Richmond. This person could be very helpful to us if we could somehow figure out who it is."

While General Butler was responsible for Fort Monroe and securing the mouth of the James River and Chesapeake region in Virginia, General Ambrose Burnside, who commanded one of the brigades defeated in the First Battle at Manassas, was now in charge of military operations in North Carolina. Burnside dispatched 3,000 soldiers in two brigades to destroy the Dismal Swamp Canal. They departed from Roanoke Island on transports, landing near Elizabeth City, North Carolina.

The Confederates, using slave labor, had constructed bulwarks to protect the canal. A brief battle ensued. The Confederates retreated, but the Union troops were unable to break through the fortifications at South Mills and destroy the canal locks. They were, however, able to cause enough damage to leave it in a serious condition of disrepair. Fearful that additional Southern troops would provide reinforcements, and exhausted from the long trek to get to the canal, the Federals did not pursue the retreating army.

Up until now, Burnside had been successful in his North Carolina campaigns. The "Battle of South Mills" was considered one of the rare Confederate successes against his army since Manassas. It helped further boost Southern morale.

The Richmond newspapers would later report that the Union attacked the canal for fear of it being used to transport enemy ironclads. Elizabeth Van Lew had no way of knowing if her letter to General Butler had prompted the expedition. Disappointed in the outcome, she rationalized, if for nothing else, it would be more difficult, if not impossible, for the Confederates to sneak future ironclads through the Dismal Swamp Canal and surprise the Union Navy.

Lincoln was once again frustrated with the performance of his military in general. Still, it was George McClellan's continued inaction that roused his ire the most. As McClellan continued to delay, avoiding conflict and making excuses for not engaging the enemy, President Lincoln quipped, "If General McClellan does not intend to use his army, may I borrow it?"

After constant prodding from Lincoln and other government officials, McClellan's Army of the Potomac launched the largest amphibious operation in North America in early 1862, with the goal of taking Richmond. The troops were transported to the tip of the Virginia Peninsula, near Fort Monroe, at the mouth of the James River. The fort would be used as the base to support operations. As word spread about McClellan's landing and march towards Richmond, many local citizens panicked. Crowds formed at the train stations and wharf, trying to get out of the city.

To disrupt the movement of this massive army of close to 120,000 men as they marched up the Peninsula, the South mounted a counter offensive. The Yankees ran into resistance from Major General John B. Magruder Confederate troops, consisting of only about 13,000 soldiers entrenched along a 12-mile front.

In the "Siege of Yorktown," Magruder's army brilliantly deceived McClellan into thinking they were a much larger force. Magruder did this by marching small numbers of troops past the same positions multiple times and skillfully moving his artillery to fire from different positions.

Instead of attacking, McClellan suspended his march. He decided not to attack without more reconnaissance and ordered his army to dig in. It became a battle of entrenchment, with high body counts and long stalemates thwarting progress. McClellan's actions astonished the Confederates. Lincoln was furious. Even Elizabeth, who had asked Chloe to prepare their guest bedroom for McClellan's arrival in Richmond, began to worry the South just might prevail.

With causalities piling up on both sides, by the end of May 1862, McClellan's Army of the Potomac had slowly pushed back the Confederates to Fair Oaks, Virginia. They were about 10 miles from the outskirts of Richmond. A renewed sense of optimism among Richmond Unionists, including the Van Lew's took hold. Perhaps the end was finally near after so many disappointing setbacks. Despite the danger for all citizens that a siege of the city would bring, Elizabeth, her family, and their trusted Unionist friends, were thrilled that the Union Army was in striking distance. Most believed taking Richmond would bring the war to a swift conclusion.

The commanding Confederate, General Joseph Johnston, was gravely wounded by an exploding Union shell during the Battle of Seven Pines at Fair Oaks. Injuries to his shoulder and chest put him out of action indefinitely. Jefferson Davis knew he needed a competent leader to replace Johnston. Someone who he believed was best equipped to save Richmond. Someone he could communicate with more easily than his other generals. Davis turned to Robert E. Lee. He was still at this time sidelined from the battlefield, providing strategic advice to Davis.

Lee knew he would have to drive McClellan's 100,000-man army away from Richmond. The Confederacy depended on saving Richmond. He renamed his forces the "Army of Northern Virginia," suggesting confidence that his army would not only break the siege, but push McClellan back across the Potomac.

First, Lee ordered his army to dig extensive fortifications around Richmond. He consolidated other units, bringing the total number of soldiers under his command to about 90,000 protecting the Confederate Capital. He skillfully placed units in strategic positions to prevent additional troops reinforcing McClellan's planned Richmond assault. As if not bad enough when McClellan heard Lee was elevated to command the defense of Richmond. Reports from scouts of the surprise appearance of Stonewall Jackson's army in nearby Mechanicsville, Virginia, further stunned McClellan.

Lee mounted an aggressive counter offensive. A series of bold attacks began against McClellan's right flank. They began forcing the Army of the Potomac back. Convinced he could no longer take Richmond, McClellan ordered a retreat to the basin of the James River where Union gunboats would protect his forces.

The abandonment of the McClellan campaign to capture the Confederate Capital of Richmond was considered a significant achievement and perhaps a sign that a Confederate victory was imminent. As Unionist aspirational wishes dissipated, a new spirit of Rebel optimism morphed into a growing presumption of Southern superiority.

Not only were war causalities mounting. So were the numbers of new captured Union soldiers, adding to the already overcrowded prisons in Richmond. Conditions continued to deteriorate. General Winder, however, decided to revoke Elizabeth Van Lew's visiting privileges with Union prisoners. He would only tell her it was orders from a superior officer.

Elizabeth was now cut off from meeting with captured soldiers. It was incredibly disappointing. On the positive side, however, she received word shortly after that Erasmus Ross did get the clerk job in Libby Prison.

The Union reversal was certainly not welcome news in the Van Lew household. The absolute crowing of the newspapers and the constant boasting of neighbors about recent Confederate exploits was hard to take. While others might have resigned themselves to the prevailing assumption that the South would soon prevail, Elizabeth decided it was time for her to do more.

After reading a particularly annoying swaggering account of the Confederate exploits in the *Richmond Daily Dispatch,* Elizabeth went to her room and opened her vanity chest, pulling out a note from a family friend, John Minor Botts, a former politician and critic of secession.

Like Franklin Stearns, he had also been imprisoned for his pro-Union views. Botts was sent to Castle Godwin, also known at the time as "McDaniel's negro Jail." He was released from prison, under the condition that he stay confined to his home, after eight weeks of solitary confinement. Botts was now living with his family on an estate in Culpeper, Virginia. He won the property in a card game. He enjoyed boasting about it.

Before going to prison, he had given Elizabeth a list of local people who supported the Union. "Just in case they can ever be useful," he had said. Elizabeth knew most of the Union sympathizers from her orbit in Richmond's social circles. These names were different. They were working class people, with their occupations scribbled next to their names. One caught Elizabeth's immediate attention, *"Samuel Ruth, Superintendent Fredericksburg & Potomac Railroad."*

Erasmus Ross arrived home late on his first day of work at Libby Prison. It was pitch black when he opened the door to his second floor boarding room. He lit the kerosene lamp and took off his jacket. He lived alone and was about to pour a glass of bourbon when he heard a knock at the door.

It was a young African American boy. As he opened the door, the boy looked behind to make sure no one else was around. He displayed no emotion as he handed a package to Ross.

"What's this?" Ross asked.

"From Miss Van Lew. She told me to let you know. What's in the package may come in handy. They will try to get you more. She also says you can trust the slave named Walter who works in the prison."

Ross took hold of the package. Before he could say another word, the boy quickly spun around, hustled down the steps, disappearing into the darkness. The package contained two sets of Confederate soldier uniforms sewn by Elizabeth's mother while helping Phoebe and her volunteer woman's group.

To avoid being suspected of foul play, Erasmus Ross from the day he started his new job, projected a harsh demeanor when doing roll calls. He was especially nasty when punishing disruptive prisoners.

When he thought the timing was good, Ross decided to pass one of the Confederate uniforms to a prisoner confined to solitary for misbehaving. He did this just when his time was up, much to the prisoner's surprise. Rather than sending the prisoner back to regular quarters, Ross led the prisoner to a closet away from the guards where he could put the uniform on.

Ross then took him to an alleyway exit, unlocking the door and handed him a note with the Van Lew address along with a hand sketched map. It was a short walk from Libby. The path highlighted on the map was a less travelled back road approach to the mansion to reduce the risk of being stopped and questioned.

Elizabeth and her mother believed with escaped prisoners disguised as Confederates it would be easier for them to blend in without being noticed. Unlike runaway slaves who needed to travel under the cover of darkness and slip into the mansion from the backdoor servant entrance, escaped prisoners from Libby dressed as Rebel soldiers could come to the house in broad daylight and enter from the main entrance without arousing any unwanted attention.

Then one day Eliza was asked by a neighbor about a Confederate soldier showing up at the front door of the Van Lew mansion. She said she sometimes gave out the address while working as a volunteer in the hospital for injured and sick soldiers. This explanation seemed to suffice, but the Van Lew's knew they needed to be more careful. Shortly after, they had a young man show up who really was a Confederate soldier.

Ross controlled who he sent to solitary and when he released them. In the early days for the prison, no formal records were kept on who was sent to solitary, or when Ross released them. With so many prisoners, it often took some time to determine another prisoner was missing.

He would space it out, doing it on rare occasions, but Ross continued to help a few lucky prisoners in solitary escape. Even after running out of uniforms, he repeated the same effort with civilian clothes he could gather up. Perhaps not as a good a disguise as that of a Confederate soldier, but as long as they could avoid conversation, or exhibiting a Yankee swagger in front of locals, it seemed to work.

Prisoners escaping the overcrowded prison were an ongoing problem. Luckily, prison officials suspected it was mostly due to low paid guards not paying enough attention, or accepting bribes. Even with all exits from the prison securely locked and heavily guarded, there were occasional escapes that confounded the prison warden.

Efforts to look and find any and all other ways out was also a constant activity the warden demanded from his guards. Even as the building became more secure over time, a small number of enterprising prisoners still managed to find escape access within the vast warehouse building. Libby was overcrowded and not built to adequately secure the facilities which extended across an entire downtown Richmond city block, between 20th and 21st Streets, with Cary Street on the north, and Dock Street off the James River to the south.

Due to the overcrowding, prisoners were given some leeway to visit other holding rooms, but were expected in their assigned room at nightfall, and for morning roll calls conducted by Erasmus Ross. Not much could be done to prevent some attrition, but roll calls and spot checks made it less easy to slip away. By building up his reputation as a harsh, unscrupulous prison official, Ross not only managed to remain above suspicion by prison officials. He was feared by the prisoner population.

"You don't want Ross to send you to solitary. You may never come back."

When early on one of the higher ranking prisoners, a Colonel Hobart, complained to Ross, convinced there was foul play involved and threatened to take it to the warden, Ross felt he had to explain what he was doing.

"You, of all people, a Unionist? Helping prisoners escape?"

"Let's just say it's in your men's best interest that they keep thinking I'm a dyed in the wool Confederate. They should believe they need to be real careful not to incur my wrath."

"Your secret is good with me, Mr. Ross."

"I can't help all of them, obviously. But if a situation arises where you think a particular prisoner should be helped, let me know."

A mild, yet overcast day as they set out. Isaac helped Elizabeth into the family carriage and they headed off for the depot station. Other Richmond ladies of Elizabeth's stature would be concerned about the appearance of being the lone passenger in a carriage with a negro driver. This wasn't done. At this point, Elizabeth was well beyond concerns about conventional behavior.

She entered the Railroad office building and requested to see Samuel Ruth.

"He's not here," the secretary said.

"Would you know where I might be able to find him?" Elizabeth asked.

The secretary looked back at her, devoid of any emotion. He got up from his desk, walked over to the window and peered out. He then looked back at Elizabeth.

"Come on over here. I'll show you."

He pointed to a man, partially bald, with a long dark beard.

Elizabeth tried to avoid the mud puddles as she walked out across the rail yard to the man. He appeared to be inspecting a train car that was sidelined off the rails. He was squatting, with his back to the approaching woman.

"Are you Mr. Ruth?" Elizabeth inquired.

He turned his head, still crouching. Noticing it was a well-dressed lady, he stood up, facing her.

"Yes, Sam Ruth," he announced. "How may I help you, ma'am?"

"My name is Elizabeth Van Lew. John Minor Botts, a family friend, gave me your name."

"Your name is familiar to me, Miss Van Lew. Church Hill, I believe."

"Yes."

"Well then a pleasure to make your acquaintance. I am a great admirer of John Botts. Shame the way they dragged him off to jail in the middle of the night. And he is still confined to his home under house arrest. An outrage."

"I agree. An absolutely terrible injustice. Is there someplace where we could speak privately?"

Ruth stroked his beard and look towards the office building. He then looked behind him and then back at Elizabeth.

"We could meet right here, in this empty railcar behind me. Can't get much more private. Wait here."

He climbed the rolling step ladder in front of the car door and pulled it open. He hopped down from the top step to assist Elizabeth in climbing up. Then slid the door closed behind them.

They sat in separate seats across from each other in what was a passenger car.

"What is this about, Miss Van Lew?" Ruth asked.

"Can I count on your keeping this secret?"

He seemed to hesitate for a moment, and then nodded.

"Good, very good. I have been working with the Underground to help Union prisoners escape across enemy lines. We have had some recent success at this."

Casting an incredulous looking squint her way, Ruth couldn't help but ask, "Pardon me Miss Van Lew, but you are being serious? Working with the Underground?

"Completely serious."

"Well, well." In a jocular tone he added, "I didn't think ladies from Church Hill dabbled in such things."

"Best if they continue to think none of us do."

Ruth was warming up to this lady of society. A friend of John Botts who had completely taken him by surprise with her revelation.

"I will not try to change their thinking. Your secret is safe with me," Ruth said.

"Very good."

"Just so I make sure I have this right. You, Miss Van Lew, are working with the Underground, and they are now helping Yankee soldiers escape?"

"Well, yes. I try to help, but I play a very small role."

"Please, go on."

"The problem is that now with the new fortifications surrounding Richmond, and larger numbers of Confederate soldiers protecting the city. Not to mention the unpredictable movement of troops along the outskirts. Made it much more dangerous."

"Yes, I could see that being a problem," Ruth interjected before Elizabeth could continue. "I have heard about some escapes, but I had no idea about the Underground."

"Not with all escapes, but a few lately. The people I know helping prisoners escape represent a small portion of these, but as far as I know, none of the prisoners they have helped have been recaptured."

"That's commendable," Ruth noted.

"We have spotters that try to help in these situations when they can. As the numbers of prisoners has grown, it has made it more difficult for the guards to supervise and control. I hear there are close to a 1,000 more in Richmond, after the recent battles along the Peninsula. These poor souls are crammed together in unimaginable conditions."

"I have heard that as well. I take it you are telling me all of this, Miss Van Lew, because you want my help."

"John Botts told me you are someone who can be trusted, and that you are a friend of the Union."

"True on both counts."

"I was wondering if you might be willing to help us transport prisoners and runaway slaves out of Richmond using your trains. Your trains could take them as far north as Fredericksburg. That is, if you are willing to help us."

Ruth smiled. "You have shared with me information that in the wrong hands could lead to your arrest. I will share something with you, as a friend of John Botts, and someone who decided to trust me. I am already doing work to help the Union."

Elizabeth was taken back. "You are?"

"Let's just suffice it to say, I was able to engineer a derailment of a train with no passengers. During the fighting on the Virginia Peninsula."

"I heard something about that," Elizabeth mentioned.

"Created quite a mess and took days to clean up and repair the rail. It prevented a large number of Northern Virginia reinforcements for Lee getting to Richmond. By the time they arrived and were ready to be transported to Hampton Roads, most of the battle was over. Otherwise, the carnage on both sides may have been much worse."

"Yes, I'm sure." Elizabeth looked around. "Was this one of the cars that derailed?"

"No, this car had some unrelated maintenance issues. I would be willing to help, but we would need to work out the logistics. Not like an escaped Union man can get on line to buy a ticket, or come into the office and ask for me."

Elizabeth smiled. "We have safe houses where we can keep escapees when they first get out, and until we believe it is safe to try to move them. There is a former slave, now a free man, who runs a newspaper stand next to the station house."

"You mean Albert?"

"Yes. He can slip you information inside newspapers, and take notes from you back to my contacts. He can give you notice when we have someone we need to get out. Rest assured, we won't do anything without your consent. If for example, you think it might be too dangerous at a given time, just pass it on to Albert. We will also assume only one at a time for now."

"Albert, of all people. I never would have guessed. Alright, I would like to help, Miss Van Lew. I am thinking it is better to use freight trains versus passenger. They're checking papers and doing frequent checks all the time on the passenger trains. I have a few trusted Union men working for me. We could slip escaped prisoners into a car when we know it is safe at night. Is there someone you are looking to transport in the near term?"

"No, but there could be one shortly. Albert will let you know. Oh, before I leave one other thing I wanted to ask you." Elizabeth pulled the list of names, which included Ruth's, out of her coat pocket. "I was wondering, do you know any of these other men?"

Ruth took the list from Elizabeth and glanced down at it. "I assume this came from John?

"Yes," just before he was imprisoned for criticizing Virginia lawmakers for leaving the Union," Elizabeth explained.

As he scrolled down the list, Ruth smiled as he said, "I see a few names that were involved in politics with John. I know several very well. Unionists to the core. Let's see, yes, you have Isaac Silver, of course. Isaac is one of my business associates. Thomas McNiven has a bakery downtown. The one on 8th Street."

"I know which one you mean. A very good bakery, but I don't know Mr. McNiven. I believe I once heard he was originally from Glasgow, Scotland."

"Yup, that's him. There are several German merchants listed here. Christian Burging. Gerhard Wolf. Frederick Lohmann and his brothers. Frederick owns a restaurant in the Union Hill neighborhood. Several of us have met there in the past to share information, or I guess you can say, to conspire." He paused to enjoy the Richmond socialite's positive reaction before resuming. "The authorities don't pay so much attention to Union Hill. Guess they rather not bother with the German immigrants and free negroes that have moved into the boarding houses there."

Elizabeth mused to herself on the irony of German immigrants, who the Richmond press consistency disparaged, from both sides of the Mason Dixon, working to thwart the Confederates. They continued to underestimate negroes and immigrants at their own peril, she thought.

Ruth continued, "A very mixed group. We have two things in common. We want to help the Union win this war and restore our rightful government. The second thing is that none of us were swooped up and jailed as suspected subversives. Like what happened to John Botts. None of us write letters published in the newspapers or give speeches. We can get away with things without being noticed. I would say those wrongful arrests is what inspired me, and at least some of the others, to act. I'm sure, not the outcome this new government intended."

'No, not at all," Elizabeth smiled as she responded.

"Just let me know how I can help. Consider me at your service, Miss Van Lew."

Chapter 6: Clandestine Network

Adding to her disappointment, after the withdrawal of McClellan's troops from the Virginia Peninsula, Elizabeth heard that General Benjamin Butler was being reassigned to New Orleans in the western theatre. His "contraband camp" had provided refuge for thousands of former slaves. She also believed he had been receptive to receiving the intelligence she and her network of spies could provide, while retaining her anonymity.

Pocketing his huge victory forcing McClellan off the Peninsula, Robert E. Lee wanted to continue applying pressure on the Yankees and keep his momentum going. He knew the prolonged war was having a negative effect on Lincoln's popularity. Lee requested permission to take the offensive and move his army north. He wrote to President Jefferson Davis that he believed it might influence the upcoming midterm elections in the North.

Lee argued that the presence of his Confederate Army on northern soil would add to the general discontent and help undermine the northern will to fight. It might influence "the people of the United States to determine at upcoming midterm elections whether they will support those who favor a prolongation of the war, or those who wish to bring it to a termination." Growing antiwar sentiment could potentially increase the number of Peace Democrats in Congress, thwarting Lincoln and the Republicans, by denying needed funding to continue prosecuting war against the South.

Both Lee and Davis also hoped that a string of victories might encourage France and England to aid the South. The Union naval blockade was restricting the flow of cotton to Europe. The Europeans professed sympathy to Confederate overtures, but had taken no overt action to assist. If the Confederates could demonstrate a decided advantage, piling up additional Union defeats, they just might formally recognize Confederate independence.

Lee engaged with the Union Army of General John Pope in the Second Battle at Bull Run, in late August, 1862. With the help of General James Longstreet, and a brilliantly executed flanking maneuver by General Stonewall Jackson, Lee crushed the Federalists. Pope was subsequently relieved of his command.

Ninety days after taking command of the Army of Northern Virginia, Lee had extricated McClellan from the Peninsula and defeated Pope. He had successfully moved the battle lines from 10 miles outside Richmond to 20 miles from Washington, D.C.

Next, Lee moved across the Potomac into Maryland, and once again his army clashed with Union forces under McClellan. This time at Sharpsburg, Maryland, before he could advance further north. Despite a 38,000 to 12,000 advantage in troop strength, McClellan moved slowly. He waited 17 hours before attacking Lee, but eventually the series of assaults launched by McClellan against the Rebel army forced Lee to retreat to Virginia. There were 3,800 Confederate causalities, compared to 2,500 Union. The Battle of Antietam became the war's bloodiest day of the conflict.

President Lincoln had been eager for a Union victory to make public a document he had drafted. Even though Lee's Army eventually retreated from the battlefield, Antietam was essentially a draw. Lincoln decided it was "enough" of a victory. He could wait no longer.

On September 22, 1862, Lincoln issued his preliminary "Emancipation Proclamation," which stated:

> That on the first day of January in the year of our Lord, one thousand eight hundred and sixty-three, all persons held as slaves within any State, or designated part of a State, the people whereof shall then be in rebellion against the United States shall be then, thenceforward, and forever free...

In effect, he was formally alerting the Confederacy of his intention to free all persons held as slaves within the rebellious states. He also warned that if 100 days later, the Rebels did not end the fighting and rejoin the Union by January 1, 1863, all slaves in the rebellious states would be free.

In his Proclamation, in addition to calling slaves in rebellious states free, Lincoln said that African Americans would be recruited as Union soldiers. Up until this point, African Americans served in noncombat roles and were not eligible to volunteer to fight with the Union army.

Until now, the primary rationale for war with the breakaway southern states was to preserve the Union. With the issuance of the Emancipation Proclamation, freedom for slaves would become a primary war objective.

Despite the massive carnage and the successful withdrawal by Lee to fight another day, The Battle of Antietam boosted northern morale. Rather than Republicans suffering a significant loss in congressional seats as expected in the November 1862 midterms, Lincoln's party gained seats. In addition, both England and France remained neutral.

There was a sign on the door "Restaurant Closed." The shades were also drawn. As they had been instructed, Elizabeth and Daniel walked down the alley adjoining the building to the opposite side of the restaurant used for deliveries.

Daniel knocked on the back door which opened promptly.

"We were expecting you, come on in," the man said, closing the door behind them.

As her eyes adjusted to the diminished light in the hallway, Elizabeth recognized Samuel Ruth coming towards her.

"Thank you for coming Miss Van Lew. And you must be Daniel," Ruth added, extending his hand. "Nice to meet you."

"Nice to meet you too," Daniel responded.

As Ruth stepped aside and motioned for them to enter the dining area, she could see tables for two placed together forming one large table. The men seated there, about six or seven, were preoccupied with the food in front of them. Another man approached, wearing an apron.

"This is Frederick Lohmann," Ruth said. "Miss Van Lew, and Daniel Gates."

"Nice to meet you. Come on in, and have a seat." Looking around Lohmann, said "There's a couple seats at the end of the table."

"Have you ever had sauerbraten before?" Lohmann asked.

"No," Elizabeth sheepishly admitted.

"Not, not me, either," Daniel said.

"It's braised beef. Marinated and cooked to perfection. We are famous for it here. Would you like to try it?"

The two newest guests both nodded.

"We have beer and wine on the table."

"Would it be possible to get a cup of tea?" Elizabeth asked.

"Yes, we have tea. Of course. That is, if you don't mind drinkin' tea bought from the black market."

There were laughs from around the table.

With no hesitation, Elizabeth retorted, "As long as it tastes like tea and I can drink up the evidence."

A few more laughs. Lohmann and another younger man, who could have been his son, left for the kitchen. They came back with plates for Elizabeth and Daniel. They were filled with the Lohmann's acclaimed sauerbraten, peeled potatoes, and cabbage.

"Your evidence will be presented shortly."

"Thank you." Elizabeth began to eat. "This is very good," she added.

Putting down his fork, Daniel grinned, affirmatively. He sipped beer from the stein he was given.

By now, most everyone had finished eating, except for Daniel and Elizabeth. Samuel Ruth got up from the other side of the table and began to speak.

"I want to first welcome our guests. They have been working with the Underground to help both slaves and prisoners escape up north. When Miss Van Lew came to see me, we talked about how we might be able to find ways we could work together. That's why I invited them here. Oh, and, I should have mentioned to our new guests. We speak openly here. You can be assured nothing you say here will be repeated outside this room. We assume by your being here, we can trust you, and you can trust us."

"Thank you for having us. Rest assured, we are very good at keeping secrets, and will keep yours" Elizabeth said.

Ruth smiled and continued. "Let me ask, both of you. Ever met any of the others here, before?"

Daniel shook his head.

Elizabeth responded, "I know Burnham Wardell, he delivered ice to us before, back when we still had dinner parties. As Wardell bowed his head acknowledging her, Elizabeth continued after looking around at the others. "I have seen some of you around town, and on occasion, I have been in Mr. McNiven's fine bakery, and recognize him from there."

"You're so kind to say, Miss Van Lew, and of course you're always very welcome in my shop, your entire family, too," McNiven responded, rolling his "r's" with a decidedly Scottish accent. "Also, I must tell you General Winder, who often visits our little shop, once said our pies can't compare to the ones you were bringing prisoners."

The group seemed to enjoy this. "Hell, I always said your pies were no good," Frederick Lohmann, still standing near the kitchen door, said.

"I think your business is safe," Elizabeth said. "Unfortunately, we are not allowed to bring pies to prisoners anymore."

"Let me introduce the others." Ruth pointed to the man sitting across from Daniel, who stood up and bowed graciously. "This is Christian Burging, who provided the pitchers of beer in front of you. Fresh from his saloon across the street."

Daniel, turned to Elizabeth, speaking loud enough so all could hear, "I think your brother, John, has been there before. More than once."

Some laughed, a few clapped. Elizabeth added between the continuing laughs, "He probably pays your rent all by himself."

"Finally, let me introduce this man sitting in the middle of the table. Joseph Mills. He works in the Adjutant General's Department here in Richmond."

Mills stood up, bowed awkwardly before sitting back down.

The younger man emerged from the kitchen to clear the table.

"Oh, and I almost forgot. This is Frederick, Jr., who you have seen sprinting about."

"Yes, hello," the young man said as he collected plates and headed back through the kitchen door.

Ruth poured himself a glass of water from a side table bottle, and then turned again facing those sitting at the extended makeshift table.

"To start things off, I have a bit of news to share. General Lee has lodged a formal complaint about my railroad company. Says he thinks operations are shoddy and the management inept. We can cope with being labeled bunglers. With so many men serving in the army, there aren't too many left who can replace us."

"Did he explain how he came to that conclusion?" McNiven asked.

"Sure did. A combination of things. Our trains were late resupplying his troops during their most recent campaign. Also, he brought up the transport of troops down to Richmond to reinforce the defense of Richmond and the battles waged in the Hampton Roads. He noted that while the derailment might not have been prevented, the response to get things rolling again was too slow. He has no idea the derailment was planned, or that we purposely delayed the supply trains headed north."

"Nice work at bungling, Samuel," Frederick Lohmann sarcastically noted.

"For our new guests, what they would call 'sabotage,' if they knew about it, would not have been possible without the advanced information from Joe Mills. He is in a most critical position to know about planned troop movements and other things."

"Brilliant," Elizabeth said.

"I have some new information to share," Mills said, nervously and apparently uncomfortable speaking in groups, at least this one. "With Lincolns planned Emancipation Proclamation coming, I am hearing Jefferson Davis is in a rage about it. Senior military commanders are talking about retaliatory measures being considered once it goes into effect. Most probably to keep slaves in check and how they will treat prisoners, especially negro soldiers and officers of negro regiments if captured. You can imagine."

"Bastards," Daniel said.

"Agree with you my friend," Christian Burging said.

Ruth continued. "Miss Van Lew, no doubt, this could have a serious impact on the efforts of the Underground to help slaves and Union prisoners escape. This is one of the reasons I invited you here. After we talked about the work you and Daniel are doing."

"Glad you did," Elizabeth commented.

"For the rest of you, when Miss Van Lew first approached me, they had already devised a way to secretly pass information to me, to work with them and use my trains. That impressed me. Miss Van Lew, why don't you share with the rest of us your thoughts?"

"Yes, gladly I will. First, thank you for letting Daniel and I meet with you today, and for the delicious meal. I think I can speak for Daniel, as well, when I say we are extremely impressed with what we have heard tonight. We need to put an end to this dastardly war as quickly as possible, and by working together, we just might be able to make a difference."

"Ja, gut gesagt," Christian Burging shouted.

"I think he said, agree," McNiven added, as others laughed and several nodded affirmatively.

"I think we all want the same thing," Ruth said. "Now when we met last time, Miss Van Lew, I told you that I am willing to help make my freight trains available to help. You mentioned last time you have safe places you can hide escaped prisoners, or slaves until we can get them on a train."

"We do," Daniel said.

Ruth nodded. "Assuming all that, my trains only go as far north as Hamilton's Crossing. From there they would be on their own to get across the Potomac. Unfortunately, that is an area that is carefully scouted by the Confederates. They could be easily rounded up."

"Not necessarily," Daniel said. "Not if we coordinate things. We have connections that can meet them off the train, provide a safe hidin' place. When it's clear, take them all the way across the river to the north."

"Daniel's Underground connections have been doing this for years," Elizabeth noted.

"Impressive, just like I told ya," Ruth commented, to the larger group.

Lohmann spoke next. "You know, my brothers and I have horse drawn wagons that we use to transport food to the Confederates, when they are in remote areas and the railroad can't be used. The Confederates have no idea about our true allegiances. That, by the way, is why my brothers aren't here today. They sometimes pick up Confederate soldiers who want to desert, hide them in the wagons and help them get away. No reason, we couldn't help, too."

"That would be most helpful," Elizabeth commented. "I also have a question. From everything I am hearing, there is a wealth of valuable information that can be garnered from this group, and obviously being put to good use. Strikes me that sometimes this information could be even more valuable to Union officers in their planning and conducting of their war activities."

Ruth responded immediately. "I think you're on to something very important, Miss Van Lew."

Elizabeth continued, "We can use escaped prisoners and runaway slaves to help us pass information across enemy lines."

The entire group was nodding affirmatively, with most smiling.

Daniel spoke next. "Like we've been sayin'. All this will only work if we can keep it a well-guarded secret."

"I think I can vouch for that," Ruth said. The other men nodded.

As they left the restaurant and started for home, Daniel turned to Elizabeth and said, "I was just thinkin' how I tried to keep you from helpin' me with what I was doin' in the shadows."

"Of course I remember Daniel, and I know you were simply trying to protect me."

"Guess we both pretty deep now. Deep in the secret shadows."

President Lincoln finally removed Major General George McClellan from his command of the Army of the Potomac, replacing him with Major General Ambrose Burnside. Burnside had turned down this position in the past. After his defeat in the First Battle of Manassas, he ran successful campaigns and won a string of impressive victories in East Tennessee and North Carolina. He participated in the Battle at Antietam, where he clashed with McClellan, who refused to respond to his request for reinforcements.

December 13, 1862, the largest concentration of troops for any Civil War engagement, over 200,000, fought in the Battle of Fredericksburg. Under the new command of Burnside, 120,000 Federal troops crossed the Rappahannock River to confront Robert E. Lee's 80,000-strong Army of Northern Virginia. Lee incurred heavy casualties; over 4,000 killed or wounded, but still turned back the Union assault. They inflicted over 12,000 Federal casualties, making it the worst Union defeat of the war.

Yet another devastating blow for Lincoln. Union morale plummeted. Confederates throughout the South celebrated. Another year closed with disturbing events for the supporters of Lincoln in his efforts to defeat the South and end the war. Even with pickups in the midterms, Republicans returned home for the holidays and had to defend a record that included

Lincoln's controversial military policies, the growing number of setbacks on the battlefield, and now plans to enforce the "Emancipation Proclamation."

This executive order from Lincoln fractured traditional party loyalty, with abolitionist supporting it, pro-slavery Unionists and those Unionists looking to compromise with the South against it. anti-war Northern Democrats, the so called "Copperheads," had also made gains in both congressional and state elections, making both Republican and Democratic Parties more divisive, reducing the number of moderates.

There were estimates that over 10,000 African American slaves escaped north across the river immediately after the Battle of Fredericksburg. The loss of a significant segment of forced slave labor would become an increasingly challenging problem for the Confederates. This received much less attention than the hyped euphoria surrounding the string of Confederate battle gains.

For Unionists in both the North and the South, the Christmas Season brought a needed respite from war. Most were happy the year was over. Many hoped and prayed 1863 would see a dramatic turn of events, but they were less than optimistic that it would. This included the Van Lew's.

Daniel sprang from his bed in the servant quarters, hearing a persistent knock at the front door. He noticed the grandfather clock in the foyer as he scrambled down two flights of stairs. A little past seven o'clock in the morning. A week or so before Christmas. Who would be calling now? It was a Confederate soldier with the local constable. They insisted on speaking to John Newton Van Lew.

They were still standing by the door when John descended from the stairs. Following behind him was his sister. John recognized the constable right away. He had been in the store a few times in the past.

"Morning Mr. and Mrs. Van Lew. Sorry to bother you this early."

"This is my sister, Elizabeth. Not my wife," John called out sternly. "What can I do for you? I am sorry, but I don't recall you name," John confided.

"Sergeant Silas Stevens, and this is Constable Jason Bailor."

"How do you do," John said, offering each man a handshake.

"Well, Mr. Van Lew, we are here on official business. You see, there is an enemy soldier missing from Libby Prison."

"I don't see what that has to do with us," John remarked.

"Well, Mr. Van Lew, we have reason to believe he could be hidden away, right here, in your home."

"What reason would we have to do this? Why would we be hiding an enemy soldier? I don't understand."

"A concerned citizen told us members of your family might be hiding an escapee," Bailor said.

"Ludicrous. A concerned citizen. Can you tell me who this was?"

"I can't. What I can do is put all this to rest if we can search your house. If we find he is not here, we will leave. Now, if you or anyone in your family is hiding him, it could be as much as a $1,000 fine, or time in jail."

"This is outrageous."

Constable Bailor said, "I am sorry Mr. Van Lew, but if you don't let us take a look, we will assume the worse. I'll come back with other soldiers and we will enter by force." Looking over John's shoulder, he added, "They may not be as careful with some of your fine things as we will be."

John protested some more but finally acquiesced. He realized that for now on the Van Lew's would be under constant suspicion, even after the search.

His sister Elizabeth was in a state of panic. Her brother John was unaware that there was an escaped prisoner upstairs. He had arrived during the night wearing civilian clothes, banging at the front door. Elizabeth, a light sleeper, was awakened hearing the noise. She met him as he climbed the stairs with Daniel leading the way.

"Give me a minute." John called out to Daniel who promptly entered the room.

"Daniel, would you please let my mother know that our home is about to be searched. When you are done, please come back here. I want you to escort these gentlemen through the house so they can have a look around."

Elizabeth was watching Daniel's demeanor as he spoke to see if she could detect any signs of concern. Daniel appeared unfazed.

"Yes sir," Daniel said.

The men went through the ground floor rooms, the family bedrooms, and the basement. At one point while looking around in Elizabeth's bedroom, the constable went over to the vanity table and started looking through opened letters.

"Excuse me sir, but those notes I believe are private," Daniel said.

"I have the constable with me and we can look at whatever the hell we want," Bailor asserted. "You better mind your own business, boy, or we might just decide to haul you in for obstructin' our search."

They entered the top floor and went through the bedrooms of the house servants, eventually stepping into the room with the false wall. Sergeant Stevens leaned against the cabinet hiding the passage entrance while Bailor looked around.

Stevens turned his gaze to the wall behind him and asked, "This wall new?"

"Yes," Daniel replied. "We had some water damage from the roof. Began seepin' through the wall. When we tried to have it repaired, found structural damage, too. Rotten wood, carpenter ants."

Still looking back at the wall, Stevens knocked on it with his fist. "What's behind here?" he asked.

"Another bedroom. Already showed it to you," Daniel replied, attempting to keep a relaxed composure.

Sergeant Stevens nodded. They moved on after what seemed to Daniel like an eternity in the room with little else but the cabinet and an unmade bed.

When they finished, John was still standing by the door.

"All done now?" John asked as the men descended the stairs followed by Daniel.

"Just about. We also want to check your carriage house and the shed out back." Bowing slightly, Bailor mumbled, "Good Day, Mr. Van Lew." Both he and Stevens shook hands with John, as Daniel opened the door.

They started through the door, when Constable Bailor stopped and looked back. Sergeant Stevens following closely behind almost walked into him.

Speaking as if he wanted the entire neighborhood to hear, Bailor announced, "I'd be very careful to follow the law, to the letter. Now that we must defend our homeland, penalties for any crime committed aiding the enemy will be very severe."

"We do follow the law," John yelled back from the front porch.

Daniel was standing next to Elizabeth inside the house, back a few feet from the open door where John was standing.

"Good thing those men weren't so smart," he whispered.

John had no idea the prisoner they were looking for was hidden away upstairs. Yet, when told later, he did not get angry. He didn't suggest they suspend all their efforts at hiding prisoners or runaways in their home. Just that they look for other alternatives whenever possible first, given their home was being watched.

In those cases where it was still needed, he asked Daniel and Elizabeth to put plans in place to ensure escaped prisoners approached the house only at night and by the backdoor entrance when they felt it was safe, just as runaways slaves did. In the future, no escapees would be given access from the main entrance. Daniel would eventually provide Ross with new plans for more potential first stop safe houses to avoid creating discoverable patterns.

These included the home of other Unionists who had been active helping the Underground Railroad with escaped slaves, such as Abigail Green, whose family also had a home close to Libby Prison, the Arnold Holmes family, and William Rowley's farm, just outside Richmond. Daniel would continue to coordinate with his Underground Railroad contacts to help the escaped prisoners make it to and across enemy lines. As disappointing as it was for Elizabeth, given the Van Lew home was now under suspicion as a possible hiding place for escapees, other homes would be used as the primary first place of refuge. The quilt would, for the most part, hang inside out. At least for the time being.

Chapter 7: The Baker

On March 14, 1863 an explosion in Richmond occurred on Brown's Island in the James River. It was in an ammunition factory where percussion caps and gun cartridges were being produced. A young woman attempting to extract black powder from a defective friction primer inadvertently created the explosion. Over 30 women were killed and 25 more injured. More than half were under 16. Word of the tragic event spread quickly through Richmond.

With the growing number of military personnel, government officials, prisoners, and wounded soldiers, from both sides of the conflict, the population of Richmond had almost tripled from what it was before the start of the war. Not only was housing difficult to come by, but now even food and clothing was becoming scarce. The effects of war were taking a toll on the citizens of Richmond, both physically and emotionally.

A few weeks after the Brown Island disaster, another consequential event rocked Richmond. In early April of 1863, the growing shortage of food for civilians was compounded by the increased number of Richmond residents who began hoarding. A crowd of close to 5,000 people, mostly women, began marching, demanding to see Governor Letcher.

One called out, "We celebrate our right to live. We are starving."

Rolling up her sleeve, exposing a boney arm, a young girl yelled, "That's all that's left of me."

They demanded bread, or they would be forced to rush the bakeries in town and each take a loaf.

"That is little enough for the government to give us after it has taken all our men," another woman shouted.

When the governor refused to see them, the mob turned unruly. They began smashing store windows. They broke into shops and began stealing food. Many more stores were looted, with clothing, as well as luxury items, such as silk and jewelry stolen. Order was restored only after troops threatened to fire on the mob. About 60 people were arrested in what became known as the Richmond Bread Riot.

Shortly after, a heavy-set man knocked on the kitchen door of the Van Lew mansion. He was carrying several loafs of bread. Rain was pouring down. He was wearing a wide brim hat. Harriet Anne opened the door.

"May I help you?" she asked.

"Yes, I have the bread you ordered," the man answered.

Harriett looked perplexed. "There must be a mistake, we didn't order any bread. At least, I didn't and I order all the food here. Not that we can't use it."

"If you don't mind, could you tell Miss Van Lew, or Daniel Gates, if either are available, that Thomas McNiven is here and would like to see them with their order." He held up his satchel so she could see the bread inside.

Harriet Anne stared back at him without responding. She shook her head and started to close the door as she commanded, "Wait here."

"Please." McNiven raised his tone as he tried to block the closing door with his foot. "If you don't mind, ma'am, it's nasty out here. Could I wait inside?"

Harriett Anne led him into the kitchen and pulled out a chair. "You can sit here, and I will check."

Harriet reappeared. "They are both coming. Would you like something to drink?"

"No, thank you, ma'am."

Elizabeth entered the kitchen first. McNiven stood to greet her. "Harriet Anne, could you please take Mr. McNiven's coat? See if you can dry it off a little. Hello, Mr. McNiven, such a pleasant surprise. What brings you here?"

Harriet Anne pointed to the bread on the table. McNiven smiled, removed his coat, and handed it over to Harriet Anne who took it, shaking her head as the coat dripped across the floor as she promptly left.

"So nice of you, but I'm sure there are others who need this more than we do. Especially now."

"Some of them already helped themselves. They broke into my store and took all my bread. What I brought you, Miss Van Lew, is one of the first loaves I was able to bake since the riot."

"How bad was the damage to your bakery?"

"Could have been worse. Broken windows, glass everywhere. Smashed plates. Hatchet marks in the counter. But they didn't damage the oven, or the baking equipment. Thank goodness."

Daniel entered the kitchen. He and McNiven shook hands.

"Hope my wife wasn't too unpleasant. She's very suspicious of folk she doesn't know. We have had a few incidents recently."

"Nice to see you again, Daniel. No, she was fine." McNiven then turned back to Elizabeth.

"The damage could have been much worse."

"I didn't mean to sound unappreciative. Thank you for the bread," Elizabeth said.

Daniel added, "Not so easy to come by these days."

Elizabeth then remarked, "I just feel terrible for all those poor, desperate women. Still, they should not have destroyed your store."

She suggested they sit down. The three of them took seats around the kitchen table. Elizabeth and Daniel waited for McNiven to speak.

"I agree, Miss Van Lew." McNiven continued, "Shouldn't have had to come to this. There just isn't enough food to go around. So much these days is now rationed to support the military."

"We are all feeling it now," Elizabeth noted.

"The only reason we still get the amount of flour we do is because we provide for the military and the Davis family at the Confederate Executive Mansion. I usually get some extra for my regular customers, but not much."

"But we are not regular customers. Why bring the bread to us?" Elizabeth looked puzzled.

"Frankly Miss Van Lew, bringing the bread was just an excuse to see you and Daniel. Can I speak candidly?"

"Yes, please do," Elizabeth replied.

"The Lohmann brothers, who you both met, are being forced to make many trips to the Lee's encampment with their wagons. They tell me the

SECRET ARMY BEHIND ENEMY LINES   111

Confederate soldiers are becoming increasingly underfed and undernourished and this despite all the rationing."

"I've heard this, too," Daniel said.

"Not only that, they have now expanded the draft so that all eligible
white men from age 18 to 45 are expected to serve.

Daniel remarked, "More mouths that need to be fed."

"Indeed," McNiven said. "This expanded draft has me worried. Makes
me wish I was pushin' 50."

"Mr. McNiven, obviously the Davis family loves your bread. That just
might be enough to save you from being drafted," Elizabeth said, as she
flashed a wink at Daniel, who reflexively winked back.

"Certainly hope so, ma'am," McNiven replied.

"I am, though, very concerned about my brother. This new eligibility
policy could sweep him up, forcing John to fight for the Rebels, even with
his bad asthma infliction."

"Hopefully he would still be disqualified by his illness," McNiven commented.

"That's what John believes. I just hope he is right."

Changing the subject, McNiven asked, "Do you remember Joseph
Mills?"

"Sure do," Daniel said. "He works in the War Office."

Elizabeth indicated she did as well.

McNiven continued. "He tells me that Lee's forces, close to Fredericksburg, are planning another attack on northern soil."

Elizabeth was taken back. Leaning forward she repeated what she had
just heard, as if she misunderstood. "Another attack on northern soil?

"It failed the first time. Why would they believe this time it would be
successful?" Daniel questioned.

McNiven nodded. "My guess? Robert E. Lee is planning something
completely different this time. From what they say about him, he is not the
kind of man who would make the same mistake a second time. If it were
successful, it would be devastating for the Yankees. A massive embarrassment. That's why I came to see you and Daniel. I was hoping with your Underground network, you could get word to Union command."

"The shame of it is, Daniel just told me we had an escaped prisoner hidden in one of our local safe homes. He could have taken the message."

Daniel explained. "He is now headed to Fort Monroe. May not be too late. I heard they had to hide him in another station before he could reach Williamsburg. I was told they ran into Confederate troop movement along the way. We can try to get something to him. This will take some time figuring out where he is. We've got other people who can deliver it, too."

"Yes, Daniel, but the escaped prisoner was a military officer. Our best chance of getting this to the right military leaders as soon as we can is most probably through someone like him." Elizabeth added, "Let's see if we can reach him with this information before it is too late."

"Yes, ma'am."

Elizabeth stood up and walked to the adjoining pantry, calling out, "Harriet Anne, could you please bring writing paper and a pen?"

"Right away, Miss Van Lew," Harriet Anne's voice echoed back.

"There is something else I wanted to share with both of you," McNiven said.

"When I deliver bread to the Confederate Executive Mansion, it's usually the cook who comes out and takes it from me. Her name is Sadie."

"I know who she is," Daniel said.

"Very pleasant woman," McNiven noted. "She sometimes shares gossip with me about the Davis family and some of their guests. She can be quite amusing at times."

"I can imagine," Elizabeth said.

"Sadie also told me that Mrs. Davis really likes you, Miss Van Lew."

At first, Elizabeth was taken aback by the remark. "Well, yes. I have seen her at a few social events. She always makes a point of coming by to say a few words to me."

"She also told me you're spending time with her seemed to infuriate some of the other ladies trying to ingratiate themselves with the First Lady of the Confederacy. Apparently, this wasn't lost on Mrs. Davis. Sadie heard her tell her husband it makes her like you even more."

Both Elizabeth and Daniel found this amusing. McNiven continued.

"I've also heard talk that while she is very loyal to her husband, she has family up north and is not very happy about the war."

"She did tell me she has relatives in New Jersey and Pennsylvania," Elizabeth said, "As I do, in Pennsylvania."

"I lived in New York when I first came to this country. I still have relatives up north. They told me Mrs. Davis is related to a very prominent family, the Howell's of New Jersey," McNiven stated. "Maybe her northern roots are why she is drawn more to you than some of the others. The reason I bring all this up," McNiven said, "Is that Varina Davis is looking for a new housekeeper. Sadie said that Mrs. Davis brought one of her own with her when she came to Richmond. Been with her from when she lived in Mississippi."

"Why does she want to make a change now?" Elizabeth inquired.

"Jefferson Davis never liked her, according to Sadie. When he couldn't find some rare coins he was saving, he blamed the housekeeper. Believed she stole them. She was then sold off. Turns out they later found the coins."

"Poor woman," Elizabeth said.

"A real shame," Daniel added.

"Apparently Varina has been looking for a new housekeeper and hasn't found anyone she likes so far. I was wondering. With all of your connections, if you might know someone we could place in the Davis' household. Imagine how useful this person could be."

"Yes, very useful. We just might know of someone," Elizabeth responded, looking directly at Daniel as they both smiled. "But I would need to check with her first. It would be very risky and I'm not sure she would want to subject herself to this."

"I understand. This would be most dangerous."

Harriet Anne returned with the writing paper and Elizabeth's favorite quill pen. Elizabeth asked McNiven, "Would you prefer to write the note for the Fort Monroe Commander, or shall I."

"Why don't I dictate, as I remember it from Joe, and you can write."

McNiven left. It was late in the day. Daniel appeared from another room, catching Elizabeth just as she was about to take the steps to retire for the evening.

"Miss Van Lew, doesn't it concern you that Mary is not trained as a housekeeper? I'm not sure she would be able to do this kind of work, even if she wanted to do it."

"Yes, it concerns me. You are right, Daniel. She is not trained, but as you know, Mary is very intelligent and picks up on things very quickly. I'm not concerned about that. We will need to convince her to do it. I'm even more concerned, assuming Mary is in agreement, that I can convince Mrs. Davis to take her. Surely by now she must be aware of some of the negative gossip about the family."

Benjamin Butler had left Fort Monroe almost a year ago. He had been reassigned as military governor for New Orleans following its capture by the Union in the early Spring of 1862. Butler had left his assignment in Virginia very frustrated. He wanted the North to capitalize more fully on the use of spies in Richmond. Butler was critical of Pinkerton and how he managed intelligence efforts.

Butler believed the Federals were missing the opportunity to take advantage of willing resources already in place. This frustrated him that no serious efforts had been attempted in this area. Butler had been reassigned before he could do anything more to cultivate Unionists in Richmond to provide intelligence for the Union. Before leaving he told his men that he hoped that one day they would be together again.

Lincoln went through with his threat. He knew from the beginning that the Confederate States would only relinquish their rebellion and rejoin the Union, if and only if, they were resoundingly defeated in battle. But he had warned them in advance of his intentions. The United States would now enact the policies he presented in the Emancipation Proclamation. Jefferson Davis issued his own response shortly after. Surprisingly, Davis opened his rebuttal proclamation with a scathing attack on General Benjamin Butler.

Davis believed northern states had no power to nullify the Fugitive Slave Act, which protected slave ownership. He rejected the "contraband of war" justification. He saw Lincoln's proclamation as exploiting this argument further. Davis called Lincoln's decree "the most execrable measure in history of guilty man." At the beginning of his own proclamation, Davis stated the following, singling out the General from Massachusetts:

> I do order that he (Butler) be no longer considered or treated
> simply as a public enemy of the Confederate States of America

but as an outlaw and common enemy of mankind, and that in
the event of his capture the officer in command of the capturing
force do cause him to be immediately executed by hanging...

Butler had no idea at the time that his refusal to return escaped slaves to
southern owners, while at Fort Monroe, would play a role in repositioning
the war in moral terms. His "contraband of war" argument had a profound
influence on Lincoln's Emancipation Proclamation.

In his new capacity in New Orleans, he earned the reputation of being
"the Beast." Butler instituted controversial ordinances. The most incendiary being his "women order." After a local woman emptied her chamber pot
on a Union Officer, Butler ordered that any woman insulting military personnel "shall be regarded and held liable to be treated as a woman of the
town plying her avocation."

In other words, bad behavior by women of New Orleans would be
punished as an equivalent offense to the crime of prostitution. This combined with other ordinances, confiscation of property, and Southern accusations of looting, made him one of the most despised generals in the Federal ranks. Jefferson Davis described him as a "felon."

Jefferson Davis and Benjamin Butler had been political friends prior to
the war. Both were active in the Democratic Party. Butler was now a dastardly villain to Davis. The Confederate President left no doubt in his response to Lincoln's edict that it was not only Butler's actions in New Orleans that incurred his rancor.

With Lincoln's Emancipation Proclamation framed in "Butleresque"
terms, applying only to slaves in the breakaway southern states, it was clear
to Davis it was aimed to provoke discord in the Confederacy. It made
the Confederate President furious. Davis believed this could disrupt the
"peaceful and contented" lives of slaves, and was meant to incite rebellion.

After excoriating Butler, Davis went on to refute Lincoln. From the
perspective of Davis, it was bad enough that in his Proclamation, Lincoln
had pronounced slaves in rebellious states free. Infuriating him even more,
Lincoln said African Americans would now be recruited as Union soldiers.

Up until this point, African Americans were not eligible to volunteer
to fight with the Union army. In the South, as slaves they were being used

to support all aspects of the war effort, working in various capacities in armories, hospitals, prisons. They built roads, batteries, and fortifications. In some cases, they were even forced to fight for the Confederacy.

In defiance of Lincoln's proposed actions, Davis argued "that all negro slaves captured in arms be at once delivered over to the executive authorities of the respective States to which they belong to be dealt with according to the laws of said States." They would be considered slaves in revolt and not given the customary privileges accorded prisoners of war. Instead, they could be executed. Davis also indicated that white Union officers in command of these units could expect to suffer the same fate.

Abolitionists would have preferred Lincoln going farther, freeing all slaves across the nation, not just in the rebellious slave states. Nevertheless, many now saw it as a positive step in making it a righteous war in support of humanitarian concerns.

Major General John Ellis Wool, the oldest officer serving in the Civil War, was now commander of the U.S. Army Department of Virginia. He had helped secure Fort Monroe for the Union in the early years of the war, a major strategic accomplishment given its position at the mouth of the James.

Wool had also successfully captured Norfolk, at the same time of McClellan's disastrous Peninsula Campaign in May 1862. Taking Norfolk with its valuable port and ship building yards was one of the few recent Union successes in the eastern theatre. Norfolk was where the Confederates were building ironclads, the most famous being the Merrimac. Wool had been a consistent outspoken critic of McClellan for his lack of aggressiveness in bringing the fight to the enemy. He was one of the few officers in uniform willing to speak out.

With Butler gone, General Wool was back at Fort Monroe when he was told an escaped prisoner from Richmond had recently arrived and said he had information concerning Lee's war plans. Wool told his staff sergeant to bring him forward.

His name was Lieutenant John Dobbs.

They met in the Commanding General's Residence at the fort. The building was a three story home, architected in neoclassic style. Built within the stone walls of the fort, the tall, elegant red brick residence was an im-

SECRET ARMY BEHIND ENEMY LINES   117

posing structure. In stark contrast from the other more modest residential structures, it was secluded away from the ever expanding number of tents, pitched for former slaves, now filling most of the parade grounds.

Dobbs was escorted to a dark wood study, with a contrasting white mantelpiece surrounding a traditional red brick fireplace. It was not in use, probably not for quite a while. Wool was sitting at his desk.

"Would you like a whiskey, soldier?"

"Yes sir, much obliged."

As the General stood and walked to the liquor cabinet he said, "I may be an old crow, but I don't drink it like General Grant reportedly does."

"General Grant drinks *Old Crow?*"

"That's what they say," Wool answered. "Not for my palette. That sweet corn candy flavored bourbon tastes more like a dessert."

"Well, *Old Crow* is a Kentucky Bourbon, if I'm not mistaken. Suppose it's easier to get your hands on a whiskey from that region when you're camped in Tennessee," Dobbs suggested.

Wool smiled. "You might have something there, Lieutenant Dobbs. Especially given I remember hearing the Confederate Government in Tennessee prohibited the sale of its local brands to anyone outside their own army."

"Maybe that's why General Grant is fighting so hard," Dobbs said.

They both laughed. The General pulled two cut crystal glasses off a shelf near the cabinet, placed on the table, and poured from a bottle of *Jameson Irish Whiskey.*

"I prefer a good malted barley base myself, but always, only in moderation. Again, not like Grant." He held up the bottle. "You won't find too many of this these days. Difficult to get up north and practically impossible from where we are here on down with our southern blockade in effect."

He handed a glass to Dobbs who raised it and breathed in, absorbing a whiff of oak from the casks used during the aging process. They both sipped, enjoying the smooth traces of blended flavor and the warm sensation of the alcohol.

"Speaking of whiskey, you might enjoy hearing this, although it is rather shameful. When I relieved General Butler from his command here at Fort Monroe, he told me the most curious of stories."

"I'm all ears, General."

"Butler noticed when his picket guards assigned to outposts over a mile from here departed for their shifts, they appeared perfectly sober. Returning the next morning, they often came back rowdy, smelling of liquor."

"Is that so?"

"Unfortunately, yes. Butler sent officers to investigate. They searched the guard outposts, canteens and their gear, turning up nothing. Then someone in Butler's command noticed something odd. The guards always carried their muskets, straight up, in a very peculiar manner. Butler told me every guard's gun barrel was filled with whiskey."

"Not *Jameson's*, I take it," Dobbs said jokingly.

"Certainly not. Luckily we were never attacked while this going on. Anyway, I was told you recently escaped from Libby Prison in Richmond and asked to see me.

"Yes, General."

"A horrible place from what we have heard. How in God's name did you manage to slip out?"

"Well, I had help, and from the most unlikely person. The clerk in the prison who did roll calls, his name was Erasmus Ross. Came on like a real son of a bitch. Excuse me, General."

Wool smiled. "That's all right, Lieutenant Dobbs. Continue."

"He was nasty as hell to us. Swore up and down. Smacked fellas around for no reason. One day he smacked me in the stomach. Called me a 'blue-bellied Yankee' and told me to come down to his office to settle some things. Thought he was gonna smack me some more."

"Then what happened?"

"Ross closed the door to this office. Reached under a counter. Handed me a Confederate soldier uniform and a wide brim hat. Told me to put it on. Then directed me to walk with him out the front door. He told me he would talk to me as if we were close friends. I was to keep my head down, only answer yes or no to his questions, and occasionally laugh at his remarks."

"This man was a clerk at the prison?"

"Yes, General."

"Go on."

"Ross suggested I walk next to him, side by side. Told me to 'act confident.' He then told me someone would be waiting for me on the outside to take me to a place where it would be safe."

He paused for a minute. They both sipped their whiskeys before Dobbs continued.

"Surprisingly, it worked. As soon as I came out, a young negro boy stepped out from the cross street and told me to follow him."

"Do you remember the address where he took you?"

"A farmhouse. Don't know exactly where. We went by way of back roads and cut through brush to get there. That's all I remember."

"What else?"

"I was to stay there until it was safe to head east with a different guide to another place. Then they hid me in a supply wagon to get me closer to here. Stayed in three different places along the way until they got me to Hampton. Walked the rest of the way until I was spotted by a soldier on guard duty."

"Sounds like a well-organized operation."

"Yes, sir. They told me same one been used for slaves, and it was mostly slaves, or former slaves, who were my guides from each stop along the way."

"The Underground Railroad helped you escape?"

"Yes sir, believe so. Funny thing, none of them would tell me anything much. Only what I needed to do to get out safely."

"That's interesting," Wool remarked.

"Yes sir, but I believe I have information that will be of more interest."

"Let's hear it."

"While I was at the last place they gave me a note. Told me to memorize it and then destroy it. Came from a person working in the Confederate War Department, I was told."

"If we have someone there helping us, this would be extraordinary. What did it say?"

"The note stated that Lee is planning another surprise attack in the North. He is convinced one more major success on Federal soil could destroy the will of us Yankees to keep fighting. Lee would be taking a big risk, according to this inside source. His troops are low on supplies, which are being rationed. Might be an opportunity to cut his army off from their lines of supply."

"Who gave this note to you? Are you sure they can be trusted?"

"The people in last house I stayed, but it didn't come from them. It was delivered to me while I was there by another negro. I assume he was a slave. Not sure who wrote it, or where it was originated."

"Then I can't be sure this can be trusted," Wool responded.

"Maybe not, General, but whoever it was, they knew where to find me. Let's assume it may have been the enemy trying to throw us off. If they knew where I was, why wouldn't they have arrested me? Why wouldn't they have broken up this group of people who helped me escape a long time ago?"

"Hmmm. Good point, Lieutenant. Maybe they let you go because they wanted you to give us a plan, as you say, to throw us off. Not saying that is the case, but we need to be careful."

General Wool began to write some notes. He then looked back up and said, "Lee tried to invade the North before. We stopped him in Sharpsburg, Maryland, in the Battle of Antietam. Sent his army scurrying back to Virginia."

Dobbs nodded in agreement as Wool continued.

"Probably could have defeated him if we kept up the pursuit. Why would Lee think his army wouldn't get stopped again this time?"

"Don't know, General."

"Did this message contain anything about Lee's objectives? Is it to surprise and confront the Army of the Potomac in their encampment? Invade Washington?"

"Nothing. Just that the plan is to advance north again. I'm sorry General, that was all I was given."

Dobbs could tell Wool was disappointed there wasn't more. So was he. The General walked Dobbs to the door of the study where they shook hands. A soldier with sergeant stripes met them at the door.

"Please show the Lieutenant to the residence exit," Wool commanded.

"Thank you, Dobbs."

"Good day General. Thank you."

Wool returned to the study and poured another drink. The General pondered what he had just heard. He remained skeptical about the sourcing, but had already decided he would pass it on to Major General Joseph Hooker, the new commander of the Army of the Potomac. An extremely frustrated Lincoln had just replaced another General. This time Burnside was sacked and Hooker was the latest installment.

Confidence in Burnside was lost after his year-end defeat in Fredericksburg, followed by the humiliating "Mud March" in January 1863 - a second failed attempt to cross the Rappahannock River and challenge Lee in his home state of Virginia. For this critical command, facing off against Robert E. Lee, and protecting Washington, Lincoln had gone through three generals in three months.

Robert E. Lee who had previously advocated rationing of food and supplies for the army, now ordered that all horses in the Confederacy be confiscated for his cavalry. While the Southern cavalry had continued to bore the cost of keeping themselves mounted, the Union cavalry rode horses made available through Federal government funding.

The early advantage of the South in possessing more experienced horsemen was now more than offset by the lack of available replacement when a horse succumbed to war related causalities. In contrast to the North's ability to provide a replacement horse, Confederates were often on their own, sometimes forced to leave their regiment, return home, and retrieve another horse.

Rationing and new restrictions impacted all residents of Richmond, including the elite. With all the new burdens the Van Lew's faced, due to the war, losing the family horses would make things considerably worse. It would be much more difficult for her brother's hardware store, where business was already down, to pick up needed supplies and make deliveries. Keeping the store running during the war had already become a challenge. On a personal level, for Elizabeth, who loved riding and who was devoted to all of the horses, this was unthinkable.

Her brother was at the store when she heard from a neighbor that government workers were going through the neighborhood, taking inventory on horses. Elizabeth called together Isaac and Daniel and asked for their help. The three of them each took one of the white carriage horses from the barn and guided them into the smoke house. They had a fourth horse, Rendezvous, a brown Morgan, Elizabeth's favorite. There was not enough room for the fourth. Elizabeth asked Isaac to take Rendezvous and hide him in a storage shack across the yard in the back corner of the property.

When one of the government workers noticed grain and fresh water in the barn, he was not amused. He barked at Elizabeth, "I could write you up for this, and you could be in deep trouble for subversive activity against the government, Miss Van Lew. Now are you going to tell me where you have your horses, or do I need to have my men search all of your property?"

Reluctantly, she said, "They are in the smoke house."

"How many do you have?" he asked.

"Three."

He wrote it down on a note pad and told her that soldiers would be around in a few days to take possession of the horses.

Realizing there was nothing they could do to protect the carriage horses, Elizabeth turned to Isaac and said, "Let's put Rendezvous in the Library."

"Ma'am? Inside the house?"

"Let's get plenty of straw, spread it around the library, get water, hay and grain too. They'll never look there," Elizabeth said.

"I'll help you," Daniel said, looking back at Isaac who appeared stunned, confused. He quickly recovered, following Daniel to the smoke house. They retrieved and secured the carriage horses back in the barn and began to collect straw. They spent the rest of the afternoon preparing the library.

Several neighborhood children were watching from behind shrubs in the adjacent neighbor's yard as Isaac put a lead rope on Rendezvous and carefully guided him up the stairs and into the house. Daniel followed from behind, hoping to prevent any missteps, as Elizabeth looked on, occasionally calling to Rendezvous to try and comfort him as he awkwardly moved up the staircase. Harriett Anne held the door as Rendezvous entered the family residence. It took a good half hour with Rendezvous in the library, before he stopped kicking and squealing.

Neither Elizabeth nor any of the servants had any idea the children had sneaked up onto the wraparound porch and were peeking through the thick interior window curtains. They started to call Elizabeth Van Lew "Crazy Bet," based on what they were seeing.

When word got back from one of her friends that some of the adults in the neighborhood had picked up on the expression and were now also calling her "Crazy Bet," Elizabeth simply said, "Better they think I'm an eccentric as opposed to a traitor."

The soldiers came a week later. They took the carriage horses away. Elizabeth waited for a few more days and then asked Isaac to take Rendezvous back to the barn. It took several more days to completely clean out the library.

When Isaac came back from the barn he asked to have a word with Elizabeth.

"Miss Van Lew. I realize we need to be real careful, now. Those damn Rebels would just love to get their hands on a strong, healthy horse like Rendezvous. I was thinking maybe we bandage one of the legs and tell folks the Confederates didn't want him. Make 'em think Rendezvous lamer than an old mule."

"My, my Isaac. That is very clever."

Chapter 8: Housemaid Wanted

She could hear the angelic sounds of the choir as they approached the First African Baptist Church, home to one of the oldest African American congregations in Virginia. Located on East Broad Street, the church was a tall red brick building in colonial style, with two white pillars at the entrance.

Isaac pulled over the horse carriage, jumping down from the driver seat, and tying Rendezvous with his bandaged leg to a post. He assisted Elizabeth as she stepped from the running board onto the ground. A white couple passed by. The man cast an unapproving eye her way. She could guess what he was thinking. Proper southern belles didn't travel without what was considered proper escort. This was just another example of Elizabeth Van Lew skirting accepted practices, with no concern about convention, or how it might be interpreted.

Sunday Service was ending. The congregation was splintering across the churchyard, where it looked like they were setting up for a picnic. She noticed Daniel in the distance, helping to arrange tables. As she moved towards the church, it occurred to her that at one time the congregation included white members, worshipping alongside of slaves and free African Americans. Some 20 years ago the white parishioners had broken off to start a separate church. The old church then added "African" to its name.

The people she passed were friendly. A couple she knew stopped and said hello. She asked them where she could find Mary Bowser, but they didn't know. She spotted the minister now standing on the church steps and approached him. The Reverend Robert Ryland, a white minister, was apparently now the only Caucasian still associated with the Church. They knew each other from community events.

"Good morning Reverend Ryland."

"'Mornin' Miss Van Lew. What brings you to First Baptist?"

"I was hoping to find Mary Bowser."

"Oh, yes, of course. Lovely young lady. Her husband Wilson is very pleasant as well. As you walk into the church, go down the stairs. You can't miss them. You will find her in the back with the children. I suspect they're just getting started."

The inside of the Church was plain, with first come first served benches, versus enclosed pews with the engraved names indicating where the important families of Richmond society sat, like her place of worship. The altar in front was also a simple wooden structure, as opposed to carved out rare stone.

The simplicity of the interior accentuated an unusual sense of reverence within her. Quite distinct from the feelings of grandeur inspired by the lofty architecture of her own church, rising atop the highest ground of Richmond, the oldest place of worship in the city. Her church was a historic building in the fashionable section of town, appropriately named Church Hill. Yet she found this humble structure immersed within the east end section of the city equally inspiring.

She could hear young voices singing as she took the stairs, but couldn't quite make out what song they were practicing. Mary was standing in front of a group of 10 or so children ranging in age from 5 to about 11. She was providing singing direction. If she noticed Elizabeth standing in the shadows of the doorway, she gave no indication.

"Let's do *Dry Bones* again, but this time, Willis, with your beautiful, booming voice. I know you know this by heart. You sing the entire song, from beginning to end, and the rest of us will sing the refrain with you, 'Come Alive, Come Alive', and then one more 'Come Alive' at the end, but first, let's try the refrain again:

As we call out to dry bones
Come Alive, Come Alive
As we call out to dead hearts
Come Alive, Come Alive
Up out of the ashes let us see an army rise,
We call out to dry bones, Come Alive

A spiritual sung by slaves, but unfamiliar to Elizabeth.

"Much better, much," Mary called out.

Elizabeth began to clap. Smiling as she looked up, Mary motioned for the children to try it again and then walked over towards Elizabeth.

"Hello, Miss Van Lew. I was looking forward to seeing you this Wednesday. This must be important."

"Hello Mary. Yes, and I couldn't really ask Daniel to speak with you about this. When you're finished with the children. I'll sit upstairs in the Church until you're done."

"Might be awhile. I could leave the children, if it doesn't keep me away too long."

"I'm happy to wait, Mary. Please, go back to the children."

She sat on a bench near the altar. It seemed like a long time. Elizabeth enjoyed listening to the sweet, singing voices. Slowly it started to come together. Finally, she heard tiny footsteps and laughing voices from the stairs. Elizabeth turned to watch as the children, one after the other, ran outside through the front doors of the church.

She walked to the back, just as Mary climbed to the top of the steps. They sat together on the bench nearest the doors.

Elizabeth spoke first. "I've told you before. I believe that the information your husband, Wilson, provided from the Norfolk Shipyard was very important. I suspect it may have prevented the Dismal Swamp from becoming a secret passage for Rebel ironclads to avoid the blockade and sneak out to sea."

"Yes, I'm very proud that he was able to get this to you. I told him at the time if anyone could help get it to the Federals, it was you and Daniel."

"Along those same lines, I'm here to talk to you about an information gathering role, but requiring an extensive commitment and fraught with risk."

"Nothing like getting straight to the point, and dispensing with any effort to make it as palatable as possible, Miss Van Lew."

"You are right Mary, I am sorry. This has preoccupied my thoughts since I first heard about it."

Mary chuckled. "Miss Van Lew, I'm just teasing a little, please go on."

"Yes, I know. Mary, I am sure you could do this, if you wanted to. Something that could make a huge difference. Frankly, few if anyone else could do it, in my estimation. I am conflicted, even just mentioning it to you. This would be extremely dangerous. The consequences if you were caught well, would be catastrophic."

"Please, tell me about this role, Miss Van Lew."

"Mary, you know you are an extremely intelligent woman. You also have an exceptional gift. Not only your reading and writing skills, or how quickly you can absorb things and learn. Your ability to see something, a page from a book for example, and retain exactly what you saw. I couldn't help but notice, even when you were very little."

Mary laughed. "I remember how surprised you were that first time."

"Remarkable. You've been doing this since you were a little girl - something most adults could never do. I certainly can't. We both know you have this gift. Yet, you seem very happy and content in your present life, working here at the church. You also have your husband to consider."

"Miss Van Lew. What is it you are thinking I could do?"

Elizabeth paused before continuing. "There might be a way, if you agree, and the decision is yours to make. There are also several things that would need to fall in place. This is an opportunity where you could apply your extraordinary gifts and help the Union, but, this is all conjecture at this point."

"Well, you have certainly piqued my interest. Even if it is simply conjecture."

"I am told the Davis family is looking for a new housemaid."

"The President of the Confederacy?"

"Jefferson Davis. Yes."

Mary stood up, stepped away from the bench, took a few steps back and forth and then jolted back on her heels. "But, I am not a housemaid. Never been one."

"I know. You could pick up on it very quickly. I am certain of this. You spent much of your childhood following Chloe around, and my guess is that you know more about it than you realize."

"Not sure," Mary uttered under her breath.

"Even assuming, things fall neatly in place, it's not going to happen right away. I have spoken to Chloe about it. She agreed to teach you what she thinks you would need to know. This would give you a chance to spend some additional time with her, which she would love."

"I would as well."

"Frankly, Mary, what I am primarily concerned about is your ability to adjust to playing the necessary role. You will be in grave danger if you ever slip up."

"What makes you think I would?" Mary asked.

"I sent you up North because I knew with your intelligence you would benefit from a good education you could not get here but, there was something else. Even as a little girl you were always quite bold, and you were never afraid to express your honest opinions. With the way things are now, you could get yourself in serious trouble."

Mary responded, "You are probably right, Miss Van Lew. Do you remember the time I decided to go into town without a pass?"

Elizabeth smiled. "How could I ever forget. I couldn't believe they held you in a jail cell for common criminals until mother and I came to take you home."

"I thought of it as a great adventure at the time."

"This is what I am most concerned about. You will need to temper your feelings and disguise your naturally inquisitive nature, playing the role of a diligent and faithful housemaid – all the while you attempt to find out things."

"You mean, playing the part, as if I was uneducated, naïve and subservient? At all times giving the impression I was unaware of whatever I might hear in conversation? Probably wouldn't hurt to come on as if I was not terribly bright, I suppose."

"Certainly you would have to hide your intelligence and intentions at all times, even with the other servants. You could trust no one. Which is even worse. You will be stepping back into a slave role."

"Yes, and treated very differently than the way you and your family have always treated your servants, even back when we were all slaves."

"Yes, but I do believe Mrs. Varina Davis is a decent lady who was also educated in Philadelphia."

"I didn't know that," Mary smiled as she said this.

"Even though you may end up liking her as I did, or feel there are others you can trust, you could not under any circumstance let them know that you are educated, or show any indication of your intelligence, or true intentions. Trust no one. Mary, I'll say it again. I have very mixed feelings even talking to you about this. I fear things could end very badly."

"I understand."

"You could never let down your guard while pretending to be someone you are not, and there may be times when you may have to lie to avoid getting caught."

Mary began to giggle, surprising a very serious looking Elizabeth.

"Chloe used to say she could always tell when I wasn't being completely honest."

"I struggled with this myself. Volunteering with mother to help the Confederate soldiers. Sometimes just by saying nothing when others would say awful things. Cajoling and wheedling General Winder for permission to meet with Yankee prisoners. Do you know what helped me?"

"Tell me, Miss Van Lew."

"Isaac. He put it in the right perspective. I have now come to terms with it, thanks to him. The so called institution of slavery is built on a mountain of lies, and so is the Confederate government established to protect it. How many more children will be born into slavery? How many more will be horribly brutalized, raped, whipped, or beaten to death? How many more soldiers will have to fight risking death before this scourge ends?"

"I can see how this helped you, Miss Van Lew. I mean coming to terms with it, but..."

Before Mary could continue, Elizabeth added, "The Confederacy needs to be defeated. I decided that anything I could do, even little things, just might help end the war a little sooner. Save more lives. Even if it means engaging in activities that make me uncomfortable. Think about how much more you could do in this position."

"If I could bring myself to pull it off, I can see how this could be very useful. I'm just not sure I'm capable of doing something like this. Miss Van Lew, it would be as if I was lying to myself about who I really am."

"I can certainly understand. It does get easier after a while."

"Exactly what I am afraid of, Miss Van Lew. What kind of person will I become? Can I ever go back, or will I be changed forever?"

"Mary, you will never be anyone else other than who you are right now. I am most certain of this. Why don't you take a day or so to think about it? Talk it over with Wilson. But I will need to know in a few days. I am planning to attend an event at the end of this week where Mrs. Davis will also attend. I haven't spoken to her about any of this, and will not unless you tell me you and Wilson are in agreement to do this."

Monday morning, Mary Bowser showed up at the door to the Van Lew mansion wearing a heavy cloth dress, covered by an old, tattered apron, and a white head wrap. She told Elizabeth she was ready to take lessons from Chloe.

Elizabeth cautioned. "I hope you are sure about this, Mary. Don't get me wrong, I am delighted that you are willing, but I only want you to go through with it if you've carefully thought this through."

"Yes ma'am, I have. Wilson wants me to do it as well. He told me he could do more for the Underground Railroad to occupy his time with me no longer living at home, but I do have a question."

Mary's husband, Wilson, was now working odd jobs in town, as well as helping Daniel and the Underground Railroad on nights when he was needed.

"Tell me," Elizabeth prompted.

"Do you think I can get Sunday's off to teach the children?"

"We'll try to make it part of the arrangement."

"Good." Mary paused for a moment and then added, "I've also decided to do this for them. The children. Maybe they can have a better life one day."

Chloe heard Mary and Elizabeth talking. She came down the stairs.

"I was just getting ready to call you, Chloe," said Elizabeth.

"Yes ma'am, mornin' Mary. Just warning you. We're both gonna be workin' real hard to get you ready."

"I certainly hope so," Mary said with a beaming smile. "I will need all the help you are willing to give me."

"No one better than Chloe for that," Elizabeth said, "but Chloe, we also need to take some time from the training and see if we can find something decent for Mary to wear at the Davis' home." Reaching and pulling at Mary's worn out apron, Elizabeth added, "this would never do."

"Yes, ma'am."

The tea for Confederate mothers was held in the former Virginia State Capitol, now the Capitol Building for the Confederate States of America. The building was designed by the renowned American architect, Alexander Parris, who would later design Boston's Quincy Market. It was built with a classical influence, popular in the early nineteenth century. The exterior was a symmetrically pleasing two story brick building featuring an extended center bay, with a four-columned portico. Escorted to the reception in the first-floor public room, guests couldn't help but admire the steep succession of arches across the high ceiling.

Varina Davis as keynote speaker helped make it a well-attended event. Elizabeth guessed about 50 people. Perhaps half were simply mothers of soldiers. The rest were wives of Richmond dignitaries and politicians. Some of them may also have had sons fighting for the Confederacy. Elizabeth wondered if so and how many. Jefferson Davis was not in attendance. As they entered the room of the event, and began to move through the crowd, Eliza lightly touched Elizabeth's arm and directed her gaze across the room.

There they could both see Varina going from table to table, talking to the mothers, joking, occasionally offering sympathy. She was wearing an embroidered white cotton muslin gown. She did not look like the mother of four children. Early in her marriage, she had lost her first child in infancy, which would have made it five. Yet Varina looked stunning, and much younger than her age.

Phoebe immediately descended on the Van Lew women, pointing out their assigned table, where they would find their name cards. She was wearing a light blue silk faille dress that was perfectly fitted to her, and as always, accentuating her most notable assets.

"Hello ladies, you both look wonderful." She leaned in and kissed Eliza on the cheek, and then Elizabeth. "They'll be serving lunch shortly," Phoebe noted. "Probably best to take your seats."

They thanked her and moved into the middle of the room to their table.

"She obviously wants to get you seated before Varina spots you. No doubt, to avoid what happened last time," Eliza quipped.

Eliza and Elizabeth did not know the other ladies at their table socially. They were polite, but spoke more to each other than the Van Lew's. They mostly gossiped about how women were dressed at the other tables.

As their cups were filled with tea, Elizabeth whispered to her mother, "I'm surprised they can still serve tea with the Union Naval blockade."

"Probably not much longer," Eliza responded. "I hear there is very little left in town."

In addition to tea, the ladies were served an assortment of cheeses, biscuits and fruit pies.

After the food was served, Phoebe spoke briefly, offering her thanks to the mothers, and for the service and sacrifice of their sons. She then praised the other women who had helped her set up the event, asking each to stand and take a bow. For Elizabeth, the talk seemed to drag on forever. Finally, Phoebe delivered a verbose introduction of the First Lady. Varina appeared uncomfortable as Phoebe rambled on.

When Varina finally got up to speak, she was brief, articulate and captivated the room with a few short stories about soldiers she had met. She spoke of one who was recovering from injuries from Manassas. With no bayonet on his rifle, he threw it away when ordered to charge with his brigade, fighting off the enemy with only a knife in his belt. He was eager to rejoin his fellow soldiers in battle. Another local soldier recovering from a leg injury had helped rout the Yankees at the Battle of Ball's Bluff by holding his ground until reinforcements could arrive. She then asked one of the ladies in attendance to stand.

"Millie's husband, two sons, brother and brother-in-law all fought at Manassas. Millie has been a devoted volunteer who most of us here know very well. Please join me in acknowledging this extraordinary contribution and sacrifice by Millie and her family."

It took several minutes for the applause to die down and Varina could continue her talk.

She then spoke of simple acts of charity she had heard about and witnessed first-hand from Richmond women helping the troops in the battlefields, in hospitals, and volunteer work, distributing food, clothing and supplies. Varina threaded her talk with well-placed humor, keeping it brief, but also making it entertaining. She ended by offering an apology for having to leave early to attend another event with her husband, President Davis.

As the speech concluded and the crowd began to applaud, Elizabeth left her mother seated and made her way around the rows of tables, following Varina, as she moved toward the exit.

"Hello Varina," she shouted as others began to leave their seats to share a word as the First Lady passed. They formed a circle, temporarily blocking Varina's exit.

Varina looked up and made her way towards Elizabeth, raising her voice as well. "Oh, hello Elizabeth."

As they got closer, Elizabeth said, "I loved your heartfelt stories, as I think everyone did. Very touching."

"Most kind of you to say so, Elizabeth. I hope you are well. Very nice to see you again."

"You as well, Varina. I was hoping to get a word with you, but obviously, impossible here."

"Why don't you walk outside with me?" Varina suggested.

As they left the Capitol Building, Elizabeth asked, "how is your baby son?"

"William Howell is doing just fine. Thanks for asking. It is hard to believe he is almost five months old already." Varina stopped at the end of the walkway, facing the street. "My carriage will come around to meet here. We can speak for a few minutes. Do you need a ride, Elizabeth?"

"No, no thank you. My mother is with me. We have our own carriage."

"What can I do for you, Elizabeth?" Varina inquired.

"I heard that you might be looking for a housemaid."

"Word travels fast in Richmond. Yes Elizabeth, I have been looking, but have not found anyone suitable as of yet. Do you know of someone?"

"Perhaps. We have two housemaid slaves, Chloe and Mary. They are both excellent. We really only need one. Chloe would prefer to do everything herself and tells me she doesn't need Mary's help."

"Having trouble getting along?" Varina asked.

"No, they get along very well. Mary gets along with everyone. Mary is very pleasant, hardworking and competent. Simply put, Chloe can be a little controlling."

"How old is Mary?"

"She is 24 and very mature for her age. And she minds her own business. This is also very important to us. I believe you would find her to be quite capable. I also think a change would do her good."

Others who also had left early passed by. They could see that Varina was engaged in conversation. A few nodded, one or two others thanked her, or commented on the speech, but none stopped or tried to interrupt.

"Sometimes when our nurse is busy, she might also need to take care of the children. Does she have any experience with them?"

"She takes care of children every Sunday at the African Baptist Church."

"Is she honest? We had a problem in the past and my husband was upset about one of the servants stealing."

"Mary Bowser is as honest as the day is long."

"Sounds like she could be ideal. Before making a decision, as I'm sure you can understand, Elizabeth, I would need to meet with her."

"Of course," Elizabeth said.

"Also, Mary will need to spend a little time with our head housekeeper. If things work out, and I certainly hope they do, she would be Mary's supervisor. Could we do this next Tuesday, morning, perhaps ten o'clock?"

"Yes, this would be fine, Varina."

"While May spends some time with Mary, you and I can have a nice chat. We see each other at social events, but it would be nice having a real visit."

"I would like that very much."

The carriage pulled up in front of the two ladies.

"Assuming we agree to bring Mary on, what kind of arrangement are you thinking we could make?"

"My family would prefer to retain ownership. This would be in keeping with my beloved father's will to never sell any of our slaves."

"I don't see why we could not work an agreeable arrangement, Elizabeth," Varina said. "We would just need to work out the fee for Mary's services."

"My preference would be to not collect any fee."

"No fee, surely we should pay some reasonable amount."

"I'd prefer that it be considered a voluntary contribution to the First Family. The President and you have taken on so much of a burden for the Confederacy. This would be a small gesture of support on the part of the Van Lew family."

"Elizabeth, this is too kind of you and your family."

"As you know Varina, so many others are sacrificing so much more. Also, I would like to eventually bring her back to work for us again. Chloe will retire in the next few years."

"Hopefully the war will be over by then and we can go home to our farm in Mississippi."

Her driver walked over to help Varina into the horse carriage.

"Let's hope for that," Elizabeth said.

"Then I'll see you and Mary Bowser on Tuesday."

"See you then, thank you so very much, Varina."

Chapter 9: Inside the Confederate White House

Some said it was because of his loyalty to General McClellan. Shortly after Lincoln removed McClellan from his command, Allan Pinkerton resigned from his post as head of the secret service. While he was credited with foiling an early plot to kill Lincoln before his inauguration, Pinkerton had been harshly criticized during the war for his habit of overestimating enemy troop strength. These estimates had provided McClellan with additional cover as to why he was not more aggressive advancing against Confederate forces.

Despite his continued skepticism, General Wool sent a communication to Hooker, Lincoln's newest commander of the Army of the Potomac. It was based on the conversation he had with the escaped Libby prisoner, Lieutenant John Dobbs.

Van Lew's identity as a potential source of Confederate intelligence and ability to leverage the Underground Railroad channels for passing information continued to allude the Federals. She preferred it this way.

In the meantime, Colonel George H. Sharpe had assumed Pinkerton's old role for Hooker. A lawyer from Kingston New York, he had fought in all major battles with the Army of the Potomac. He would now serve as the Army's Intelligence Chief.

He was medium height, with neatly trimmed short brown hair, and matching brown eyes that projected a steady alertness. Sporting an inverse "V" moustache that angled out across both sides of a long chin, combined with a wide-brimmed Union hat he generally wore slightly angled, Sharpe projected more the image of a Texas Ranger than a northeast lawyer turned soldier.

One of the first orders Hooker gave Colonel Sharpe was to see if he could verify the information passed on by Lieutenant Dobbs, or at least find other corroborating information.

"This is highly suspect in my judgment, George. General Wool feels the same, but I want you to see what else you can find out."

"Yes sir."

"Impossible for me to believe Lee would attempt to invade the North a second time. Especially after what happened when he tried at Antietam and failed."

Unlike Pinkerton, Sharpe was determined to make contact with Unionist supporters already living in the South and was planning to send scouts to help recruit them as spies. Early attempts failed and the veracity of the communication from Richmond could not be established.

Hooker realized President Lincoln was anxious for his new commander for the Army of the Potomac to score a victory and turnaround the series of defeats in the eastern campaign that were continuing to add up. Hooker, who had been critical of the previous commanding officers who held the same post, wanted to launch an aggressive offensive that would destroy the Army of Northern Virginia.

He asked Sharpe to help on this as well. Sharpe was to come back as soon as possible with estimates on comparative troop strength. Hooker knew that he had a sizable advantage. His 130,000-strong force would be almost double that of Lee's Army of Northern Virginia. He also knew based on the intelligence received second hand from another spy, that the Confederates were short on supplies.

Hooker's plan was to send his cavalry to destroy Lee's supply lines in April, 1863, hindering his ability to move north. Hooker would follow with the bulk of his army across the Rappahannock River – just as General Ambrose Burnside had done in the Battle of Fredericksburg. This time, however, it would not be a frontal assault.

From their encampment in Falmouth, Virginia, on the northern bank of the Rappahannock, Hooker sent his troops 40 miles further west to cross upstream, near Kelly's Ford, and execute a wide sweep to attack Lee's left flank, outside Fredericksburg.

Hooker's advance was spotted early. Rather than order a retreat, Lee decided to attack Hooker's much larger force while they were still in a wilderness area after crossing the river. As the Confederates advanced, the Union soldiers could hear the shrill sound of the "rebel yell" echo through the woods. Yankee soldiers turned and ran.

Lee's aggressiveness led to Hooker pulling the rest of his men back. For a commander previously hailed as much more aggressive than McClellan, it was a surprising decision early in the campaign. Lee capitalized, stealing away the early initiative.

Lee and General "Stonewall" Jackson devised a bold, high-risk plan, splitting the Army of Northern Virginia in two. With about 30,000 troops, Jackson would follow country road paths to swing around, surprise and confront the right flank of the Union infantry. Lee, with less than 14,000 soldiers, would attempt to divert Hooker's attention from the counter assault along a three mile stretch.

The Battle of Chancellorsville ended with another stunning victory for the Confederates, forcing Hooker's Union soldiers to retreat across the Rappahannock River. Both sides incurred heavy losses, over 17,000 Union causalities, and more than 13,000 for the Confederates. This included Stonewall Jackson, who was mortally wounded. The groundwork was laid for his legendary status to grow.

News of the battle outcome sent morale soaring once again in the Confederacy. Although the loss of Stonewall Jackson, one of Lee's most trusted generals, was considered a significant blow. In the North, morale now seemed to be in free fall. Lincoln was reportedly shocked by news of another devastating defeat. Republican defeat in the next election now appeared very likely.

Mary Bowser's interviews with Mrs. Davis and May, the Irish head housekeeper for the family, had gone extraordinarily well. Mary impressed both ladies during their discussions. May then put her to the test. She required that Mary clean a guest bedroom with dirty floors, windows and an unmade bed with folded sheets and blanket stacked on a nearby table.

She was left with a bucket, cleaning brushes, rags, a broom and asked to do as much as she could to tidy up. May said she would stop back in thirty minutes. When May returned, not only had Mary scrubbed the windows, floor and made the bed to May's satisfaction. She also had dusted a cabinet, cleaned the cabinet glass window, and polished brass figurines of a horse and lion displayed in the cabinet.

"Chloe had me well prepared," Mary mused as she left with Elizabeth.

"I know Mrs. Davis wanted to talk with May first, but I'm sure you will be offered the job."

"How was your talk with Mrs. Davis?" Mary asked.

"Conversation comes very easily for me with Mrs. Davis. It would be hard for me not to like her. She is very progressive in her thinking."

Mary startled Elizabeth when she asked, "What about her thinking on slavery?"

"I would not be surprised if she has mixed feelings about it, but not sure. She has never indicated one way or the other. I think her loyalty to her husband supersedes any of her personal feelings on the war. Sadly, slavery too, I suspect."

In addition to the intense training from Chloe, Elizabeth worked with Mary on various scenarios that might develop and how best to handle. Also, they concocted consistent story lines about her past.

Elizabeth introduced her to Thomas McNiven. He who would be her main conduit for passing information received back to Elizabeth. She could also share information with Daniel at Sunday services, but she would be limited to passing it along once a week.

"As long as the information is not as time sensitive, that could also work," Elizabeth assured her.

The arrangement was made for Mary to start in a week. Varina Davis told her she would be given time away to spend with her husband, but felt it was important that she live on the premises, given the housemaid responsibilities she would have.

Isaac pulled up in front of the Executive Mansion in the Court End neighborhood. Built originally in the early nineteenth century as a family residence, it was designed in a federal style of architecture. Now it was the home of the Confederate President who was preoccupied with waging war against the Federals.

Soon after it became the residence of Jefferson Davis and the Confederate First Family, local Richmond folks would occasionally refer to it as the

Confederate White House. Word spread quickly never to do so in the presence of Jefferson Davis. He disliked the comparison to the White House of the enemy, and let people around him know it. Although one of the more opulent residences in the downtown section of Richmond, it was demonstrably less grandiose in comparison. Also, it was rebel gray, not white.

Along with Isaac, Daniel helped Mary Bowser as they began to carry her things from the carriage to her new residence on East Clay Street. Isaac and Daniel followed Mary as she walked around the mansion. "Not a bad looking place to live," Isaac cracked.

Mary turned and pronounced, "Yes, but not where I'll be living."

Her new home was a squared off flat roof wooden bungalow. Along with two other bungalows, it was behind the Davis family home, blocked from the street view. Other servants with more seniority inhabited rooms over the kitchen which was a later extension, built out from the back of the house.

"Nasty hot in here," Daniel mentioned. "Gonna be even hotter on those dog days of summer."

"Yeah, and for winter we better get you lots of extra blankets for those windy cold nights," Isaac added.

Mary would share her living quarters with two slaves owned by the Davis family, Melissa and Gaby. Melissa was warm and friendly upon meeting her. Gaby, on the other hand, was far less friendly.

Gaby went to bed early. Melissa stayed up with Mary, helping her arrange her things, and sharing information about the Davis family and working there. Melissa told her she worked in the kitchen, helping Sadie the head cook, doing dishes and cleaning. Gaby, she told her, helped Sadie preparing and serving meals.

"Mrs. Davis is very nice, most of the time," Melissa said, "She can also be demandin'. Especially when it comes to takin' care of the children. The young fella, little William Howell, is a handful himself. I think that makes it tough for her. That and her husband. He seems stressed most all the time."

"Does President Davis conduct business from the home?" Mary asked.

"He's got another buildin' he go to during most days, but yeah, he also works from his office at home, too. You don't want to get on his bad side. Got quite a temper."

As she lay in bed the first night, she thought about the advice she had received from Elizabeth Van Lew. Foremost, she was told, don't trust anyone, even if they appear to be friendly, or sympathetic. Elizabeth had also told her that while it was important to demonstrate her innate confidence, alertness, ability to quickly learn new things, to be guarded and not show off her true intelligence.

"Above all," Elizabeth had noted, "Show no indication of your reading or writing skills."

Mary had been told to join the other servants in the main house the next morning at seven o'clock, sharp. Melissa and Mary were among the first to arrive. They sat in the west parlor where they were told to go. Mary looked around. There were statues facing across from each other on both sides of the room, each holding masks. One comic, the other a mask denoting tragedy.

Varina joined them as other servants started to enter the room. Both Mary and Melissa rose to greet her.

"Mornin', ma'am," Melissa said.

"Good morning, Mrs. Davis," Mary immediately added.

"Good morning to both of you," Varina said. She was beaming as she turned to Mary. "Could you follow me, Mary? This will take just a second or two." Turning to Melissa and the others gathering in the parlor, she noted, "We'll be right back."

Following the First Lady, Mary crossed the hall and took the stairs. They walked through the master bedroom before Varina stopped at a closed solid red oak door and knocked.

"Come in," came booming from a deep modulated voice behind the door.

As they walked through the door, Mary recognized Jefferson Davis from a portrait she had once seen. He had those long, sharp features, just as in the portrait, but the man sitting at his desk looked older, weary, and his eyes appeared glazed. Different from the piercing, unnerving stare she remembered from the portrait. He did not stand up to greet her. Not surprising to Mary, but he hardly acknowledged his wife either, keeping his gaze solely on the newspaper laid out on his desk.

"Dear, I wanted you to meet our newest housemaid, Mary Bowser. She comes highly recommended by the woman I previously told you about, Elizabeth Van Lew."

Davis looked up at Mary. "Welcome," he said. Turning to his wife, he added, "Miss Van Lew, yes I know about her. Isn't she the woman who was visiting enemy prisoners in Libby?"

"Yes, we have talked about this before," said Varina. "She has also visited our boys wounded in battle and sick in Richmond homes and hospitals. I happen to know she is involved in several activities supporting the Confederacy."

"I seem to recall there were several accusations made about her alleged support for the Union," her husband noted.

Mary felt like Davis was talking as if she wasn't in the room.

"There have been baseless allegations made against many that haven't held up. You know as well as I do that people in Richmond are paranoid. Some see Unionists around every dark corner."

For the first-time Davis smiled. "Yes, there is some truth to that."

"Miss Van Lew was simply doing what she believes is her Christian duty to help those in need. That includes Union prisoners. Besides, I like her. The Van Lew's are a good family, well respected in Richmond. Others have confirmed my impression that her slaves receive the best of training as domestic servants. Also, we will not be paying for Mary's services. The Van Lew's are providing her at no cost to us."

"Hmmm," Davis mumbled.

Varina continued. "I was told it was General Winder who extended to Miss Van Lew the privilege of visiting Union prisoners back when they were short on help at Libby."

Mary would have liked to say something, but thought better of it. Instead she tried her best to project an indifferent countenance.

"Well Mary, I hope you are as good as Varina believes you will be. Welcome to our home." He continued to sit. "Now Varina, if you don't mind. I do have a full day ahead of me. Kindly close the door behind you."

Following Mrs. Davis back to the parlor, Mary now counted nine servants, in addition to herself. She recognized Wilbur, the coachman, from the church choir, as he approached and greeted her warmly. As Melissa had explained the night before, there were all together 13, with one recovering from illness.

They were a mix of free servants, slaves owned by the Davis family, and slaves loaned from others on a fee basis to work for the first family. Mary Bowser had seen a few of the slaves before, at Sunday Services, or around town, but not the others.

Unlike the Van Lew household, there was a hierarchy of workers, as Melissa had explained. Edward, a German immigrant was the steward. May, who tested Mary during her interview, was an Irish immigrant. She was well respected by both Mr. and Mrs. Davis in her role as their head housekeeper. There was Sadie the cook. The children's nurse, Catherine, a white Irish American came next, followed by the domestic house slaves, including Jefferson Davis' manservant, Robert, and the butler, named Henry. Wilbur came next, semi-retired, at an advanced age, with little to do, now that Varina had donated the family horses to the war effort. He was well liked by the family who intended to keep him, even with his diminished responsibilities. There were the young slave girls, Gaby and Melissa who did housework. Lowest in ranking was a slave who took care of the property.

"I asked all of you to join us here today to welcome our newest housemaid, Mary Bowser. She comes highly recommended, and I am sure will perform her duties very well. Both May and I are convinced she will fit in nicely. I ask that each of you, who haven't met her already, to introduce yourselves to Mary, and help her in learning her new responsibilities and getting familiar with her new surroundings."

A few claps in one corner, followed by more clapping across the rest of the room.

"May, if you don't mind, after we finish here, I'd like you to meet with Mary and Melissa, who will be sharing some of their work, and explain to them their individual responsibilities."

"Yes, Mrs. Davis," May said, betraying her Irish brogue.

As the others left the parlor, Mary and Melissa followed May into a small side room, just off from the parlor where they sat in upholstered high-back chairs around a white marble table.

As May closed the door, Melissa spoke first. "I remember when General Lee came to visit with President Davis in this very room. Sat in same chair as me. Got mud from his boots all over the floor. Right where my feet are."

"I'll never forget. He must have had other things on his mind. I thought Mrs. Davis was going to smack him," May said jokingly.

"Took me long time to clean that mess up," Melissa added.

May pulled a couple sheets of folded paper from her pocket. "I've already spoken to Mrs. Davis, and here is how we are going to divide up the domestic duties. Mary, you will be responsible for taking care of the bedrooms, including the children's room. As you saw, President Davis has an office, next to his bedroom. Mrs. Davis has her own office on the opposite side. You will take care of those, and the library and sitting rooms downstairs. Upstairs hallway as well. This means, making beds, cleaning carpets and draperies, dusting, replenishing linens. I have no doubt after the little test, you will do just fine. When there are social functions, you will help me in preparing for them."

"Yes, ma'am," Mary said.

"Melissa, in addition to your kitchen cleaning duties, you will be responsible for polishing furniture, cleaning the fire places, and taking out the trash. You will also have primary responsibility for cleaning the servants' rooms, including mine, and Edward's." May turned and looked at Mary. "Edward is our house steward."

Mary and Melissa went into a side room off the kitchen where the slaves ate. They were late, the others had already eaten, but there was still some left over gingerbread.

Mary spent the rest of her first day meeting individually with the other servants. The others for the most part were friendly and welcoming.

When they were alone, Wilbur the coachman asked if he could have a word.

"Mary, I had no idea you were a housemaid."

"I've been doing it most of my life, and then when Wilson and I lived in Norfolk. Miss Van Lew loaned me out to one of her relatives who needed help."

She hoped Wilbur would leave it at that and not get overly curious.

She viewed meeting Sadie the cook as most important. She knew from Elizabeth and meeting with Thomas McNiven that it was Sadie the cook who met his cart every morning in front of the mansion when he delivered bread and other baking goods.

Sadie was very pleasant. Older than she expected, but high energy and an enthusiastic woman, who seemed to know how to make the best of things. She shared with Mary her favorite meals to cook and how she liked to be creative in the kitchen, which Mrs. Davis encouraged. Although there were limitations. Certain foods President Davis could not eat, or simply didn't like. Leafy vegetables, for example, were to be avoided.

After casual, light conversation, Mary asked, "I'm just curious, what kind of things do you need to do to get started every morning?"

"I make sure Gaby and I clean the dining room before goin' to bed," Sadie said. "In the mornin' I'll begin to prepare things and make sure I have the right pots and dishes for that day's upcoming meals. Sometimes President Davis or someone else comes down at night and eats somethin'. Gotta clean that up, too. Henry the doorman usually fetches me eggs. I then start my cookin'."

"You've got a lot of mouths to feed." Mary said. I'd love to know how you prepare a typical meal." When Sadie looked back at her obviously surprised by her request, Mary, added "Just curious. Always was very interested in cooking."

"On a typical day, I might start by cooking pork, bake cornbread and things for the servants. Mr. and Mrs. Davis usually don't come down until later. They get, eggs, meats, breads. Sometimes griddle cakes. The children usually eat last. Sometimes griddle cakes or cornmeal, sometimes eggs."

"Do you bake all of you own bread?"

"Nah, just the cornbread. Owner local bakery brings more than I can bake from his oven. The Davis family likes its bread," Sadie confided as she grinned. "He comes every mornin' in his horse drawn cart. He's usually waiting before I do anything in the kitchen. I go out and meet him first thing."

"Well, I get up early. If I can pick it up for you, when you're busy. Just let me know," Mary said. "I just love the smell of fresh bread."

"You'll have plenty to do young lady just learning your new job here. You'll want to make sure you take care of that before offering to do other things. Mrs. Davis can be very strict."

Mary spent the next few days with May who provided guidance and watched her as she performed her regular duties. By the end of the week, she was on her own. While performing her chores, she paid particular attention getting to know the typical daily activities of Jefferson Davis and his wife.

Davis would work early morning from the office near his bedroom, and then leave to spend most of the day at his official office on Bank Street. When he left, Mary was usually finishing up her assigned downstairs work and about ready to head upstairs to attend to the family bedrooms.

If she were nearby, as the Confederate President left for his office, he would say, "Good day, Mary." She would reply, "Good day, Mr. Davis."

Varina usually had breakfast with her husband, spent the rest of the morning with the children, and then worked from her office. She would often leave the house in the middle of the day, sometimes before lunch to perform civic duties, attend meetings and accompany her husband at official events. When home in the late afternoon, she often played the piano. The children would eat an early dinner. Varina typically waited for her husband to get home to have dinner with him.

It was a nice, mild evening. Melissa and Mary sat together on the stoop outside their bungalow. Gaby was inside, mending a dress.

"How's things goin'?" Melissa asked.

"Pretty well, pretty well," Mary said.

"I hear Mrs. Davis likes you. You must be doin' well."

"Not sure about President Davis. He is always polite, but seems very stern."

"He's like that with most of us," Melissa said.

"He works long hours." Mary mentioned. "Even after dinner, he goes into his office and works. Look, you can see the light on in his office now."

After looking up, Melissa said, "Uh-huh. The President works most all the time. Office, home, don't matter."

Mary commented. "One thing I'll say, he cleans up after himself. This makes it easy for me. He always puts his papers away before I clean. Takes some, puts in his satchel to take to his work office. The rest he places in the safe in his office. Never anything left out."

"There's a reason for that."

"Oh?"

"Yes. President Davis use to conduct meetings in the dining room. All kinds of meetings, even about the war. That all ended 'bout half a year ago."

"Why, what happened?" Mary asked.

"Maybe nothin'," Melissa said. "Just 'bout a year ago there was a meetin' in the dinin' room. Bunch of generals there with President Davis. Papers, maps all over. I was helpin' in the kitchen, with dishes and such. Sadie and Henry our butler were goin' in and out of the dining room, as they served President Davis and the generals."

"Was General Lee there?"

"He was one of 'em. Didn't get all the other names. Anyway, these generals and the President were talkin' back 'n forth 'bout their plans to stop McClellan comin' to Richmond. While in the kitchen, I hear Henry tell Sadie, 'They act like we're part of the furniture. Like we not there.'"

"Yeah, I've run into that myself," Mary said.

"Well, one day Henry heard somethin'. He came up from Mississippi with President Davis. Probably the only one of us President Davis trusts. Henry heard the President talkin' to Mrs. Davis. Says one of the generals thinks there was a leak from the day they had the meetin' here. No other way the Union could have known about their plans, why we lost at Antietam," he said.

"I see. Do you think it came from one of the servants?"

"Nah. Who would we tell? We'd be shipped down the river so fast. Just like Daisy, the servant you're replacing." Melissa then said, "Since then, President Davis locks all his papers away when not workin'. In his safe. Now he also always closes the door to his office when talkin' 'bout the war."

"Well, we should get ready for bed," Melissa suggested as she started to rise from the stoop.

Mary reached out and gently touched her arm. "One other question, Melissa," she whispered, "If you don't mind. Maybe it's nothing, but Gaby is not very friendly with me."

"I've noticed that too. She's not very friendly to begin with. I think it's also 'cause she wanted your job. May told her she wasn't ready yet."

Sunday, after church services and teaching the children, Mary and her husband Wilson met with Elizabeth Van Lew and Thomas McNiven. They met inside McNiven's closed bakery. The ladies were elated to see each other. McNiven served fresh baked muffins.

"They workin' you hard, Mary?" McNiven questioned.

"Harder than Miss Van Lew and Chloe ever worked me," Mary responded. They all laughed.

Elizabeth asked, "You holding up alright?"

"I am," Mary said. "Not so bad. Most of the other servants are pleasant. Varina Davis can be strict, but she seems pleased with my work."

"What about Jefferson Davis?" McNiven asked.

"He doesn't pay much attention to me. I'm told he is that way with most of the servants." Looking at Elizabeth she added, "He mentioned when we first met that he heard complaints about you visiting enemy prisoners. Mrs. Davis told him you were very supportive of the new government, and did many charitable things for both Confederate soldiers and Union prisoners. He seemed to accept that."

"Good," Elizabeth said. "Any indication that he knew anything about you? Your education up North, or anything else?"

"No, nothing."

McNiven spoke next. "I know, Mary, you haven't been there very long, but any luck learning anything about Lee's plans?"

"No, but I will keep trying. I know..."

"Even more urgent now," McNiven blurted out, interrupting Mary. "Sam Ruth heard that a Union scout met with a cousin in Fredericksburg who is against the secession. A local merchant. He told Sam after talking to his cousin that there have been rumors that officials up north have been hearing about Lee planning another assault. I don't know if this came from the message you and Daniel sent along with the escaped prisoner."

"It could have come from other sources, as well, Elizabeth noted."

"True, Miss Van Lew, the point is, Union leadership is skeptical, but worried. Sam was told they sent scouts into Richmond as well to try and find out more. He asked if Sam could direct his cousin to Union friendly people who might be able to help. Sam said he wasn't close with anyone like that, but would pass the request on to others who might be able to help. Sam is always very careful. He says you never know if it could be a Confederate scheme to try and trap him."

"Do they now know in Washington about Mr. Ruth's secret activities?" A perturbed looking Elizabeth questioned.

"No, don't think so. Sam doesn't share what he has been doing with his trains with anyone else. As for the few folks he has helped you and Daniel get out, Sam says he tells them he was just doing a favor for someone else, and asks them not to tell anyone. So far, seems to have worked."

"Hopefully, he hasn't shared anything about Miss Van Lew, or Mr. Mills either, Daniel interjected.

"No, he guards these things very carefully, Daniel, about himself, and the rest of us as well." McNiven added, "Not even many of his close acquaintances who are sympathetic to the Union have any idea what he or any of us are doing."

"Good. As we agreed when we met at Lohmann's restaurant, we all need to be very careful sharing anything with others outside our little circle," Elizabeth asserted.

Mary spoke next. "If you are hoping I can find out more about this invasion, I must confess, I think this is going to be a problem."

"Why?" Elizabeth asked.

Mary explained how Davis kept everything in his safe when he was not working, and always closed his door when discussing battle plans with guests. She also indicated that she had tried listening through the door, but could not hear anything.

"You must keep trying," Elizabeth said. "If at all possible, try to find a way."

"I will, Miss Van Lew."

"As you know, Mary, I deliver goods there every morning. If you do pick up something, you need to let me know," McNiven noted. "Like we discussed."

"Yes, of course," Mary said.

"Guess we are lucky they haven't confiscated your horse," Wilson said, sarcastically. "I heard they are starting to do that."

McNiven smiled. "Yes, but they think I'm a loyal secessionist, delivering food and condiments to Confederate officials and the military. Should not be a problem for me."

"I was hoping Sadie might let me meet with you to get your deliveries, with everything else she has to do mornings, but she's not going to budge on that. She insists on being the one who meets your cart. At least for now."

"Darn," McNiven blurted.

"Here is what I was thinking. There is a vase with two handles in the sitting room across from the pantry. Sits on a table high enough that it is easily visible from the street. If I have information, I will turn the vase so that one of the handles is pointing out from the window. If you pull around to 12 Street, I can sneak out the back and meet you there. There's a jewelry store on one corner, and the local apothecary on the other."

"Why down there?" McNiven asked.

"It is close by. Less likely we would be noticed talking together. I can get there and back through side alleys without being seen. I would simply tell the others I wasn't feeling well and went to get some fresh air."

"Alright, I'm fine with that," McNiven said.

"The other thing I was wondering..." Mary turned to look directly at Elizabeth. "I know you told me not to trust anyone, not even the other servants, but having an additional helper inside the house could improve our chances of finding things out. Melissa, who I share a room with, might be able to help."

"Perhaps," said McNiven.

"I think it is too risky. You don't know any of them well enough to assume you can trust them," Elizabeth said. "As I told you before, I would trust no one."

"Yes, you are probably right," Mary said.

"Well, hopefully we'll get a break in the near future. Something unexpected could happen. Davis could be distracted, leaving his papers behind to attend to something."

Elizabeth nodded in agreement. "This is really important, Mary, that you stay alert and look for one of those opportunities."

Chapter 10: Plans for Northern Invasion II

Vicksburg, Mississippi, resting on a high bluff, was considered the gateway of the Mississippi River which extended over 2,300 miles, beginning at the end of Lake Itasca in northern Minnesota and pouring out to the Gulf of Mexico. Vicksburg was a strategic military location, halfway between Memphis, Tennessee and New Orleans, Louisiana.

"The Big Muddy" served as a critical demarcation point, separating east from west. More importantly, Vicksburg was the last Confederate stronghold on the Mississippi River. If the North captured Vicksburg, the Union would gain control of river transportation and sever the Trans-Mississippi Confederacy from military operations and communication channels with the east.

Capturing the Confederate stronghold of Vicksburg was a primary objective of General Ulysses S. Grant. Grant was the commanding officer for the Union Army of Tennessee in the western theatre of the war. His first attempt to take the city had failed back in the winter of 1862 through 1863, when the Confederates ravaged his supply lines. His second attempt began in the Spring of 1863.

Union Brigadier General Benjamin Grierson's cavalry conducted a raid through central Mississippi, and into Louisiana, helping to divert additional enemy forces. Naval Captain David Porter made possible the landing of Federal troops south of Vicksburg.

Caught completely by surprise, Confederate Lieutenant General John Pemberton first retreated to the perimeter area surrounding Vicksburg. Pemberton lost his last chance to make an escape run with his men as the surrounding city was completely cut off. After successfully rolling them back, and bottling up Pemberton's forces within Vicksburg, Grant launched his major siege against the city.

The city was now completely cut off. The Confederates had to severely ration food supplies with soldiers close to starvation based on the miniscule portions they were allocated. The only hope was a counter offensive from General Joseph Johnston. In early May 1863, Judah Benjamin, former War Secretary, now serving as the Confederate Secretary of State, directed Johnston to "proceed at once to Mississippi and take chief command of the forces in the field."

Johnston told Benjamin that he would obey the order, even though he was still 'medically unfit,' continuing to suffer from a wound during the Peninsula campaign. Time for the Confederate soldiers and citizens trapped in Vicksburg was running out.

Thomas McNiven continued his deliveries for the Davis family at the Executive Mansion. A week passed, then a few more days. The vase was still in its original place. He had received word that Mary was still looking for a way to learn what she could, but nothing so far. On this particular morning, she was by herself, looking out the window and shook her head as McNiven passed by in his horse drawn wagon. Mary felt discouraged, but was determined to keep trying.

She knew she needed to continue to look for an opportunity to go through the Confederate President's desk when he wasn't there. Lately Jefferson Davis was leaving earlier for his downtown office and returning later. He seemed to always take most of his papers with him. The rest were placed in the safe when he was not there.

She had also tried to listen in to conversation between Mr. and Mrs. Davis without making anyone else aware. So far, nothing of importance was discussed when she happened to be close by. Trying to listen in on closed door conversation was risky.

It was only a few days into her new job, when Varina Davis asked to see her. They met in her office near the bedroom. Door closed. Mary took a seat as requested. Varina continued to stand.

"Did I do something wrong, Mrs. Davis?"

"I'm not sure. Don't get me wrong. I'm pleased with your work, so far, but I must know about this. Did you ask several questions to Melissa about my husband's work habits?"

"Did Melissa tell you this?"

"It was not Melissa."

"I see."

"Please be honest, Mary. Tell me if this is true or not."

"There was a night when Melissa and I were talking. I simply said that cleaning President Davis' office was easy. He always puts everything away and tidies up before I come in to clean. That was it, Mrs. Davis. I wasn't trying to pry. I think Melissa would tell you the same."

Mary was stunned. She wasn't sure if Varina could detect her high level of anxiety and general discomfort in what she felt was, at best, a feeble attempt to rationalize a defensive justification for the conversation with Melissa.

"She already has, but I wanted to hear it from you as well. I know she didn't have a chance to speak with you before I could. I just talked with her before asking to see you. You both said pretty much the same thing."

"Yes, ma'am."

"Another servant went to my husband and said that they overheard you talking to Melissa. You were asking lots of questions. I wanted to talk with both you and Melissa first before we jumped to any conclusions. Please don't take it the wrong way, Mary."

"No ma'am."

"We simply need to be very careful and can't have anyone, especially servants, snooping around in areas that are none of their business. I will chalk this up as a misunderstanding. Some things you said were misinterpreted. From now on, keep what I've told you in mind."

"I understand, and I will. Thank you Mrs. Davis, but this is not why I was talking about cleaning President Davis' office. May I ask..."

"I'm not going to tell you who it was."

Mary already knew. It had to have been Gaby. She had been inside the bungalow when she and Melissa were sitting on the stoop where the conversation took place. No one else was anywhere near enough to have heard anything.

She tried to keep her composure. From now one, she had to assume she would always be under suspicion. Not a great way to start. It would make finding things out all that more difficult. As she began to descend the stairs, Gaby came through the foyer and started up the winding spiral staircase.

"Morning, Mary," she said as they passed by.

"Good morning."

No snickering or, for that matter, any display of emotion, which Mary found surprising. Surely, she must have known that Mary had been, or soon would be, called to task after her talk with President Davis.

After cleaning the main sitting area, including the grand piano, that Varina Davis played, Mary moved into the side room where Melissa told her Lee caught hell from Mrs. Davis for messing up her carpet with his dirty boots.

She was dusting the furniture when she became aware that someone was watching her from behind. She kept working, as if oblivious to the observer. As she moved to the window sill to continue dusting, she heard steps and the door to the room close. It was Henry, the butler.

"How did it go with Mrs. Davis?"

"You know I was meeting with her?"

"I saw her ask you to follow her."

"She thought I might be prying to find out things about President Davis. It was a misunderstanding."

"Get it cleared up?"

"I think so," Mary responded.

"Good, good. I didn't mean to startle you. Just wanted to have a private word myself."

Mary continued to stand with her back pressed up to the window. She was uncomfortable in this small room with Henry whom she didn't know, and who had closed the door behind him. She had been in similar situations before where she had to be firm and push back.

"About, what?" Mary inquired.

"You were a slave with Miss Van Lew. The lady you first came here with."

"What do you know about Miss Van Lew, Henry?"

"Some of the guys I play cards with on my day off. Local guys from around here. They told me slaves who work for Miss Van Lew could help me escape."

"Don't know what you're talking about, Henry," Mary said.

"Oh, I think you do. I need to get out of here. Can't take it no more."

"I heard from some of the others that you have always been very loyal to President Davis. Came up with him from Mississippi."

"With him in Louisiana, too. Didn't have much of a choice, but to go with him. My wife stayed in Louisiana workin' at another farm. She then got sold off to somebody else. No idea where she is now."

"Listen Henry, I think you are wrong. There are people around here who help runaway slaves, but I don't know any, and none of them are slaves working for the Van Lew's."

Mary started for the door, attempting to walk around Henry who stepped away. As she passed him, he reached out, grabbing her arm. "Please help me," he said. "I know you can."

She had trouble sleeping that night. Given everything that had happened, she reasoned it was quite possible Henry had been told to try and set her up. Nonetheless, Henry's plea for help was consuming her thoughts. Preventing needed sleep. So was Miss Van Lew's coaching not to trust anyone.

Time was running out. Late spring already, and she had been told that it was believed Lee would make a move very soon. Anything she could find out could be helpful. She tossed and turned before finally dozing off. Still groggy as she began to wake from a predawn catnap, Mary weighed the pros and cons of what she should do.

She went about her daily chores. It was nice weather and in the late morning she was in the yard behind the Executive Mansion. After pulling carpets from the children's room over a clothesline, she began to beat out the dust with a wicker broom. Mary noticed Henry coming through the gate. He was carrying a paper bag.

Henry asked, "Can I help you with those carpets?"

Mary nodded. He slowly walked over to her.

"I could use your help folding them" Mary said.

"Sure, Mary Bowser, I can help you." Henry put the bag down on the nearby stoop.

"What's in the bag, if you don't mind my asking?"

"Oh, had to go to the apothecary, around the corner. Picked up medicine."

"For the children?"

Henry looked at Mary. Then shook his head, "No, he said." After another pause, he continued, with his voice trailing off into a whisper. "I'll tell you, but you can't tell nobody else. For President Davis. I picked up his quinine. The President been sick for a while. He got malaria. But nobody else supposed to know."

"Malaria, how awful."

"Shhh. Yeah, his first wife died from it. Every once in a while he gets a bout of it. Bad stomach cramps. I think it is why he sometimes get so mad so easy."

As they folded the carpets and stacked them over an old blanket Mary had placed on the ground nearby, Mary was also now whispering. "I can't make any promises. I will see if I can help you escape. I do have a favor to ask you, though."

"Mary Bowser, I would be so grateful. Anything, anything I can do."

The next day, to his delight, as Thomas McNiven pulled up his carriage to deliver his baking goods, he noticed the vase had been turned with the handle facing out. To minimize anyone taking particular notice, he pulled his carriage around to 12 Street, a little further down the road. He tied his horse to a post and walked back to the designated place where they agreed to meet.

She was already there, standing in the shadows of the alley, behind the jewelry shop. McNiven looked around to make sure there was no one nearby before approaching Mary.

"Hello Mary. Tell me what you've got."

"Nothing yet," she said. "I know both you and Miss Van Lew told me I shouldn't trust anyone. Problem is, that if I'm going to get any information, I need to trust somebody else inside the Davis home."

"Well, before you do that."

"I already have."

"Who is this person, another servant?"

"Yes, his name is Henry," Mary responded.

"Henry? I know who Henry is. He sometimes meets me to get the bread when Sadie is busy. He has been with Jefferson Davis forever. Mary, this could ruin everything."

"I don't think so. Henry wants help to escape north. He says he heard about Miss Van Lew. In my gut, I believe him. If he was setting me up, he already has enough to turn me in."

"Yes, but..."

"With Jefferson Davis so careful with his papers, the only chance I have to get a look at them is for someone else to create a disturbance to make Mr. Davis want to immediately leave his office. While his papers are still out."

"What kind of disturbance?" McNiven asked.

"We are still trying to work this out. Perhaps make it look like somebody broke into the house, a burglar, a potential assassin. Or maybe, something to do with one of the children, taking sick, or missing. I could not do this alone. Henry agreed to create the distraction, but then he can't stay. He will need for us to help him escape."

"When are you planning to do this?"

"Tomorrow morning."

"But you don't even know what you're going to try and stage as of yet."

"Has to be tomorrow. About same time as now. Jefferson Davis leaves the next day. We think he may be meeting someplace in northern Virginia with his generals."

"Which generals? Will Lee be there? Do you know where?"

"Don't know."

"Alright. We'll get somebody to try and follow him, scout it out. You sure about this, Mary? I wouldn't want to see you get in serious trouble."

"I'm sure. Oh, and something else. Not sure this is important, but Jefferson Davis has malaria. Occasional attacks, but he has been dealing with it for some time."

"Malaria? That is probably of interest. I'll pass that on."

"Can you also get word to Daniel? Need to get Henry to a safe house right away after tomorrow. He won't be able to stay where he is."

That night, Mary met Henry in the backyard, behind the bungalows used for slave housing. There they finalized plans. Henry packed the meager belongings he planned to take with him in a gunny sack made of burlap. He woke early, and while everyone else was sleeping, he left his quarters.

After opening the lock on the basement door from the outside, he placed his bag behind a shed in the backyard. He then walked to the park.

He carried his bed sheet folded under his arm. He was careful to stay as much in the shadows as possible. He laid out the sheet and began to pick up and fill it with twigs, damp after a recent rain shower under a clump of red oak and nearby maple.

Mary also woke early. She dressed and walked over to the main residence. She was standing by a side window and watched as Henry came back through the yard, and pulled back the basement door, stepping down and closing it behind him. It was probably 15 minutes later, when she heard Henry climb the stairs and open the inside door from the basement. It was six o'clock.

The rest of the morning was uneventful. She and Henry joined the other servants at breakfast in the kitchen area, eating cornbread freshly baked by Sadie. They talked about a neighbor caught stealing chickens, and about a local slave girl who had given birth to twins.

Mary went about her chores, as did the others, starting with the downstairs. Nearly eight o'clock, Mary headed to the staircase, making sure she was unnoticed. The children, who shared one large room, on the northwest side of the house, across from their parent's room, were all downstairs eating breakfast. The parents had eaten before and were both back upstairs, sitting at their desks in their respective private studies on opposite sides of the bedroom.

She slipped into the children's room and was pretty sure neither of the parents saw her. Mary squatted behind one of the beds and waited for almost half-an-hour, which seemed like an eternity, before she heard it.

"Fire, fire," Henry yelled. "Sadie, Gaby, make sure all the children get out." He ran to the stairs. "Fire, Mr., Mrs. Davis. You need to come down. Now. The whole basement is on fire."

By now smoke accentuated by the crisp damp twigs was rising up from the open basement door. Davis followed his wife down the stairs. "Where are the children?"

With his voice cracking, Henry hollered, "They're all outside with Sadie and Daisy. You and Mrs. Davis should get out, too. I'll see what I can do to put it out."

"You should leave too, Henry," the Confederate President said.

"Don't worry about me. Just gonna go look. Mr. & Mrs. Davis, leave it to me."

Davis looked at the black smoke rising up from the basement. He wrapped his arm around Varina's shoulders and escorted her through the front door.

When she heard the door close, Mary pulled herself up from behind the bed and headed for the President's home office. The door was wide open and the desk was filled with papers. She leaned over the desk and began looking through the documents.

Mostly non-military government operational reports, budgets and a letter about conditions in the City of Richmond. The smell of smoke had begun to permeate the upstairs, even in the office behind the master bedroom. She shuffled another stack to the side. There it was. A map with markings. There was also a letter underneath from General Lee, a week or so old. She read the letter and studied the map.

Mary was still looking through the papers, carefully placing them back as she had found them, when she heard the front door open. She had thought it would be a little longer before help showed up. She waited. There was no one on the stairs. Mary kept searching, reading what she believed might be important.

She heard Jefferson Davis call out from the front door. "The fire is out. It's safe to come back in."

He apparently didn't wait for help to arrive. Mary had hoped she would have had time to sneak back downstairs and out the back. She could now hear the others coming back into the house. There was talking, but she couldn't make it out.

"Anybody see Henry? I have to get to my office downtown. Have an important meeting."

She then heard Gaby say, "Don't see Henry. Don't see Mary, either."

Then she heard footsteps on the stairs. She quickly placed the papers she was studying back on the desk. Looking around, she panicked for a moment. No way out. No good place in this small room to hide. She spotted the drawn, thick golden curtains that hung to the floor. She moved quickly toward the window and pulled the heavy curtain around her.

Davis entered the room and sat down at his desk. He started gathering up his papers, one pile for the safe, the other to take with him. A few moments later, his wife stepped into the room.

"There is still no sign of Henry anywhere. Do you think it was him who set the fire?" she asked.

"I do. Must have been someone in the house, and clearly did not intend to set the house on fire. It was started in a metal can with a bucket of water and a folded blanket nearby. Just to cause a distraction, I suppose. Henry spotted the fire, told the rest of us to leave, and then seemingly disappeared. He is the last one I would ever have suspected doing something like this. He must have done it to try to run away."

"Strange. He didn't need to set a fire to try and get away. He could have slipped out of the house while everyone else was sleeping," a puzzled looking Varina pointed out.

"You are so right, Varina. I was thinking the same thing. None of this makes any sense right now. After all we have done for him. He'll pay dearly when they catch him, which I'm sure they will."

"Do you really have to leave?"

"Unfortunately, I do, but I'll get Francis from next door to stay in the house until I can get one of my officers to come by. You and the children will be fine."

She could hear Varina walk away and back down the stairs. Davis continued sitting at his desk. Mary's legs felt weak. She had to resist scratching an itch on her nose. He finally got up, put papers in the safe and locked it. He went back to the desk, took his work bag and left. Thank God, he didn't notice her.

The children, along with Catherine the nurse were now upstairs. How could she get out and down the stairs without being spotted? She would have to go out through the window and hoped no one would see her. She opened it, and stepped onto the roof of the newly built extension, with the kitchen below and the servant quarters on top where May, Edward, and a couple other servants slept.

Mary walked along the ledge until she reached a window. It was May, the head housekeeper's room. She slipped through the window, took the backstairs and headed across the backyard.

She took a walk around the block, gathering herself before heading back to the mansion, through the backyard.

"Where were you?" Varina asked as she entered the front door. Standing behind her was May. Arms folded and an angry expression on her face.

"Oh, Henry asked me to pick this up from the apothecary."

She handed Varina the package with the medicine Henry had picked up the day they met by the clothes line. He had kept it and told Jefferson Davis they were out of the needed ingredients and he would have to pick it up later. This would be his alibi for leaving the house if things didn't work out. He told Mary he had left it in the backyard shed. Now it was her alibi.

May turned to Varina and said, "I reckon maybe Henry asked Mary to pick it up when he decided he wasn't coming back."

Mary looked first at May, then Varina, and back at May. "Did you say Henry? Not coming back? He just told me he had some other chores he needed to do and asked me to go for him."

Varina took the package. She stood peering at Mary for several moments. Never said a word. She then turned, clutching the package, and walked away. Mary wasn't sure either of them believed her.

Next morning she turned the vase handle, facing the window. Underneath her apron in a dress pocket were the notes she wrote up the night before, based on what she had seen. She was about to walk through the downstairs to the back door of the mansion, when Varina appeared on the stairs.

"Mary, can you come upstairs, please?"

She was frozen for a moment. Hopefully it would not take long. Surely McNiven would wait for a while.

"Yes ma'am, I'm coming."

Mary followed Varina into her office where the First Lady shut the door behind her.

"Please, have a seat, Mary."

"Yes, Mrs. Davis."

"My son, William, is sick. Catherine is going to stay with him."

"What's the matter with him?"

"We're not sure, but he has a high fever. We're going to move him into the guest room. Don't want any of the other children to get sick."

"You want me to help you get the room set up?"

"Well, yes. That would be most helpful. The doctor will be here shortly. Would be nice to have it set up as soon as possible. There is something else I wanted to ask you. I know you didn't come here to take care of the children, but I know from Miss Van Lew, that you are good with children, and have experience."

"I don't know how good I am with young children, to be honest…"

"I was hoping that while Catherine is with William, you can tend to the other children. Take care of them, play with the younger ones, Joey and Jeff, while the tutor is here for Margaret. I'm guessing for only a few days, until William feels better, God willing."

"Mrs. Davis, I'll do what you want me to do, but what about my regular chores?"

"I'm going to ask Melissa and Gaby to pitch in. Once William is better, you'll all go back to your normal house duties."

"Yes ma'am."

"Now if you could help Catherine prepare the guest room."

How would she pass on the information to McNiven now? Mary was beside herself. She helped with the guest room, dressed the children, and sat downstairs with them as they ate their breakfast. William was coughing. What if he was still sick for some time?

Mary tried to hide her feelings and stay upbeat with the children. She showed them games she played as a little girl. They were laughing, having fun. The two boys seemed to like her. Mrs. Davis looked in a few times and also appeared pleased. Mary was resigned that she would have to try again. She overheard Catherine tell Mrs. Davis he would need to stay in bed for several days. This would make sneaking away more difficult.

The day dragged on. Late that afternoon, Mary heard a knock at the main door downstairs. With Henry gone, Wilbur the semi-retired coachman had agreed to help around the house until a new butler could be obtained.

She heard Wilbur say, "I do it until you get a real one again, or that rascal Henry returns, n' clears all this up."

Seemed as if everyone was in a temporary role. She heard Wilbur call out, "Mrs. Davis, you got company. Elizabeth Van Lew."

Continuing to play with the children, Mary tried hard to listen. She could only pick up parts of the conversation at the door.

"What a lovely surprise. Nice to see you again, Elizabeth."

"You as well, Varina. I don't want to intrude, without an appointment. Knowing how busy you must be. I just wanted to drop off a few things for Mary."

"Oh, how sweet. Well come in, please, Elizabeth. Sadie just made a fresh batch of lemonade. Let's go into the parlor room and visit." Moving into the hall, motioning for Elizabeth to follow, Varina stopped for a moment and then called out, "Melissa, would you go upstairs, ask Mary to come down for a minute, and please if you would stay with the children until Mary comes back."

"Yes ma'am," came from a distant part of the house.

The room was beautifully furnished with elaborate Axminster woolen carpeting and colorful, exquisite drapes. Elizabeth was particularly impressed by the piano. It was a rosewood grand piano in empire revival style. There were twin candle sticks on both sides of the piano top with symmetrically arched crystal branches that looked like upside down mini-chandeliers. Centered was a fresh bouquet of pink hydrangea.

"Do you still play, Varina?"

"Every day. Playing the piano has a calming effect on me."

When Melissa reached the children's room and relayed Varina's message, Mary left immediately, moving down the stairs at a brisk pace. The two ladies were discussing recent news reports about the Polish uprising against the Imperial Russian Army as she entered the room.

"The Poles are fighting for their God given right to freedom, just as we are," Varina noted.

"Yes, let's hope they are successful," Elizabeth responded.

She stood up as soon as Mary entered the room, walked to her, and they embraced.

"Mary, I hear you are doing well in your new job."

Varina concurred. "She certainly is."

"Still have lots to learn," Mary noted.

Elizabeth continued. "I have some things for you," as she turned and stepped back toward the seat where she had been sitting. Varina sipped her lemonade. Bending over, Elizabeth pulled up a bag made of carpet and extended it towards Mary. "You left these behind. With the increased heat of summer almost upon us, I thought you could use them."

Mary opened the bag and reached in to explore the contents. "I really need these, thank you so much, Miss Van Lew."

Looking back at Varina, Elizabeth said, "This contains a few summer dresses, light linen petticoats, chemises and pantalets. It would be much more comfortable than those wools you are wearing now."

Varina smiled. "Absolutely," she stated affirmatively.

"Let me take these over to my quarters, and I'll bring you back the bag, Miss Van Lew."

"Well, actually, I do need to be going. I have an appointment downtown this afternoon, and I don't want to be late. I'll walk out with you, Mary. Thank you so much for the lemonade, Varina. It was delicious. Come and visit us in Church Hill when you have more time. Always a pleasure."

"I will Elizabeth, and thank you again for your kindness dropping these essentials off for Mary. My youngest is under the weather today."

"So very sorry to hear this."

"Our family physician was here, Dr. Alexander Garnett. He believes William needs lots of sleep and to drink plenty of fluids. Should be better in a few days. In the meantime, I asked Mary today to take care of the other children while our nurse takes care of William. She has been doing a splendid job."

"Children have always been very fond of her."

Varina walked them to the door. In a kidding manner, Varina stated, "Now hurry back, Mary, before the children get the better of Melissa."

All three smiled and Elizabeth extended her hand in farewell. "Until next time."

"I will look forward to that, Elizabeth, indeed."

As they stepped around the side of the house, Mary whispered, "I take it this is not a spontaneous visit."

Also whispering, Elizabeth replied, "Tom McNiven came to see me. He said you gave the agreed signal that you had something. He waited as long as he could, but you never came. We were all worried."

By now they were just outside Mary's ram-shackled new residence.

"Where did you get the clothes?"

"We already had your measurements. Chloe made the petticoats. I bought the rest. We were planning to hold them until we saw you next."

"I have important notes in my pocket, but I think it's best if you wait here. We are probably being watched." She held up the bag. "I'll empty the content and bring it back."

Mary disappeared into the shack. She came back with the bag and handed it to Elizabeth. Mary walked her to the gate in silence. They hugged and parted.

Chapter 11: The Ghost Army

General Joseph Hooker was the grandson of a Revolutionary War captain. He was another of the Civil War generals fighting on both sides of the conflict who had attended the Military Academy at West Point. He had earned the nickname "Fighting Joe Hooker." Yet after his humiliating defeat to the seriously undermanned army of Robert E. Lee in the Battle of Chancellorsville, he had lost the confidence of Lincoln and his war cabinet. His competency as Commander of the Army of Potomac was in serious doubt.

He must have suspected this, but Hooker continued to focus on trying to improve his Army of the Potomac, preparing his men for the next conflict. Since taking over from Burnside, Hooker had reorganized, consolidating his cavalry, improved rations and was able to reduce desertions. He also cleaned up corruption among officers. For this, he continued to be well regarded by most of his men.

Another of his priorities was his new Bureau of Military Information, and Colonel George Sharpe, who Hooker had put in charge. Rather than focusing primarily on relative troop strength of the enemy, as McClellan and Pinkerton had done, Sharpe's primary objective became the gathering of intelligence on fortifications and troop movement.

Sharpe began experimenting with hot air balloons to potentially monitor enemy advancement. He made more extensive use of the telegraph, invented by Morse over 20 years ago, hiring telegraph operators and making it possible to speed up communications between generals and their field commanders. He expanded the Signal Corps, developing cryptography techniques to encrypt and decrypt messages from spies. He also took it upon himself to explore multiple avenues of intelligence, not just cavalry scouts or northern spies attempting to infiltrate Confederate strongholds.

He was also still determined to find and recruit Southerners with Union sympathies as spies.

The Army of the Potomac was back near Falmouth, Virginia, near the north bank of the Rappahannock River. Hooker believed they were strategically positioned between Lee's Army of Northern Virginia and Washington. He was also within striking distance of Richmond, should the opportunity arise, under more advantageous circumstances.

Colonel George Sharpe asked to meet with Hooker on an overcast early morning, just after sunrise. They met outside the General's tent but decided to walk several yards across the encampment to a cabin on the western side of the city of tents. This was where Hooker conducted his business and met privately with his officers. The less said where others could hear, the less risk of it falling into enemy hands, either from spies within the camp, or captured prisoners. Hooker sat at his desk with Sharpe taking the seat across.

"I have something for you to look at, General," said a beaming Sharpe. Remember the unsubstantiated information from Lieutenant Dobbs?

"You mean the information about a second invasion by Lee?"

"Yes, General." Unfolding the notes he was carrying, Sharpe declared, "I now have a written correspondence with a bit more information. If it is credible, and I am not yet convinced that it is, this provides war plan communication between Lee and Davis that is unprecedented."

"A correspondence between Lee and Davis?" a mesmerized Hooker asked.

"No, I suspect something someone else may have copied from the original, but if what this says is true, this would give us a significant advantage." Pointing down at the notes, Sharpe added, "This appears to disclose Lee's plan to invade the North." He then passed the notes across the table to Hooker.

Hooker put on his spectacles and lifted up the first page and read:
Letter from General Robert E. Lee to President Davis, May 10, 1863

Mr. President, We have positive momentum on our side, and I recommend that we take full advantage of it while we can.

My recommendation, which I plan to discuss in detail at our upcoming conference, is to take the offensive, once again, and move swiftly through Maryland and into Pennsylvania with the objective of capturing the Pennsylvania capital of Harrisburg, a city not nearly as well defended as Washington. We would expect to face local militia, only. I firmly believe this will increase the negative sentiment in the North against the War and could bring things to a speedy conclusion.

Taking a deep breath, Hooker looked up at Sharpe and shook his head. "Harrisburg? The city must be over 100 miles north from Washington. From Lee's camp in northern Virginia, probably another 60 to 70 miles. Even assuming they could somehow get there, I don't see the strategic advantage for Lee in capturing the capital of Pennsylvania. Does he think we would let him march straight up past our army?"

Before Sharpe could respond, Hooker held up the palm of his hand suggesting by this motion for the Colonel to hold his thought. He then turned it over and read the second page:

If we move swiftly, we will have a decided advantage. By the time Hooker learns about our advance, and gives chase, we can be strategically positioned around Harrisburg. Capturing the city would be another humiliating defeat for the North and further erode the willingness of northern citizens to support the war.

The morale of my men is still good. If we are forced to fight on the defensive with limited supplies, I fear the worse.

Hooker looked up, pulled his spectacles down on his nose to glance across at Sharpe. "If limited supplies are a challenge holding a defensive position, marching to Harrisburg would be nothing short of lunacy. I'm not convinced, either, George. This clearly is not an original. An unusual handwriting. I doubt this is Lee's. No signature. Could very well be a forgery. Trying to send us off in the wrong direction. For all we know, the real objective could be to attack Washington."

"Or, it could have been transcribed from an original letter," Sharpe suggested. "There's more. Look on the back of the first page."

Hooker turned the page over. There was a handwritten map sketched on the back. It showed two advance lines, one making what appeared to be a circular advance, first west, and then north, ending at an "X" marked point on the paper, labeled Harrisburg. The second went slightly east and then north directly to the same endpoint. Both lines crossed state lines labeled "Maryland" and "Pennsylvania."

"Assuming this is accurate, it is not clear from this sketch how far west he plans to go."

"No sir. It very well may be a diversionary tactic. That is, if we first assume this is reliable information. My guess, Lee may want us to think he is moving west to come to the aid of General Pemberton, trapped at Vicksburg."

"Where did you get this?"

"A negro, sir. He crossed enemy lines. He pulled off the heel of his shoe and removed the note. That's why it was folded with so many creases. Handed it to one of our pickets. He told him it came from a well-placed spy. Asked the soldier to make sure it got to you."

"I hope the soldier brought him in for further questioning."

"He tried sir, but the man made a break and went back into Confederate territory. He didn't want to shoot him."

"Why would he go back over to a hostile government, fighting to keep his people in chains? Why, when he had made it to where he could always be free and so much better off? Makes no sense. Unless maybe he was working for the enemy."

"I'm told it's not the first time, General. Information received in the past has been reliable. We believe these are couriers who worked for the Underground Railroad before the war. A combination of free negroes and slaves. They are now helping to pass intelligence information, sometimes hidden in their boots, like this man did, or sewn into their clothes. They are also helping some of our captured soldiers escape north who also sometimes bring us useful information on the enemy."

"We need to find out who is running this network, and make direct contact with them," Hooker noted.

"Yes sir. One of my top priorities. Although I do believe it might be a decentralized group."

"Well, if we assume the information in this note is accurate, Lee certainly doesn't hold much respect for me."

"This could work to your advantage, General."

Hooker grinned.

Sharpe then said, "I think Lee recognizes that the South cannot win in a prolonged conflict, given their lack of industrial output compared to us. Whether the letter is accurate or not, I do believe it could be possible Lee wants to attempt another stunning victory in the short term to sway opinion in the north and turn most northerners against the conflict."

"Before we commit to anything, I want verifiable corroboration."

"Yes, sir."

It didn't take long. After making inquiries, Sharpe learned that a Confederate scout had been captured, near Chambersburg, in Pennsylvania Dutch Country in early May. The man's name was Josh Wilcott. So far he had refused to talk. Sharpe went to interrogate the prisoner himself. After hours of intense questioning, Wilcott still refused to say anything consequential. Sharpe got up to leave, explaining that he would be back later.

"Something you should think about in the meantime, Captain Wilcott. You were apprehended wearing civilian clothes. This means you could end up being hung as a spy. Now if you were to cooperate, answer my questions, I just might recommend some leniency in the charges filed against you."

The tactic worked. When Sharpe came back to the holding cell, Wilcott indicated he was ready to talk. He told Sharpe that Lee was in fact planning a second advance into the North. It would probably happen in the near future, now that the winter thaw had subsided.

Wilcott disclosed to Sharpe that the approximate timing for the advance was uncertain. Sometime in the Spring, based completely on improving weather conditions, he insisted. Wilcott went on to mention that there were several scouts like himself evaluating different approaches across enemy lines. He indicated that all possible routes were being considered, from western Virginia to eastern Maryland.

Sharpe pressed him, but Wilcott swore he wasn't privy to what route had been chosen, or if it was still under consideration. His assignment was only to scout possible crossing locations across the Potomac, north of Leesburg, Virginia. After hours of interrogation, Wilcott held fast to his original story.

Sharpe still knew very little. Only that Lee planned to invade the North a second time. He still did not know where or when. Harrisburg could be the primary military objective of the planned assault, or it might not be. He worried by picking one route over others, with so little definitive information, that this would be the equivalent of making a high risk wager against a highly skilled, unpredictable player. Except worse.

After sharing what he had learned from Wilcott with Hooker, Sharpe concluded his briefing by saying, "Needless to say General, this is deeply concerning."

"Not to belittle what you did manage to find out, George. Thanks to you, we are now more certain of the old man's intentions, but we must find out more."

"Yes, of course, General. There is something else you should know. Our sources monitoring Lee's Army haven't picked up anything happening there out of the ordinary. The weather has improved considerably. However, the Army of Northern Virginia is still encamped at their winter location. There is no indication, from what we have been told by our local spotters that they are preparing to move out anytime soon."

"What are you saying George?" Do you think Bobby Lee is up to another of his old tricks? Sending us bad information and planning a very different type of action?"

"No, I do believe Lee is planning a second invasion. It's just that, well, things aren't adding up. I'd like to send two of my very best scouts down there to take a look."

"By all means."

The Union already had spotters in place, keeping tabs on Lee's army since they pitched winter camp near Culpeper, Virginia. They were local southerners against the secession. A small group of local farmers. Not experienced spotters, and most certainly naïve to the art of spy craft.

Sharpe's scouts first arrived in early June at the residence of one of the volunteer observers.

"Far as we can tell, they show no signs of moving out anytime soon. Just heard that again today from one of the other men. We take turns checkin' things out."

"Get you somethin' to eat or drink?" The man's wife had poked her head into the room.

"No thanks, ma'am" the first scout said.

"I think we want to have a look for ourselves," the second one added, after the wife had left the room.

When they got close enough to the encampment, much closer than the others had ever ventured, they realized there was only a small contingent of men left. It was after sunset. The men had lit fires across the camp and were making considerable noise, making it appear as if the camp was still full of soldiers.

"We've been duped," the first scout mumbled under his breath.

"DANG," the other scout exclaimed, a little too loudly as he threw his cap on the ground. "Sorry," he added in a whisper, working to regain his composure.

"Not the first time Lee has done that. My guess is that the bulk of Lee's Army slipped out at night. Could have been weeks ago, too. No way of tellin.'"

"Nah. Surely not that long. One of the spotters would have noticed by now. Either that, or word would have leaked from somebody, making a delivery, for example."

They dispatched a courier working for the Union who had successfully passed information back to the Federals in the past.

After being briefed by the courier, Sharpe had the unfortunate task of telling Hooker.

Hooker erupted. "Bastards. How long ago do we think they broke camp?"

"We think first couple days of June, as best we can tell," Sharpe answered.

"We have to find them as soon as possible. Whatever it takes."

"Yes, General."

"What about his cavalry?"

"Still near Brandy Station, General. 'Bout six miles north from Culpeper. Positioned as if they are still protecting Lee from Union forces across the river."

"Maybe he is going to bail out the Confederates trying to hold on to Vicksburg."

"I don't think so," Sharpe declared. "Too late for that. They'd be relinquishing the eastern theatre and hastening the end of all hope for a Southern victory. I believe his objective is someplace in Pennsylvania and possible Harrisburg. We'll find them."

In the meantime, Sharpe's scouts set out promptly, fanning out at the crack of dawn to spot and catch up with the advancing army. Other scouts were also dispatched. Each taking what they believed were the most likely routes. The Army of Northern of Northern Virginia was nowhere to be found.

As on scout said to another when their paths finally crossed, "It's like a ghost army. Where the hell are they?"

Sharpe decided to put one of his reconnaissance ideas into action. He sent out a hot-air balloon. The crew included a pilot, lookout and captain. Luckily, the weather appeared to be good, with stronger than usual prevailing winds from the southeast and visibility was decent. They canvassed a stretch of land northwest of Culpeper. No sign of the Confederate troops.

The frustrated pilot said, "As if they just disappeared."

"Keep looking," the captain ordered, turning to the lookout.

The lookout put down his telescope. "Don't see them. If the estimate we were given on when Lee left camp, they couldn't have gone that far. I should have spotted them by now. Unless..."

"Unless what?" the captain asked.

"What if they swung further west and around the Blue Ridge Mountains? They could be using the mountains to shield their movement as they advance into Maryland."

The captain turned to the pilot. "I was told we received information at headquarters that the Rebels might first swing west and then turn north. Never verified, though. What if they went much further west around the mountains? Can we make it across?"

The pilot shook his head. "I'm not sure. Very risky to attempt that."

"Maybe so, but we just might be able to do it," the lookout suggested. "Seems like the wind is moving in the right direction. Could push us west over the mountains."

"We're already starting to drift too close," the pilot barked, shooting a wicked grin at the lookout. "You can feel the shifting gusts of wind as we get closer. Dangerous to continue."

It was a gamble and they all knew it. Movement of the balloon was dependent on the direction of the wind. The pilot could increase or decrease altitude to exploit some variation in air pressure impacting the direction of air currents, and at times provide some minimal navigational agility, but not much else.

Complicating it further, the mountains were drawing wind from different directions, intensifying the air velocity as it was forced up, making it extremely unpredictable and hazardous. If they were able to use the prevailing southeastern winds to successfully cross, they could easily be stranded on the other side. That was assuming a successful landing after clearing the mountains was possible.

The small crew disagreed on what to do. The lookout implored the captain to take the balloon over the mountains. The pilot strongly objected.

"You're a fool," the pilot yelled at the lookout.

"Foolish or not, there's too much at stake to not attempt it," the captain fired back.

"There's an even bigger problem. Our level of hydrogen gas may get us over, if all goes well, but not sure we will have enough to get back, the pilot in a desperate plea informed the rest of the crew. "We can't keep going much longer."

"How long?" The captain asked.

"Few hours, maybe. Not much more."

The order was given by the captain. "Cross the Mountains."

The pilot adjusted the tank valve, releasing more gas for the burner. The hot air forced the balloon higher. They encountered higher gusts of wind as the balloon elevated to clear the nearest peaks. The crew was bouncing from side to side from the choppy wind.

Thick green forests of spruce took over the mountain terrain at the higher altitude, supplanting mixed forests of oak, maple and scattered birch at the base of the range. Getting across seemed to take forever. The air was cooler. There was an eerie silence. The only sound was a high pitched wheezing caused by the wind.

Finally, passing over the mountaintops, they began to descend. The winds had shifted again. The lookout noted that they were now drifting due north.

"The mountains are keeping those westerly gales on this side. When combined with that stiff breeze that seems to be coming from the south, the wind is forced into a sharp left turn," he suggested, speculating aloud.

"This is very good news," the captain said.

The pilot weighed in. "Well, actually it depends on where and when they crossed over. Assuming they did cross over. They could still be south of us and we wouldn't know."

"Let's hope not," the captain firmly responded. He was obviously annoyed by the pilot's negative attitude.

As they descended beyond the peaks they noticed the thick cloud bank below, draped along the eastern ledges of the Blue Ridge.

The captain called out again. "Those low hanging clouds down there. Going to be a problem. Son of a..."

"Those mountains are definitely trapping those clouds from moving further east," the lookout pointed out. Adjusting his telescope, he added, "This cloud cover extends out pretty far west, too."

They would need to descend below the clouds, if they stood any chance of catching any sighting of the ghost army – if they were anywhere to be found. The pilot realized his cautionary warnings would be ignored again, but he decided he should still voice his concerns.

"You realize, Captain, this looks like a very thick cloud cover. Not sure how far down it goes. We will lose all visibility for some time. We could get pushed in closer to the mountains and not even know it. No telling if there may be treetops that rise up into those clouds below, or boulders, cliff ledges that could be extending out."

The captain gave the order. Reducing the flow of gas, the pilot lowered the balloon into the mist of clouds. The passenger basket tossed and turned, at times violently, until they eventually dropped through the cloud cover, with the thick forest of the Shenandoah Valley now visible below.

The shrubs in the valley became less dense as they floated north. None of the crew members said anything, but they all knew this would compound the risk they faced. It would make it easier for the enemy to see them. They could be shot down at this much lower level.

They were sailing parallel to the mountains, heading north at enough distance where they felt safe from encountering any wind shear turbulence that could potentially force them too close into mountain edges. They did not want to venture too far west from the mountains either, given the fuel situation.

"Is it possible if they could be way ahead of us by now?" the pilot inquired, as he tried his best to keep the balloon steady.

"I don't think so," the captain stated. "It would have taken them some time crossing the Blue Ridge and getting through the trees and brush on both sides. Lee is obviously using the mountains and the valley forests for cover."

The lookout continued to peer through his telescope while the captain used his less powerful binoculars, in a sweeping motion from side to side, hoping to catch something indicating troop location. Precious minutes were racing by.

Up ahead they could see a large patch of cleared farmland in the distance. The lookout shouted, "I see them."

It was Lee's Army. The men in the balloon were elated. The captain patted the lookout on the back with a congratulatory smack that almost knocked him forward. He then turned and shook hands with the pilot. His face was beaming.

With his eyes still pressed against the telescope he was holding, the lookout pointed with his free hand. "Over there. Looks like they are encamped." He handed the captain his telescope.

The captain looked and said, "Yeah, there they are."

"Any idea how many?" the pilot asked.

The captain gasped as he scanned more of the area over the horizon. "Holy. Hard to say. Must be thousands of them. Can we get a closer look?"

"Not much fuel left. We'll be lucky if we make it back from here. Never make it back if we keep going," the pilot pleaded with the captain.

The captain handed back the telescope. He said, "Much larger number of soldiers than I would have expected. Let's try to get an approximate estimate. As best we can."

"I'd say somewhere between seven to eight thousand men."

"How much time would you say before they could make it from where they are to the Pennsylvania State line?"

"Hard to say, Captain. I'd guess three to four weeks," the lookout replied. "Assuming they meet no resistance along the way."

"Let's try to get back over the mountains," the pilot ordered. "God pray we make it."

The lookout observed an area up ahead close to a waterfall where the mountain slopes were lower.

"Could be our best opportunity to try and cross back," the lookout commented, as they approached the dip in the range. "May not have to go too much higher. The less we climb, the less gas we need to dispense."

"Assuming the wind cooperates," the captain pointed out.

"Precisely," the pilot acknowledged. "May just be possible to catch some unobstructed airstreams, hopefully creating a wind tunnel. Just might be able to move us through that gorge up ahead. However, it's also possible those unpredictable currents force us into a vortex. Could also be a deathly spiral if things don't go right, Captain."

"Noted," the Captain said as he tried to scrutinize the opening in the mountain canyon. Turning back to the pilot, he commanded, "Let's try it."

General Hooker, was still upset about his stunning defeat at Chancellorsville. Yet he remained singularly focused on preparing for the next engagement. Hooker continued to drill and condition his men. He reorganized his cavalry units into one unified command, as opposed to the way they had been parceled out in the past to various infantry units. This was designed to make his cavalry a much more formidable striking force. Hooker still held the respect of his men.

Briefing General Hooker on the intelligence from the balloon team and other sources, Colonel Sharpe concluded his summary by saying, "There can be no other conclusion. Sweeping west, General Lee is trying to hide the advance of the main corps of the Army of Northern Virginia. Lee is about to invade the north a second time. With the bulk of his army approaching Pennsylvania through the valley, I believe the movement of specific divisions or units left behind we can assume is primarily diversionary."

"I concur with your analysis, Colonel. Lee is attempting to get an early jump, leaving us in the dark long enough to penetrate deep into Union territory and force us into a scramble, trying to pursue. Let us not forget, however, there was on that map we received a second line of attack from the east. Perhaps Stuart's cavalry?"

"Yes, General. I suspect so. Oh, and one other thing. Harrisburg may be his objective as we heard from our Richmond source. A softer underbelly than other targets. But the city, as you know, does provide a major railroad gateway between the Atlantic coast and the west. We must also consider, based on the direction they are moving into Pennsylvania, the Army of Northern Virginia could easily change course. Attack Washington, or Philadelphia instead."

"A well thought out plan," Hooker confided with Sharpe. "Lee takes the city and establishes a strong defensive position in the surrounding hills. This could be a catastrophic embarrassment for the Union if we allow this to happen. A potential death blow after so many other unfortunate losses. We need to move quickly.

"Yes sir. I now have scouts tracking the Rebels. They will report back as soon as possible on potential intersection points were we could cut him off. Assuming we can get there in time."

"We will," Hooker stated emphatically. "Lee, the old fox, marching his army through the heart of the region's bread basket, where they can strip the Maryland and Pennsylvania countryside to sustain themselves. No longer constrained by slow moving supply lines as they swiftly advance."

"Seems to me there could be a backlash," Sharpe suggested. "They are no longer simply defending their homeland when they invade the North. If the Army of Northern Virginia ravages its way through the countryside, ruining property and stealing produce and livestock from local farmers, I don't think that will be taken very kindly."

"Perhaps a backlash in Maryland. A border state with plenty of secessionists who could turn against the Confederacy. Knowing Lee, he will probably order his men to 'tread softly,' as Shakespeare put it, as they push forward. Asking versus taking. With rifle in hand, of course. My guess, though, all this would be of a secondary concern. I now believe, as that letter was transcribed, Bobby Lee wants to scare the hell out of people all over the north so they demand an immediate end to the war."

"Yes, General. I see your point. Probably hoping to get more people to vote for anti-war Democrats in the next election."

Lee's plan had been exposed. Not only was he attempting a second time to secretly launch a massive invasion into enemy territory. He had devised a solution to advance completely unencumbered by his undependable, slow moving supply lines that had reduced his effectiveness in the past. This, combined with the successful naval blockade by Union Navy had depleted almost all options to provide the needed rations and supplies to sustain the Army of Northern Virginia.

By first entering the Shenandoah, and then the Cumberland Valley, his army could gather fresh food and supplies as needed, as they continued to move swiftly through Maryland and Pennsylvania to inflict a decisive blow that could potentially bring the war to a close.

Hooker knew he could not do the same without infuriating Unionists. With his army living off the land, pilfering from northern landowners could turn more citizens against the war and assist Lee in attaining his objectives. He couldn't help but wonder if Lee had also thought of that. That crafty bastard must have, he thought.

With the new information Sharpe shared, Hooker was in a position to develop his own plan to move north, confront Lee and stop his advance. He studied maps and consulted with Sharpe and his scouts on the most optimal paths to catch and stop the Army of Northern Virginia. The Union, he was convinced, had superior scouts, familiar with this terrain. This could prove to be an increasingly deciding factor as Lee continued to move north.

Hooker knew his men were well trained, in peak condition, and believed they were up to the challenge. Morale was good. They wanted another crack at defeating the Confederates. He was reasonably confident they could give chase with minimal supplies, overtake the enemy, and cut them off before Lee's full plan could be executed. He was willing to bet they could do so, and without having to pillage the countryside in their path.

General Stuart, commander of the Rebel cavalry, had been instructed by Lee to move north across the Rappahannock River to raid Union positions and disrupt operations. This, Lee reasoned, would further confuse Union command as to his real intentions. He believed Union leaders would assume the bulk of his army would follow in the same direction. Eventually, Stuart would swoop west to join Lee's infantry crossing into Pennsylvania.

Just before launching the attack, Stuart decided to conduct a grand review in downtown Culpeper of his 9,000 horsemen. Perhaps he believed when Union leadership heard about it, as surely they would, it would add to the impression that there were no immediate plans to take the offensive.

Sharpe brought the news to General Hooker.

"I would say, General it is highly likely, based on the intelligence we've collected, that Stuart, following his charade of a parade, will mount a diversionary attack with his cavalry very soon."

"Yes, George, I have been considering various options on the best way to prepare a counter offensive. I have decided that our cavalry should cross the Rappahannock and attack him first."

"General, with all due respect, are you sure about this? Should we not be more concerned about Lee's infantry invading Pennsylvania? I can understand preparing to defend and repulse Stuart with sufficient resources when he comes at us, but do you really want to attempt another crossing? Especially General, forgive me for being blunt, when the last time it went so badly?"

"It was you, George, who told me that it could work to my advantage with the Confederates thinking I could be easily fooled. What better way to keep them thinking we are unaware of their primary assault than to launch a limited attack, crossing the river again? There goes Hooker repeating his mistakes of the past. However, this time, it will be our diversionary action, cavalry led. Hit them before they can hit us."

As Stuart prepared to execute his mission, Hooker sent his cavalry of 8,000, along with 3,000-foot soldiers, across the river from the north. Although the Union withdrew after approximately 10 hours of fighting, it successfully disrupted Stuart's plans and impacted his timeline moving north. Some called it a draw. Others argued that the South prevailed, given the Union eventually retreated.

Nonetheless, what became known as the Battle of Brandy Station demonstrated that the Yankees now had a formidable cavalry that could hold its own against the Rebels. This also gave the appearance that the Union had taken the bait, assuming an impending attack would be launched behind Stuart's cavalry. Confederate leaders continued to assume Hooker and the rest of Union leadership was unaware of Lee's top-secret progression north.

Moving in a more direct route than Lee, Hooker hoped to overtake and defeat his Rebel forces, long before reaching Harrisburg. Stuart's cavalry began moving into Maryland, swinging east, approaching dangerously close to Washington. What if the accepted assumptions of attacking Harrisburg were incorrect? There was little at this point the Army of the Potomac could do to prevent a cavalry attack on the U.S. Capital.

Hooker knew it was a high risk calculation. Knowing Lee depended on his cavalry for scouting and flanking maneuvers in battle, he was convinced Stuart would eventually loop in a circular motion towards Lee. The Army of the Potomac moved swiftly into Maryland, with the objective to slice between Lee and Stuart's cavalry, stopping both from coming together and advancing further into Pennsylvania.

Lee still assumed that by moving behind the mountains of western Virginia, the Confederate infantry was gaining a significant time advantage in its invasion of the north. They might run into pockets of resistance, but these would be no match to the advancing Confederate regiments.

Leading the advance was Ewells' Second Corp. They reached the Union garrison at Winchester, Virginia, the northern end of the lower Shenandoah Valley, close to Harper's Ferry, made famous by John Brown. They easily defeated the Yankee soldiers stationed there, capturing 4,000 men and 23 cannons. Crossing the Potomac, Ewell's men marched unobstructed through Maryland and into Pennsylvania, using South Mountain, the northern extension of the Blue Ridge, for additional cover. Lee was delighted with the progress the Second Corps was making.

Unaware that the Union Army of the Potomac was already in hot pursuit, Lee sent the following message to Ewell:

If Harrisburg comes within your means, capture it.

Hooker's Twelfth Corps led the Union advance. They crossed the Potomac on pontoon bridges near Edwards Ferry and travelled close to 100 miles over a period of eight days, with the summer sun beating down on their backs. They carried rifles, ammunition in their belts, knapsacks with sleeping blankets, personal items, and haversacks with extra food they were given, or whatever else they could scrounge. The combination of heat while carrying heavy gear caused soldiers to constantly stop to refill their canteens, but they pressed on with little rest. Most of Hooker's Army had reached Frederick, Maryland, by June 25, 1863.

The war effort in the eastern theatre continued to be a grave concern, both militarily and politically. Lincoln was well aware it was weighing heavily on troops and citizens alike, impacting morale and raising doubts about the prolonged conflict. As with previous commanding generals of the Potomac Army, Lincoln now had doubts about Hooker.

The President left the White House and walked to the War Department, housed in a two-story brick office with a huge portico overlooking Pennsylvania Avenue. He often did this to consult with his General Chief-of-Staff, Henry W. Halleck.

Sympathetic to the South before the War, Halleck had always remained a staunch advocate of the Union and was determined to fight to preserve it. He looked more like a bookkeeper then a general, but was considered a master of logistics. He tended to be cautious and methodical in planning and had frequent clashes with several of his top generals during the war.

Lincoln had dark circles under his eyes as he entered the office. He towered over Halleck. Always energetic by nature, the General rushed from behind his desk to greet the President. They sat at opposite ends of a small round table across the room from Halleck's desk. Behind Halleck was a framed letter from one of his instructors at West Point. The General pushed to the side several neat piles of paper between them.

"I'm worried Henry. We cannot suffer another devastating defeat. Particularly not in our own backyard."

"Agree, Mr. President."

"I am deeply concerned that 'Fighting Joe' may have lost his nerve after the humiliating defeat at Chancellorsville."

"Yes, I can see how you might feel that way. It is not only that, Mr. President. I'm sure you will recall how soon after Chancellorsville, General Hooker sent me several requests asking for reinforcements, which of course I denied."

"I do."

"In addition, I realize he is a strategic thinker and likes to develop alternative proposals, evaluating their relative strengths and weaknesses. He shared several of these with me once we learned of Lee's planned offensive. This could be an indication of lack of resolve."

"I believe this was early on, before we could confirm Lee's plan from multiple sources."

"Yes sir, but in my opinion it is still relevant. One of Hooker's proposals was to capture the undefended Richmond in Lee's absence, should he move north.. You responded to him yourself."

"I had to remind him that Lee's Army, not Richmond was his objective. I thought we had been very clear on this from the beginning."

"We were. He also proposed that I should let him take the command at Harper's Ferry, assuming Lee's advance north would be in that general direction. When I turned him down again, it must have frustrated the hell out of him."

"All of this concerns me deeply," Lincoln said.

Halleck continued. "After I rejected his last request, General Hooker sent me a letter offering to resign. My suspicion is that he never thought I would accept it. He must have believed he was simply making me aware of his frustration. I still have his resignation offer and can accept it NOW. With your concurrence."

"Stunning and quite sad, Henry. He is, after all, the fourth general I appointed to command the Army of the Potomac. We have discussed General John Reynolds before."

"Yes sir, but I'm not sure he would accept the position. If not, General Meade would be my recommendation for a replacement."

"I concur. Let's assemble the War Department."

With the confirmation from multiple sources on Lee's plans, and with what he believed was complete concurrence from the War Department,

Hooker was resolute to aggressively confront the enemy. His army was on the march. They were less than 50 miles from the Pennsylvania border.

To his surprise, Hooker was awakened while sleeping in the Union camp at Frederick, Maryland, to be handed the letter of acceptance of his resignation. Hooker hoped he could redeem himself after Chancellorsville. One more shot at defeating Bobby Lee. He would not be given the chance.

After John Reynolds turned the appointment down, George Meade was asked to assume command immediately. He was astonished when he received notice that Lincoln had appointed him head of the Army of Potomac. Well-liked by his fellow officers, he was referred to as the "Old Snapping Turtle" by many of his men who found him to be "irascible and uncharismatic." This came up in the War Department meeting to discuss Hooker's replacement, but was not considered disqualifying. There was a sense they were running out of good options.

Meade, who had been under the command of Hooker, was highly critical that his troops were primarily left in reserve at Chancellorsville. When he had asked for permission to resume the attack against Lee, his request was dismissed. Assuming command from his post in Frederick, Maryland, he had little knowledge of the disposition of his troops. Yet Meade was determined to continue Hooker's advance, aggressively pursuing and confronting Lee in an effort to stop and defeat him.

He ordered his scattered army to advance north from Frederick, Maryland and concentrate near Gettysburg, Pennsylvania, not far from the Maryland border. Gettysburg was a hilly, heavily wooded crossroads town, where Confederates, left unfettered could easily advance to Harrisburg. He had received Sharpe's intelligence report. Meade also knew if conditions changed, Lee, the master strategist but also opportunist, could change course at Gettysburg, if needed, and march his troops to Philadelphia, Baltimore, or even Washington, D.C.

By now, General Ewell's units, still leading the advance, had reached Carlisle, about 25 miles from Harrisburg. Other Confederate units were still moving into lower Pennsylvania. On June 30, Confederate General Henry Heth sent a reconnaissance unit of soldiers into Gettysburg to scout the area and search for supplies. Due west of the town, they spotted armed horsemen. They reported back to Heth and other commanding officers.

Facing local militia is what they reported, but as a precaution, they planned to send two divisions to investigate further. Instead, they found the Army of Potomac cavalry, under the command of General John Buford.

Realizing he was facing superior numbers, Buford ordered his men to take and hold defensive positions in the high ground until additional Union forces could arrive. Dismounting, armed with quick firing carbines, his men took position on a few ridges west of Gettysburg. The disposition of his troops, combined with their ability to counter the Confederate barrage of attack, gave the time needed for reinforcement from Union troops under the command of General Reynolds. Reynolds, who had turned down top command, was killed during the fight.

By midday July 1, Lee had reached the site of the battle. He had been determined not to escalate the conflict until his full army arrived. He ordered Ewell to turn from his position outside Harrisburg and advance south to Gettysburg. Lee was unfamiliar with the terrain and had no idea as to the strength of the opposing troops. The Army of the Potomac success at creating a wedge between Lee's infantry to the west and Stuart's cavalry from the east, deprived Lee of his ability to augment the attack with horsemen, or to receive critical reconnaissance reports.

The battle quickly escalated. Rebels attacked Union lines from the northwest. The dreaded rebel yell could be heard across the battlefield. Some of the same Union troops that turned and ran at Chancellorsville, did the same, running through the street of Gettysburg. They gathered to the south, at Cemetery Hill. Lee decided not to pursue, but to wait until the next day. Causalities the first day were estimated at 6,800 for the South, 9,000 for the North.

Overnight, additional reinforcements arrived for both sides. Meade continued to line his troops along the fishhook line of hills to the south of Gettysburg. By the second day of battle, both armies had reassembled. Lee no longer had his favorite general and confidante, Stonewall Jackson. He and Jackson communicated well, shared similar convictions and understood each other. It was different now.

After losing Jackson at Chancellorsville, Lee had split his army under three commanders, Generals Longstreet, Hill and Ewell. His new commanders often found Lee's orders ambiguous and confusing. Regarding capturing the Pennsylvania Capital, Lee's previous message to Ewell read, "*IF* Harrisburg comes within your means, capture it." With regard to attacking Cemetery Hill, Lee said, "*IF* practicable, but to avoid a general engagement." His new generals were at times not clear if Lee expected them to take action, or if the decision was being left to their own discretion.

Now, Longstreet and Lee disagreed about the plan of attack at Gettysburg. Longstreet wanted to avoid the Union left flank and attack further south. They argued for much of the morning of July 2, the second day of the battle. Finally, late afternoon the Confederates launched their next assault, attacking both the Union left flank, as well as the right. The North incurred heavy losses, but this time the blue coats held their positions.

Lee essentially ordered the same attack on the third day of the battle, against the Union left and right flanks. Stuart's cavalry had finally showed up. Stuart's order was to attack from the rear. Ewell's assault on the right failed. Longstreet was late establishing position of his troops for the attack of the Union left flank. He then held off, reporting back to Lee that the Union defenses were too formidable. Instead, Lee ordered a massive attack of 12,500 infantry, supported by 150 cannons against the Union center. He believed that by applying constant pressure from his superior troops, eventually the Union front lines would collapse and fall back as they had done in previous clashes.

The questionable frontal assault became known as "Pickett's Charge," named after Major General George Picket under Longstreet's command. Despite his disagreement with the revised plan, he was commanded to lead the charge. At first, the Confederates pierced the Union front lines, but causalities were severe, and they were eventually repulsed. Stuart's cavalry attack from the rear also failed. Lee ordered retreat to Virginia.

The North had finally won a consequential battle in the east. However, when Lincoln learned that Meade did not immediately give chase to Lee, he was furious. Like the others before him, Lincoln was convinced his latest Commander of the Army of the Potomac had squandered an opportunity to finish things off.

Lincoln did not consider how the Army of the Potomac had marched with limited supplies over extensive tough terrain in record time to catch Lee and reverse his advance. Survivors had fought for three days in one of the bloodiest conflicts imaginable. The amount of battle causalities was incomprehensible. Gettysburg easily surpassed all previous battles of the war.

There were close to 100,000 soldiers fighting for the North who suffered over 23,000 causalities. For the South, with a troop size estimated at about 75,000, there were 28,000 causalities. A tragic slaughter for both sides.

The day after the Union victory at Gettysburg, Grant's 47 day siege of Vicksburg ended. The city fell, July 4, 1863. The entire Mississippi River was now controlled by the North, with the Confederacy split in two.

Two recently formed regiments of untrained African Americans, armed with old muskets, and assisted only by a Union gunboat, drove off a Confederate brigade, attempting to disrupt Grant's supply line in the final siege of Vicksburg. This was at Milliken's Bend on the Mississippi River in Louisiana, just above Vicksburg. African American soldiers were captured and executed. "I heard prominent officers who formerly in private had sneered at the idea of negroes fighting," reported U.S. Assistant Secretary of War Charles A. Dana. He went on to note that they now "express themselves after that as heartily in favor of it."

Several days later, Elizabeth spotted an article in a publication on the carnage at Gettysburg. She read that Paul Joseph Revere, grandson of the Revolutionary War patriot, was among those killed. Elizabeth was terribly upset. She eventually wrote a long note to his family expressing her deepest sympathies. When she was done, she asked Daniel if he could help through his clandestine contacts to smuggle it across enemy lines.

"It will be done, Miss Van Lew," Daniel assured her.

Harriett Anne walked into the room.

"I am wondering, would it be a good time to continue our reading lessons?" Elizabeth asked.

They both nodded. Elizabeth left to get the book she was using.

Chapter 12: Escape from Morgue

The Van Lew's were delighted by the news from both Gettysburg and Vicksburg. They, like other Unionists on both sides of the Mason Dixon, hoped the recent Union success would hasten the end of the war with the South's imminent surrender. At the same time, they mourned the death of soldiers on both sides, and attended several local funerals. The loss of Paul Joseph Revere was particularly upsetting for Elizabeth.

When Elizabeth next saw Mary she asked if she had seen or heard anything that might indicate a change in Confederate thinking after the devastating major defeats.

"No Miss Van Lew. When Mr. and Mrs. Davis were speaking one night after dinner, I did overhear Mr. Davis mention that General Lee was thinking of offering his resignation after Gettysburg. Mr. Davis told his wife he was determined to talk him out of it. He told her he still had confidence in Lee, but not in General Johnston. He made it clear he blamed General Johnston for the loss of Vicksburg."

"But, I take it he does not blame Lee for Gettysburg," Elizabeth noted.

"Apparently not," Mary replied. "He told his wife he thinks a spy must have tipped the Yankees off about Gettysburg."

"Oh, no."

"That's alright Miss Van Lew. I don't think they suspect me. At least not yet."

"You have already done so much. Remarkable. I can talk to Varina. Tell her we need you back immediately. Make something up. Chloe can't work anymore. Mother is sick."

"I am not leaving."

"Dear, dear Mary. There may not be another opportunity to do this before they do suspect you."

"I am sorry, Miss Van Lew. The war is not over. I'm staying where I am. Please don't get me wrong, I appreciate your concern.

On July 11, 1863 it was reported angry mobs of mostly Irish immigrants started a violent riot in the lower Manhattan section of New York City. Congress had passed a conscription act earlier in the year, which would begin the first military draft of United States citizens. The Confederate Congress had passed a conscription act the year before. Rioting started after draft officers in lower Manhattan began drawing names.

There was deep discontent with the inequalities associated with conscription. Affluent draftees could buy their way out. Immigrants were primarily in support of the Union war effort, but they felt neither party represented their interests. Concern that the emancipation of slaves would result in a large influx of negro workers was also behind the discontent of many. A recent New York longshoreman strike, where African Americans replaced white stevedores, had contributed as well to a festering resentment.

The riot surged onto the streets where people were harassed and assaulted. Buildings burned. The police and the returning 7th Regiment from Gettysburg had to be called up to put it down. The riots lasted for four days. Some estimates indicated over 1,000 people were injured, and 120 killed, with close to 100 of them African American. Property damage was estimated at $1,500,000. The name drawing was suspended until August when it was conducted peacefully.

Several months later, a prominent physics and chemistry professor at Columbia College in New York City abruptly resigned from his seat. He wrote the following in a letter delivered to Columbia President Charles King:

September 25, 1863
Gentlemen,

I hereby resign the Chair I have held at Columbia College. It should incite (sic) no surprise (sic) that one, born and reared a southerner, prefers to cast his lot with the South.

Permit me to thank you for all your generosity and consideration you have for nine years extended to me; and to assure you that I have always endeavored to justify the same, by zealous devotion to duty...

Very truly your Obedient Servant
R.S. McCulloh

The letter was curiously dated from Richmond, Virginia. The College Governors balked at accepting his resignation. They viewed his words and action as treacherous and voted to expel him, instead. When they announced a replacement for the Department of Mechanics and Physics, they wrote the following in the Course Catalogue:

> Ogden Rood, A.M., ...Appointed in the place of R.S. McCulloh, expelled from his Professorship by a Vote of the Board of Trustees of Columbia College, ...for having abandoned his post of duty and gone to Richmond, Va., and allied himself to those now in rebellion against the Sovereignty of the United States.

McCulloh's expulsion from Columbia for the stated reason of allying with the enemy was picked up by local New York newspapers. One of the men working for Colonel Sharpe's intelligence organization reached out to a friend at the college. He also learned that McCulloh may have had some connection with the New York City Riots. He passed it on to his boss. Sharpe decided to pay a visit to Columbia. He would talk to the College President and other professors who had worked with, or had been associated with Professor McCulloh.

Sharpe met with the Columbia President, Charles King, and Professors John Joy and John Torre. They were all strong opponents of slavery, based on Sharpe's preliminary inquiries into their background. They met at the campus building at 49th Street and Madison Avenue. The building was enormous, constructed with gray stone, architected in Greek Revival style, but undergoing renovation to give it a more up to date Neoclassic look, more like other Ivy League Schools.

When Sharpe asked about Professor Richard S. McCulloh, all three men tried to talk at once. The floor was finally ceded to King.

"Professor McCulloh stained the reputation of our fine institution. He has betrayed his country in support of the rebellion."

"President King, when you say betrayed, what do you mean?"

"He resigned his chair at the college to flee to Richmond. I have been advised that before he left he had begun to express his support of the Confederate South, very openly, to many of our patriotic professors and students."

Professor Tory stated, "one of our professors saw him just before the riots broke out."

"Any idea what he was doing?"

"Just that he saw McCulloh with a group of Copperheads moving along with the crowd."

"I am convinced he was a 'secret agent of secession,'" Professor Joy said.

Before Sharpe could ask why, Professor Tory interjected, "Several of us believe he left to start some type of military laboratory to help the Confederates prosecute war against the Union."

After additional discussion about McCulloh's curious habits, President King said, "Oh, something else, I just remembered. McCulloh is married to a cousin of Robert E. Lee."

Sharpe then met with the police station commander for the downtown 13th Precinct. His name was Captain Thomas Steers. He was first generation Irish, with no trace of a brogue.

"My understanding, Captain, is that your men were called in to help break up the recent Draft Riot."

"Yeah, we did. Took four days to fully restore the peace. Never seen anything like it before. Hope we don't ever again."

"The papers I read suggested it was caused when they announced the names picked from the lottery for the draft. Soon after heavy causalities from Gettysburg were released."

"A helluva a lot more to it than that, Colonel."

"How so?"

"There were agitators that helped work up the crowds. Like there usually is."

"Any idea who they were?"

"Sure, Copperheads. Started chanting anti-war slogans and bigoted remarks. Stirring up the crowd. We had reports from witnesses. They saw Copperheads joining in with the violence, too. Breaking windows, starting fires and such."

"Any Copperheads arrested?"

"Plenty of arrests. Maybe some of those we arrested were. To be honest with you Colonel, not sure. Those Copperheads were smart, and I believe were organized for this. Helped get things started. Most of them left early. Before things got out of hand."

"Have you heard the name, or did anyone mention the name of a Professor Richard McCulloh?"

"Yes, now that you mention it," Steers replied. "From Columbia College, right?"

"That's him."

"I remember his name because we thought it very strange that a professor from a prestigious school like that would be joining in to help provoke a violent riot."

"Do you remember anything about what the professor was up to?"

"Yeah, but not much I'm afraid. Somebody reported he saw this McCulloh fella who he knew scurrying around lower Manhattan, nailing anti-war posters up everywhere, just before the draft. When he tried to stop him, McCulloh pushed him away, and then ran into the crowd. We tried to locate the professor for questioning, but we were told he left the college and had gone to Richmond."

In the eastern theatre, Charleston continued to be a strategic Union target. They had made some gains, eventually taking Fort Wagner, a beachhead fortification on Morris Island, where the 54th Regiment, an African American regiment from Massachusetts, had fought bravely in the first wave. These men fought knowing that Confederate President Jefferson Davis promised that they would be sold into slavery, and white officers leading these units would be executed if caught.

Six hundred men from the 54th were ordered to storm a superior Confederate force of 1,700 men in fortified positions. Almost half of the regiment were killed, wounded or captured. The valiant effort of this regiment inspired Union forces and helped dispel disparaging rumors about fitness of African Americans in military combat roles. Efforts to recapture Fort Sumpter and take the city became a long, costly conquest.

Frederick Douglass was a major advocate for allowing African Americans to serve and fight for the Union Army. Two of his sons volunteered to serve with the 54th Regiment. One of them saw action in the Battle of Fort Wagner.

In the late summer, Union engineers under the command of Major General Gilmore constructed an inland battery about five miles from Charleston for the purpose of bombing the city. A 200-pound Parrott rifle was installed, called the "Swamp Angel." As if directly bombing the city wasn't enough, it was later learned that a modernized version of an ancient incendiary weapon, known as "Greek Fire," was launched, along with regular shells, from the battery at Charleston.

First used by the Greeks, the original combustible compound was believed to contain elements of sulfur and petroleum mixed with molten iron to create a flaming weapon that would burn immediately when lit, even when hitting water. This proved effective in ancient naval battles. Considered also highly resistant to being extinguished.

Attacking Charleston, the North used a version of Greek Fire containing saltpeter, charcoal, asphaltum, naphtha and sulphur. General Gilmore's official report noted that the shells, a version of Greek Fire, exploded prematurely "and worked very poorly." A few structures were damaged. Only one fire resulted from these shells, and they were easily extinguished.

Local newspapers in Richmond hyped and decried the bombing of Charleston with unconventional incendiary weapons. They pointed out that this conflicted with a decree issued by President Lincoln regarding the conduct of war. In early 1863, Lincoln had issued a general order for instruction for the United States military. It was prepared for Lincoln by Francis Lieber, a lawyer and ethicist. The order became known as the Lieber Code and contained the following:

> The use of poison in any manner, be it to poison wells, or food, or arms, is wholly excluded from modern warfare. He that uses it puts himself out of the pale of the law and usages of war.

Whether Lincoln and his War Cabinet didn't view the Greek Fire weapon used at Charleston, as falling within the banned substances covered in the general order, or it was a direct violation of the decree, was left to speculation.

In late October, Jefferson Davis went by train to visit with the Confederate Army of Tennessee. He stopped in Charleston upon his return to see first-hand the battle waging in Charleston, and to visit with Brigadier General P.G.T. Beauregard. Beauregard was now responsible for the coastal defense of South Carolina, Georgia and Florida. Along with Lee, he had been one of the favorite generals. His relationship with Davis had become strained as the war lingered on.

Davis inspected the defenses with Beauregard and his staff. He also saw the terrible destruction in the downtown section where historic churches, houses and graveyards were ruined by Union bombardment.

Local residents had nicknamed this area the "Shell District." What he witnessed infuriated Davis, making a lasting impression. Yet he would subsequently declare, "it was better the city be reduced to a heap of ruins than surrender."

When Davis was working from his home office, he was always careful with his papers. What he didn't take with him to his executive work office on Bank Street, a few blocks away, he methodically placed into the locked safe in his office before leaving.

Mary watched while he was away how Robert, Davis' personal manservant, would take received mail and pile it neatly, unopened, in a stack on the desk in the President's office, adjoining the bedroom. Oldest on the bottom, newest on top.

She was constantly on the lookout for the best opportunity to rummage through the entire pile and see if it were possible to pick up anything that might be useful to pass on.

From previous occasions she knew that she could hold some of the envelopes containing letters up against light and make out sections of the content. Not always, many envelopes were too thick, or the writing impossible to decipher from the folded pages. Nothing so far on her occasional spot checks provided any insights she thought worth mentioning.

Mostly the ones she tried were administrative in nature concerning government activities, letters from friends and concerned citizens. There were two communications from war generals, one from General Joseph Johnston, but the envelope was too thick. A second was a telegram from a General Bragg that had just arrived. Mary knew Jefferson Davis had been critical of Johnston, Department Commander of the West. Bragg reported to Johnston. She wanted to do a more thorough, detailed inspection of the pile now sitting on the Confederate President's desk.

There were generally too many people around during most days to get adequate time to look without being seen. From evening to daybreak, the Davis' bedroom, along with offices on both sides for Jefferson Davis and his wife were off limits – even when they were travelling. She would have to do it during regular working hours.

Mary was convinced the following Friday morning provided the perfect opportunity to try since Mr. and Mrs. Davis were at a government function. Catherine had also left the house with the children. The other house servants were all downstairs. Bringing several cleaning rags and a bucket of water with her for cover, she climbed the stairs and entered the office. Mary opened the curtains and let the brilliant rays of light stream into the room. She grabbed the letters from the desk, put them on a side table near the window, and pulled over a chair.

Mary counted 28 letters. She eliminated almost half as personal, based on the references handwritten above the wax seal. She began by holding the envelope from General Bragg up to the light from the window. His title on the envelope was "General, Army of Tennessee." After thanking Davis for visiting his troops, the telegram read:

> As we discussed, I will send 15,000 of my men to assist Longstreet in the assault on Knoxville.

Mary knew this could be important. She kept looking through the other envelopes. She found it much easier to read content of unfolded letters within the envelopes. In some, she couldn't see anything. Those she could read appeared to be mostly personal correspondence or about affairs of state, unrelated to the war. She kept digging until she came across a letter from Christopher Memminger, Secretary of Treasury. Inside she could see the following:

> I recommend that you order the use of force, to collect taxes, including confiscation of property. In areas like North Carolina, citizens are now refusing to pay....

She couldn't read the rest. A few more. Nothing. She then spotted a note from another Confederate Cabinet Officer, James Seddon, Secretary of War. At first, it appeared unimportant:

> I have approved Charles Sengstack as Ordnance Sergeant.

As Mary quickly scanned down further, she found something most curious:

> ...issuing $100 in Federal notes to finance his mission across enemy lines to destroy enemy property.

She was about to hold up another promising looking envelope with a British seal when she heard someone on the steps. She quickly gathered all the letters and hid them behind the side table she had placed by the window. She grabbed her bucket and a rag and stepped onto the chair and began wiping down the window glass.

May, the head housekeeper walked into the room. "Ah, there ya are, Mary," she said in her thick Irish brogue. "So what are ya doin'?"

Mary turned around and stepped down from the chair. "Hello Ma'am. With all the light today, you can see how dirty these windows are. I finished the rest of the morning chores you gave me early, and thought I would clean them before Mr. Davis gets back home."

"Hmm. Well, I wanted to see if you could give Melissa a hand cleaning the downstairs kitchen and pantry floors. They're a mess. Need a good scrubbin'."

"Yes ma'am. I can do the rest of this later."

Mary noticed May give a casual glance down at the desk. No indication if she noticed the missing pile of letters. When she left, Mary quickly retrieved the letters from behind the table and stacked them in the order as she had found them back on the desk.

As she was doing so, she noticed there was an open letter in the pile addressed to Jefferson Davis from John Minor Botts, who she knew was a Unionist friend of the Van Lew's. She also had heard from Elizabeth that he had been active in politics before the war and his anti-secession sentiments had led to his being jailed for a short period of time.

She walked back over the window and held it up. Botts had written to Jefferson Davis a letter of accommodation for a Professor John Sears Mc-Culloh.

> I take the liberty of introducing to you acquaintance, the bearer of note, Professor Richard S. McCulloh, a gentleman of rare scientific attainments, whose wide spread reputation is probably not unknown to you...His talents and attainments qualify him for extraordinary usefulness to you...I take pleasure in making him known to you and commend him to your favorable considerations.

She knew nothing about McCulloh, but found the note curious. By the sound of it, McCulloh must have met with Davis and brought the introductory letter with him. Somehow, it had gotten mixed in to the unopened letters. Perhaps, she thought, Robert, responsible for tending to Davis' personal affects, had found it in one of the suits Davis wore.

Leaving the property grounds early mornings without permission to hand off intelligence to Thomas McNiven had become problematic. Mary couldn't get away at this time of day without being noticed. She passed the information she collected in a note she had written to Daniel at Church Service the next Sunday. With Elizabeth's tutoring, both Daniel and his wife Harriett Anne's reading abilities were improving, but he still asked Mary to explain some of her writing.

"More of your scribbling I can't make out. Not 'cause I can't read," he joked.

After hearing about Sengstack, Daniel was anxious to bring this latest information back to Elizabeth.

"Makes me wonder if they decided to change their tactics," Daniel said. "Last couple of big battles didn't go so well."

"You might be right, Daniel," Mary said. Also, let me know if Miss Van Lew knows anything about this Professor McCulloh."

"I will. Take care of yourself Mary."

Another opportunity developed for passing more timely intelligence. In addition to her other remarkable capabilities, Mary had the skills of a practiced seamstress. She had watched and learned from Chloe as a child. In Philadelphia, her formal education included needlecraft. Although she found it tedious, and only did it out of necessity in the past, she was quite good at it.

Using left over yarn and other material from Gaby, Mary began knitting and sewing evenings when she could not sleep. She made socks for Margaret Howell Davis, the eight-year-old daughter of the Davis family. Margaret loved it. The other children each wanted their own.

Varina Davis employed a seamstress who came once a week and used the sewing machine in the Davis' home. This was an advanced lockstitch sewing machine recently purchased by Jefferson Davis at the request of his wife. A practical necessity, she had assured her husband, given the children were so quickly outgrowing their outfits. It was kept in a backroom off the kitchen.

Recognizing Mary's talent, she asked the woman to spend a little time teaching Mary to use the machine. Mary never used this type of sewing device before. She picked up on it more quickly than she let others know, careful not to give away her educational experience, or ability to grasp things quickly.

After a while, Mary began to make an assortment of children's clothing, dresses, undergarments, short pants. It didn't matter that they had closets filled with some of the finest children's clothing in Richmond, or that the oldest could easily pass clothes down to their younger siblings. They wanted things Mary made especially for each of them.

While it endeared her even more to the children, it made others from the household staff, particularly Catherine, the family nurse, and Gaby, who had also knitted garments for the children. Varina, on the other hand, was delighted to see the enthusiastic response from her children, several of whom could be quite difficult. She gave Mary a pass so that when time allowed she could leave the premises to go by herself to order and buy what she needed for sewing from the local dry goods store, close by. She could also charge it to the family account.

The proprietor of the Richmond Dry Goods Store was Wayne Evans. At one time, years ago, he had been close with Elizabeth Van Lew. Elizabeth was much younger than Wayne. Back then, she was a striking young lady. She cut a petite but lovely figure, with her refined facial features. Ocean blue eyes, accentuated by thick, copper brown hair, which she usually pulled up tightly in a thick bun. This made men callers wish they could hang around past proper calling hours, just to watch as she let it down. She had many suitors, but men her own age bored her.

"They're simply boys," she told her parents.

Wayne, like other young men of the day, tried courting her favor. He was over six feet, with reddish hair, piercing brown eyes, a strong chin, and a friendly, unexpectedly kind smile. He was one of the few Elizabeth allowed to get close. Something more may have come from it, but Elizabeth's father put a stop to it. He viewed Wayne Evans as a nice man, but not only was he too old for his daughter. This man, he told his daughter, was not of the right pedigree. Wayne was still a bachelor.

Using Daniel as her intermediary, Mary first checked to make sure Elizabeth was comfortable with Wayne as a contact source for exchanging confidential information. Daniel encouraged Mary to hold off until Elizabeth could talk with Wayne.

Elizabeth had not been in Wayne's store since the war began. His display window from the street contained several items most certainly less in demand given the blockade restricting trade across most of the southern coast. Items such as coffee grinders, tea pots, and a spice rack with matching canisters now seemed more quaint than practical.

The bell on the front door clanged as she entered the store. She noticed that very little had changed inside. The shelves were full of cooking utensils and assorted household items on one side, bolts of cloth and sewing material on the other. Consumables were in the middle.

An elderly man was browsing in the food section. Elizabeth walked over towards Wayne Evans behind the counter. He was sitting in a chair, checking items on a delivery list, completely oblivious to her approach. He was older, but still possessed boyish good looks. She picked up a jar of molasses, studied it for a few seconds, put it back down, with a thud, and moved across the room to look at the soaps.

The bell on the front door jangled again as the other patron walked out of the store. Elizabeth immediately put down the bar of soap she was holding and walked back up to the counter. Wayne finally looked up and sprang that smile she remembered so well.

"Elizabeth Van Lew. What a pleasant surprise."

"Very nice to see you, Wayne. It's been too long. Would it be possible to speak in private?"

Wayne walked to the front door, locked it while turning the "Open" sign around, and closed the window shade. Walking back, he motioned with his hand, inviting her to follow him to the other side of the store where there were two stools and a matching table for sale. She sat, back straight, hands folded on her lap. Wayne pulled his seat closer and waited for Elizabeth to speak first.

"I can remember years ago how you told me you feared the country might one day split apart, and how if it came to that, you hoped Virginia would stay with the Union."

"Sure, Elizabeth, I do recall that conversation. I believe you at the time were convinced Virginia would never leave."

"I was wrong and you were right. Never did I fathom Virginia would take part in the rebellion. With Richmond becoming the capital of the rebellion at that."

"If only you were right and I was wrong."

She then opened up to her old friend. She shared with Wayne how Mary came to work as a servant for the Davis family and how she was in a position to provide valuable information on Confederate war plans. Elizabeth went on to explain how Mary had recently been given a pass from Varina Davis to buy sewing materials from his store.

"Elizabeth, you were always full of surprises. On one hand, I'm glad to know you haven't changed very much. Nonetheless, what you are talking about would be considered treasonous by this government, if you were ever caught. Both you and Mary are putting yourselves in grave danger. But you already know that."

"I do. So does Mary. We have both come to terms with that in our own different ways. My hope is that you may be able to as well. Given you have been doing business with the Davis family..."

"Strictly business. Mrs. Davis has been a very good customer. A lovely lady, even if she is the First Lady of this loathsome Confederacy."

"She is lovely. I often wonder how Varina Davis really feels about all this."

"I have noticed at times as she browses the shelves of my store, there is a certain sadness in her temperament."

"So this is why you are here? To ask for my help?"

"Wayne, you could be of tremendous assistance. All I am asking is that when Mary comes to the store, you secretly accept information she gives you and then pass it on to me. That is if you can come to terms with this, and are willing to do so," Elizabeth bluntly suggested.

"I reckon that you then pass it on to someone else."

"The less you know, Wayne, the better for you, and the rest of us. You could be making a significant contribution to restoring our rightful government and helping to make freedom available for all."

"Or I could be signing my own death warrant, just like you and Mary."

"I can't imagine you are resigned to accepting the status quo. For nothing else, it can't be good for your business. I was hoping..."

"I'm not saying I won't do it. Just that this request is so abrupt and unexpected. Especially coming from you, Elizabeth."

She was about to get up and leave. Wayne broke out in a wide grin.

To be perfectly honest, I still think of you often, Elizabeth. I may regret it, but I'll do it."

They discussed how best to discretely exchange messages, with Mary occasionally visiting the store and delivering notes to Wayne. If Wayne couldn't do it himself, he would have his nephew take them to Elizabeth's Church Hill residence while doing his regular deliveries. Wayne noted the boy was trustworthy and mature for his age. He need not know what was in sealed messages, and not the type to pry.

Wayne began to nervously fidget in his chair. Elizabeth feared he may have had second thoughts.

"I saw something in the *Daily Dispatch* the other day. Thought it might be of interest to you. While I don't know much about it, I do know you've always enjoyed the theatre."

"Yes, always have. A great way to get one's mind off the hardships we all must endure, especially these days."

"Well, I read that the famous British actress, Miss Bella Vaughan, is planning to perform right here in Richmond. Guess that's assuming they can figure out how to get her through the blockade."

"I read that as well. I believe she will be performing in *Lady Audley's Secret*. I don't know how much you know about it, but I read the book by Elizabeth Braddon. It's quite controversial. Touches on themes that have traditionally been taboo for literature."

"I didn't know. Maybe then this wasn't such a good idea. I was going to ask if you might like to accompany me to the performance."

"That would be lovely, Wayne. Oh, and, I know you put up the 'Store Closed' sign. May I still buy a few things?"

Mary would begin leveraging Wayne as another source for communicating sensitive information. Elizabeth Van Lew, with Daniel's critical assistance, continued to send messages across enemy lines. Sometimes a courier or an occasional escaped Union prisoner, moving from one secret location to another to reach Union encampments. Sometimes using Sam Ruth's help with his railroad for part of the journey.

Whether they thought the communications were important or not, they rationalized that the Federal officials could potentially piece loose ends together with other information they possessed. Perhaps cull it for items of significant value, recognizable only by them. These messages were always delivered anonymously. Despite previous clues, the identity of Van Lew and her network of co-conspirators eluded the Union top command.

With the continued influx of new prisoners from all the recurring battles, many injured and in need of medical attention, compounded by the decision of Jefferson Davis to suspend prisoner exchanges, Richmond was reaching a saturation point. By the Fall of 1863, there were over 4,000 in Libby Prison, with 700 or more often sharing the same room.

Castle Thunder, which was created when the military commandeered three separate buildings on Cary Street, had a reported capacity of 1,400. Now it housed over 3,000. Belle Island, a strip of land in the James River, was purchased from Old Dominion and Iron Works to deal with the additional capacity. Whereas the other prisons were brick structures, Belle Island was an open-air stockade. There were now over 6,000 prisoners held there as well. Dysentery, smallpox and other diseases were common across all prisons, and spread easily.

Clerking at Libby Prison, Erasmus Ross had continued to work with Daniel and the Underground helping prisoners escape. Because Elizabeth Van Lew was under constant suspicion, they were most often put up in other homes sympathetic to the resistance, but where the residents were less likely to be suspected. With the outskirts of Richmond more carefully guarded by a combination of Confederate troops and local militia, it had become more challenging moving escaped prisoners from safe houses to other locations outside Richmond.

Upon the advice of Daniel, Ross had recently helped place an African American girl trained in nursing in the Libby Prison hospital. Her name was Dolores Halsey. She was an attractive young girl, with deep brown eyes and a dazzling smile. Dolores had been working at the Chimborazo Hospital for wounded and sick Confederate soldiers when a doctor there tried to take advantage of her.

Dolores was a slave. She had previously worked at the downtown Richmond Hospital for civilians before the war and was contractually loaned to the government to assist with the large number of wounded soldiers. Ross convinced government officials to transfer her to Libby where nurses were scarce. They were happy to let her go. When she tried to complain about the doctor, she was labeled troublesome, given to fantasy, and a devilish flirt.

Ross was concerned that he too might be falling under suspicion. He was determined to find other more discrete ways to help prisoners escape. Daniel had informed him that Dolores Halsey could be trusted.

Dolores was assigned to a rotating shift of days and nights. Ross had heard the supervision in the hospital room was much more lax. Guards leaving doors open. Things like that. He mentioned to her that there was one prisoner in particular he was hoping to try and get out. Ross wanted her to see if by moving him into the hospital room as a patient it might be easier to find a way out.

During one of her breaks, she made a point of walking by the office of Erasmus Ross. He was a good-looking man with a thick mustache sitting behind his desk.

"Excuse me, sir, might I have a word?"

He looked up and nodded. Standing, he motioned with his arm for her to enter and take a seat.

She looked around to make sure no one was watching, stepped into the office and shut the door. She remained standing. He again offered her a chair to sit, this time verbally, but she turned it down.

"Thanks Mr. Ross, but need to get back before I'm missed. You asked me to let you know if I see anythin'."

"I did."

Ross didn't expect to hear from her this soon. Dolores had only been working in Libby for a short time.

"The other day, I noticed one of the patients in the hospital died. When I went to the head nurse, she told me to get Walter to help me take him down to the morgue."

"You know you can also trust Walter. He has helped us before."

Dolores smiled. "Sure, Mr. Ross, I know that." She continued. "Surprised me she didn't tell me get the doctor. She didn't want to look herself, either. When I asked 'bout it, she told me, doctor too busy with the livin'. So was she, she told me. Took my word he was dead."

"Is that right?"

"Yes, sir. Then she told me to make an 'X' on the clip board over his bed. For the sake of the other patients, I was told, they move the body as soon as possible to the morgue. One of the doctors goes down later and certifies the patient is dead."

"This is hard to believe."

"I bring this up, 'cause you asked me to look for ways we could get a prisoner out."

"Interesting," Ross replied. His initial serious, inquisitive look had been replaced with a smile.

"Well, Walter and me took 'em down. I noticed that there is a door to outside in that room they been using for the morgue. The inside door to the morgue is locked with a key. Only the guard on duty has a key, but the door inside the morgue to the outside has a simple bolt lock. When I mentioned it to Walter, he says, 'guess they don't think no dead people gonna get up and go walkin' out.'"

"Dolores, this might just be the answer. Maybe help this man I told you about escape. Shame we can't help everyone, but we really need to help him out. As soon as possible."

As Dolores walked through the door, he whispered, "I still need to see if I can work a few things out on my end. Will let you know. Thank you for this. Well done."

Several days earlier a young girl named Josephine Holmes had gone to Elizabeth about a prisoner at Libby. The girl had been given temporary permission to visit captured Union soldiers, privileges Elizabeth Van Lew had enjoyed until they had been revoked.

Unbeknownst to prison officials, she too was a member of a Richmond abolitionist family against the war who had helped runaway slaves escape in the past. During one of her visits, she met a man who called himself Captain Harry Howard. She shared with him her negative feelings about the Confederacy and its policies. The man decided to trust her.

He explained that he had been a scout, spying for the North. Wearing civilian clothes, he was close to the battle lines at Chickamauga. He knew his capture was imminent. For fear of being hung as a spy when caught, he took a uniform off a dead Union officer. He confided that his name was not Harry Howard, but Harry Catlin.

"Can you help me get out of here?" he begged her. "Other prisoners know I was a spy. We're all in desperate straits. Some less conditioned to take all the abuse. If any of them decide to trade that information for special treatment from the guards, I'm as good as dead. I had an argument with one of them who already threatened to rat on me. Cost me my pocket watch."

"What makes you think I can help you?" the girl asked.

"I heard others have gotten out with help from people here in Richmond. Even if you can't, you may know who can."

Elizabeth told her to go see Erasmus Ross at the prison and tell him privately what she had shared with her. "Tell him, you were sent by me," Elizabeth suggested.

Thanks to Ross, for her next visit, Josephine had received permission to dispense bags of Virginia tobacco. Making the rounds, she handed them out to several prisoners, including Catlin. He was highly disappointed when she simply handed him the bag and turned to continue passing other bags out to the crowd of prisoners forming around her.

"Any chance you can stop back and visit when you are done?"

"Not today, I'm sorry. Need to get back home."

Calling him by his alias name, one of the other prisoners mischievously ribbed him. "Why should you get any special treatment, Howard? Captain Harry Howard, right? That's your name?" Luckily the guard standing nearby didn't appear to pick up on it.

Catlin went back to his cot and sat. He eventually pulled out his pipe and opened the bag. He began pinching tobacco from the bag, first sprinkling it from his fingertips, and then packing it into his pipe. When he reached in for a second pinch, he felt something at the bottom of the bag.

There was a slip of paper. No one appeared to be watching. He pulled the bag further apart with both hands, and without lifting the paper from the bag, tried as best he could to unfold the creases and spread it out. It read:

Would you be free? Claim you sick. Get to prison hospital.

The next evening Dolores was working the night shift. Catlin was pulled into the hospital, shivering and groaning. He fit the description Dolores had been given. When she moved over to the bed to take his pulse, she also checked his chart to make sure it was "Harry Howard."

The night shift jokingly referred to themselves as 'the skeleton staff." Under the dire circumstances, Dolores didn't appreciate the macabre humor. On slow nights like this one, only one of the nurses, or staff members, would be in the room with patients during the later hours, while the others caught some needed sleep. At least one non-medical male slave was always on duty there. A guard was posted outside the door, at night, but he often was not there. Sometimes going off someplace to catch a nap or a smoke.

Before working her first night shift, Dolores had asked other staff workers about what to expect. She learned there was a bell they could ring if additional help was needed. The room was dimly lit by a few lanterns to help patients sleep.

The door to the hospital room was supposed to be locked when the guard stepped away. One of the staff members also confided that the night shift guard hated being around when "stiffs" needed to be moved from the hospital room to the morgue. He would often step away, leaving the door to the hospital room open, as well as the door to the morgue, coming back later to lock them both back up.

Dolores waited until the early morning hours when all the other patients appeared to be sleeping. She went straight for Catlin's cot. Checking his pulse, Dolores sighed as she let go of the arm, and unrolled a sheet over his entire body. Marking an "X" on the clip board, she signaled to the non-medical staff worker standing close by. The staff worker, another slave, went to the door and knocked for the guard to open it.

"Got a corpse, got to move," the staff worker said after the guard stepped into the hospital room.

"I'll go open the morgue," the guard said as he turned and left.

The worker came back a few minutes later with Walter carrying a stretcher. Just as she had been told, the guard had stepped away, leaving the door, closed but unlocked. They lifted Catlin's body and lowered him onto the stretcher. The two men began to carry the stretcher over to the door. As Dolores opened it for the men carrying Catlin into the hall, another patient sprung up from his bed and bolted in their direction. They were all standing in front of the door, but in the hallway.

Walter and the other worker immediately put the stretcher down. Dolores closed the door behind them. The staff worker, a big man, grabbed the patient and pulled him around. He placed him in a restraining lock with one muscular arm wrapped firmly around his upper body and the other covering his mouth.

Looking around to make sure the guard was not in view, Walter also grabbed him, by the collar, saying, "you gonna ruin everything."

Catlin sat up in his stretcher, pulling the sheet from his head. "Let him come too," he said.

"I knew you weren't dead," the other man said.

"Let's go," Catlin demanded.

Dolores nodded at the men restraining the other patient. Catlin climbed off the stretcher. "Might as well both walk now, save time."

Walter motioned for the two prisoners to follow him down the hall. The other man picked up the stretcher and followed. Dolores moved back into the hospital room where she closed the door behind them.

"What's all the noise?" came from one of the other beds.

Walking toward where she heard the voice, in a soft tone Dolores muttered, "Shhh, everything is alright. Don't want to wake the others now, do we?"

Someone else was coughing. Another patient was waking. Dolores hoped none of them saw anything. The guard was back. He stuck his head through the door.

"Everything OK? Walter took the body to the morgue?"

"Yes," Dolores replied.

She heard the door lock behind her. She immediately went to the second empty bed and marked another "X".

The smell was indescribable. It was even more revolting for the prisoners who hadn't experienced it before. It was dark with the only light coming from a small window. As their eyes adjusted, they could see dead bodies lined up next to each other across a table. Each had a clip board on the chest. Walter pulled back the bolt to the outside door and swung it back.

He gasped for fresh air. A light from the street spilled into the room. The men could see the loading dock and back alley that had been used as a delivery entrance since the days the building had served as a tobacco warehouse. This area of the dock was now being used for moving dead bodies. The prisoners were about to move to the door, but Walter said, "wait."

He closed the door again. Several minutes passed. The two prisoners were getting antsy. When Walter opened the door a second time they spotted a couple of African American men carrying a corpse appeared from the alleyway. They hauled the corpse up onto the loading dock. Following Walter's direction, they carried it over to a long table where other dead bodies were lying. Walter put Harry Howard's clip board on top of the unknown corpse.

"Where did you get the replacement corpse?" Catlin asked one of the new arrivals.

"Easy to find these days," Walter responded.

He took out a knife and tape from his pocket. He cut the name band from Catlin's arm and taped it onto the corpse. You could hardly see where it had been taped.

He then walked up to the second prisoner, cut his band and stuck it in his pocket.

"No corpse to replace you," Walter angrily noted. "You put the rest of us at great risk. Guess we'll just have to dream up somethin'. Say you must have got out some other way. Now follow these men. They will help you escape."

The guard let the non-medical slave worker back into the makeshift morgue before locking the door once again. The worker immediately walked over to the empty bed where Dolores was still standing. He pulled down the medical sheet she had just altered and quietly ripped it up into small pieces before tossing it into a waste basket.

"What are you doin'?" she asked.

In a low voice he said to Dolores, "things so crazy busy here. They won't remember if he was here, or if so, when he left. If they do question us, we'll just say he must have slipped out when the guard left the door open. Must have taken his personal chart too, hoping no one would notice. When they finally figure out he is gone from the prison, maybe after a roll call, they'll just figure he found some hole someplace to climb out of the prison. Happens more than you would think."

"I'll strip the bed and put on some clean sheets."

Wayne knocked at the front door of the Van Lew mansion. Daniel opened it.

"Yes sir, may I inquire who you are and what your intentions might be?" Daniel asked, jokingly.

"Wayne Evans. Here to see the lovely Miss Van Lew. We have an appointment at the Marshall Theater. My intention is to escort her there."

"I see. I shall inquire the lovely lady of the house to determine if she is available."

As they left the house together, Wayne mentioned to Elizabeth. "I notice Daniel's use of language seems to have improved quite a bit lately. You wouldn't know anything about it, I guess."

"I have no idea what you are talking about, Wayne."

Around the same time the Lincoln's attended a play at the Ford Theatre in Washington, D.C., along with Mrs. Ben Hardin Helm, the President's sister-in-law. John Wilkes Booth, a popular actor of the day, was on stage performing. Mrs. Helm noticed Booth glaring at the President while on stage. She leaned over, whispering:

"Mr. Lincoln, he looks as if he meant that for you."

Lincoln replied, "He does look pretty sharp at me, doesn't he?"

Chapter 13: Bomb Making Factory

Mary Bowser slipped into Wayne Evans' store late in the afternoon. Wayne spotted her immediately, but continued to act preoccupied in conversation with a regular customer. The store was more crowded than usual, with six or seven people. With the war's dire impact on the local economy, this was about the largest crowd Wayne could expect.

Mary began to hold up some of the silk and wool fabrics on one of the display shelves.

She picked up a few balls of colored yarn, some ribbons and thread and walked over to the cash register. Wayne excused himself from the customer he was speaking with and circled around the counter.

"Same charge as last time, right ma'am?"

"Yes, thank you sir."

She handed him the envelope containing a slip of paper authorizing the charge to the Davis' account. Also contained in the envelope was Mary's latest intelligence report, folded discretely behind. Leaving the store, Mary took her time heading back to the Executive Mansion. Strolling down Broad Street, she would occasionally stop to look at the varied store front display windows.

"Mary Bowser, you left something you paid for in my store." It was Wayne.

He handed her another ball of yarn. Before Mary could say anything he explained, "Not really, but needed to speak with you."

"I don't understand," Mary responded.

"Don't worry, my nephew Timothy is minding the store." A woman shopper was passing by. After making sure no one else was coming, he added, "I hope you don't mind, but I read your notes. Knowing Miss Van

Lew, I think she will want more explanation. You mentioned some important things."

"Sure. Maybe we can go someplace nearby to talk."

"Frankly, I think you should talk directly to her."

"Yes, but Miss Van Lew suggested that I not be seen coming or going to see her. She told me there were too many suspicious people in the Church Hill neighborhood."

"I saw her the other night. She planned to be in town today. Why don't you go back to my store, if you can spare a little more time. I'll see if she can meet you there."

Elizabeth and Mary met alone in Wayne's cluttered storage room in the back of his store. They had to wipe the dust off a couple stools before sitting.

"Sorry you had to leave your scheduled event. Wayne felt it was important that I not only delivered this," she held up the note Wayne gave back to her and handed it to Elizabeth. "He suggested we discuss it."

"He actually saved me. Mother wanted company. We were attending an exhibit. What passes for art these days is quite disturbing," Elizabeth mused as she put on and adjusted her reading spectacles.

"Sure seems that Varina Davis is more comfortable and trusting having you around."

"Yes, Miss Van Lew. She's happy that the children like me."

"Good, very good."

Mary began to discuss her latest information. "As it says in my note, the President was just back from visiting with his generals across the South. He had a dinner party with some members of his cabinet and other politicians. I was asked to help serve."

Staring at the note, Elizabeth commented, "These look like some of his most trusted advisers, Judah Benjamin, James Seddon, Alexander Stephens. At least that's what I've read in print."

"I didn't know all their names. Jefferson Davis still looked tuckered out from his trip. Alcohol was flowing. They talked more openly than usual. Lot of talk about the squabbling among his generals. James Longstreet they said was sent to the western theatre because he was critical of Lee at Gettysburg. Now he was bickering with General Braxton, and none of them seemed to get along with their senior commander, General Johnston. One of the Congressional guests I didn't know said, 'seems our general would rather fight each other than the Yankees.'"

Elizabeth began reading out loud:

> Mr. Davis said they only have limited raw materials outside Richmond. The blockade has further reduced our ability to procure these resources from abroad. It is critical that we continue to control the Virginia and Tennessee Railroad, even though West Virginia, with so many Northern sympathizers, had split from the rest of the State of Virginia to join the Union. We need the railroad for the new weapons we are developing.

Looking up, Elizabeth asked, "Any idea what type of weapons he was referring too?"

"I don't know, I couldn't hear. Picked up what I could as I walked in and out of the kitchen. You will see further down that they are expecting a large shipment of potassium nitrate on this railroad at the end of the month. Somebody else explained that it was needed for experiments to be conducted at the Richmond Nitre and Mining Bureau."

"Potassium nitrate. If I'm not mistaken, that's another name for saltpeter. Used to make bombs."

"I guessed as much."

"A very good idea that you decided to get this information to us right away," Elizabeth scanned further down the note. "Charles Sengstack," she said aloud. "I remember from your last note, something about destroying property up north."

"All I heard was that Sengstack made it successfully to Maryland. I believe it was Mr. Seddon who was talking. He called Sengstack 'the Pharmacist.'"

"Seddon is the Secretary of War."

"Did you hear anything more about Richard McCulloh?"

Mary's eyes shifted. "No, nothing comes to mind. Nothing about Richard McCulloh."

They could hear voices. A few people had entered the store. They both sat without speaking for a few moments before Elizabeth broke the silence.

"Sam Ruth did talk to John Botts about his recommendation letter that you saw," Elizabeth said in a hushed whisper.

Somebody in the storefront was laughing.

After another pause, Elizabeth continued. "I thought John was simply trying to play the part of a loyal Confederate, so as not to get thrown back in jail. Sam said not the case. He met McCulloh when he was a guest speaker at the University of Virginia. John was trying to help him relocate back south and thought his previous work in developing better fertilizer could provide agricultural assistance to local farmers who right now need all the help they can get to produce more."

"Guess we both suspect it was not about fertilizer," Mary sarcastically mentioned, also speaking in a whisper.

Elizabeth concurred with a partial smile and approving nod. "I will add my own note to provide additional context based on what you just said and we will get this to our friends up North. I'll say it again. No one else could do what you are doing. I pray to God you stay safe, my dear."

"Will you and Daniel try to send this to the Army of Potomac Headquarters, like last time?"

"Remember General Benjamin Butler? I sent him the information Wilson provided on ironclads before the North captured Norfolk..."

"Yes, I sure do."

"Well, General Butler is back. He has been named the new commander of the Department of Virginia and North Carolina. He became known as the 'Beast of New Orleans' from when he briefly served down there. Guess he'll be the 'Beast of the East,' now. The Confederates loathe him. We will try to send it to him."

"Oh, something else. I heard Mr. Davis ask his guests not to share anything about any of this until more testing on these potential new weapons could be done."

"This is most useful information, Mary. You really have become quite good at this, as I knew you would."

"Perhaps, but I must also tell you, Miss Van Lew. You once said telling lies would get easier after a while. Well, it hasn't. Not for me."

Harry Catlin and John McCullough, the man who insisted on escaping with him, followed behind the two African Americans, taking alleys and back roads where possible. Working to their advantage, Jefferson Davis had issued an executive order to extinguish the gas lights in downtown Richmond to conserve fuel.

They were ushered into the basement entrance to a large mansion, not far from the Van Lew's. The home belonged to the Holmes family. They were Unionists to the core, and friends with Elizabeth's family. Josephine Holmes, the young girl who had first delivered the message to Catlin hidden in a sack of tobacco, greeted them warmly.

They were given food and civilian clothes. The next evening one of the same men from the previous night guided them to William Rowley's farm. They would stay there until Sam Ruth could secure passes for the train out of Richmond. A week later they safely arrived in Washington, D.C.

Benjamin Butler read the latest notes from Richmond, but still had no idea about the source. Still using the Underground Railroad discrete linkage between stops, the couriers who delivered messages across enemy lines only knew the last individual who passed it to them. The same held true for all the couriers down the line.

Butler immediately passed it on to the Union War Department, but he was now more determined to make direct contact with whomever it was providing these dispatches from Richmond.

He would later hear about Catlin and McCullough's escape from Libby. He immediately summoned Catlin, who had been a scout for him in the past, to a meeting at Fort Monroe. Catlin recounted the events that led to his escape.

After he finished, Butler noted, "I doubt the young girl who delivered the message to you came up with this scheme on her own."

"When I saw her again in her father's house, I asked about that. I assumed her father was behind it."

"My dad and I did this as a favor for Elizabeth Van Lew," she said.

"A woman?" Butler asked.

"A lady well respected in Richmond society, I was told" Catlin noted.

Butler was convinced it had to be the same person who sent him the anonymous letter before he left for New Orleans regarding the movement of Confederate ironclads. He called out to his secretary, "We need to send a message to Colonel Sharpe."

Sharpe and Butler shared a consistent view that they needed to more effectively employ the services of Unionists living in the South, especially Richmond. They knew there was a Unionist network, working in conjunction with the Underground Railroad, to help soldiers escape and had provided the Union with confidential information back across enemy lines several times in the past.

Up until now, there was no effective coordination between the army and the Richmond network of spies, and no clue how to establish contact. Sharpe was completely on board with Butler to change this and decided to take immediate action.

After receiving Butler's communication, Union War Department Headquarters contacted General William W. Averell, Commander of the Department of West Virginia. He received the following order:

> Proceed with all your available force now at New Creek, without delay, via Petersburg, Franklin, and Monterey, and then by the most practicable route to the line of the Virginia and Tennessee Railroad, at Bonsack's (sp) Station, in Botetourt County, or Salem, in Roanoke County.

He was told to destroy all the bridges, water-stations, depots for the railroad, and to remove rails to render them useless. His troops reached Salem, Virginia in a surprise raid, and were able to cut telegraph wires, tore up railroad tracks and set fire to depots.

The Virginia and Tennessee Railroad ran west from Lynchburg, Virginia to Bristol, Tennessee. While it was generally known to be used by Confederates for troop movement, it was also moving raw materials to support the war effort. Copper and lead were transported from mines in Tennessee. Saltpeter from caves in West Virginia.

Averell left from New Creek, West Virginia with 2,500 cavalry and mounted infantry and a battery of artillery. Despite bad weather, they reached Salem in three days, over 200 miles.

A captured group of Confederate soldiers told them a train was coming from Lynchburg loaded with Confederate troops to protect the rails. They created an ambush, opening fire at the train, forcing the conductor to turn back. Knowing more sizable cavalry and infantry units would soon be on their way, Averell ordered withdrawal.

They encountered pockets of Confederate resistance during the retreat, but most of his men made it back safely, travelling close to 400 miles to reach Beverly, West Virginia. He lost seven men to drowning, seven were wounded, and one went missing. The damage would delay Confederate movement of supplies and material for weapons, but not for long. The North would continue to mount attacks against the railways in West Virginia to disrupt these vital routes into Richmond.

Saturday mornings, Elizabeth often visited the Farmers' Market in the downtown area. Sometimes she would go with Harriet Anne to help her pick up fresh produce for Saturday evening dinner. When feeling up to it, Eliza at times came as well. On this particular Saturday, Elizabeth was alone.

Richmond boasted one of the oldest public markets in the country, dating back to 1737. It was situated on the corner of 17th and Main. The location was ideal. Main Street was the primary access route to Williamsburg. Also, it was close to the James River, where fresh seafood and shellfish became a market staple, when in season.

Elizabeth worked her way through the crowd, she bought some winter squash and greens. She walked over to a stand piled high with potatoes and began to hold a few up, squeezing to determine firmness. Once a potato passed this test, and appeared relatively free of blemishes, and with no protruding sprouts, she handed it to the merchant who placed all of them together on a scale. Elizabeth then dropped the potatoes into her satchel, along with the other vegetables. She had just finishing paying when someone tapped her from behind.

"I thought I might see you here, my dear, hello Elizabeth." It was Sam Ruth.

"Hello, Sam."

Pointing to her bag, Ruth asked, "Do you need help carrying that?"

"No thank you, Sam. I can manage fine."

Taking her arm and lowering his voice, he said, "Let me take your bag, anyway. Please walk with me. We need to talk."

They crossed through the market, away from the crowd and over to where several merchants were packing up their things. When he was sure there was no one close by, Sam stopped and faced Elizabeth.

"A scout working for a Colonel Sharpe came to see me. Colonel Sharpe is running a new military intelligence organization for the Army of the Potomac. His organization figured out that I had helped those last two prisoners escape by rail out of Richmond."

"Oh no, Sam. I always felt we were better off when no one knew what we were doing. Not even the Union. Timothy Webster was caught and hung when they sent other spies to talk to him. They blew his cover."

"Well, they now know about you as well. I was told General Butler wants to establish ongoing communication directly with you," Ruth said.

Elizabeth was fuming. "You didn't give them my name?"

"No, Elizabeth, they already know about you."

"But how?"

"One of the escaped prisoners knew your name. The young Holmes girl, Josephine, told him while helping him escape. I don't think she meant any harm. Sooner or later it was bound to come out. They say this Sharpe fella is relentless."

Elizabeth nodded.

"They came to me first. Wanted me to let you know in advance before they made contact with you directly."

"You know Sam, I always wanted to keep my activities, and more importantly, those of Mary secret. More people knowing could land all of us at the foot of the gallows."

"Can't be changed. That is just the way it now is, Elizabeth. Frankly, with all the prisoners you helped and knew you by name, it is amazing to me it had not gotten back to Butler, or one of the other Yankee Generals. Mary still is an anonymous source. Although they must know we have somebody inside close to Davis."

"Let's make a pact that neither of us will ever divulge her name."

"You have my word. Promise."

"Why do they have to talk with me directly? Why can't they just go through you?"

"I did suggest that, knowing how you would react to this, but they insisted they need to make contact with you personally. They want a direct channel between you and Union Command."

"How will they contact me?" Elizabeth was still fuming.

"One of the prisoners, Harry Catlin, is a Yankee scout. He now works for General Butler. He will meet with you and propose a plan for future communications."

"Any direct line of communication could more easily be intercepted."

"I was told he will brief you on using coded messages so others would not be able to decipher it."

"I am not comfortable with this," Elizabeth firmly stated.

"We have precious little time. Harry Catlin is right now back in Richmond. Sent by General Butler to meet with you. Please Elizabeth, at least hear him out."

"When does he want to see me and where?"

A couple women carrying shopping bags filled with market goods strolled by.

"When was the last time you had someone clean your beautiful cast iron cooking stove? Never too soon to recheck the dampers, air flow, clean and adjust the flue and burners. He can come to your home on Monday." After the women had passed Ruth added, "I'm told Catlin could actually do all this if he had to as part of his cover."

"Tell him early afternoon would be best. My mother has a luncheon event, and my brother will be working. I don't think either of them would be very pleased by this latest development."

Elizabeth reclaimed her satchel from Ruth. As they began to turn and part ways, Ruth reached out to her again, tapping her shoulder.

Speaking again in a low voice, Ruth said, "Oh, and I wanted to let you know, and please get word to Mary as well. Charles Sengstack, the druggist sent to Maryland to create havoc? The one Mary told you about?"

"Yes, I recognize the name."

"Thanks to that information, Colonel Sharpe's men picked him up in Baltimore. Good thing too. They believe his plan was to attack shipyards and railroad bridges with some type of chemical weapon."

"I'm sure Mary will be pleased to hear about the capture of Mr. Sengstack. What will happen now? Will he face trial for treason?"

"He should, but Maryland, even though a Union State, it has a large number of Peace Democrats, as you know. The word is that some politicians are talking about releasing him back to the South provided he doesn't come back."

"Maryland is a hotbed for malcontents. Plenty already there. I do remember the Baltimore riots led by the Copperheads early in the war and Lincoln invoking Martial Law. So close to Washington, as well."

"A slap on the wrist sends the wrong message," Ruth noted.

Elizabeth responded, "I have no doubt that if we were arrested, based on our activities, we would not be facing a slap on the wrist."

"Good day, Miss Van Lew," Ruth said, this time, loudly.

"Good day, Mr. Ruth."

Upon returning to the house, her brother, John Van Lew shared a reprinted article from a New York paper he was reading. The article was about Lincoln when he was confronted by several congressmen, suggesting Grant, the hero of the Vicksburg campaign, was a drunkard and should be replaced. Lincoln asked if they could tell him what brand of whiskey Grant drank. According to the article, the congressmen were perplexed by Lincoln's question. John read aloud the published quotes:

"Why do you ask, Mr. President?"
"Because, if it makes him win victories like this at Vicksburg, I will
send a demijohn of the same kind to every general in the army."

"I take it President Lincoln is not a big believer in temperance," Eliza cracked.

Shortly after, on November 19, 1863, President Abraham Lincoln delivered his 'Little Speech,' as part of the commemoration event at the Gettysburg battlefield, the bloodiest battle of the Civil War. The event was purposely scheduled to take place after some time had passed from when the battle had been fought.

The crowd listened to the famous orator, Edward Everett, for two hours. Everett's speech had been promoted prior to the ceremony as the anticipated highlight of the day. Almost all reports of the ceremony indicated he was underwhelming. Lincoln's "Gettysburg Address" lasted for less than three minutes:

> Four score and seven years ago our fathers brought forth on this continent, a new nation, conceived in Liberty, and dedicated to the proposition that all men are created equal.

> Now we are engaged in a great civil war, testing whether that nation, or any nation so conceived and so dedicated, can long endure. We are met on a great battle-field of that war. We have come to dedicate a portion of that field, as a final resting place for those who here gave their lives that nation might live. It is altogether fitting and proper that we should do this.

> But, in a larger sense, we cannot dedicate—we can not consecrate—we can not hallow—this ground. The brave men, living and dead, who struggled here, have consecrated it, far above our poor power to add or detract. The world will little note, nor long remember what we say here, but it can never forget what they did here. It is for us the living, rather, to be dedicated here to the unfinished work which they who fought here have thus far so nobly advanced. It is rather for us to be here dedicated to the great task remaining before us—that from these honored dead we take increased devotion to that cause for which they gave the last full measure of devotion—that we here highly resolve that these dead shall not have died in vain—that this nation, under God, shall have a new birth of freedom—and that government of the people, by the people, for the people, shall not perish from the earth.

Abraham Lincoln

Chapter 14: Dear Aunt Eliza

Harry Catlin was escorted though the back door by Daniel, carrying assorted wire brushes, a bucket containing a large bottle of what looked like vinegar, other containers, a small shovel, some spare parts and tools, including a knife, a scraping device, and a hammer. He was unshaven, wore a hat low on his forehead, and overalls that were badly worn.

Daniel brought him into the kitchen. "I don't think you are going to need them. Why don't you leave your stuff over in the corner and have a seat? In the meantime, I'll get Miss Van Lew," Daniel added, as he pointed across the table, "Help yourself to the cookies over there. My wife Harriett Anne baked them. Fresh from this morning."

Catlin stood when Elizabeth came into the room. He was an average sized man, stocky build with inquisitive eyes. Elizabeth had the impression this man didn't miss much. Unlike so many of the soldiers she met, Catlin had no facial hair.

"It is a pleasure, Miss Van Lew."

"I didn't expect you'd ever want to come back to Richmond," Elizabeth said.

"I follow orders, ma'am."

Only the two of them remained in the kitchen. Both Daniel and Harriet Anne had cleared out to give them privacy.

"Would you like some tea? Very hard to come by these days. We are down to our very last can."

"Then I should leave it for you and your family. Those cookies are delicious."

"I'll boil some water. We'll both have tea." Elizabeth walked over to the wood burning stove, often kept burning during cold weather as a source of heat. She placed a pot over a lit burner and walked back over to the table where Catlin was sitting. "We actually just had it repaired. Think we are good for a while."

"Well then I won't have to bill you," Catlin responded.

Elizabeth smiled. "I'd pay any price if I could stay incognito."

"We will protect your identity," Miss Van Lew.

Elizabeth then said, "My understanding is that General Butler wants me to send intelligence information directly to his headquarters."

"You and your connections have already been of great service for the Union. He wouldn't request this if he did not think it's even more critical now."

"Let's assume I decide to do this. Send notes back and forth, directly, as General Butler requests. I first would need to be convinced that all the necessary precautions will be in place."

"Of course, ma'am. We believe this will be safer for you."

"I don't see how."

"Right now, you are passing some highly confidential information from one person to another, at least that's what I've been told," Catlin said.

"Correct."

"Not only does it take longer, which could be an issue, depending on the time sensitivity of the information. With several hand-offs along the way, there is more of a chance of something going wrong, and the information never arriving."

"How do you propose we communicate?"

Catlin reached into an inside pocket and pulled out a letter addressed to "Whom it may concern." He handed it to her. "Open it," he said.

Elizabeth opened the letter and put her glasses on. She began reading aloud:

> My Dear Aunt Eliza: I suppose you have been wondering why your nephew has not written before, but we have been uncertain whether we should be able to send a letter. The Yankees steal all the letters that have money in them through flag of truce, so that we would wait until we got a safe chance.

I am glad to write that Mary is a great deal better. Her cough has improved, and the doctor has some hope. Your niece Jenny sends love, and says she wishes you could come north, but I suppose that is impossible. Mother tells me to say that she has given up all hope of meeting you until we all are in heaven.

Yours Affectionately, James AP. Jones

She was perplexed. She placed her glasses on the table as she gazed up at Catlin. He stood and walked over to his pail and pulled out a tiny bottle and a rag.

"This is a special type of acid. Need to be careful. I'll leave this with you. In a pinch you can also use the acidic acid from a lemon, but this works best."

He took back the letter from Elizabeth and laid it out flat on the base of the stove. He poured a small amount of the acid liquid into the rag and rubbed it against the letter.

"Would you mind if I relight your stove?"

"No, please go on."

Elizabeth stood up and took a few steps closer. Catlin held the letter over the lit burner and gently moved it back and forth. He then pulled it away. He turned off the stove and began to blow on the letter to cool it off.

"Would you mind reading it now?" he asked.

Elizabeth took it back with her to the table, retrieving her glasses. "This is extraordinary," she commented as she looked at the letter. "It's completely different." She started reading:

My Dear Miss:

Would you be willing to aid the Union cause by furnishing me with information if I would devise a means. You can write me through Flag of Truce, directed to James AP. Jones, Norfolk, the letter being written as this is, and with the means furnished by the messenger who brings this. I cannot refrain from saying to you, although personally unknown, how much I am rejoiced to hear of the strong feeling for the Union which exists in your breast and among some of the ladies of Richmond. I have the honor to be,

> Very respectfully, your obedient servant

Elizabeth was astonished. She continued to stare at the letter.

Catlin finally broke the silence. "What I just did was remove the part written with standard ink. What you just finished reading, the hidden note from General Butler, was written in invisible ink."

"Fascinating, and of course under Flag of Truce, it would make it possible to send a letter through to Union controlled Norfolk. At least the Confederates still allow us to pass communication through enemy lines, but we know they open anything that looks suspicious."

"We must always assume this," Catlin stated.

"I just pray we can communicate this way without being discovered."

"Miss Van Lew, it is in our mutual interest to do this as carefully as possible. We know that you have successfully placed people where they have access to information that can be very useful to the Union. We have no intention of doing anything that could compromise them, or you."

"Well, I hope you haven't overestimated my abilities, or yours."

"Also, General Butler would like to pay you for your services."

"Pay me? With what? Confederate dollars?"

"We can make arrangements..."

"Please tell General Butler I appreciate the offer, but I do not wish to be financially compensated. All I want is for your army to hurry up and win this war. This has been going on way too long." Elizabeth added, "You need to get back. We can help you, like last time."

"Thank you Miss Van Lew. I came this time on my own, from Fort Monroe, right after seeing General Butler, and I should be fine getting back. I have forged papers to get out of Richmond, and a man who can navigate the river at night. By the way, when you spoke with him, did Sam Ruth share with you his concerns?"

"No, what concerns?"

"Sam recently heard from another contact in the Confederate Administration. Lee has suggested to Confederate officials that he can site numerous examples where he believes Sam Ruth has purposely delayed his trains carrying troops and military supplies between Richmond and Fredericksburg."

"I know Lee has been very critical of Sam Ruth for some time."

"Sam thinks they may have put him under surveillance again, as they have done in the past. As you know, Sam helped me escape north."

"Sam Ruth has helped others, too. He has been a vital link in many of our previous communications. He has shared vital information on things such as Virginia troop strength and movement, as well as reporting on supplies delivered from blockade runners brought to him for rail transport."

"I am aware of that. He needs to be extremely careful, especially right now."

"As far as I know, I'm suspected of being against the secession and displaying poor taste. That is from when I was visiting with Yankee prisoners. I don't believe they suspect me of passing information to the enemy."

"Frankly, neither did Union Command. With all due respect, ma'am, they never suspected it was coming from someone like you."

"You mean a woman?"

"Well, the point is, with Sam Ruth and others who have helped us in past under suspicion, we need your help more than ever."

As new commander in charge of Union forces in the west, Grant immediately ordered his troops to forcibly take the initiative in the Battle for Chattanooga. They first successfully opened a new supply line to feed starving infantry trapped in the city. They had been surrounded by the Confederate troops under the command of General Bragg.

Now, with the knowledge that Bragg had reduced the size of his army, sending troops to support Longstreet in the Knoxville assault, Grant ordered the attack on Confederate positions around Missionary Ridge and Lookout Mountain. A series of poorly conceived orders and tactical mistakes in execution proved costly for the Rebels.

For the Union Army, it became the "Miracle of Missionary Ridge." Northern troops under the command of General George Henry Thomas exceeded their orders for a limited frontal assault. They ended up completely sweeping enemy forces under Bragg from the ridge, forcing a Confederate retreat, and ending the siege of Chattanooga.

This eliminated the most vital rail link from Richmond to the west. Bragg's friend, Jefferson Davis, could no longer defend him. He was relieved of his command.

General Longstreet's Knoxville campaign turned out to be inconsequential.

On December 8, 1863, President Lincoln presented to Congress a "Proclamation of Amnesty and Reconstruction" as a proposed peace offering for Southern States to rejoin the Union. The North had captured and now controlled strategic portions in the South. The recent success in Tennessee offered the potential opportunity to advance through Tennessee to Atlanta. An effective naval blockade for most of the war had helped send the Confederate economy into a tailspin. Now with limited access by rail to the west or to the deep south, rations available for troops and many civilians in the battleground states had to be drastically cut even further. The threat of starvation on a large scale was a stronger possibility.

The Confederate Capital of Richmond had been effectively isolated. The Union controlled the port City of Norfolk, the Peninsula surrounding Fort Monroe, as well as West Virginia. The Army of the Potomac continued to threaten the city from the North. Richmond residents feared that their city could be the next Vicksburg.

Lincoln believed the time was right to test a trial balloon. His peace offering was nicknamed "the Ten Percent Plan." It would require approval by only 10 percent of eligible voters in any of the rebellious states to rejoin the Union. If adopted, it would re-establish federated state governments, offering full pardon and restoration of property to all engaged in the rebellion with the exception of the highest Confederate officials and military leaders. Lincoln made this conditional upon an oath of loyalty, and an agreement to accept the emancipation of slaves.

Lincoln's intention was to further weaken support for the Confederacy and abolish slavery. Radical Republicans, those in favor of repressive measures against the Rebel southern states, thought Lincoln was being far too lenient.

His proclamation to Congress stood in sharp contrast to how Jefferson Davis addressed his Congress the day before. After laboring with several rewrites, Davis had asked his close confidante, Judah Benjamin to weigh in. Benjamin indicated it might be perceived as too negative, but in the end Davis ignored his suggestions to tone it down throughout most of his speech. He decided he would be honest and direct.

Davis openly discussed the recent military reverses, the weakened economy, and the failure in foreign affairs to solicit additional help. He talked about the "barbarous policy" and "savage ferocity which still marks the conduct of the enemy," whom he claimed were "hardened by crime." He went on to say the Union refused to listen to peace proposals, and failed to recognize the "impassable gulf that divides us."

He also detailed the many economic challenges, poor conditions and setbacks in the war, and went on to castigate the enemy for its conduct; including the use of incendiary weapons used in Charleston.

With his voice booming, Davis concluded his congressional message with the following:

> The patriotism of the people has proved equal to every sacrifice demanded by their country's need. We have been united as a people never were united under like circumstances before. God has blessed us with success disproportionate to our means, and under his divine favor our labors must at last be crowned with the reward due to men who have given all they possessed to the righteous defense of their inalienable rights, their homes, and their altars.

Ending by complimenting the citizens of the Confederacy, and encouraging them to carry on despite all the hardship, did little to change the prevailing mood. This had been a very bad year and most were well aware it could get worse.

Any hope of a peaceful restoration based on Lincoln's terms was clearly inconceivable to Davis. On the same day Lincoln presented his proclamation to Congress, one Confederate Senator, and long-time enemy of Jefferson Davis, Henry S. Foote, severely criticized the military and civilian policies of the Confederate President. He believed the war was doomed and that the Confederacy should negotiate a settlement. If other congressional leaders harbored similar views, they kept it to themselves.

A hard freeze set in to Richmond, just before Christmas, 1863. A cover of fresh white snow helped to disguise the overall shabbiness and deterioration of the city, now three years into supporting a war most mistakenly thought at the onset would be over quickly. Ice covered the James, and a bitter wind from the west made it feel colder making the already harsh conditions for prisoners, especially those in the outdoor Belle Island prison, even more intolerable. Further north, Robert E. Lee's Army of Northern Virginia had settled in to winter camp near the banks of the Rappahannock River.

Lee left his troops for Richmond days before Christmas to confer with Davis. Most conversation was outside the Executive Mansion. There was a brief meeting at the Davis residence.

As they sipped whiskey in the parlor, before withdrawing behind closed doors, Mary heard Lee say that he concurred with Davis' choice of Joe Johnston to replace Bragg. He was less enthusiastic about Davis contemplating an operational military advisor to the President role instead for his old friend Braxton Bragg.

She heard Lee tell Davis, "I have no issues with Braxton, but I'm afraid my peers would not take kindly to this type of influential role. Particularly after Chattanooga."

Most of the ensuing conversation on military tactics, was done behind closed doors. Mary had no available way to listen in.

"I'll give it some more thought," Davis responded.

Mary made a mental note on this and would pass it on.

With Christmas a week away, shopkeepers decorated their windows more dramatically than the past few years. Families took Confederate soldiers from distant places into their homes for holiday leave. Baked goods were distributed, and Christmas carols were sung in the Confederate military hospital. General Winder made an exception and allowed Elizabeth and Harriett Anne to provide eggnog to Union prisoners.

The Van Lew's received an invitation to join John Minor Botts with his family for a dinner party a few days before Christmas. They enthusiastically accepted, despite the long trip to get to Culpeper and the anticipated on-going stretch of inclement weather. They were also invited to stay the night. As John said, "Probably would do all of us some good to get away from Richmond."

The Van Lew's took the Richmond to Fredericksburg train, operated by Elizabeth's friend and fellow "conspirator," Sam Ruth. John Botts arranged for a carriage to take them from Fredericksburg to his plantation house in Culpeper. Luckily, the carriage was supplied with plenty of blankets.

They were greeted warmly at the door by the accomplished statesman. Servants carried their things to the designated guest rooms for each of the Van Lew's. After exchanging pleasantries, Botts led them through the house and upstairs where they could freshen up after the long journey.

"We have a lot more available space than we ever had in our previous home," Botts noted.

The three Van Lew's agreed to meet in a few minutes at the top of the stairs, so they could join the party together. John also wanted to help his mother who was less sure of her footing in unfamiliar surroundings.

They could hear Botts booming voice and the sound of laughter as they left their respective rooms. The Van Lew's entered the large downstairs room where other guests were gathered. Mary Botts stepped forward to welcome them as they entered the room.

At least half the guests were Unionists. John Botts, his wife and two daughters most certainly were. Sam Ruth was there, as was Mr. and Mrs. William Rowley, and the Palmers. Charles Palmer, like Botts, had been imprisoned as a suspected ringleader of an assumed group looking to overthrow the Confederacy. He had been released the previous year with not a shred of evidence obtained. He still looked frail from his time in prison. The other guests were mostly neighbors. John whispered to his sister that one of the neighbors had a son who was a Confederate officer in the Army of Northern Virginia.

Greetings were exchanged. A house slave served apple cider with a touch of bourbon. John Botts made a few brief comments about the long tradition of celebrating Christmas in the Botts household, and the importance of gathering with family and friends. Botts proposed a toast to the ending of hostilities, and a returning to normality in Virginia. Several children from the area, as well as the Botts grandchildren entered the room. They gathered together near the front archway and sang Christmas Carols before bowing to enthusiastic applause. They departed immediately.

Elizabeth had noticed that the room around her was decorated meticulously with garland and holly on the window frames and mantels. After speaking with several of the guests, including some of the local guests she did not know, Elizabeth walked over to admire the Christmas tree, elevated on a corner table, filled with gingerbread men, golden apples and crocheted ornaments shaped as snowflakes. She didn't notice John Botts come up behind her.

"The grandchildren helped make some of the ornaments and also with decorating the tree," he said.

"Very lovely," Elizabeth responded.

"I'm so glad you came. Looking forward to having a talk later."

Dinner, given the shortage of food as a result of strict rationing provisions, was unexpectedly bountiful. The table was filled with boiled ham, roasted geese and partridge, apple sauce, beets, potatoes, and winter squash. Sherry and Madeira wine were poured. For dessert, they were served cornmeal pudding and pecan pie.

"Another advantage to living away from the city," Botts said.

"Yes, thank God for this meal," Mary Botts added, "We are so thankful to have all of you here with us."

Glasses were raised once again.

"Merry Christmas."

"Merry Christmas."

There was little talk about the war or its consequences. It was obvious to Elizabeth from a few of the conversations and a couple brief comments before and during dinner that most of the neighbors supported the Confederacy. Any pro-Unionist views or argumentative positions she or the others at the table might have had, including Botts, were not shared.

The party moved to the parlor. Botts oldest daughter played a few popular tunes on the family piano and the others sang along. Sam Ruth was the first to leave. He had urgent business in Fredericksburg early the next day. The Palmers left with him. All of the neighbors lived close by. They were gone by early evening. Only the Rowley's and Van Lew's would stay overnight at the Botts' home.

Assuming the men wanted to move to the study to drink and smoke alone, the ladies decided to withdraw to a separate room to play cards. The men stood as the women began to leave.

"Elizabeth, would you mind staying with us for a few more minutes?" John Botts politely asked."

"Not at all."

The other ladies smiled. They all knew Elizabeth very well and were not the least bit surprised. Their full-length gowns swiveled as they turned and left.

In the study, Botts closed the door and poured a glass of port wine for Rowley and himself. Elizabeth declined his offer. She sat in a red tufted baroque style chair that rose up behind her like a throne. The two men settled into leather backed walnut desk chairs across from her.

Botts began. "I am sorry Sam couldn't stay, but he does know all this. Told him earlier when he first arrived. I got together with Professor McCulloh last week. The man who quit his post at Colombia to move to Richmond."

"Oh, yes, the man you recommended to President Davis," Elizabeth said.

"Knowing you Bet, I'm sure you'll never let me forget. We were supposed to meet before that, but he cancelled twice. What he told me was very disturbing."

"How so?" Rowley asked.

"He is working as a consultant at the Nitre and Mining Bureau. Mostly what they do there is making gun powder and land mines. McCulloh is testing materials for building new, more powerful explosive weapons."

"Nothing to do with fertilizer as you initially thought," Elizabeth noted.

"Absolutely not. He said he was working on things, and I quote, 'it will bring the Union to its knees.'"

"God help us," Rowley mumbled under his breath. "John, how in the world did you ever get him to admit to this?"

"I served him a few glasses of whiskey. I also made him think I was a staunch supporter of the Confederate States. Recently coming back South, he had no idea about my pro-Unionist speeches in the past, or that I was jailed."

"He probably does now. I'm sure he must have told someone he met with you," Rowley said.

"Perhaps, but I am now considered a model Confederate citizen since I was released, and that comes from friends inside the government."

"What else did he say?" Elizabeth inquired.

"The good news is that McCulloh confided that several recent shipments of needed materials never arrived. He expressed real concern that they don't have access to all they need. He said recent Union attacks have disrupted freight by rail and it is impacting his research."

"A real shame," Rowley sarcastically commented.

"He also told me that his research includes experimenting with cats. He said he has lots of strays to use, but needs more of the chemical compounds to conduct his experiments. In meantime, he has to keep feeding and taking care of all these 'damn cats,' he said."

"How awful," Elizabeth commented, sarcastically. "Did he say what compounds he needed?"

"Yes, he specifically mentioned saltpeter, sulphur and phosphorous. He gripped about one other thing too. He confided that he needs more help. I told him that I might know of someone. I told him I have a nephew who was a chemist who used to work at the Richmond Arsenal. What I didn't tell him is that he is also a Unionist and quit after Virginia seceded."

"What's his name?" Rowley asked.

"Mark Rivers."

Neither Rowley nor Elizabeth knew of him.

Botts continued. "I've already talked with Mark and he is willing to go in and report back on things. Maybe he can help slow down the research."

"He would do this?" Rowley asked. "Must be a brave young man."

"He is. Has the right motivation, too. Not only was my nephew upset with what they did to me. Imprisonment and defaming my reputation. His younger brother was forced to fight for the Confederacy. He was killed in the second battle at Manassas. Mark wants to do this."

Elizabeth was delighted when Wayne Evans brought a shipment she had ordered through his store to the house. The package came from New England and she wasn't sure it would arrive before Christmas. Most deliveries crossing into the Confederacy were checked.

After they embraced at the door, she asked Wayne to carry it to the library. Closing the door behind her, she asked for his help opening the package. Wayne pulled a pocket knife from his jacket and carefully went to work cutting through the paperboard box. It was filled with embroidered woolen blankets and overcoats.

"One for each of our servants. As no one seems to expect this unusual cold spell to break anytime soon, these coats will come in handy," Elizabeth explained. "I had no idea when I ordered them we were in for this kind of winter."

"I'm just glad they made it through. You can tell it was opened. Guess they decided it was alright. We were lucky this time. I can assure you, it really is hit and miss when I try to do this for other customers. Things ordered from up north often go missing."

"Can't thank you enough Wayne. Looks so much nicer than in the advertisement I read in the newspaper."

As Elizabeth held up a few items, Wayne agreed the items were of a superior quality. She wrapped them back in the package and asked Wayne to place them behind a corner chair.

"Just for now," she said. "Would you like some eggnog?" Elizabeth asked, as she walked over and opened the library door.

"No thank you Elizabeth, I really must get back to the store. As I'm sure you can understand, this is one of the busiest times of the year for me. But before I go, my visit has a dual purpose, in addition to seeing you. I have some important information to share. Mary came into the store, just before I closed yesterday."

Shutting the door again, she retook her seat. "Is everything alright?"

"Yes, Mary is fine," Wayne responded, trying his best to hide any of his personal feelings about her precarious and potentially perilous position. Elizabeth, he realized, worried enough. No need to add to her concern.

Elizabeth's sighed, yet her look of distress betrayed her true feelings.

Wayne continued. "I will try to tell you this the way Mary told me. Before she came to the store, she never had a chance to be alone and write it down. Mary overheard a conversation between Davis and his wife. Quite a heated discussion, she said. Jefferson Davis wanted his wife to tell him where she heard a piece of confidential information. Mrs. Davis would only say it came from the wife of one of the legislators."

"Did either of them indicate what it was about?"

"Not immediately. Mary said Davis was angry. He told her only a small group of his cabinet members and a handful of congressman knew. Then it is true, Mrs. Davis asserted. This made Davis angrier, she said. He insisted they were all told it was highly confidential and not to tell anyone else, not even family members."

"Did Varina indicate who she had heard it from?"

"Mary said no, at least not while she was able to listen. According to Mary, Davis kept asking, but his wife wouldn't answer. Instead she insisted on knowing if what she heard was true."

"There are rumors their marriage has been difficult at times. Two strong willed people who don't always see eye to eye," Elizabeth noted.

Wayne related more of what Mary had told him. "She indicated Jefferson Davis got quiet for a while, before saying it had become evident to him and other Confederate leaders, after the devastating losses at Gettysburg and Vicksburg, the South could not hope to win a conventional war against the North. He added this group he had confided in believed they could win an unconventional war."

"Extremely disturbing, where all this seems to be heading," Elizabeth commented.

Wayne shook his head, agreeing. "At that point, Mary noted that Varina kept badgering him on what he meant by unconventional. She suggested it might be best to just give up. Davis became belligerent again. Yelled that he never would give up the fight."

"Is that it?"

"No. Davis finally did open up a little more to his wife. He told her that they were thinking of mounting a series of guerilla warfare campaigns, not to replace but to augment traditional military combat. His armies were undermanned and under supplied, as compared to the enemy. Davis tried to explain to his wife that this is what the colonists did against the British in the Revolutionary War."

"They keep trying to make this comparison which totally misses the mark. Absurd to compare what they are doing to the founding of our Nation. How did Varina respond?" Elizabeth commented, as she leaned more forward on her seat.

"Mary said that Jefferson Davis tried to explain that by conducting a series of surprise attacks across enemy lines they could break the will of the North to fight. Mrs. Davis asked if this would be directed at both military and civilian targets."

"Varina is very perceptive. She also has family on the other side."

"Well, Davis answered the primary targets would be military. He then went on to say that in war, civilian causalities are often an unintended consequence. This was one of the inescapable tragedies of war, he asserted. Mary told me that at that point it sounded like Mrs. Davis was getting up to leave. She heard nothing further."

"We already know, thanks to information from Mary, they were able to pick up a man they called the pharmacist in Maryland. He was looking to destroy property and was funded by the Confederate government. We also know they are working on some type of secret weapon at the Nitre Mining Bureau."

"God help us," Wayne exclaimed. "Something else Mary wanted me to pass on. She wasn't the only servant listening in on the conversation between Jefferson and Varina Davis. I guess you could say at least it wasn't only her. May, the head housekeeper, spotted Mary and the two other servants close by to the room where the Davis couple were arguing."

"How unfortunate. Mary has indicated before that she thinks May is suspicious of her," Elizabeth noted.

"She told me this as well. May went on to say if she catches anyone of them doing something like this again, she will tell the President and they will be sold off on the spot. She said they could end up picking cotton in the Deep South."

"Mary will have to be even more careful now."

Elizabeth walked Wayne to the door. They extended Christmas greetings and said goodbye. Wayne leaned awkwardly over and gave Elizabeth a peck on the cheek.

"Hope to see you soon again," Elizabeth called out at, as Wayne departed.

"I'll send your warm regards to our mutual friend. Next time I see her," he replied back.

Chapter 15: Killing Cats with Lethal Gas

U.S. military command had been made well aware of the deplorable conditions captured soldiers had to endure in Richmond's Confederate prisons. They heard it directly from escaped prisoners. Northern newspapers also reported on the many alleged abuses. Political pressure was mounting on Lincoln to do something.

General Benjamin Butler summoned Colonel George Sharpe.

"I just received some disturbing news from Aunt Eliza Jones on the latest Flag of Truce boat," Butler stated. "The Rebels are planning to move our men in Richmond prisons further South, farther from the battlefield."

"Where they think they will be more secure, no doubt," Sharpe noted, "avoid more embarrassing escapes, like Harry Catlin."

"Moving further South would make any large-scale effort to rescue them exceedingly more difficult," Butler added. "In the same letter, Miss Van Lew also provides additional information from the source she calls 'Quaker.'"

"We believe he works in the Adjutant General's Department in Richmond. Van Lew has developed an impressive group of agents with access to very valuable, sensitive information. Truly remarkable, sir."

"Here is what the note says." Butler read aloud:

From Quaker: No attempt should be made with less than 30,000 cavalry, from 10,000 to 15,000 infantries to support them, amounting in all to 40,000 to 45,000 troops. Do not underrate their strength and desperation. Forces could probably be called into action in from 5 to 10 days 25,000, most(sic) artillery. Hoke's and Kemper's brigades gone to North Carolina; Pickett's in or about Petersburg. Three regiments of cavalry disbanded by

General Lee for want of horses. Morgan is applying for 1,000 choice men for a raid.

Butler asked Sharpe, "Do you think we can trust this? Miss Van Lew has been reliable so far, but we have no idea who this 'Quaker' is…"

"Always a concern, General, but my instinct tells me it's reliable intelligence. Van Lew hasn't let us down yet."

"I concur, Colonel. I'm going to send this on to Army Headquarters and recommend that we move quickly on this."

"They may frown on doing something quickly, General, given our armies are in winter camp and the weather has been unusually bad this year."

"Yes, however, as part of my request I will tell them if we wait, our Union prisoners will no longer be in reach. I'll suggest I would like to have approval to attack as soon as there is a bit of a break in the weather. The Confederates will not expect it."

Sub-zero weather in early 1864 had brought most military operations on both sides to a halt. The extreme conditions also impacted citizens of Richmond. When there was finally a break in the frigid cold streak, Elizabeth went into town to do some shopping.

She stopped by to see Thomas McNiven at his bakery shop. No one else was in the store.

"Miss Van Lew, I am very glad to see you."

After a brief exchange on how the declining economy was impacting everyone, and especially local merchants like McNiven, he asked about Mary.

"I'm glad we found a safer way for her to provide sensitive information. Way too dangerous for her to try talking with me. Too many people watchin.'"

Elizabeth shared with him what she had learned about the Confederates moving prisoners to Georgia.

"I heard this as well," McNiven said. "Things keep getting worse for those poor boys. They were already overcrowded in Libby Prison. Now that they've added the captured soldiers from the fighting in Tennessee, I hear their practically crammed on top of each other. Still, moving further South.

Can't believe any of them want to be loaded up in cattle cars and sent further south."

"This would make any effort to escape back North much more difficult."

"Miss Van Lew, do you remember Frederick Lohmann?"

"Sure do," Elizabeth responded.

"Well, he and his brothers are still deliverin' food for Confederate troops. They also continue to exploit their access to help Confederate deserters and runaway slaves escape. Rarely are they pulled over for a spot check."

"Yes, Daniel had shared with me some of their exploits helping both runaways and Rebel deserters."

"Well, Frederick told me a week or so ago that he was asked to deliver several cases of turpentine received from North Carolina to that place we've been wondering about..."

"You mean the Nitre Mining Bureau?"

"Yes ma'am. Not sure why turpentine, but that's beside the point. Frederick said that while he was waiting for someone to sign off on his delivery he heard a few men talking near the loading dock, while having a smoke. Frederick figured they smoked outside, given all the combustible chemicals they work with there. He thinks they were scientists the way they dressed and spoke. Three or four of them."

"Did you know John Botts has a nephew who works there?"

"Yes, William Rowley told me, but Frederick didn't know. Not sure if he was one of these men, either."

"Not much you don't know, Mr. McNiven."

He smiled. "Don't worry, I only share what I know with people I know can be trusted."

"What did he hear?"

"Frederick said this one man, who was feeble looking, was really upset. He said all the cats got out of their cage the night before, and that it would take days to find any of the ones still left in the building."

"John Botts' nephew mentioned they were conducting experiments with cats."

"What kind of sick people are these? Well, as I was saying, according to Frederick, the man said he wanted to know who was last in the cage. Somebody said it might have been one of the slaves who fed them."

"Always blaming the poor slaves," Elizabeth commented.

"Then supposedly, another man, younger looking, said that the cage had a barrel bolt lock. He said he had heard of cats tinkering with locks over and over until eventually one of their paws slid it up and over and they got out. This made the older man even more upset. 'Somebody did this on purpose' he said, 'I'm going to find out who.'"

"Is that it?"

"Frederick told me these men he thinks were scientists eventually put out their smokes and left. Shortly after the facility manager came along to sign off on his delivery. He asked him about the cats. The manager thought most got out of the building. Frederick asked him what kind of experiment they were planning. Something to do with lethal gas, he was told."

"A lethal gas. This is diabolical. Those poor cats. I hate to think what else they have in store."

"The facility manager went on and on, according to Frederick, how much he disliked this new scientist running the experiment. Well, I won't say the word he used, but it was not kind. He told Frederick he was demanding that this facility manager drop everything else, get his workers together, and get him more cats right away. He said he didn't care if they had to chase them down in alleys or steal them away from backyards."

"Did he mention the name of this head scientist?"

"Just that he was a professor from New York City."

General Benjamin Butler began his appeal to Edwin Stanton, United States Secretary of War, with an aggressive request. The primary purpose was to rescue Union prisoners in Richmond before they were moved. He went on to argue that the released prisoners could augment his troops in an assault against the Confederate leadership and potentially the capture of Jefferson Davis and his cabinet.

Stanton, like Lincoln and other senior officials in the Federal government, was well aware of the horrible conditions Union prisoners faced and his inclination was to support the mission. He and other members of the Lincoln administration were appalled by reports and first-hand accounts from escapees. With 1864 a Presidential election year, they were also sensitive to the political implications. Many believed the prolonged war with weakening public support would ensure Lincoln's defeat at the ballot box later that year.

Ongoing stories in the press on the hardship of prisoners in Richmond didn't help. The *New York Herald* helped lead the charge. This was printed in late 1863:

> The suffering of the unhappy prisoners are set forth in most painful terms by the reports of the surgeons released from Libby prison. The mortality in the hospitals amounts to 50 a day, and the food supply to the sick is wholly inadequate and unfit for the patients.

A subsequent article in the same newspaper noted that General Butler had reported that the Rebels were no longer accepting supplies from the North for Union prisoners. They saw it as "an imputation on their honor." There was also this from another *New York Herald* edition:

> But if the Rebels are too poor to feed their prisoners, or give them shelter, they know that an honest confession of this inability to any Union officer, with an intimation that supplies will be accepted from Washington, would instantly be answered by a shipload. The failure of the enemy to adopt this course fully justifies the conclusion that they have deliberately adopted the policy of starving their Union prisoners of war to death.

The editorial staff weighed in, and may have telegraphed Union plans: "They should not be permitted to perish," and they "must be rescued by forces of arms."

Whether Stanton, like Butler, truly believed these men who had endured so much, many who were obviously suffering in terrible health and close to starvation, could augment an attack on Richmond in their present condition was unclear. Capturing the Confederate President and Cabinet must have seemed equally far-fetched. In any case, Stanton approved the request.

The approval received to conduct the raid called for 6,000 men to execute the mission. This was considerably less than the 40,000-45,000 of combined infantry and cavalry in the secret letter Butler received from Elizabeth Van Lew. In any case, plans were drawn up to proceed. General Isaac Wistar was assigned by Butler to execute the mission.

Assuming it would work to his advantage and potentially compensate for a smaller attacking unit, Butler had received a scouting report indicating that Rebel forces protecting Richmond had been recently stripped to provide reinforcement to Confederate defensive operations in North Carolina.

In addition, Union command had also received intelligence reports that the Bottoms Bridge crossing of the Chickahominy River, 13 miles northwest from Richmond, had a small number of posted guards. As a diversionary tactic to throw the enemy off, units from the Army of the Potomac crossed the Rappahannock, sixty miles east of Richmond, as if the plan was to attack Lee.

Wistar's cavalry leading the charge were hit with unexpected heavy fire as they approached Bottoms Bridge in early February, 1864. Four batteries of Confederate artillery and three infantry regiments had been deployed to protect the crossing. They were already in place before the Yankee horsemen arrived. The bridge had been destroyed and they easily repulsed the advance from their defensive positions behind felled trees and rifle pits along the banks of the river. Wistar's entire regiment was forced to retreat.

Shortly after, General Butler received a copy of the *Richmond Examiner* arriving at Fort Monroe via a Flag of Truce boat. An article he read indicated that the Confederates had been tipped off in advance. A Union soldier being held after killing his commanding officer had been caught attempting to get away after the murder. He was tried and confined to prison, where he managed to escape. Crossing enemy lines, the convicted Union soldier disclosed the plan for the surprise attack to the enemy.

When the news of the failed rescue attempt reached Elizabeth, she was devastated. It seemed to her that the Union continued to blunder and was consistently outplayed by the Confederates in its numerous efforts to attack Richmond.

Only a few days after General Wistar's failed rescue attempt, Daniel asked to see Elizabeth in private. They met after breakfast in her favorite room, the family library. They sat across from each other in front of the wall with built-in walnut shelves covered with books her father began collecting from when he and Elizabeth's mother first moved into the Church Hill mansion.

"You've heightened my curiosity, Daniel. What is it?"

"Miss Van Lew, we still have a chance to help, at least some of those Union prisoners, escape from Libby."

"I wish we could help all of them, as you know so well, Daniel. Helping one of two at a time has always been a challenge. What makes you say we could help *some*?"

"There's plan for a prison break. I was told the ringleaders don't want to get shipped out to Andersonville, Georgia. They're workin' hard to finish faster. Ever since they heard the bad news."

"How are they planning to do it?"

"There been attempts before to dig tunnels, but the guards always found them. The diggers were severely punished. They're diggin' a new one and think this time it just might work. Nobody payin' as much attention, and they think no one suspects anything. Guessin' they might be focused more on shuttin' the place down."

"Do you know when they are planning to escape?"

"I don't, Miss Van Lew. Not exactly, but I have been told they are close. Tunnel now goes out under the prison property, out towards Canal Street."

"Incredible. They must have been working undetected on this for some time. Any idea how many are planning to escape?"

"Don't know, but there is a way we can find out. Remember Walter, the slave who works in the prison?"

"Sure I do. I met Walter several times back when they were still allowing me to visit."

"He wants to meet with us, but he wants us to meet him at his place. Not in public. Not here. I tried to convince him to meet just with me, but he insists on you comin' too."

"That's perfectly fine."

"But, here's the thing. Walter's lives in that real bad Birch Alley neighborhood in Shockoe Bottom."

"Happy to go, and I'm not worried, I'll have you with me."

"Yes, but Miss Van Lew. You'd be noticed there. It's where mostly slaves workin' factories, hospital and prisons stay. Some free negroes, too. Not the kind of place you often see ladies like you. Don't know why he's askin' for you to come too..."

"I have heard it is a terrible place to live. Someone once told me the poor people who live there are close enough to hear the slave auctions. Awful. I'm going with you, Daniel."

"Afraid you'd say that. I'd like to suggest you wear some kind of disguise. So you don't stand out. Harriett Anne just might have some old clothes you could use."

Walter's slave owner used to run one of the old tobacco factories in downtown Richmond. The government paid him for Walter's services in the prison. Part of that payment covered Walter's room in a broken-down boarding house, also owned by his slave master.

The entire neighborhood was badly run down. Rickety wood frame buildings were dangerously adjoined, making the entire street a serious fire hazard. Walking down the street required maneuvering around piles of garbage. There was no regular removal in this section of town. Only the unusually cold winter with gusts of northeasterly winds from the direction of the river kept the stench at bay.

Elizabeth and Daniel crossed the street to the boarding house where Walter slept most nights – the nights he was not asked to work or bunk at the prison. Elizabeth was wearing a shawl covering most of her head, and an old woolen overcoat. The coat was slightly ripped at the center back seam. Also, it had a few visible moth holes, and plenty of loose threads. She walked arm in arm with Daniel.

"Even I don't recognize you," Daniel joked.

"I'm glad she never threw it out, but why did Harriett Anne hold on to this? We gave her a new coat."

"She's very sentimental. Belonged to her momma."

Walter greeted them at the entrance. He invited them in, looking both ways down the hall before shutting and locking it behind them.

His home was one tiny room, shaped in a symmetric square. The room was sparsely furnished with a crude boxed bed, a wooden table and four broken down chairs, none of which matched. There was no place to cook and no wardrobe for clothing. Walter had an open suitcase in one corner of the room that served as his closet, and a bucket close by that he must have used as a sink.

After exchanging greetings, Walter explained why he requested the meeting in his place.

"There gonna be a prison escape and we need your help."

"So I've heard, when? How many prisoners?" Elizabeth asked.

"Next couple weeks, we think, ma'am. Don't know how many. Best guess is 10 to 15. Mr. Ross wanted me to talk directly with you, Miss Van Lew, 'cause he knows you and trusts you. I know I can trust Daniel to tell you, but Mr. Ross made me promise. Would have done it himself, but he knows he is being watched."

"I understand," Elizabeth assured him.

Daniel spoke next. "But why meet at your place?"

"I thought and thought where I could meet up with Miss Van Lew. I don't want to draw suspicion on me or you folks, either. I would be noticed goin' up to Church Hill, and I'd be doin' it without a pass. Just figured nobody watchin' this area very closely. I knew I could count on Daniel to come too. Show you the way."

Elizabeth had kept her coat on and was shivering from the cold inside the flat. She jolted back, her chair snapping back against the wall when she saw a rat run across the edge of the far side wall.

"They more scared of you than you are of them," Walter noted. "Sorry ma'am, you get used to it living here."

Changing the subject, Daniel requested, "Tell us what you can about the planned escape."

"At first there was two, then four. Workin' nights diggin' in the basement out to the street. In a section of the prison they closed down. They been usin' an old fireplace chute on the other side of the kitchen, not in use, to slide down to the basement."

"Not in use" Daniel repeated.

"Yeah. They already started moving prisoners out. Don't need as many for cookin' no more. Anyways, the opening in the fireplace wasn't big enough to fit through, but two of the men who were home builders snuck out of the holding room, workin' nights. Opened up the back using a kitchen knife and chisel. When they placed the bricks back when done, can't tell nothin'."

"Necessity, the mother of invention," Elizabeth commented. Both she and Daniel were intrigued by Walter's account of the ingenious effort behind this planned break out attempt.

"Rose nicknamed the two men 'Brick and Mortar'. They worked every night carefully takin' out bricks. One at a time to open up the first-floor fireplace not in use. It was behind a couple big kitchen stoves no longer in use, and a storage area that gave them some cover so as the guards wouldn't spot them when walkin' by, doin' their rounds."

Daniel spoke next. "That gets them access to slide down the chute to the basement, but how do they get back up?"

"They have a knotted rope I got 'em to climb back out. Also helped them steal tools for diggin' from the carpenter shop. Snuck some others in from outside. Also got them towels so they could remove the soot before goin' back to their prison rooms. Lots of candles, too. The further out that tunnel goes, the less air for candles, or breathing either. Even with one man as part of a team fanning air in."

"How much more they have to dig?" Daniel asked.

"I been told, last time I checked, 'bout 5 to 10 feet from Canal Street."

Elizabeth asked next. "Do you think, a few more weeks?"

Walter replied. "Yes ma'am. They were workin' only nights. Takin' too long. Decided to do in shifts. Figure gotta dig about one-hundred feet to get out of the prison grounds."

Daniel bared an incredulous grin. "That's a long way. How do they get away with workin' during the day? Don't the guards notice them missin?"

"Mr. Ross takin' care of that. He goes room to room doin' roll calls. I've watched it. After their names called out, a few of the men already marked present circle around and sneak into the back of the line and shout out when the other digger names are called. In one of the room, they dug a secret passage to another room. Behind a storage bin where they keep extra blankets. In this way they can cover for men in the adjoining room, too."

"I know Erasmus didn't want the prisoners to know he was on their side, helping some escape when he could. Guess they know now."

"Well, ma'am. That's the funny thing 'bout it. I been helpin' Mr. Ross for a while. He told me, better for the prisoners to think he is a bastard, oh, 'cuse me ma'am. He asked me not to say nothin' neither. I've been there when Mr. Ross does it. The prisoners just think he don't know what they doin', but he sure do."

"They don't realize he knows about the escape plan?" Elizabeth asked.

"No ma'am. He don't let on. Mr. Ross don't only hear about it from me, either. Colonel Hobart keeps him abreast. So does a free negro prisoner named Ford. The others don't know any of these other men be talkin'."

"You think a couple weeks, right?" Elizabeth asked.

"No one really sure," Walter said. "Been lots of setbacks. One day part of wall collapsed. Huge 'bang'. Lucky no one hurt. Guards heard it. Thought it was caused by workman doin' repairs day before, but for lot of reasons Guards doin' spot checks more often these days."

Daniel looked puzzled. "Don't the guards check the basement too? Wouldn't they find the dirt from the dig someplace?"

"As I said, that part of the prison is closed off, locked up. The guards don't like to go in there. Call it 'Rat Hell'. Lots bigger than the one you just saw, Miss Van Lew, but they do check it now and then. The floor is covered with straw. So far none of them guards noticed the dirt they been smoothin' out underneath."

"We can certainly help once they get out of the prison," Elizabeth said...

Before she could continue a smiling Walter interrupted. "Mr. Ross said you would."

"Knowing the planned date is very important," she quickly added.

Daniel weighed in, "So is getting as close an estimate as we can of the number of prisoners so we can arrange safe houses for the first leg of getting them back across enemy lines. Sounds like we will need four of five places and maybe a few more, just in case we run into any problems."

"All of this will require careful coordination," Elizabeth pointed out.

"Yes ma'am. Somethin' else where I can use both your help," Walter stated. "There's a tobacco shed on the other side of the wall between Libby Prison and Canal Street. If they come out where supposed to, they will be right behind it where can't be seen."

"Outside the prison lot?" Daniel asked.

"Yes, but property owned and used by the prison. Part of my job is to leave new prisoners things that belong to them but can't keep with 'em. Even though I lock it, guards break in all the time and steal anything worth somethin'."

"Not surprising, I'm afraid," Elizabeth commented.

"Can you get me a bunch of civilian clothes, coats, hats, pants. Different sizes? I can leave 'em inside the shed in a big storage box where we put extra clothes and things. None of them guards bothers with it and I can add more things there for them to put on to blend more in with town people..."

"We can take care of that," Elizabeth responded immediately.

Daniel nodded, "I can get them to you." He then inquired, "But how will you let us know when we can expect it to happen?"

"As well as the expected number," Elizabeth added.

"For the clothes, yes Daniel, bring them to me, here. The sooner the better. The problem is that it is more than likely I won't have enough time to get out and back once they decide to go without being noticed. Better for me to be on inside as they get close. They'll need my help."

Elizabeth and Daniel both looked perplexed. Daniel spoke first. "If not you, who will let us know?"

"The free negro I mentioned before? Name is Robert Ford. Was workin' as a teamster for the Union when captured. He takes care of the warden's personal things. Also his horse. Gives him more freedom than the others. Both in prison and running errands for the warden in town."

"I've seen him once or twice," Daniel said.

Walter continued. "Also passes what he hears back to Mr. Ross. That's one reason Mr. Ross tryin' to be so careful. Ford told him they gettin' suspicious of him. Mr. Ross wanted me to tell you that Ford will be the one who can let you know when and how many. Just got to work out who he should contact. As Mr. Ross said, somebody who can be trusted and somebody nobody would ever guess would be up to doin' somethin' like this."

"I can take care of that," Daniel suggested. "He often stops at a local grain store on Valley Road. The people who run it can be trusted. The owner has helped the Underground in the past, hiding runaways back in his stalls."

"Speaking of the Underground," Elizabeth noted, "We will then need to get word to the prisoners, not only where to go, but what to look for." Looking at Daniel, Elizabeth added, "Maybe the way you have used quilts as a signal for runaway slaves?"

Daniel nodded.

Walter spoke next. "Once you let me know, which safe houses we can use, Daniel, I can get word to the diggers."

As they left, Elizabeth turned to Daniel and asked, "What is Walter's last name? Assuming he has one. I know in the past many slaves weren't given surnames."

"No last name. You are right, Miss Van Lew, some slaves never got one. Less common these days. As our numbers grew, last names became more common, so slave owners could keep track. Imagine when the slave owner on the plantation calls out a first name and 10 slaves come 'round. That's when they started givin' many of us last names."

"Is that how you got yours? Gates?"

"No. If slaves were not given one, some made it up, like my papa did. He was a doorman, too. In Lynchburg."

"How come Walter never made one up?"

"I asked him about that once. He said he would take one the day he became free."

One time, I asked a friend who did this. He was an escaped slave helpin' the Underground. He told me he did this so that he would never forget."

Guess Walter decided he didn't need one, or was better off without it."

The next day Elizabeth and Daniel worked their connections to establish the multiple routes and the secretive accommodations needed along the way. Despite her family being suspected of helping prisoners escape in the past, Elizabeth overruled Daniel and insisted they add the Van Lew house to the list.

"You sure, Miss Van Lew? They been watching this house for some time."

"We have the advantage of being closest to the prison. If they are careful, like we talked about, coming at night, making sure they're not being watched, and using the back entrance, I think we will be fine."

"Even if so, we will need to move them out very soon after. Take them to Rowley's farm or somewhere else. We were lucky they didn't discover our secret room last time. Also, not much room there. Just enough for one person, maybe two."

Daniel also began recruiting for six to seven guides that would meet the escaped prisoners in a back alley off of Cary Street. They would be responsible to take two or three prisoners to the prearranged safe houses.

The plan was to get the escaped prisoners safely to Williamsburg, now controlled by Butler's army. This would be the primary route. Separate guides would then help them move from one safe house to another until they arrived safely there.

Elizabeth arranged for her and Daniel to meet at the farmhouse with William Rowley to discuss plans. Samuel Ruth agreed to meet there as well. Ruth was willing to use his railroad and his connections in northern Virginia, if an alternate route became necessary.

Elizabeth shared the latest information on the timing and the estimated numbers they expected. Daniel talked about his plans for moving the escapees from the Van Lew home and other in town residences to Rowley's farm. He also discussed moving them from the farm to the next shelter, as well as additional logistics and contingencies, should things go wrong, as they often did.

A free African American servant knocked at the door and entered with hot cider and biscuits. He recognized Daniel and they exchanged warm greetings. The conversation regarding the prison break continued after he left.

At one point Ruth changed the subject. "Elizabeth, I also wanted to tell you that I saw our mutual friend John Botts last week."

"We so miss him being so far away from Richmond these days," Elizabeth commented. "How is he?"

"Doing well. He told me the latest about his nephew, Mark Rivers. I'm sure you remember. Mark's been working for the Nitre Mining Bureau."

Elizabeth said, "Yes. Experimenting with a new kind of dangerous weapon. Testing first with cats before using on humans. How evil. I loved hearing the story about how somebody left the cage open and many got away. They haven't yet figured out who did it?"

"Apparently not. Took them days to find new strays. Heard they also stole cats from backyards. Well, Rivers continues to be a fly in the ointment. John Botts told me that Mark's boss, Professor McCulloh is very difficult. Puts them under extreme pressure to deliver. Keeps telling everyone they are not moving fast enough."

"Sounded like he was fit to be tied when the cats got loose," Elizabeth noted.

Ruth said, "No doubt, and you are so right, Elizabeth. They are continuing to experiment with the cats to create a new chemical solution that can kill large numbers of people. Mark told his uncle John they believe it could change the entire calculus of the war."

"Bastards," Daniel blurted out. "Pardon me."

Ruth laughed. "No apologies necessary, Daniel. Bastards they are. John told me his nephew is doing everything he can to slow them down. When no one else is around, he oxidizes the experimental chemical compounds, or does other things to dilute them so they are ineffective."

"They haven't figured that out, either?" Daniel asked.

"Not yet, but according to John, Mark thinks his efforts to do this can only slow things down. Not stop them. He also realizes at some point he just might get caught."

Chapter 16: Libby Prison Break

It was one of those days when Jefferson Davis, slightly under the weather, decided to work from home. Mary Bowser had just finished her morning chores in the family bedrooms, hall and adjoining rooms. As she began to take the stairs down to continue working the parlor, and other first floor rooms, most named after specific Confederate States, her least favorite the Texas Room with its longhorn furniture, she heard the doorbell ring. William, who was still filling in as doorman since Henry left, answered the door.

"I came this morning as President Davis requested. Long journey ahead of me. Please tell him Captain Thomas Hines is here."

He was a good-looking man who could have passed as a thespian. Some thought he resembled the well-known actor of the day, John Wilkes Booth. Thin, medium build, ocean blue eyes, wavy raven hair with chiseled forehead and cheekbones, and a somewhat out of place Roman nose. He had an ivory complexion and a thick mustache with bushy edges that hung well below his chin.

Mary picked up on his slight drawl, not from the Deep South, but not from Virginia either. William suggested he take a seat in the reception room while he went to announce his arrival to President Davis.

Davis and the man called Hines met in the small side room off from the west side of the parlor. This was where Davis often met with small groups, no more than four, mostly for personal conversations. It was also where Lee once caught hell from Varina Davis for leaving a trail of mud in and out of the room from his boots.

Mary usually finished her downstairs work assignment in the parlor, but decided to start there, despite her uneasiness of being caught eavesdropping again. Mary had no doubt this time May would surely turn her in.

Luckily, May was upstairs with Varina Davis in her office working on household bills. However, Mary knew May could appear behind her at any moment without warning.

She could hear Hines voice easily, so to make it less obvious she was trying to listen in, she put her pail down and knelt several feet away from the door to the separate room where Davis and Hines were meeting and started to scrub the floor.

Hines was recounting his adventures, first as a cavalry raider under the command of a man named Brigadier General John Morgan. He was eventually caught and sent to a Union penitentiary in Ohio. He bragged about his remarkable escape, hiding in an old mattress being discarded from the prison. She could hardly hear Davis who was speaking more softly, but she could tell he was enjoying Hine's relating his escapades.

They were both laughing.

The conversation eventually turned more serious. Hines thanked Davis for "Accepting my proposal to finance Canadian Operations."

Davis said something she couldn't quite hear. Mary then heard Hines say, "I believe we can have maximum impact by creating incidents around well attended events."

She thought she heard Davis say that he agreed, but she couldn't be sure. He was still talking at a much lower timbre than Hines. Davis continued talking, but Mary couldn't make out what he was saying. She would have to take the gamble she wouldn't get caught. Mary hopped up and moved closer to the door. Davis was still speaking.

"Of immediate importance. We need to suppress the will of the majority of northern citizens to support Lincoln's war. The worse possible scenario for us would be for Lincoln to win reelection. I am confident that your team in Canada, working with our friends in northern states, can help ensure this doesn't happen. What the Copperheads need is organizational management and more backbone. That's what I'm hoping your proposed plan can help."

"Well, as you know, Mr. President, the newly formed 'Sons of Liberty' operating in Ohio, Indiana and Illinois have plenty of backbone. I believe working with my team in Canada we can mount successful campaigns to disrupt the Federals and turn even more northerners against the war during the upcoming election cycle."

"Absolutely this is what is needed. I know some of the men personally who are now in Canada. Good, dependable men."

Hines speaking again. "Yes sir. I'm sure you know Clement Vallandigham who escaped to Canada. The leader in exile for the Sons of Liberty. Elected last February."

"Yes, I know Clement well. We have been in secret communication since he made it to Canada. He can fill you in when you meet with him there. Don't take it personally Captain, but it's better for all of us, especially you, that you do not know more about this in case you are apprehended by the enemy before reaching your destination."

"I understand, Sir. You should know, you can count on me to never waver from my mission, and I would never divulge anything to the enemy, even if they tortured me."

"Captain, I know you are committed to the Cause, loyal and very brave. Still we must take every precaution."

"Yes, sir. I can also vouch for the loyalty of the other men in my unit. I conducted raids with several of these boys who also escaped northern prisons and are now in Toronto. Some of the others I know by reputation. A strong team. We will not be thwarted from completing our mission."

"Good," she heard Davis say. Then they were both speaking with lower voices. She couldn't make out what next was said. Mary thought to herself that she remembered hearing something about the Sons of Liberty in the Revolutionary War. This was obviously very different.

She could hear Davis speaking again. "Canada, as part of the British Monarchy has remained neutral, at least until now, but their sympathies are clearly with us. The blockade is hurting their textile industry. If the Federals find out about the Canadian operations and attempt to strike across the northern border, it just might give the Crown a convenient excuse to come to our aid and declare war against the North."

Hines speaking again. "Hopefully they will not learn about us before it is too late, but if they do, either they elect to leave us alone in a neutral country, or they risk Armageddon."

"Very convincing, Captain. I have a list here I want you to study," Davis stated. "These are additional contacts who you will meet in Canada and other key individuals who are part of the new organization we are constructing. This list contains their names and corresponding code names we will use for communications. Memorize it and then destroy it before you attempt to run the blockade."

"Yes sir, I will," Hines replied.

Davis spoke next. "Make sure you share this with Jacob. Oh, and one of the names you will see here is Cassius Lee. Robert E. Lee's uncle."

Cassius Lee had lived in Alexandria, Virginia and had been against secession. He decided not to join the Confederate Army, but with Union forces close by at Fort Ward in Alexandria to defend the capital, and his relation to Robert E, Lee, he fled to Canada to avoid possible arrest.

Mary heard Davis say, "Let me give you his address. Again, as a precaution, he will then provide the location of the others." This was followed by, "Thank you sir. I believe I already have Mr. Cassius Lee's address, just outside Toronto." Davis speaking again. "Oh, and ah, one other thing. I have something I want you to give Cassius from me. It's upstairs, let me go get it. On second thought, why don't you come with me, I can give you a tour of the Executive Mansion along the way."

Mary bolted back to her spot on the floor where she left her bucket and brush and fell quickly to her knees. She began lightly humming, "Go Down Moses," another gospel song she had taught the children. She scrubbed the floor as if completely oblivious to the two men walking across the parlor.

She waited until she heard them go up the stairs. She immediately headed for the room no longer occupied. She hoped to find the list with coded names, but it wasn't on the circular marble table in the middle of the small room, and it was nowhere else to be seen. She was extremely frustrated. Hines must have placed it in his pocket.

She pulled the door open further to survey more of the room for one last scan. Something banged up against the back of it. Looking behind the door, she noticed the satchel Hines was carrying when he first entered the mansion. It was hanging off a hook. She unbuckled it and found the note folded inside. Mary glance at the names on the list:

At Cassius F. Lee - Hamilton, Canada

Napoleon – J. Thompson
Fide sed cui vide - Reynolds
John S. Williams signs N. N. Simpson
Woman of the South – Baxley
Harris will sign Alexander
McCulloh will sign Richard

At the bottom of the list was written "key word is Constantinople." Mary wondered if this was a code name for another individual, not identified. Or was it perhaps meant to represent a city or town?

After skimming down the list for a few brief seconds, Mary had the names and their respective alias' committed to memory. She placed the list back in the satchel as she found it and returned to the parlor, assuming her previous floor cleaning position.

Shortly after Davis and Hines came back down the stairs. The Confederate President waited by the door as Hines crossed back through the parlor to retrieve his satchel. The two men shook hands.

"Wishing you safe passage, Captain Hines, and great success in your mission, so important for our cause. Don't forget what I told you."

"Thank you sir. I won't forget, President Davis, and we will do all in our power to make it successful."

As she continued to wash down the floor of the parlor, Mary was thinking about writing out the list of names as she saw it, as well as notes from what she heard in the Hines conversation with Davis. Probably safest not to take another trip to Wayne's Dry Goods Store for at least another day or so. She had just been there.

Mary knew there were more questions that would be asked, and more danger of being exposed as a spy if she asked to go again this afternoon. After carefully weighing the risks, Mary convinced herself that she would still attempt to do so anyway. The sooner the information she just learned was passed on, the better the chances that Hines could be apprehended as he tried to run the Federalist blockade. Perhaps others on the list could also be rounded up expeditiously.

Mary made something up about forgetting to get some additional sewing materials last time. To her surprise, Varina agreed to let her go. No questions were asked.

Upon receiving Mary's latest message from Wayne, detailing all she heard, Elizabeth was deeply disturbed. She shared her thoughts with Wayne.

"This sounds to me that they are looking to open a new, more nefarious phase to this awful war. One targeting civilian populations. Dreadful."

"I'm afraid I would have to agree with you, Elizabeth," Wayne said.

"Time is of the essence. I will make sure this gets passed on promptly. All this is very hard for me to fathom. That they think of themselves as fighting for freedom, like the real Sons of Liberty, our forefathers. When their ultimate objective is preserving the practice of slavery. Makes it all the more despicable."

"So much for the 'Peace Democrats,' sympathetic to the Confederates from up north in their fight for 'freedom,'" Wayne sarcastically remarked.

"Ironic isn't it? The height of hypocrisy and duplicitousness," Elizabeth added.

Pressed by Robert Ford to provide a date he could share with his new external contacts, Colonel Thomas E. Rose, the acknowledged leader of the digging teams, could only provide a best guess estimate; sometime in the middle of February. Ford passed it on to the grain store owner.

In desperate need of new recruits, President Jefferson Davis expanded the Conscription Act, making all men in the Confederacy up to 50 years old eligible to fight. This included those who in the past had been ruled exempt due to health or other physical limitations.

John Newton Van Lew, Elizabeth's brother, was subsequently drafted, despite his debilitating case of asthma. He was told to report for training to assume a front-line infantry role. Elizabeth and his mother knew he was conflicted. Even John wasn't sure what he would do until the very last moment as he left that morning and was expected to report to his assigned training camp.

When they didn't hear anything, his family was distraught. Late the next day Elizabeth received news about her brother. This came from another of Daniel's connections. He did indeed desert, and was now in hiding with a poor farmer and his family on the outskirts of town. They had helped the Underground in the past. Elizabeth asked Daniel to take her to see him. She assumed it would be the last time she would see John before he tried to escape north.

Once more she donned the old overcoat received from Harriett Anne, along with a wide bonnet, to avoid calling attention to herself. She thought she could easily pass as a servant leaving the home. They arranged for Frederick Lohmann to meet them at the bottom of Church Hill with one of his carriages to take them the rest of the way. As they set out, they passed a group of four or five neighborhood boys.

"Crazy Bet, it's you, ain't it?" one of the boys shouted. "Why you dressed like that?"

"Why? 'Cause she's crazy," another boy said, as they all began to laugh.

"Just keep walkin'," Daniel whispered.

The gang of boys began to follow them. More name calling and taunting. Daniel took Elizabeth's hand as they increased the pace of their strides. The boys began to drop back. One of them yelled, "There goes Crazy Bet, stepping out with one of her negro slaves." More laughing. Eventually they peeled off as Elizabeth and Daniel reached the end of Church Hill.

"Guess you were right Miss Van Lew. Thinkin' you're crazy is probably a good thing."

John was delighted to see them. It was late in the day. The poor Unionist family was gracious and offered to provide overnight accommodations for Elizabeth and Daniel, as they had done the night before for John. The siblings talked past midnight in front of the center room fireplace, where John methodically continued to add a new log to keep the flames from dying out.

The others had gone to bed much earlier. John expressed his regrets about leaving the hardware store with no one to run it. Elizabeth pointed out that business had been bad anyway, thanks to the senseless war. She assured her brother that she and Eliza would get along fine. Finally Elizabeth called it a night. John asked her to try and explain why he had to leave without having a chance to say goodbye to his beloved mother. He promised his sister he would come back to Richmond as soon as it was safe for him to do so.

STEPHEN ROMAINE

In the morning, Daniel was about to leave. He planned to reach out and work his connections to help John evade the Confederates and make the trek north to safety. Isaac showed up with the family carriage, bringing provisions for John's journey. He also brought more disturbing news.

"I'm so sorry Miss Van Lew. I thought they weren't supposed to come for another week or so, and we would be told when."

"Who, Isaac?"

"The prisoners. Three men showed up at the front door last night in civilian clothes. They claimed to be from Libby. They were supposed to come to the back door, like we talked about. I thought at first they might be spies workin' for the Confederates, tryin' to trick us. Also, I saw neighbors across the street watching. Told those men at the door to go away."

"You were right to be cautious, Isaac."

Before Isaac could continue, Daniel, staring at Elizabeth asserted, "This may have been a blessing you weren't there to take them in. We all may have been arrested, along with the escaped prisoners."

"Perhaps. This was not the way the plan was supposed to work. I just hope those poor men haven't been apprehended," Elizabeth responded.

"They weren't, at least not yet," Isaac replied.

"How do you know?" Daniel asked.

"Well, after thinkin' 'bout it, I went out after and caught up with them on Franklin Street. They didn't see me right away. Stayed in the shadows. After listenin' to them, decided they really were Yankees. Got them off Franklin just before a couple Confederates showed up. Looking around."

"How did you know they were Yankees?" Daniel asked.

"Didn't know where they were goin', and sounded like Yankees. When they didn't think anybody was listenin'. I took them back roads to Miss Abby Green's house where we entered through the servants entrance. There were four others there already."

"Hope none of them get caught carryin' maps or instructions to safe houses," Daniel said.

"These men were all officers. I would assume they wouldn't be that careless," Elizabeth commented.

Isaac continued. "Miss Green wasn't sure but she suspected some of them may have managed to get to a couple other homes like hers without guides as originally planned. She figures most just moved out of Richmond as fast as they could. On their own."

"I wonder why they decided to go early," Elizabeth said. "So much more dangerous this way without giving us any advance notice."

"I would guess somethin' happened that forced them to try now," Daniel responded.

Daniel was first to leave. "I'll be back, Mr. Van Lew, once we have your passage north figured out."

The Libby prison break happened the day before. Just two days after Robert Ford had heard the Prison Warden talking to his guards. A prisoner informant must have told them he heard talk about the tunnel, but they still didn't know where the tunnel was.

The men working it had tried to keep it secret. But other prisoners surely knew. Their coming and going from their holding rooms at all hours could not have been missed. Rose was amazed that so far they had kept the location secret from prison officials.

Ford had just come back from running errands for the warden outside the prison. His first stop was to meet with the grain store owner. He had told him the escape would not happen for at least another week. He would get back to him as soon as he had precise information on the exact date of the planned break. Back in Libby, it was now late morning when Ford went to see Rose.

Just before dinner, guards pulled him aside and ordered Ford to go immediately to a solitary holding room. An armed guard was posted at the door. Perhaps Ford thought, someone overheard him talking to Rose and reported it. But why didn't they come after Rose?

Walter was also forced to stay on the premises "for the next few days." Both he and Robert Ford were worried. They knew they were now suspected of helping the diggers, but neither knew for sure how the prison officials found out.

Hearing this, Rose realized if they had any chance of getting out, they needed to finish digging and move the plan up to leave earlier. They would have to take their chances with no one on the outside alerted in advance to be of assistance.

His concerns had already been heightened a week or so before. Erasmus Ross prepared to do his daily roll call across the prison rooms filled with men. This time, two guards stood beside him the entire time, paying close attention. Rose panicked. He had just gotten back, but two of his teammates were still in the hole. They worked in shifts, three members per team.

With the guards keeping a close eye, there was no chance other members of the tunnel crew could cover for them, circling back and calling out the missing prisoner names, after already calling out their own, as they had done so many times before. Ross never seemed to notice. This time, with the guards closely watching, he counted two men missing.

After roll call, Rose decided to head down the chute and to personally deliver the bad news. Rose had nicknames for these men as well. He called one of the men "Tiller". He was the man responsible for moving dirt on the Rose team. Tiller, like the others, moved the dirt with a large spittoon stolen from the kitchen from out of the hole and spreading it evenly under the straw covering most of the Rat Hell section.

The other man he nicknamed "Cyclone". His job was to blow air into the tunnel. The tunnel teams had started by using a large umbrella Walter gave them. As the tunnel extended farther, it became ineffective. One of the new men came up with the idea of using a rubber blanket stretched over a light frame for fanning more air farther back into the hole.

Rose told the men there was no good alternative. They could take their chances, heading back up where they were sure to be reprimanded and interrogated. If they did go back to their holding room, they would need to come up with a plausible excuse and convince the guards. Or, they could stay in the hole. The others could snatch extra food and drink and bring it to them, "But, rest assured. It will be hell in Rat Hell," Rose warned.

Cyclone decided he would go up. "I could never stay there for long. I'll come up with something to tell 'em," Cyclone assured Rose. The other, Tiller, said he would take his chances staying in Rat Hell. Rose warned him that he would have to deal with complete darkness until the day of the break and that could be several more days. These days would pass slowly. He would also have to contend with all the rats. Did not take long before Rose could see it was getting to Tiller.

Making matters worse, as part of their search for the tunnel, the guards had opened the door to the closed part of the basement and walked into Rat Hell. Tiller heard them removing the barricade and dislodging the locks on the door, giving him just enough time to bury himself under the thick bed of straw covering the floor. The same straw he and others had used to hide the excess soil from the dig.

They walked around, one of them stepping close to where Tiller lay. Rats scrambled and the guard heard it. He started poking with a rifle through the straw. More scrambled, a few ran across Tiller, making him cringe as he tried hard not to budge.

The other guard laughed. "Just the rats."

They moved on without noticing him. They also didn't spot the entry hole to the tunnel which was hidden behind piles of no longer in use cooking vats, pots, pans and other assorted cooking equipment. Tiller surmised they wanted to be able to say they checked the room and get out of there as soon as possible.

Tiller was completely spooked and Rose worried he was close to cracking. Making matters even worse, Rose knew at some point they would be back to do a more thorough search when they couldn't find the tunnel anywhere else.

The other digger, Cyclone, who went up also had a close call. He was immediately spotted by a guard when he tried to join the roll call line the next day. When asked why he went missing yesterday, the prisoner said he felt sick and went to the hospital room. The guard wasn't convinced. He pulled Cyclone along to the makeshift hospital and asked the head doctor to call his staff over.

"Anybody remember seeing this man here? Claims he was sick and came down here yesterday. Any record he was here?"

None of the doctors or nurses could vouch for him. One of the nurses went back and pulled out a roster sheet. The guard was told there was no record.

"You got a lot of explaining to do," the guard said, indignantly, as the hospital staff began to step away.

"All I said was I came down here with a bad belly ache." Cyclone bawled, as the guard grabbed him by the arm. "One of the nurses, don't see her. She told me they were too busy. So I just went back to my room and fell asleep," he added.

"About the time you would have been here yesterday." He then called out to one of the doctors still nearby. "Is this the same shift that worked yesterday? Anybody missing today?"

"Don't think so," the doctor replied.

"I'm tellin' ya, I came here," Cyclone insisted.

"But there's nobody here backin' your story up," the guard hollered back.

As the guard began to take Cyclone away, one of the nurses who had been comforting a patient, and not been part of the conversation looked up. She overheard the loud, cantankerous exchange between the guard and prisoner.

She called out, "I remember him. It was me. Told him to come back later."

The nurse was Dolores. The relief Rose felt when he first heard this was obliterated a few days later. After learning that the guards were looking for the tunnel, one of his other diggers came to him with disturbing news. Cyclone had been bragging to a group of other prisoners about his bamboozling the guards. Rose confronted him immediately, pulling him into the water closet where they were alone.

"We agreed not to tell anybody else," Rose asserted.

"Colonel, I didn't say anything about the tunnel. I just told them I missed roll call and talked my way out of trouble," Cyclone retorted.

"Maybe, but you don't want to call attention to yourself, or any of us, especially now. You know they are looking for the tunnel. The searches have intensified. What if one of the guys you mentioned this to puts things together? Figures it out? Decides to tell one of the guards? You know some of the men here will do anything to earn special treatment."

With all these threatening events heightening his fears and concerns of the tunnel being discovered, Rose felt the only good alternative was to go as soon as possible. Even though the 15 men as part of the tunnel crew had been sworn to secrecy, the longer it went on, the greater the odds of someone leaking information to the guards.

Rose was not only the leader of the tunnel crew, he was the best digger by far. He also turned out to be the best worker in dealing with the lack of air and inability to use candles for light as the tunnel extended further out. Prior to the war, he had worked in a coal mine in Allentown, Pennsylvania where he worked within deep, hazardous shafts under grueling conditions.

Taking the lead in digging the next few critical yards, Rose knew he would have to do so in record time. He asked Cyclone to come with him. With Tiller already in the basement, Rose was confident he had the best team to finish the tunnel. That night the three worked a double shift.

The tunnel was now about 50 feet long and 4 feet deep. In the early morning hours, Rose started to dig upwards. He could no longer breathe. He would need to punch through the surface or he would suffocate. Effectively using gravity to help dislodge the dirt above him, Rose worked frantically. Soon, he was smothered by top soil as it caved in. Pulling himself free, he could finally see the opening. As he dislodged himself and adjusted his eyes, Rose looked up at the sky and took in a deep breath. It was still dark in the early morning hours. While continuing to breathe heavily, Rose noticed he was between the prison wall and the shed. They had miscalculated.

"Damn it," Rose mumbled under his breath, frustrated with himself.

He broke through about seven feet short. In front of the storage shed, not behind. Rarely did anyone pass through this area between the wall and the storage shed, but as they climbed out they could be spotted from the upper floor windows, or from the street. Still, it would have to do.

Cyclone retrieved a wide board previously cut in anticipation along with another two by four board, long enough to support it underneath. As best he could, Rose covered it with the soil that had fallen through and wedged it into the earth surrounding the top of the hole with the supporting board to balance it.

They climbed back out of the tunnel, only large enough for one man to pass at a time, into the Rat Hell basement. Tiller, who had been blowing air with the blanket to little effect, helped pull each of them out, one at a time.

Rose spoke first. "We'll go tonight in groups of five. I'll tell the others." Cyclone nodded and started towards the chute.

Rose called out to him. "You stay here with Tiller."

"I don't think I can. What if something goes wrong? Then I'm stuck here too."

"If something goes wrong, we'll all be in trouble. Frankly, I am more worried that if you go back, the guards may grab you and torture you until you tell me all. Besides, Tiller can use the company."

Colonel Hobart, who had maintained a secret contact with Erasmus Ross, agreed to stay behind. Someone had to replace the bricks after the last man went down the chute. He helped the first group of five enter the back of the "Not in Service" fireplace.

The first batch of escapees approached the door to the shed. The lock was broken, again. They went for the civilian clothes stashed inside. A prisoner by a window caught sight of the first few prisoners as they had surfaced from the hole and ran behind the shed. Word about the escape spread quickly to other prisoners.

Hobart was about to close it up when a couple of the men who knew about the tunnel entrance approached him, begging to also go down. More men started to show up. Hobart was astounded. All these men knew about the tunnel and had never said anything. Hobart decided to leave it open for as many that could escape before it was discovered. He too, would slide down the chute and escape.

One hundred-and-nine officer prisoners escaped before guards found the tunnel and closed it off. Of this number that escaped on February 9, remarkably, only one was caught within the city limits. The Confederate military was pressed to provide extensive search parties and to close off possible routes and passages to northern lines.

Forty-eight were captured outside Richmond, and brought back to Libby, including Colonel Rose. Among those who made it to safety were Colonel Hobart and the two men missing from roll call. Tiller, the one who stayed in the hole, and Cyclone, who Dolores helped by supporting his excuse about going to the hospital, Brick and Mortar also managed to make it back to Union controlled territory. None of the Richmond area safe houses were exposed.

After he was told about the escape, the warden, T.P. Turner, called in Erasmus Ross and the head jailor on duty. He told them this was an embarrassing disgrace for all of them. He was convinced the only way that high number of men could have escaped was with help from the sentries.

He told the head jailor he wanted all the sentries on duty the previous night sent to Castle Thunder. There they should be searched for any greenbacks that may have been used to bribe them. He wanted them all punished with jail time hoping one of them would give the others up.

As Ross and the head guard began to leave, Turner said to the jailor, "One other thing. I want you to tie up and whip Robert Ford. Whip him good. Let's see what he knows about all this."

Ford received exceedingly harsh punishment. Five hundred lashes. Yet he never divulged a thing. He did learn during interrogation how they found out about him. Someone overheard him talking to the owner of the grain store, outside the prison. This was not a leak from another prisoner. Walter was also questioned, but he was allowed to go home and received no punishment. He knew he was lucky that they somehow believed he had nothing to do with the prison break.

Considered a complete debacle by Confederate sympathizers, The Libby Prison escape boosted Union morale and received considerable attention from the northern press. From the *Chicago Tribune*, February 24, 1864:

> The lions of the day here are the 25 gallant officers who escaped from Libby Prison on Tuesday of last week and arrived here this evening from Fortress Monroe...They look as if their escape involved much privation and suffering, and their different statements of the perils through which they passed sound like romance...It is believed more than half of those who got out of the prison will reach our lines.

> The officers who are now in here were from five to eight days getting from Richmond to Williamsburg, and we think many more will follow successfully down the Peninsula, that some will escape via the army of the Potomac, and that others will eventually be heard from in North Carolina.

Harpers Weekly, recounted the escape "that abounds in details of thrilling interest," in its March 5, 1864 edition, concluding:

> They were aided by negroes, by Union citizens, and by cavalry detachments, which were sent out by General Butler for that purpose as soon as he heard of the escape. We can hardly imagine what were the feelings of these refugees when, hotly pursued by the enemy and almost exhausted, they beheld the old flag which had come to find and protect its soldiers.

Citizens in the North could not get enough. At the same time, they were well aware that conditions for captured Union soldiers still in southern prisons continued to deteriorate as the prison population exploded. Escaped prisoners and the ongoing communication, including those between Elizabeth Van Lew and General Butler, and letters from other concerned Unionists, helped fan the outrage.

One reason the prison population was over bloated was that President Lincoln had suspended regular prisoner exchange until the South would agree to return black prisoners. Instead, they were often killed or forced back into slavery. As stated in Lincoln's executive order dating back from July 30, 1863:

> It is the duty of every Government to give protection to its citizens, of whatever class, color, or condition, and especially to those who are duly organized as soldiers in public service.

Lincoln threatened that for any indignities visited upon black troops, an equal number of Confederate prisoners would be placed into hard labor. Neither side would give in, except for very rare "one-off" exchanges, such as the one for Robert E. Lee's son, Rooney, in early 1864, followed by one a few months later for Colonel Thomas E. Rose.

Pressure mounted for the Lincoln Administration to do more to free federal prisoners. This did not go unnoticed by the President's most trusted advisers that 1864 was an election year and as the war dragged on, support for the embattled incumbent continued to erode.

As bad as Libby was for officers, the outdoor overcrowded camp of Belle Isle for enlisted non-officers was considered even worse. It was also becoming common knowledge that prisoners in Richmond were beginning to be moved to the new Confederate prison at Andersonville, Georgia.

This was a way to accommodate larger numbers, but also to make escape or rescue less of a threat. Andersonville would soon become known as the most notorious of all Confederate prisons. In Camp Sumter, its official name, overcrowding and unhealthy conditions would account for over 13,000 deaths.

The combination of the escape narratives, the relaying of the harsh conditions prisoners faced, and the spectacle of prisoners being moved further South where escape or rescue would be exponentially more difficult, may have been what inspired Brigadier General Hugh Kilpatrick to propose one more audacious plan to try and save the remaining Richmond prisoners before they were moved.

A massive cavalry raid on Richmond was his proposal. Given this was only three weeks since General Wistar's recently failed attempt, this was startling. Kilpatrick's plan called for freeing the prisoners in Libby and Belle Isle, and then using them to help defend against local militias and Confederate soldiers until Union troops could arrive.

Called the "Boy General" and "Kill Cavalry" by his men, he was considered ambitious to the point of being reckless with soldiers' lives. General Sherman called him "a danged fool." Through political connections Kilpatrick was able to present his proposed plan to Secretary of War, Edwin Stanton. Kilpatrick claimed he spoke directly with President Lincoln as well.

Kilpatrick based his argument on previous battle experience. He took part in the Chancellorsville conflict, the humiliating defeat for the Yankees in what became known as Lee's "perfect battle." Kilpatrick led a cavalry raid, behind enemy battle lines on his mission to cut off supply routes. He claimed his unit advanced within two miles of Richmond. Only home guard boys and old men were left to defend the city, according to the young general.

General Meade was furious that Kilpatrick went over his head, but decided, despite his personal misgivings, that he needed to go along. Unable to regain favor with Lincoln after his decision not to pursue Lee's retreating army after Gettysburg, Meade decided he was not in a strong enough position to weigh in. He told Kilpatrick, "No detailed instructions are given you, since the plan of your operations has been proposed by yourself, with the sanction of the President and the Secretary of War."

Kilpatrick's plan had three objectives. Cut off Confederate communication lines to Richmond. Free Union prisoners at Belle Isle and Libby. Spread the word in Virginia of Lincoln's amnesty proposal for Southerners, inspiring them to repudiate the Confederacy and pledge allegiance to the Union.

Critical to executing his plan, was Colonel Ulrich Dahlgren, another well connected young officer. His father was Rear Admiral John Dahlgren who developed the smoothbore howitzer for naval vessels, as well as a muzzle-loading caste iron cannon that became the standard armament for the Navy. It was known as the "Dahlgren Gun."

By all accounts, Ulrich Dahlgren was a dashingly handsome young man. He lost his right leg at Gettysburg, but had no intention to leave his command. He was fitted with a wooden one and was still eager to reengage and make a name for himself.

The plan called for Dahlgren to advance to Richmond from the south with 460 men. Kilpatrick's 3,000 additional troops would attack Richmond from the northwest. They would provide cover for Dahlgren's detachment, as they began to free northern prisoners. A feigned attack across the Rapidan River against Lee's west flank by General George Custer's cavalry of 1,500 would be used as a diversionary tactic.

The attack commenced on the evening of February 28. They encountered below freezing temperatures as they pulled out, with a sweeping wind chill that felt like an unusually bitter arctic blast. Things went well in the beginning. Major Kilpatrick's advance scouts captured Confederate pickets at Ely's Ford, east of Lee's Army. They cut telegraph wires and destroyed railroad tracks along the way. This, and with Lee's Army distracted by Custer, Kilpatrick's troops were able to ride unobstructed for 12 hours until they reached the outskirts of Richmond.

By now, Richmond citizens had been alerted. As Kilpatrick predicted, his cavalry faced young boys, old men and soldiers on furlough who had volunteered to defend the perimeter. However, a stronger defense by them than expected was mounted. This, combined with heavy snow slowed his advance. The next day General Wade Hampton's southern cavalry, which had been in hot pursuit, arrived.

Some of Kilpatrick's men began to scatter in separate directions, as most dismounted and tried to take up the fight as infantry. There was no sign of Dahlgren, and no clear path forward. Kilpatrick ordered his remaining troops to retreat back to the Peninsula, behind Butler's lines.

Dahlgren had been delayed, proving costly to executing the planned attack. When his detachment reached the ford of the James River at Dover Mills, it was too deep to cross. In a furious rage, Dahlgren concluded that his guide, an African American former slave, had purposefully mislead him and was a spy. Inexplicably, he had the man hung on the spot.

The approach had been accessible in the past. It was likely the unusually harsh winter snow and rains of 1864 that had made this area temporarily extremely difficult to navigate. Dahlgren's rash decision to hang the scout after he concluded must have purposely tricked his unit, was most likely based on misguided assumptions.

Unaware of Kilpatrick's retreat, Dahlgren ordered his small contingent of cavalry to push forward. He decided to circle back and approach from the east, believing he could still converge with Kilpatrick's larger army.

After meeting stiff resistance from the Richmond militia, he too decided to withdraw toward the Peninsula. Ambushed by Confederate cavalrymen as he attempted to retreat, Dahlgren was killed. Most of his men were captured. Little was accomplished by the Kilpatrick-Dahlgren raid. Only minor damage to communication lines, railroad tracks and bridges resulted.

Soon Richmond was consumed with outrage over the astonishing news. It was reported that a member of the Home Guard found papers on Dahlgren that included orders to burn the city and kill Jefferson Davis. The papers looked official. This was considered against the long held rules of war.

Dahlgren's body was brought to a York River railroad depot were many local citizens were allowed to view it. His wooden leg was gone. So was one of his fingers, apparently where a ring had been taken. Dahlgren's corpse was then placed in an unmarked grave. The captured prisoners from the raid were paraded through Richmond where locals could yell insults at them.

An article in the *Richmond Daily Dispatch* shortly after the raid noted the following:

> The miserable wretch whose orders to hang Jeff. Davis and burn and sack the city, have brought down a storm of deserved excretions upon his head, it ought never to be forgotten, and was no worse than the rest of his Yankee comrade in crime, and not as bad as the monstrous villains of the Washington Cabinet, under whose express and explicit orders he was of course acting.

After reading copies of Richmond newspapers several days later, followed by a letter of complaint from General Robert E. Lee, General Meade ordered an inquiry. He subsequently wrote a letter to Robert E. Lee claiming the charges were false and that the killing of Davis and his cabinet, along with the burning of Richmond, were never sanctioned. Lincoln and Stanton both denied giving any such orders. When asked, Kilpatrick also claimed no such orders were ever given, let alone written down.

Northern press lionized Dahlgren and attempted to discredit the accusations. Newspapers sympathetic to the Union pointed that even if one assumed the orders were legitimate, it would be preposterous to think an officer would carry them on his person into battle.

Others sympathetic to the North claimed that while some of his other papers had what appeared to be official signatures, the part referencing the Davis cabinet and burning Richmond did not. The last words of the last sentence read, *"...and once in the city it must be destroyed and Jeff. Davis and Cabinet killed."* It was argued that this could have been easily added and altered by those who came into possession of the dead Colonel's papers.

Secretary of State for the Confederacy, Judah Benjamin had photographs of the Dahlgren papers smuggled around the Union blockade to Paris. He hoped to discredit Lincoln and his administration with European governments. Lithographs were created from the photographs.

Eventually, Dahlgren's father, the Rear Admiral, was able to view the lithographs when they were sent to the United States. He claimed they must have been forged, as his son's name was misspelled, with the 'h' and 'l' in 'Dahlgren' reversed. Confederates argued that it was a mistake made by the lithographer attempting to 'touch up and reformat' the photograph.

The controversy continued to play out with the partisan press from both sides, firing up their readership, and the public at large. The originals were never again presented for validation of their authenticity, and were never recovered from within Confederate leadership inner circles.

For Southern leaders, the Dahlgren papers, whether real or forged, provided useful rationalization. Confederate press argued that covert operations against the north were warranted in retaliation. Experimentation with nonconventional war methods at places such as the Nitre and Mining Bureau, in the eyes of Confederate leadership, became justifiable.

Elizabeth Van Lew, like most Unionists in Richmond, believed the Dahlgren papers were a forgery used to demonize the Union officer, and to discredit President Lincoln. She also believed that the young man was a heroic figure. If she had been made aware of the imprudent decision to hang his African American scout, it might have tainted her general opinion of the man, but not her outrage at how the entire incident was fueling Confederate propaganda.

She was particularly infuriated when Admiral John Dahlgren's plea for the return of his son's remains was ignored. Instead, the Colonel's body lied in an undisclosed place, sanctioned by military leadership. Elizabeth found the editorializing on the disposal of Ulrich Dahlgren's body in local papers particularly cruel. As described by the *Richmond Examiner,* March 8, 1864:

Where that spot is no one but those concerned in its burial know or care to tell. It was a dog's burial, without winding sheet or service. Friends and relatives at the North need inquire no further; this is all they will know – he is buried that befitted the mission upon which he came...

Shortly after, on a pleasant Sunday afternoon, Daniel came back to the Van Lew home after attending Sunday Service at the African Baptist Church. Elizabeth noticed he was in good spirits.

"Good afternoon, Daniel."

"Good afternoon, Miss Van Lew. I spent some time with Mary this morning."

"I suspected as much. How is she?"

Daniel nodded. "Fine. Told her the information about Hines was passed on, but hope you don't mind Miss Van Lew, I told her as far as we know, he was never caught. Probably in Canada by now. Still, what she provided had to be of good use for the Union Army."

"Perfectly fine with that, Daniel. You must have something else to tell me. I couldn't help but notice you seemed to be in a jovial mood as you came through the door," Elizabeth noted.

"Yes ma'am."

"Well then, please don't bite your tongue any longer. News reports of late have not been very inspiring. Out with it, Daniel."

"First off, Mary says the Davis family seems to trust her more. She's been able to listen in on more conversations. Just recently, Mary overheard a conversation between President Davis and General Bragg."

"I know Davis has received quite a bit of criticism in the local newspapers for making his friend Braxton Bragg Chief of Staff."

Daniel relayed what he had heard from Mary. "General Bragg was havin' dinner with President Davis and his wife. They had come from a meetin' with Longstreet. Longstreet came to Richmond. Mary said the President had a meetin' with his generals. Bragg, Longstreet, Lee. Somebody else there too. Oh yeah, Seddon..."

"Secretary of War, James Seddon."

"Yes, ma'am, right. They were talkin' 'bout another general. General Johnston."

"He replaced Bragg at the end of last year," Elizabeth said. "Now in command of the Army of Tennessee. No love lost there."

"Hmmm, well, Mary says it sounded like all the others are mad with him, too."

"Well, I know from reading about it in the papers, Longstreet was never a big fan of Johnston, either. Why are they so riled up this time?"

"They want him to attack in middle Tennessee, go after the enemy, but he keeps givin' excuses."

"Did Mary say what kind of excuses?"

"She did, ma'am. Not enough men. Not enough horses. Low on supplies."

"Did she hear anything else? How they would try to resolve things? Anything about battle plans? Sacking Johnston for Lee, or maybe another general?"

"No, ma'am. That's all Mary heard. They did rest of talkin' behind closed doors."

"I see. Well, this is still very insightful information to pass on. Thank you, Daniel."

"I've got more, Miss Van Lew. I think you will want to hear. Not from Mary. From somebody else I saw at Church today. Knows about what I've been doin'." He had Elizabeth's undivided attention. She leaned over her chair as he continued. "What this man told me. Well, it practically knocked me on my can. Pardon me, ma'am..."

Elizabeth smiled.

Daniel continued. "This 'bout Ulrich Dahlgren. The Confederates think they kept it a secret where he's buried. Well this man, a slave, was passin' thru the graveyard late that very night. Told me it was a short cut and 'cause he had no papers to be out on his own, it was a safer way for him to go. He saw them diggin' a hole with soldiers standin' around. Hid behind a tree to watch. Heard one of them say to another 'Nobody gonna find him now', Well, I won't say what he said next, Miss Van Lew, but they were talkin' badly bout Dahlgren."

"Poor, Admiral Dahlgren, his father, I've read he has been so beset with grief. The Admiral they say has been asking for his son's body to be returned. As you can imagine, he would be relieved to know that his son's remains have been discovered. Confederate authorities insist that no one knows where he was buried. This man can find this location again?" Elizabeth asked.

Daniel nodded. "Says he'll take me to the exact spot. Wants me to first go alone with him. Then I can bring others to help dig him up and take him to someplace else. Everybody deserves a proper burial, this man said."

Daniel went with the man to the secret grave. The next day a team was assembled that would help exhume the body. It would include Daniel, and an African American gravedigger Daniel knew. Also the Lohmann brothers would then use one of their mule drawn carts to transport the body to Rowley's residence.

Under the cover of darkness, Daniel took them to the exact spot that he had been shown. It was a stormy and windy night, which made the macabre circumstances even more creepy, but also shielded them from drawing unwanted attention. If caught, the entire Unionist network in Richmond could have been exposed.

They approached the entrance of Oakwood Cemetery and followed the gravedigger. He easily found the grave, marked solely by a sapling, as described. They dug as quickly as possible until they reached the wooden casket. Next, they disinterred the body to ensure it was Dahlgren. The leg was missing and so was one of the fingers, as had been reported in the papers. They loaded Dahlgren's corpse into the cart provided by the Lohmann's and whisked it away to William Rowley's farm without incident.

Dahlgren's corpse was hidden in a store room on the property. The next day, the Lohmann's brought a metal coffin. The decision was made to try and move the body in its new metallic coffin closer to Union lines. They loaded the coffin into a wagon owned by Rowley and covered it with peach trees, as if packed by men working in the Rowley nursery.

The plan was to drive across newly fortified picket lines around greater Richmond to a safer resting place at a farm owned by Robert Orrick, some 10 miles northwest of Richmond. Orrick had on several occasions acted as a Union "middle man," moving secret communications between Unionists on both sides of the battle divide.

With the Lohmann's heading out first to provide reconnaissance, William Rowley set out. He was stopped by sentries protecting the greater Richmond.

"Where you goin'?" the guard asked.

"Making a delivery. Peach trees."

"That all you got in dare?"

"Yes, sir."

Rowley dropped his reins, letting them fall to his side, attempting to convey a sense of indifference. He slowly stroked his long beard.

One of the guards, who was holding a rifle with bayonet, walked around his wagon. The other guard stood a few paces back. Rowley kept his eyes locked on his horses. One of them started to shake its head. The horse then kicked out one of its hind legs.

"Wow boy, wow. Calm down," Rowley yelled.

The guard circling his wagon came back around, stopping in front of him. He stared at Rowley for a few moments and looked back at the other guard. He then said, "Go on."

Rowley drove off, relieved, catching his breath. Surely if the guard had poked inside his wagon he would have hit the metal coffin. It would have been over.

Colonel Ulrich Dahlgren was once again buried. This time in Orrick's orchard. One of Rowley's delivered peach trees was planted over the spot.

Upon returning home from William Rowley's farm, Elizabeth Van Lew took it upon herself to pen a letter to General Butler regarding the recovery and transport of Colonel Dahlgren's remains to a safe place.

Rear Admiral John Dahlgren had pleaded to the Confederates to return his son's body via a "flag of truce" boat. After mounting an aggressive campaign and sending numerous letters, they finally attempted to recover Dahlgren's remains. They found that his unmarked grave in Oakwood Cemetery was empty.

General Butler sent the following to Admiral Dahlgren:

> I have reliable information from Richmond that Colonel Dahlgren's body has been taken possession of by his Union friends, and has been put beyond the reach of the Rebel authorities. I propose to take in the matter the course indicated in my last conversation with you. Please advise me if you wish any other. Benj. F. Butler, Major-General.

Admiral Dahlgren wrote the following in response:

My dear General: Accept many thanks for your kind note of 18th received by last mail. It renews no grief, for that can never leave me; the memory of my son is ever present as well as the remembrance of the last sad offices to his remains. One of the parties who was privy to the removal came to me just before my return here, narrated what had occurred, and handed me a paper with some relics of hair. It was some satisfaction to think that the precious body was no longer in the power of the atrocious ruffians, who had so basely desecrated it. You see how consistent they are in the barbarous exposure of Union officers at Charleston to the cannon of their own friends. If a prayer will help the Army, it is mine most earnestly that the banners of the Republic may speedily wave over what may be left of Richmond, and may the traitors have no more mercy meted out to them than they have accorded to others.

With my best wishes for your success I am Most truly yours,

J. Dahlgren

Chapter 17: Grant Comes East

Before the harsh winter of 1864 turned to spring, Lincoln promoted Ulysses S. Grant to Lieutenant General, and appointed him General-in-Chief of the United States Army. Only George Washington and Winfield Scott held this rank in the past. This made Grant only answerable to Lincoln.

Lincoln had no previous experience in managing military affairs. By necessity, he quickly became self-educated, and quite accomplished, as a de-facto war analyst and general, challenging his appointed generals in their strategies and methods, which continued to disappoint.

He needed someone he could trust, particularly with an upcoming presidential election the experts predicted he would lose, badly. More importantly, he needed an aggressive fighter. Lincoln was frustrated that his previous commanding generals seemed to consistently fail to take initiative. Lincoln had been impressed with Grant and the campaign successes he kept rolling up.

Shortly after the appointment, Lincoln wrote the following to Grant, demonstrating his confidence in his new General-in-Chief:

> Not expecting to see you again before the Spring campaign...I wish to express...my satisfaction with what you have done up to this time. If there is anything wanting which is in my power to give, do not fail to let me know it.

Wanting to seize the initiative, as the harsh winter receded, Grant immediately appointed his friend and confidante Brigadier General William Sherman to succeed him as head of the Military Division of the Mississippi. This made Sherman chief commander of the Western Theater.

General Meade passed on information to Grant that he had received from Butler's trusted spy in Richmond:

> Petersburg, about 25 miles south of Richmond, is where 5 separate railroads bring most of the needed supplies. They come from all over the deep South to Richmond, and the upper James River Region for Lee's Army. Cut off the supply lines from Petersburg and it should hasten the end of this terrible war.

Grant initially proposed a strategy to attack Richmond from the south of the city, near Petersburg. Lincoln rejected it, instructing Grant that, just as he had before with Hooker and Meade, his primary objective was to defeat Lee. Richmond was the secondary objective and would inevitably fall when Lee was forced to surrender.

The new General-in-Chief then devised a three-prong plan of attack with the objective of implementing maximum pressure on the remaining Confederates forces, and preventing them from moving infantry and cavalry back and forth to respond to these separate assaults.

Grant would do this with an army of soldiers in the east who knew him only by reputation. They had heard he would be aggressive in battle, and certainly not as cautious as some of their previous commanders. Grant himself had concerns. He would also be leading an army with generals reporting to him he had not fought with in the past.

The plan was for Grant and Meade to attack Lee's Northern Army of Virginia. Sherman would attempt to break through the defenses of General Johnston's Army of Tennessee and march through Georgia to the Atlantic.

General Butler would approach Richmond from the southeast. His mission was to move up the James River and cut off Lee's supply line from Petersburg, as suggested in the communiqué from Elizabeth Van Lew. It was also designed to confuse the Rebels by diverting attention and potentially troops from the main assault against Lee from the north.

Lincoln must have felt overjoyed when Grant assured him, "Whatever happens, there will be no turning back." He also told Lincoln he intended to insert himself and participate in the attack with Meade's Army of the Potomac, as opposed to commanding the Union Army from Washington.

Sherman wrote to Grant before starting his advance, "If you can whip Lee[1] and I can march to the Atlantic I think ol' Uncle Abe[2] will give us 20 days leave to see the young folks."

While Sherman was massing his troops near Chattanooga to cross the border to Georgia, Confederate General Nathan Bedford Forrest mounted a counter offensive to disrupt Sherman's preparations and gain more rations, horses and supplies for his army. Forrest attacked Fort Pillow on April 12. The fort was defended by Southern Unionists, Confederate deserters, but mostly African Americans.

The Federals lost their commander, killed in the early action, and were outmanned, and outgunned. They attempted to surrender, but were shot down as they tried to do so. Estimates were that close to 300 men were killed, all the African American soldiers and the white officers. Forrest, who Sherman called "the Devil," became responsible for the most notorious massacre of African Americans during the Civil War.

As Sherman's troops prepared for their march, "Remember Fort Pillow" became a rallying cry. This hardened the resolve for Union soldiers to bring the war to conclusion. The emancipation movement was also bolstered by this inexcusable slaughter.

Prisoner exchanges had started up again, but after Fort Pillow, Grant issued an ultimatum: "No distinction whatever will be made in the exchange between white and coloured prisoners." If Confederate authorities rejected his conditions, prisoner exchanges would be halted once again.

After the "Libby Great Escape," followed by the "Dahlgren Affair," the Van Lew home, like many other homes of suspected Union spies, was under increased surveillance. On a few occasions, strangers were seen spying into the house windows, or hiding behind the tall columns supporting the back portico. One morning Daniel found a disturbing note addressed to "Miss Elizabeth Van Lew" under the door. A skull and crossbones were drawn on the top of the note.

When Elizabeth joined Daniel and Harriett Anne in the kitchen, Daniel told her about the note.

1.   https://en.wikipedia.org/wiki/Robert_E._Lee

2.   https://en.wikipedia.org/wiki/Abraham_Lincoln

'I don't think you should read it, Miss Van Lew. Take me at my word. It's bad."

"She needs to know," Harriett Anne said sternly to her husband. "Why don't you read it to Miss Van Lew? If you don't, I will."

Daniel unfolded the note and began to read:

> Old maid. Is your house insured? Put this in the fire and mum's the word.
>
> Yours Truly,
> White Caps

"I'm sorry, Miss Van Lew." Daniel passed the note over to Elizabeth who pulled her spectacles from her pocket and read it herself.

Looking up, she said, "Don't be sorry, Daniel. I believe this it is important for all of us to be much more aware, so we can take necessary precautions, and be prepared."

They now knew that the house was being even more carefully watched than in the past. Hiding additional prisoners or slaves was no longer possible without accepting serious risks for all involved. The quilt on the rail to the servants' entrance would remain inside out.

This did not stop Elizabeth from continuing to communicate with General Butler and passing him information from her established network of spies. He sent her a note prior to his planned attack on Richmond to take place at the same time Grant struck at Lee from the north. When acid and heat were applied, Butler's note indicated that he had information from another source that spies in Richmond were being rounded up. She needed to be very careful. He also asked the following:

> Will there be an attack from North Carolina? How many troops are there? Will Richmond be evacuated? If any thought of it, send word at once at my expense. Give all possible facts.

Elizabeth provided all she could from her sources. There were 25,000 troops poised to counter attack any offensive moves against the Confederate Capital. The only evacuation in Richmond was a constant stream of prisoners being sent to Georgia – at least so far. If she held any concern about being arrested as a spy, she didn't share it with others. Nor did it interfere with her conviction to maintain ongoing activities helping the Union.

By now Elizabeth Van Lew was hard pressed to keep funding her clandestine activities, and those of her associates. The closing of John Van Lew's hardware store compounded the problem. Her mother Eliza was becoming more feeble with age. With no money coming in to support the family, savings were being depleted.

With limited financial support and using what little personal finances she had left to support escaped slaves and Union prisoners, Elizabeth finally accepted Butler's offer of financial support. He began sending money to keep the Van Lew spy network operational.

Just before the Union would launch another major assault against Lee, a Union scout spotted a man in Confederate uniform approaching. He pointed his rifle and yelled, "Stop. Identify yourself. What is your purpose?"

"My name is John Van Lew."

Elizabeth's brother had successfully made it across Union lines. When brought to camp, he informed the men around him:

> I will tell you something that may be of value to you. If you can
> get into communication with my mother or sister, they are in a
> position where they might furnish you valuable information.

This was passed directly to Grant. He was already aware of Van Lew and the value of her network of spies and intelligence gathering. John Van Lew would end up in Philadelphia. With his store closed and the Van Lew women close to broke, they were still grateful when word was received that John was safe, and no longer in the Confederate Army.

Grant met with Butler in April at Fort Monroe to discuss battle plans. Before Grant could ask about Van Lew and her intelligence network, Butler brought her name up, sharing with Grant the importance of his contact and the trove of valuable information she was gathering from well-placed sources within the Confederacy. Butler provided details on Elizabeth Van

Lew's latest intelligence and shared the method they were using for information exchange.

Grant knew that Butler was a politically appointed general, very popular with "Radical Republicans" against slavery after his "contraband of war" argument for not returning runaway slaves to the South. Butler, however, lacked formal military training. Grant appointed two proven war generals to support him. Major General William Smith, and General Quincy Gillmore were assigned "to command troops sent into the field."

In planning his advance, Butler recognized that Fort Darling, the Confederate stronghold on the James River, could be a significant obstacle his army would need to confront. He sent a message to Elizabeth Van Lew requesting as much information as her spy network could provide.

Joe Mills came to see Elizabeth at her home, entering from the back-door entrance under the cover of darkness. They met in the drawing room, behind closed doors. Mills looked more like a schoolmaster than a war department administrator. Roundish shoulders, a thin receding head of hair parted in the middle, a clean shaven book-worm countenance, with thick spectacles hanging off the lower tip of his nose.

Elizabeth said, "Coming here represents a big risk, Joseph. You know they are watching our home."

"I tried to bring it to Wayne Evans like we talked about this afternoon, but the store was crowded with people coming and going. I waited outside the store for a while, but then I saw a few people who know me from work passing by. One asked why I was standing around. Made somethin' up, but he looked skeptical. I know the store is closed tomorrow."

Mills pulled out a set of marked up maps of Fort Darling and surrounding Drewry's Bluff and laid them on the giltwood table in the middle of the room. The markings showed troop positioning and corresponding estimates on numbers of soldiers.

"For your friend, Miss Van Lew. Also important to note what is unknown. I can't predict how the Confederates will respond with additional reinforcements."

"This I'm sure will be exceptionally helpful for the Union in their planning."

"I hope so, Miss Van Lew. You are right about the risk. In fact, my boss, Robert Kean, the Bureau Chief, has launched a concerted effort to plug up what he called obvious leaks in our department. This was after one of his bosses told him, 'the enemy seems to be fully informed of everything transpiring here.'"

"Do they suspect you?"

"Don't think so, at least not yet. They interrogated all of us. We were told they are convinced we have, what was referred to, as a 'mole' in the department. Anyway, a long way of saying, I'll try my best to go to Wayne next time, for both our sakes."

"Yes. This will be the safest way to exchange messages between us for right now. Have you heard anything about a mission being planned out of Canada?"

"No ma'am, but I do know that when captured Confederate soldiers are able to escape from northern prisons, several of them have ended up in Canada. If I do hear anything, I'll let Wayne know."

"You could also pass it to Thomas McNiven, the baker. Do you know him?"

"I know Mr. McNiven. I'll keep that in mind as another alternative, if I need it. I know we all need to be very careful."

Another of those days came when Jefferson Davis was not feeling well and decided to work from his home office in the Executive Mansion. The children were playing in their room across the hall. Varina Davis climbed the stairs, bringing a basket lunch to her husband.

When Catherine, the family nurse, had stepped out momentarily from the children's room, four-year-old Joseph managed to wander out onto the balcony. He climbed over the rail, slipped and fell onto the brick walk below. His older brother, Jeff, ran down the stairs and out the door. When he couldn't get his little brother to "Wake up," he went running for his nurse.

Catherine's screaming alerted Jefferson and Varina to the horrible tragedy. Joseph was dead. The couple knelt on the walk over their son. Davis was in shock. He kept repeating "Not mine, oh Lord, but thine."

Jefferson Davis had lost his first wife, close to 30 years earlier, and his first son with Varina, Samuel, had died as an infant 10 years ago. Joseph, considered a bright and fun-loving child, had replaced Samuel as his father's favorite.

Three children were left, Margaret, nine; Jeff, seven; and William, three. Davis would need to contend with his physical ailments due to malaria, this latest of these deep personal tragedies, and comforting his now hysterically depressed wife, Varina. All this, in addition to managing the war and his other presidential duties.

Richmond elite were well represented at St. Paul's Episcopal Church for the funeral services of Joseph Davis. It was an early day in May and the sun shined brightly above the somber crowd pouring into the church. St. Paul's dominated the skyline near Capitol Square, with its gigantic octagonal spiral and Corinthian portico that adorned the stucco and brick base, architected in Greek revival design.

St. Paul's, where the Davis family worshipped, was completed in the 1840's, almost a hundred years after Elizabeth Van Lew's beloved St. John's, about a 20 minute walk from each other, straight up along Broad Street most of the way.

Elizabeth, much like most citizens, regardless of their position on the war or politics, was horrified by the news. She prayed for the Davis family and attended the funeral.

After the service, she noticed Mary Bowser standing in the churchyard next to several other African American slaves working at the Davis executive residence. After paying her respects, and offering condolences to the First Family of the Confederacy, Elizabeth started to walk over towards Mary.

Catherine, the Irish nurse for the Davis family, got there first, with the children walking behind her. Elizabeth could hear her voice, breaking with sorrow, as she said, "Mary, would you please watch the children while I help with Mrs. Davis."

"Yes, ma'am," Mary responded.

The nurse was beset with grief and didn't acknowledge Elizabeth as she hurried back towards the church.

Elizabeth and Mary embraced.

"How terribly awful this is," Elizabeth said.

"Yes, it is horrible, but I am still glad to see you here. Thought I might." Mary's eyes were welled up which caused Elizabeth's red eyes from crying earlier to do the same. "Poor Catherine, she blames herself."

William, the three-year-old, too young to fully comprehend the gravity of the situation, began to play, running around a nearby magnolia tree in the church yard. The other children sauntered over.

The two ladies talked for a few minutes. There were others standing around next to them, mostly slave servants. There were other children, in addition to the Davis family children. Mary assured Elizabeth she was doing well, all things considered.

Mary mentioned that she had heard a visitor tell Jefferson Davis that Hines did make it to Canada. Elizabeth noticed Mary's jaw tighten as she looked behind her. Elizabeth turned around. There was a tall, gaunt faced woman walking over. She recognized her immediately.

"Hello, Miss Van Lew," May's loud, lilting voice seemed to echo across the yard. "We met when you first came over with Mary."

"Yes, I remember. I wish we were meeting again under different circumstances."

May nodded respectfully, maintaining her stoic disposition. She immediately looked back at Mary.

"You should be more mindful of the children. Especially given what just happened. Mrs. Davis wants you to take the children back home, right away."

"Absolutely. I will. Right now."

"I've already talked with Wilbur who will go with you, along with one of the soldiers."

Mary and Elizabeth embraced each other one more time as May looked on, contemptuously. At home, as Elizabeth began to take off her jacket, she noticed a folded note in the outer pocket. As she suspected, it was Mary's handwriting. She read the following:

Conversation between President Davis and General Bragg:

Jefferson Davis and General Bragg are very concerned about General Joseph Johnston as Commander Army of Tennessee.

Davis told Bragg he needed Lee in Virginia and Beauregard in the Carolina's, and there were no other good options. He said he blamed the surrender at Vicksburg on Johnston. Davis told Bragg we lost due to "want of provisions inside, and a general outside who wouldn't fight." Both expressed concern Johnston was not up to the task at hand. Whether against Grant or now with Sherman.

On May 5, the same day Grant launched his attack, Butler transported his army of 33,000 men on a flotilla of vessels, moving up the James River to the Bermuda Peninsula. This was a small strip of land, 15 miles south of Richmond, at the confluence of the James and Appomattox Rivers.

His objective was to cut off the supply line between Richmond and Petersburg via the Richmond and Petersburg Railroad. Grant and his generals hoped this would force Lee to send reinforcements south of Richmond, softening his resistance from Grant and Meade's primary attack from the north.

Based on the intelligence received, Butler knew he would initially face a small number of Confederate forces and militia between Richmond and Petersburg, perhaps several thousand. They would be under the command of Major General George Pickett, who led the failed "Pickett's Charge" at Gettysburg. Time would be critical, given the potential threat presented by the proximity of General Beauregard's larger force in North Carolina.

They landed on the peninsula unopposed. Based on Grant's directive, they moved west across Bermuda Hundred and started construction to establish a defensive position near Cobb Hill, overlooking the Appomattox River.

From the start, Butler became extremely critical of Gillmore, accusing him of "timidity" and "disobedience." He was furious that he did not take immediate initiative to attack the Richmond and Petersburg Railroad, only several miles to the west.

While the infantry stalled, Butler's cavalry under General Kautz swung south, attacking the railroad nexus between Petersburg and Wilmington, North Carolina. After disrupting this major southern supply line to Petersburg, they headed north, destroying bridges and telegraph lines.

Beauregard sent his additional troops from North Carolina to sure up defensive lines. Concerned his window of opportunity would soon close, Butler gave orders for his army to take the immediate offensive.

"The enemy is in our front with cavalry, 5,000 men, and it is a disgrace that we are cooped up here," Butler complained. As more Confederates continued to move in to position against them, Butler ordered his brigades to attack and destroy the Richmond & Petersburg Railroad.

They successfully wrecked sections of rail, at the midway point between Richmond and Petersburg. Butler's army repulsed a counter offensive, where the Confederates suffered 140 causalities, but failed to pursue the fleeing Confederates.

That evening, Smith and Gillmore proposed an alternative plan of sweeping south and attacking Petersburg versus a frontal assault on Beauregard's troops forming a position to protect the rails. Seizing Petersburg, they argued, would be more disruptive for Richmond. They also reasoned it would be less costly in causalities. This would, however, defy Butler's orders from Grant.

Butler received a communication that proved incorrect indicating that Grant was making progress in his advance. He decided they should not change their approved mission of destroying the railroad and moving toward Richmond in support of Grant's advance. A golden opportunity was missed. It was highly unlikely the thinly defended city of Petersburg could have withstood the onslaught of a concerted assault from Butler's army.

Beauregard's reinforced troops now numbered near 18,000, but were still less than half of Union strength. They met and successfully stopped Butler's Army of the James at Drewry's Bluff. The cannon fire could be heard in downtown Richmond. Union forces withdrew to their fortified camp on Bermuda Hundred.

The thin strip of land worked to the advantage of Beauregard's smaller units as they "bottled up Butler." Several hundred Virginia Military Institute cadets had joined the fight with the Confederates and were hailed as heroes. The objective to divert resources from Lee's main body of army failed.

Telegrams Butler received from the War Department on Grant's progress indicated the Union had won a major battle against Lee. The report indicated that Lee was in full retreat and the Army of the Potomac was moving on Richmond. Edwin Stanton, Lincoln's Secretary of War sent a message to Butler suggesting "General Grant is on the march with his whole army to form a junction with you." None of this was accurate, either.

Grant first crossed the Rapidan River unopposed in north central Virginia. His plan was to move 118,000 troops as quickly as possible through the dense underbrush near Spotsylvania, Virginia and slip behind and flank Lee's right wing. Lee's forces numbered about 65,000. They were camped outside the "Wilderness," south of the Rapidan.

Not only were the Confederate outnumbered, they were less sheltered through the most recent cruel winter months, and their rations had been reduced to cornmeal and mush. Some were now calling it a war of "Feds and the Cornfeds."

The Rebels were still motivated to fight. They loved their commander, Robert E. Lee. Also, they knew it was an election year for President of the United States. They were told another devastating defeat for the Yankees could help swing votes for a peace advocate to win the Democratic nomination.

Lee's signal stations notified him of Grant's movement. He ordered an advance, confronting Union forces before they could pass through the Wilderness. The thick brush and terrain were problematic for both sides. The Confederates had a decided advantage being familiar with the terrain.

The conflict was bloody, chaotic. This resulted in high numbers of causalities, primarily for the Union. When faced with similar clashes in the past, Federal Generals retreated. Grant did not.

Battered but not defeated, he ordered his troops to continue to advance. After two days of battle, Federal troops, exhausted from intense fighting continued to keep pushing south, reaching the edge of the Wilderness.

Many were still unsure about Grant, new to the Eastern Theatre. As they left their trenches to advance, Grant rode to the front line of the troops. Their new commanding general was still ordering an advance, not retreat. The soldiers broke out in cheers.

They marched to the vital crossroad town of Spotsylvania Courthouse. Lee's advance guard was already there and, once again, helped stall the

Union advance. There were more than 17,500 Union casualties over the two days of fighting. The Confederates suffered approximately 7,000. Disappointed Union leadership now grasped that the effort to defeat Lee and march to Richmond would be a long, slow slog.

Davis hoped Johnston and his Army of Tennessee would prove his latest concerns misplaced. Unlike Vicksburg where he failed to mount a counter offensive, it was critical that Johnston confront the new Union threat from the west. He implored him to stop General Sherman. To bolster Johnston's confidence to engage, Davis increased Johnston's troop strength to 65,000, versus Sherman's 100,000, by adding General Polk's 16,000 men from Alabama.

As the third leg of the multi-prong Union assault, Major General Sherman struck first before Johnston could react. Launching his offensive in early May, Sherman's advance coincided with Grant and Butler's moves in the east. Sherman's troops successfully maneuvered around Johnston's defensive positions, orchestrating simultaneous flanking movements in northwestern Georgia.

Within days, Sherman's Division of the Mississippi pushed Johnston's troops back 20 miles to Calhoun, Georgia. By the middle of May, Johnston was pushed back another 20 miles.

With Union troops moving closer to Richmond, Confederate officials feared another raid to free prisoners might occur. The approximately 1,000 officers left in Libby Prison would need to be moved to Georgia.

Just before the move, Robert Ford, the African American prisoner, brutally whipped when suspected of helping white officers escape, escaped himself. He was assisted by Walter on the inside, and Daniel, who had bribed a guard, helped him through his trusted contacts, to make it safely to Fort Monroe. There were now thousands of escaped slaves living in tents at "Freedom Fortress."

Shortly after, Elizabeth went to visit Sam Ruth in his office behind closed doors. He had requested the meeting.

"Thank you for coming Miss Van Lew. Very difficult for me to go anywhere these days, but between work and home. I hope you didn't mind, but I assumed your coming here to the depot is less conspicuous than if it were me going to your home. As you know, Albert no longer has his stand. Another casualty of the bad economic conditions due to the war."

"Very unfortunate for Albert, and a host of others. You are correct, Samuel. Meeting at my home would not be a very good idea these days. I see you are intrigued by the coat I am wearing."

"Well..."

"I have developed my own cover. They may think you are incompetent. I have worked hard to give them good reason to believe I'm crazy. While they continue to watch the house, to make sure no one suspicious enters, they must have decided there is no need to tail a crazy middle-aged woman moving about town dressed like a beggar."

Elizabeth laughed as she looked down, grabbed at a ripped seam area in her coat and held it up. Ruth mustered a polite smile, still appearing slightly confused.

"Several of the neighbors now call me Crazy Bet. The adults do it behind my back. At least the children are honest enough to call it out to my face."

"In any case, I'm glad you are here. I was so sorry to hear about your brother," Ruth said, changing the subject. "Have you heard anything since you last saw him?"

"Not a thing, at least not yet, but thanks for asking, Samuel."

"Let me explain why I asked to see you," Ruth stated.

"Please do."

Ruth replied. "As you know, I periodically meet with one of Colonel Sharpe's scouts. We get together when there is news to exchange, just outside Fredericksburg. I have relatives who live there."

"Yes, I am aware of this," Elizabeth said.

"Sharpe is most grateful for the intelligence you continue to provide. This is about the most recent information. The operation being set up in Canada, and the plan to help the militant offshoot of Copperheads in the Midwest."

"The Sons of Liberty?"

"Correct. A militant group of northern Peace Democrats."

Elizabeth shook her head. "Isn't that a contradiction?"

Ruth nodded as Elizabeth continued.

"I'm so afraid they are planning to do terrible things up north targeting property, and perhaps civilians, too."

"The challenge is that the Rebels in Canada supporting this appear to be disbursed between Toronto and Montreal. They've been very tough to track down, and while the U.S. Consuls in both cities have gone to the Canadian government, they haven't as of yet done much to help."

"Is that so?" Elizabeth asked.

"Yes, apparently the Canadian government has told U.S. officials they wish to remain neutral. I suspect they are more sympathetic to the Confederate States given the importance of cotton to the textile industries in Canada and Great Britain."

"Probably still bad feelings after the War of 1812 as well."

"Maybe so. In any case, the Lincoln Administration does not want to cause an international incident. Needless to say, anything more you, through your well positioned contacts can learn would be extremely useful."

"Understood," Elizabeth said. "My sources are already working on this. To find out as much as possible."

"Good. I passed on some information myself recently. From John Botts nephew, Mark Rivers. The Nitre Mining Bureau is increasing its spending for the production of sulfuric acid."

"They must be planning something big."

"Yes," Ruth said. "You should also know; Mark Rivers is no longer there. Unfortunately. This was one of the last pieces of information he was able to provide to his uncle."

"We lost Mark Rivers? I hope they didn't catch him spying, or disrupting their experiments. Seemed like he was doing a great job at that..."

"No, lucky for him," Ruth responded. "They fired him thinking he was like me. Incompetent. A huge loss for us."

"I have a feeling finding a good chemist to replace him can't be easy, either."

Chapter 18: Rebel Raiders from Canada

After his impressive victory in Vicksburg, where Grant had marched his army over 200 miles in 18 days, limiting casualties to about 7,000, his star power continued to rise as he assumed the position of General-in-Chief over all U.S. Armies.

As he began the Wilderness Campaign, Grant's name was being floated as a potential replacement candidate for president, given the "divisive" nature of Lincoln's politics, and a growing concern Lincoln would lose the November Presidential Election. It didn't seem to matter that he and Lincoln shared similar political views. The Republican elite wanted to exploit Grant's popularity to offset the growing chorus of discontent with the current Republican Administration.

Not only were those who advocated giving up the fight vigorously opposed to Lincoln. Radical Republicans, who advocated no compromise until slavery and secessionism were completely eliminated, thought Lincoln was a weak, incompetent buffoon.

After the bitter clash between Grant and Lee at the Spotsylvania Courthouse, Grant ordered a withdrawal. He then attempted to flank Lee once again, continuing to push forward. The Army of the Potomac approached Cold Harbor, a critical railroad hub for Richmond. Lee's Army of Northern Virginia was already there and had established an entrenched defensive position.

Grant ordered a frontal assault. The 13 days of battle in the middle of May racked up more causalities than all other Union campaigns combined, with over 37,000 killed, wounded or missing. Lee's Army suffered 22,000. The renowned Confederate cavalry leader, J.E.B. Stuart was one of those mortally wounded.

Lee's troops held their defensive position and successfully thwarted Grant's attack. Grant would later say that he regretted his Cold Harbor assault, admitting that "no advantage whatever was gained to compensate for the heavy loss we sustained."

Despite Lee's victory, Grant was able to surprise him by making it look like a retreat, but instead slipping south, crossing the James River. Grant's Army was able to free Butler's forces pinned on Bermuda's Hundred along the way. The Union armies established position close to Petersburg. A prolonged back and forth campaign with causalities building up with little demonstrative progress in gaining ground ensued.

News of the disastrous consequences of Grant's march with the Army of the Potomac through "the Wilderness" of Northern Virginia was a crushing disappointment for northern citizens. One again, their hopes for an imminent end of the conflict were misplaced. The apparent stalemate that followed, as the 1864 presidential election campaign heated up, diminished the enthusiasm for a Grant replacement at the top of the ticket.

It was late afternoon. Wayne came to see Elizabeth Van Lew. He waited in the parlor where Daniel left him to get Elizabeth. Wayne pulled a canister out of the bag he was carrying and placed it on the table next to where he was sitting.

As she entered the room, Elizabeth exclaimed, "I keep getting things I didn't order from the bakery, the general store..."

"Let's just say, things haven't been normal in Richmond for a while," Wayne replied. "We've all gotten a little confused. I'll just take this fine tea from India back."

"Tea, however, we can definitely use. I can't imagine what you went through to get it. How much do I owe you, Mr. Evans?"

"Well, let's see." As he tapped his fingers on the canister, Wayne said, "There's about 200 grams of tea in this, that's almost half a pound. I would have charged about $5 in Confederate currency in the past to cover my costs. Now that runs about $25, but I won't take a cent. This is a gift from me to you."

"I had a feeling you would say that, Wayne. You're too kind."

"Any excuse I can use to drop by, especially when I have something else for you, I know you will want to hear."

"Something from Mary?"

"No, from Joe Mills. Came around earlier today."

"He seemed very flustered when I last saw him. He said they suspect someone in his department of leaking information. I was afraid we wouldn't hear anything more back from him."

"Yes, he told me the same. About the leak. I'd be flustered too. Yet he came upon the information he said you requested last time."

"About Canada?"

"Precisely. He told me senior officials are rattled with the Union Armies of Grant and Butler so close to Richmond. Joe Mills said he recently discovered something they were trying to keep very quiet. The War Department has a fund for spying operations."

"How did he find out?" Elizabeth asked.

"He said he saw some documents recently he wasn't supposed to see. A Secret Act of Congress last month approved an allocation of one million in gold to support secret service operations in Toronto."

"One million in gold?"

"Yes. Certainly worth way more than Confederate paper." Wayne then pulled a note from his pocket. "Joe copied this from the file record." He read it to Elizabeth.

> The proposal of Captain Thomas Hines is approved to work with our northern state allies to instigate incidents that will help influence the outcome of the 1864 elections, by increasing public sentiment against the war and making the U.S. government more predisposed to ending the conflict with the Confederate States of America.

"Joe also said the one million will be distributed to Jacob Thompson to be used at his discretion."

"Napoleon."

"Napoleon?"

"We believe that is his code name in their secret communications. Guessing by the nickname and the funds placed in his charge, he must be the leader."

Wayne asked, "Wasn't Jacob Thompson a former U.S. Cabinet member?"

"He was. Secretary of the Interior, I believe. I remember Horace Greeley called him a traitor for joining the Confederacy. One million in gold can pay for a lot of bombs. Did Joseph have any idea what it was for? Based on what he saw, or perhaps heard?"

"No, I'm sorry, Elizabeth, that's all I have from Joe. But, something else I wanted to share with you. I ran into Thomas McNiven in town before coming here. Can't seem to get away from your spies these days. Told Thomas I was going to be seeing you. He said I could save him the trip."

"As much as I like Mr. McNiven, we certainly don't need any more un-ordered baked goods delivered."

They both smiled. Wayne continued. "Thomas told me he still talks with Sadie, the Davis cook, when he delivers bread to the Executive Mansion. She says Varina has Mary taking care of the children more often and is giving her additional responsibilities. Sadie says she is working out well."

"That's great news. I suspect Varina may have lost some of her confidence in Catherine the nurse. She was supposed to be watching their son when he fell to his death."

"Maybe. Terrible what happened. Sadie did mention something else, though. She doesn't think May, the housekeeper, cares for Mary. Wasn't sure why, but she said May is keeping a close eye on her."

"I noticed she wasn't quite right with Mary at the funeral," Elizabeth noted.

"Do you think she has an inkling as to what Mary might be up to?"

"From some of the things Mary has told me before, I think that is a real possibility. Mary knows it and is trying to be very cautious around May."

"I sure hope so. Having Varina Davis in her corner can't hurt. Probably acts as a buffer May can't get around. As long as Varina likes her and doesn't suspect anything. Well, that's all I have. Should get going."

"Do you have dinner plans, Wayne? I'm sure we have extra portions. I can have Harriett Anne add another plate to the table."

"Well, ahh, I'd like that, but do you think your mother would mind?"

"I think she is getting used to you by now, and she definitely appreciates what you are doing to help pass information to the Federals."

"Then I'll stay."

"Wonderful. You know, Wayne, when we first talked about using your store for Mary to bring information, you said you would have your nephew, Timothy, deliver it to me at the house. I'm glad it's mostly you."

"Me too."

The Republican Convention was held in Baltimore, in June, 1864. There was a clear risk the party would splinter apart. Cold Harbor may have reduced enthusiasm for a Grant candidacy, but he still had important supporters within party ranks. Most still believed with Lincoln on the ticket they were headed for defeat. In keeping with precedent, Lincoln did not attend the convention.

Many residents of Baltimore were antiwar. Riots had first broken out in Baltimore at the beginning of the war. While the border state of Maryland stayed with the Union, it also remained a slave state. Maryland had more Copperheads than most of the northern states.

Colonel George H. Sharpe was apprehensive about the upcoming convention. It had been about a half year ago that Charles Sengstack, "the Pharmacist," had been apprehended in Baltimore, on his mission to burn shipyards and railroad bridges, hoping to stir up dissent. Perhaps it was a prelude to more disruptive agitators attempting terrorist acts during the Convention.

Sharpe contacted the Civilian Provost Marshal of Maryland, James L. McPhail to warn him that radical elements of the Copperheads in Maryland with the help from outside agitators might try to stir things up. McPhail had already developed a reputation as a hardnosed Unionist who had previously arrested Southern agents and secessionist sympathizers in Maryland. Police security was increased. Under McPhail's leadership, a strong showing of force before and during the convention took place. Whether this had an impact or not, there were no major incidents.

As representatives assembled and the event proceeded, the more moderate block of the Republican Party argued for toning down the rhetoric in an attempt to expand the party's base. The party name was changed to the "National Union Party," in an effort to attract War Democrats to their platform.

Both conservative and radical leaders of the Republican Party continued to confide in Lincoln that he could not win. The intent of highly influential party leaders was to convince the delegation to nominate someone, anyone, other than Lincoln. Their plan didn't work. When Missouri decided to switch its 22 delegates from Grant to Lincoln on the first ballot, Lincoln won the nomination unanimously, with three delegates abstaining. Lincoln's running mate would be a pro-war Democrat, Andrew Johnson.

Radical Republicans who advocated complete and immediate emancipation and equal treatment of all slaves across the north, south and U.S. territories, decided to launch an independent party campaign. They held their own convention a few weeks later. They considered nominating General Benjamin Butler, but decided on John Fremont. Fremont had been the first ever Republican nominee from the 1856 election. A third party with Fremont as the candidate, even if he could not be elected, was sure to peel votes from Lincoln, making his reelection even more unlikely.

Grant's initial thrusts at Petersburg to capture the critical railroad junction to Richmond continued to be repulsed by Beauregard's much smaller army in established defensive positions. The assault melds further into a drawn out battle of trench warfare.

The march through Georgia by Sherman started out well. His army traveled seventy miles and now was within thirty miles of Atlanta, having faced minimal resistance from Johnston along the way. Sherman, frustrated by Johnston's reluctance to challenge his advance, could no longer flank the long line of defense protecting Atlanta.

Sherman ordered a frontal assault on the enemy near Kennesaw Mountain. His army encountered an unfamiliar 100 degree heat, with unanticipated dense brush and high, rocky terrain. Sherman suffered over 3,000 casualties. Johnston's forces, about 1,000. Sherman would concede failure, explaining his actions by stating:

> I perceived that the enemy and our officers had settled down into a conviction that I would not assault fortified lines. All looked to me to outflank. An army to be efficient, must not settle down to a single mode of offence, but must be prepared to execute any plan which promises success. I wanted, therefore, for the moral

effect, to make a successful assault against the enemy behind his breastworks, and resolved to attempt it at that point where success would give the largest fruits of victory.

The heat was unbearable. More like a typical hot, sunny August day, than a late spring day in mid-June. Jefferson Davis was still distraught over the loss of Joseph. This, combined with the early uncomfortable heat wave, made his decision to stay home an easy one to make in his typically highly stressful days. He was doing it more often.

Mary Bowser, was dusting the downstairs furniture when she heard a knock at the door, followed by Wilbur's heavy steps as he went to answer it.

Wilbur said, "Mr. Judah, nice to see you sir. President Davis is expecting you. I will take you to his office, please follow me."

From the corner of her eye, Mary could see another man with the Secretary of State, but did not know him. They climbed the stairs. She continued dusting, moving from the wall to wall bookcase across the room to the gold trim portrait frames.

"Mr. President. We bring some very good news."

She could hear as the door shut. She knew from past experience it would be almost impossible to hear anything with the door closed. This would surely arouse the attention of May if she left her work assignment and tried to sneak up the stairs. May was in the room next to her.

Not until the second time she called her, did Mary realize Sadie the cook needed her. Mary stepped away from the portrait of Varina Davis and walked to the kitchen.

"Hi Mary, can you get me some peas and lettuce from the garden? I can't leave the kitchen right now."

Mary went to the garden behind the mansion. She was carefully inspecting each vegetable before making her selection, and placing her picks into the bucket she carried with her.

The voice of a man called out to her. "You look pretty darn warm out there."

There was a man slouched against the nearby garden shed. It was hard to see him with the glare from the sun. His form was obscured in the shadow cast from the shed. Taking a step forward, she could make out that he was a white man wearing a Confederate uniform.

"Why don't you take a break and come sit over here in the shade?" he suggested. "Got some roasted peanuts. Happy to share."

"What are you doing here? This is private property."

"I'm waiting on Mr. Judah Benjamin, meeting inside."

"You surprised me."

"You don't gotta worry 'bout me, hell, if I ever did anything and it got back to Benjamin, he'd have my...well, he'd send me back to the front lines. Especially with..."

"A colored girl?" Mary hesitated, but then walked over into the shade, next to the man. He extended his hand with the bag of nuts. She took some and then stepped back.

"OK if you don't wanna sit next to me. That's OK. You can just stand there. Nice here in the shade though, huh?"

"You've been with Mr. Benjamin for quite a while?"

"Yeah. I was assigned to him when he was Secretary of Defense. When he became Secretary of State and James Seddon took over as Secretary of War, Benjamin asked me to stay on with him. So I did. Works out good for me. He has his hands in almost everything and has the confidence of President Davis. It beats sleeping in the trenches."

"Who was the man with Mr. Benjamin?"

"You must mean Brigadier General Thomas Harris. Retired now."

Mary remembered the name from the list she saw from Hine's satchel. His code name was Alexander.

"You said retired? He didn't look old enough to me to be retired," Mary commented.

The soldier laughed. "Yeah, especially compared with some of the old war horses we have as generals. He's doin' something very different now."

"Oh, what's that?"

"Can't tell ya. It's a big secret. You speak pretty good."

"Pretty well. That bothers you?"

He reached out again with the nuts. Mary took another handful.

"Sounded like you have an important job working for Mr. Benjamin. I heard him say when he came in that he had good news. Maybe 'bout the war?"

"Good news on the war, I wish. Nah, that's not why we're here."

The soldier pulled a flask out of his pocket and took a big gulp before continuing. "Want some? Kentucky Bourbon. Might do you some good."

"No thanks," Mary said. "I did hear Mr. Benjamin say he had good news..."

"Killin' cats. That's the good news."

"Cats?"

"Yeah, cats."

"What do you mean by that? Killing cats, why? With what?"

"You sure ask lots of questions. Forget what I said. What's your name?"

"Mary Bowser."

"Better be careful, Mary Bowser. People get suspicious real easy these days."

They met on July 20, 1864 in Chicago in the upstairs meeting room of a downtown hotel. The Democratic Convention would be held in Chicago a month later. It was early morning. Representatives from four other states were present. In addition to Illinois, they came from Indiana, Kentucky, and Missouri. Also attending was Captain Majors, commissioner representing the Confederate Government.

There were 11 of them seated around several square tables pulled together in the center of the room. Robert Holloway from Illinois, the acting national leader of the assembled group stood up to address them.

"I think most of us know each other. I want to introduce you to our newest member, Mr. Felix Stidger," Holloway said, pointing to Felix who stood up, bowed awkwardly, before sitting back in his seat.

"Welcome, Mr. Stidger," one of the others said. A few more repeated similar greetings. "Where are you from?" another asked.

"Kentucky, sir," Stidger said.

"Not only that, but Mr. Stidger served in the Federal Kentucky Regiment. Yes, I said Federal. His conscience got the best of him fighting an unjust war, with all the gross injustices he witnessed. Isn't that right, Mr. Stidger?"

"Yes sir. That's why I asked for a discharge. Told them I was tubercular, but that wasn't true. I was able to fake the symptoms. Fooled the doctor."

Holloway continued. "Dr. Bowles, owner of French Lick Springs Resort, who is also with us, recommended him to me. He was very impressed with his skills, experience and passion for righting the wrong the United States Government is doing. Infringing on his state, and other state rights and freedoms."

"He's as committed to the 'Cause' as I am," Bowles called out.

A man sitting next to Stidger patted him on the back, as he exclaimed, "You're on the right side now, son. Better late than never."

Bowles stood and asked for the floor. Holloway nodded.

Bowles proudly noted, "Felix Stidger also comes highly recommended from Joseph Bingham, Editor of the *Indianapolis Sentinel*, among others. Needless to say, Mr. Bingham has been a strong vocal advocate for ending the war. After he met with Mr. Stidger and me in the *Sentinel* office, Mr. Bingham did some checking around and he told me Mr. Stidger passed with flying colors."

Another man shouted out, "Mr. Stidger's has already been initiated, correct?" This came from Joshua Bullitt, Chief Justice of the Kentucky Court of Appeals.

"He has, in our Indiana State Chapter," Bowles answered.

"Welcome to this special regional meeting of the Sons of Liberty," Bullitt shouted. "We're all patriots here, just like the original Sons of Liberty during the Revolutionary War."

Holloway spoke again. "Dr. Bowles has convinced me that Mr. Stidger can provide invaluable service to us, given his good reputation and many influential connections. He can travel without raising suspicion from the enemy and coordinate our communications across state lines."

Bullitt crossed the room, walking over to Stidger and extended his hand. Stidger clasped it in the secret grip handshake he learned in his orientation. The others clapped.

"I take it then, that you are also familiar with our goals, Mr. Stidger?" Bullitt questioned.

Shaking his head in the affirmative, Stidger answered, "Yes, Sir." He then recited, "To prevent four more years of succession of the Republican

War Party. To force recognition of the Confederacy. To resist all military actions of the Federal Government."

"Well said, my boy," Bullitt noted approvingly as he reclaimed his seat. More clapping.

"Let's get started with our meeting," Holloway said, cutting off the discussion.

They stood and recited their secret oath, ending with: "...In the presence of my fellow members of the new Sons of Liberty, I pledge my most sacred honor."

The secretary of the group recited the minutes from last time before Holloway shared with the group that they now estimated the number of members to be well over 100,000. The latest plan was to start an insurrection in Chicago, just before the Democratic Convention.

At the same time, other members of the Sons of Liberty would raid arsenals, Confederate prison camps across the region, as well as attack railroads and Union ships in the Great Lakes. The intent was to create a Sons of Liberty uprising across the Midwest, scare enough people and influence the convention delegates that things could get even worse if they didn't nominate a candidate to end the war.

Bullitt called out, "last time we met there was quite a bit of debate whether we act first, or wait until we have support from the Rebel army. Do we have a decision yet?"

"Yes," Holloway responded. "We have confirmation that General John Hunt Morgan's Confederate cavalry will coordinate its raid into Kentucky at the same time we begin to seize arsenals and supply depots in the four states each of you here represent. At the same time, guerilla forces of about 20,000 in Missouri will create a diversionary attack to occupy the Northern Army."

"But do we have an exact date and time?" Bullitt questioned.

"As you all know, I'm only the acting leader in the absence of Clement Vallandigham after he fled to Canada, shortly after he was released from prison. As some of you may already know, Vallandigham is back in the country. He has been invited to speak at the Democratic Convention next month."

"Vallandigham is here, in the States?" someone asked.

"He is," Holloway said, as others clapped and hollered approvingly.

"The Federals will arrest him for sure," Bullitt declared.

"Exactly what he wants," Holloway responded. "He is willing to let this happen as he believes, and I agree, it will create a huge uproar. That's when we need to act. This will allow us to gain maximum effect in gaining overwhelming support."

"Just what you might expect from a great man like Vallandigham," Harrison Dodd, the Grand Commander for Indiana said.

Holloway nodded and then continued. "Now, what we need to know from each of you is how many men from each State represented can we depend on?"

They went around the room. Bullitt was first to pledge 20,000 from the Commonwealth of Kentucky. Harrison Dodd estimated 30,000 in Indiana. The overall numbers were estimated to be about 80,000."

"That doesn't include the additional men from Canada."

Overall logistics were summarized, with, as Holloway noted, details on specific orders to follow shortly. Holloway then yielded the floor to Harrison Dodd to talk about his recent meeting with Clement Vallandigham. Dodd, the commander of the Indiana operation, had met with Vallandigham, the Supreme Commander of the clandestine Sons of Liberty, at an undisclosed location in the Midwest the previous week.

An Ohio politician and former representative of Ohio in Congress, in 1863 Vallandigham received a military court martial. He was found in violation for "sympathy for those in arms against the Government of the United States, and for declaring disloyal sentiments and opinions, with the object and purpose of weakening the power of the Government in its efforts to suppress an unlawful rebellion."

Considering Vallandigham a "wily agitator," and concerned that he was becoming a martyr figure for those opposed to the war, Lincoln ordered that he be sent across enemy lines to the Confederacy. He then managed to slip through Union territory and join Jacob Thompson in Canada. An outspoken Copperhead from the earliest days of the conflict, he remained highly critical of Lincoln and his war against the South.

Dodd walked to the front of the room, carrying a box which he placed on the table where he was standing. In an effort to maximize dramatic effect, he stood silent, as he peered across the inquisitive faces in the room.

"What's in the box, Harrison?" asked one of the Illinois representatives.

"Fire like you've never seen before. Greek Fire."

Dodd pulled a conical shell from the box. "Don't worry," he said. "This hasn't been set to detonate. Just for you to see what we'll be using once Vallandigham gives us the final word to act."

"So this is what sets off Greek Fire, one of the others said. I heard it is supposed to be almost impossible to stop from burning once ignited, even when it lands in water."

"Quite true," Harrison Dodd said as he continued his explanation. "Something like this was first used by the Greeks when they attacked Constantinople, but how it was made was lost to antiquity. Many have tried to figure it out, including Union scientists. They tried it during the Battle of Charleston with a very crude version. Didn't work. They had to rely on conventional weapons instead to destroy the city. No one has had much success. Until now." He pointed at the devise sitting on the table.

"How do you know this will work?" A representative from Kentucky asked.

"I met with Jacob Thompson in Niagara Falls last month. He assured me that the scientists working in Richmond have figured it out. They have tested the formula both in Richmond and in Canada."

"How will we use it?" another asked.

"We will launch it against steamboats on the Ohio River at the same time we attack designated Federal facilities in Illinois, Indiana, Kentucky and Ohio." He held it up so they could all see."

"How much does it weigh?" Bullitt asked.

"Not much more than thirty pounds." He began unscrewing the bottom of the shell. "As you can see this is where the powder compound would be stored."

"I'll be damned," someone else said.

Pointing to a round aperture above the lower compartment, Dodd added, "This is where the liquid Greek Fire would reside. Will explode immediately when thrown at any object."

He made a gesture as if he were going to throw it across the table. One of the men tried to duck. The others laughed. Placing it back in the box, Dodd continued.

"More about this later. Vallandigham was able to secure a commitment of $500,000 from Jacob Thompson and our friends in Canada for guns and other supplies. In addition, and I know each of you will appreciate this, he negotiated for a reward of 10% of the value of any Union property you are able to destroy."

"Thank you Harrison," Bowles shouted. Others clapped.

"Just before the convention, each of you will be contacted by Captain Tom Hines, or one of his close associates, to determine what you need, including the number of incendiary devices, like the one I just showed you."

"Captain Hines rode with General Morgan before he was captured, didn't he?" One of them asked.

"The same. A highly respected cavalry officer who met with President Davis after escaping prison and who has his utmost confidence. He and his associates will be responsible distributing funds for additional weapons, supplies, and also to help make any final arrangements."

Chapter 19: Unholy Alliance with New Sons of Liberty

Continuing his successful flanking maneuvers, General Sherman's Union Army had pushed General Joseph Johnston back to the outskirts of Atlanta. Jefferson Davis, fearful Johnston would withdraw from Atlanta leaving its defenses to state militia, replaced him with John Bell Hood. Under newly promoted General Hood, the siege of Atlanta turned into another costly stalemate.

At the same time, Lee was continuing to hold off Grant, despite smaller troops size and inadequate provisions for his soldiers. By blowing up a section of Lee's trenches using gunpowder planted inside an old coal miner tunnel, Grant was able to create a huge crater, opening a gap in the Confederate line near Petersburg. A combination of white soldiers and African Americans charged through the hole, yelling *"Remember Fort Pillow."* The assault, however, was met with a strong counter offense by Lee.

With Grant preoccupied in his Petersburg campaign, Lee realized Washington was unprotected. He dispatched Confederate General Jubal Early who led 15,000 men from Lynchburg, Virginia, through the Shenandoah Valley. Crossing into Maryland, pushing back weakened Federal resistance along the way. They were now only five miles from the White House. Washington's residents were spooked. All this fueled a new round of pessimism and increased anti-war sentiment.

These latest developments were also discouraging for Elizabeth Van Lew. Yet, she quickly grasped an opportunity based on the new campaign strategy for the Union. With Grant, who relied extensively on Colonel Sharpe and his Secret Service now engaged more closely with Butler in the Virginia campaigns, she and her network of spies were becoming more indispensable for relaying enemy intelligence.

With the vast majority of prisoners moved out of Richmond, Elizabeth Van Lew could shift her entire focus to providing military intelligence information gathered by Mary and her other spies. Unfortunately, Joe Mills at the War Department had to be more careful. Less information on military plans was being shared at his level. Also, Mark Rivers was no longer at Nitre.

With Union forces now in closer proximity to Richmond, and closing in on Confederate strongholds, information on enemy troop disposition and movement was even more critical. Elizabeth would need to rely more heavily on Daniel's contacts to scout Rebel movement, and Mary to provide what she could from inside the Davis home.

Recognizing the increasing importance of the intelligence gathering by the Van Lew network, Sharpe decided the "Flag of Truce" passage was too slow and unreliable. To expedite the receipt of information from Van Lew, he sent one of his agents to instruct her on the use of cipher code for future communications.

Elizabeth kept a scrap of paper with a code translator chart. She sometimes carried it inside her watch case. Daniel would use his network of Underground workers to transport her communications. This became so effective; soon Elizabeth Van Lew was delivering flowers and Richmond daily newspapers directly to General Grant, along with her coded messages.

One of the most recent messages came from Mary Bowser who overheard Davis talking to a guest about Clement Vallandigham sneaking back into the United States from Canada to address the Democratic Convention in Chicago.

President Davis, she noted, sounded gleeful about Vallandigham's planned appearance at the Convention. She heard Davis talk about his proven ability to inspire others and push a peace agenda "to help us end the war under acceptable terms." She also heard him say if things went well, Vallandigham had an outside shot to become a Presidential candidate, or a cabinet pick for the new administration.

The guest said, "Things are already in motion to help this along."

Weeks before the convention and the date of the planned insurrection, the Sons of Liberty friendly journalists from newspapers such as the *Indianapolis Sentinel*, published articles supporting the South and printing encouraging words for those who might attempt to resist the Federal Government and its pro-war policies.

To the surprise of the leadership of the Sons of Liberty, Vallandigham made himself highly visible in Chicago prior to the convention. Yet no attempt was made to arrest him.

Then another unanticipated surprise. The office of Harrison Dodd, the founder of the Sons of Liberty was raided, just before the Democratic Convention. Press outlets less sympathetic to the southern cause published incriminating letters found in his office. These included correspondence from Vallandigham, Bullitt and other members of the Sons of Liberty. As the *Evansville Daily Journal* wrote in an article entitled "Revolution in the North" on August 24, 1864:

> At the head of the order in this state is Harrison H. Dodd of Indianapolis. This secret cabal is sworn to assist the secessionists and Rebels of the South in destroying the Union.

> Arms and fixed ammunition are found in the printing establishment of Dodd, the president of the order, and a large quantity have been seized *in transit* while arrangements have been made for enough guns and pistols to supply an army. Rumors come to us of unlawful gatherings in several localities that a Northern rebellion is in preparation.

> Union soldiers had raided Dodd's office. He disappeared before he could be apprehended.

A few days later the 1864 Democratic Convention kicked off. It was August 29th. As noted in *The New York Times,* August 30, 1864:

> From Chicago:

> There is already much excitement in our city, growing out of the large number present, who are here for the purpose of participating in the Democratic National Convention which is to commence its session on Monday.

Many of the great lights of the party are here, and the wires are being industriously pulled. VALLANDIGHAM is here, and excites as much curiosity as a loosed elephant would in our streets. Crowds follow him wherever he goes—they enter his hotel with him, and are clamorous for a speech. Loyal men are indignant that such an arch traitor is permitted to stalk through our streets, trampling upon the authority of the Government and defying its power.

The event was every bit as contentious as the preceding Republican convention. Hard edged partisans on both sides, representing those both 'for' and 'against' the war with the South led to heated debate and in a few cases, representatives came close to blows. The "War Democrats" became alarmed as they saw numbers of unrecognized hordes pouring into Chicago, many surrounding the convention days before it started.

Many of the delegates were shocked to see Vallandigham walking freely inside the convention hall in the Chicago Amphitheatre, especially after the Sons of Liberty plot was exposed prior to the convention. They wondered why he had not been arrested once again.

At the same time, news began to spread that Sherman was gaining on Atlanta. Sensing he might not get a chance to speak, Vallandigham had approved a revised plot to begin hostilities anyway. Despite efforts to move ahead, the expected uprising never happened. Word spread quickly that the arrests of suspected members of the group and seizure of arms shipments were continuing in Illinois, as well as in other states.

Indiana Union troops arrived by train just in time to confront and thwart the advance of Rebel guerillas, giving chase, deep into Kentucky. Confederate forces, who originally planned to provide additional support decided to stand down.

Days before the convention, additional Union troops had arrived in Chicago to protect arsenals, depots and local prisons housing captured Confederate soldiers. A General Order was declared the day before the convention preventing the sale or distribution of arms or ammunition within Chicago.

A plan to set fire in five Chicago locations was abandoned. Hines, who was in the city to help coordinate terrorist activities safely slipped away once again, back into Canada. Other collaborators fled as well.

All of this unexpectedly helped strengthen the hand of the War Democrats. Lincoln's former commander, whom he had fired, Major General George McClellan, won the nomination for Democratic candidate for President as a pro-war candidate.

As an attempt to bring the party together, George Pendleton, a "Peace Democrat," and close associate of Vallandigham, was nominated as his Vice Presidential running mate. Vallandigham would not speak, but he did write the party platform which was decidedly anti-war.

The party platform called for the immediate cessation of hostilities so that "at the earliest practicable moment peace may be restored on the basis of the Federal Union of the States." The delegates promptly adopted the party plank.

Despite Vallandigham's best efforts to get the former General to take a firm stand in support of the peace platform, McClellan rejected it, insisting a Union victory was a prerequisite for peace. In the end, the contradiction of nominating a War General as the Presidential Candidate along with a Peace Democrat running mate and an anti-war platform weighed heavy on delegates as the convention concluded. As related in the *Chicago Tribune*:

> The delegates have returned quite grieved in the heart and sore in the head. One half of them are open and avowed secessionists and can hardly be expected to pull the nomination of McClellan with delight. Some of their constituents announced their determination to bolt and cast a scattering vote on the day of election.

Shortly after the convention ended, with none of the planned major uprisings across multiple states occurring, Felix Stidger called on Judge Joshua Bullitt in Louisville, Kentucky.

Bullitt was indignant from the moment Stidger showed up at his door carrying a large briefcase. "What are you doing here? Don't you realize how dangerous meeting like this could be?" Bullitt motioned him in to his office, slamming the door shut behind them.

"Dr. Bowles sent me."

"I hope no one's been following you."

"Don't think so, your Honor. Besides, I'm only a note taker for the group. Why would they follow me?"

"Actually, your title is Secretary of the Indiana Grand Council and they'd love to get their hands on whatever you are carrying in that briefcase. We are all at risk of being hauled off to jail."

Stidger nodded before responding. "Maybe so, and you're the Secretary for Kentucky, but neither my name, nor your name was printed, like the others. Dr. Bowles thought it would be safer to leave these documents with you."

"Safer? Your coming here could get both of us arrested."

"We believe they are planning to raid other Sons of Liberty activists living in Indiana. As Dr. Bowles told me, you are very respected in Kentucky. 'Beyond reproach,' he said. That is, unless you think we should suspend our activities, or you want to quit the Sons of Liberty."

"No. Never."

"Let me show you what I have here," Stidger asserted as he starting pulling stacks of papers from his briefcase and placing them on Bullitt's desk.

"These are documents that were *not* seized. Dr. Bowles insisted that I get them to you. They include notes from meetings, contact information for new friends we made in Chicago, old friends in Canada and Richmond, naturally, too. Bank notes. Our Secret Lodges throughout the Region. Where guns and ammunition are stored. At least the ones not yet seized." Pointing to the pile now on Bullitt's desk, he added, "As I said, Dr. Bowles felt for the time being, these would be safer with you."

"One of our brothers in arms might think one of us was the leak. A turncoat. You and I might be under suspicion already from the others. They may have concluded that it is one of us who betrayed them. With you coming from Indianapolis where it happened, how do I know it wasn't you?"

"Wasn't me. Couldn't have been. I stayed in Chicago after our July meeting. Been with Sons of Liberty comrades most of the time. Stayed with several of them in a downtown boarding house, planning events that, unfortunately, never happened. Only got back to Indiana a week ago."

"Maybe it was Bowles, setting both of us up."

"Don't think so. If you want to speculate, Judge, it could have been Mr. Dodd himself. They must have been watching him before the raid. How is it he so easily got away? Now none of us know where he is. By raiding his office rather than him simply handing our secret correspondence over, makes him look less suspicious, but maybe not."

"Hmmm. That never occurred to me. Dodd? Nah, that's too hard for me to believe."

"I don't know who it was. Could have been one of many people within the organization," Stidger noted. "Judge, you do agree it is vital that we carry on, correct?"

"Yes, I think, despite this terrible setback, we should continue. We need better coordination with Canada and the Confederate Government, but I do believe we need to fight on. Try again. When the timing is more conducive for carrying through."

Felix Stidger left the brief case with Bullitt and returned to Indiana, arriving after sunset. He stopped first in a country home on a back road, just outside of Indianapolis. This was not a Sons of Liberty lodge or safe house. As he climbed the porch steps he was stopped by a man in a Union uniform with a rifle. The man recognized him at once.

"He's inside waiting for you," the man said.

Sitting behind an old wooden table in the center of the room was General Henry B. Carrington of the United States Army. He was responsible for the secret service operations in Indiana. Stidger had met with him before visiting Bullitt. Everything Stidger left with Bullitt had first been meticulously copied by agents of Carrington.

"General, good to see you, sir," as the two men saluted.

"You as well Felix, please have a seat."

"Did things go as we planned?"

"They did, General. They are all suspicious of each other and afraid of being arrested."

"Splendid. I, frankly, was very pleased that you were first able to infiltrate the Sons of Liberty the way you did. I am amazed that you were able to gain the confidence of Dr. Bowles and other leaders so quickly that they appointed you General Council Secretary."

"I do hope we can now move quickly, making arrests. Just a matter of time before they realize it was me all along. My life is in danger."

"The authorities have begun to do just that."

"I certainly hope so. General, one thing I still do not understand. Needless to say, we were able to prevent the planned insurrection. Thank God, but why didn't anyone move to arrest Vallandigham when he arrived in Chicago as a delegate to the convention? There he was, walking around with impunity. Violating a military court ruling to never return to the United States. We're lucky he didn't provoke a mass riot on his own."

"We knew from Colonel Sharpe when Vallandigham first left from Canada. He left from Montreal. John Potter from the U.S. Consul Office in Montreal alerted Sharpe. Sharpe had a man shadowing him when he arrived by ship from Windsor to Detroit. Followed his movement by rail until he arrived in Chicago. Ironically, Vallandigham was in disguise which didn't fool our agent at all. He had no idea he was spotted and being followed the whole way."

"But he wasn't in disguise walking around Chicago, or at the convention."

"No, because, he was goading us to arrest him and cause an incident that would spark the uprising. Credit our President for that. President Lincoln gave explicit orders that he be left alone."

"Guess looking back now that makes sense."

"We also intercepted a note from Jacob Thompson who runs the Canadian operation. He used his code name, 'Napoleon' in the correspondence. The note was meant for Thomas Hines, who I know you met in Chicago. Another of their plots was to seize the Union Warship, *Michigan,* in Lake Erie. They intended to use their Greek Fire weapons they devised to attack and free Rebel prisoners on Johnson's Island. That would have been a terrible disaster if we weren't able to stop these in time."

"I wonder if they got the idea from what had been tried unsuccessfully a few times by us to free Union prisoners at Libby Prison."

The General smiled. "Maybe, Felix. Luckily, based on our intelligence from you and another source, we were able to arrest the man Jacob Thompson sent to capture the *Michigan* in advance. He provided critical inside information. When those who were left approached the *Michigan* they found it crawling with Union soldiers. Forced them to back off."

"Thank God. This would have been disastrous across the Midwest. It could have impacted the Chicago Convention, too. Many might have assumed only Vallandigham could restore the peace. He may have won the nomination if the rebellion was successful. Not only would the Confederates have been granted their independence, slavery would have continued to expand, whether the South stayed separate or not."

"Do you really think, Felix, there were thousands of men ready to rise up if things went according to their plan?"

"I heard there were over 110,000 men who joined the Sons of Liberty. There are lodges across 15 states, including New York, Pennsylvania, New Jersey and Connecticut. Would all of them have risen up? Probably not. But, I do believe if they had successfully pulled off some of the planned raids, many would have joined and thousands of innocent, non-military people could have been seriously hurt or killed."

"Agreed. One other thing from that list with code names. Colonel Sharpe believes 'Constantinople' may have been Chicago. Let's hope this puts an end to these efforts to incite insurrection in our country."

"Yes sir."

"Felix, what you have done, and placing yourself in extreme danger to do so, has been of enormous help to the citizens of our country. I can tell you that I, and the entire command, are eternally grateful. So is your President."

"Let's just continue to keep it secret for now. They won't think twice about killing me if they find out I was behind it."

"As we round up and arrest your fellow members, what if that means arresting you, too? So no one suspects you as a spy."

"Do it."

Eight leaders that plotted the Midwest rebellion of the Sons of Liberty would be arrested. Dr. William Bowles and Judge Joshua Bullitt. Harrison Dodd, escaped to Canada, but was subsequently arrested as well. Felix Stidger was also arrested but let go, based on "lack of evidence." He would later testify in a trial leading to the conviction of Dodd and Bowles, but their sentences were subsequently commuted. Bullitt would be swapped in a prisoner exchange.

Thomas Hines successfully escaped back to Canada. The Feds continued to leave Clement Vallandigham alone. His name appeared on the 1864 Democratic Ticket as "Secretary of War." But his influence quickly dissipated. U.S. officials were relieved that they were able to thwart Confederate and their northern operative plans to create havoc just before the Democratic Convention. There was a sense the Confederates had overplayed their hand and that the worse of the off battlefield covert efforts they could devise was over.

At this same time the entire country was riveted by the recent developments in Atlanta. Like Richmond, Atlanta had become a stirring example of Confederate resistance against the onslaught of Union aggression. Atlanta housed a sizable war industry critical to the fight, as well as providing critical railroad connections to lower South cities of the Confederacy.

The replacement of Johnston with General John Hood by Jefferson Davis had been controversial from the beginning. Johnston's reluctance to engage with Sherman, and finally signaling his intentions to withdraw his army from Atlanta, gave him no other option. Only militia would be left to defend the city, essentially ensuring capture by the Union.

Yet Davis was also aware of the potential backlash by removing Johnston. Similar to Lincoln's earlier problem with George McClellan who refused to take the initiative, missing opportunities to engage, Johnston was popular with the public and his men.

Hood was considered aggressive, but also reckless. He immediately took the offensive, attacking Sherman, crossing Peach Tree Creek, north of the city. This proved costly, with his army suffering double the amount of casualties as inflicted on Union troops. Two days later he initiated another attacked east of Atlanta. Rebel casualties were double those of the Union again. Hood tried a third time which resulted in seven times the number of casualties over Sherman.

After two of his cavalry advances upon Atlanta were repulsed, Sherman began to shell the city and moved to cut off the railroad supply line from Macon, destroying supply depots, tracks, and blowing up ammunition railroad cars filled with ammunition.

On September 3, Sherman sent a telegram to Washington, "Atlanta is ours, and fairly won." Hood's Army had evacuated the day before, burning military facilities as they withdrew. It was estimated that the combination of extensive Union shelling and the burning of military assets by retreating Confederates, resulted in over 37% of the city being demolished.

Elizabeth Van Lew, using a combination of abolitionist and African American couriers, both slaves and former slaves, continued to send regular reports on Richmond defenses to Grant and Sharpe. They provided the most recent information on picket posts, fortification, supplies, troop strength and movement. They identified seven regiments encamped outside Richmond, eight cannons put in place south of Richmond at Chaffin's Farm and New Markets Heights.

Sometimes this intelligence, encrypted with cipher code, was hidden in courier shoes, or sown into their clothes as they travelled to cross enemy lines, avoiding detection. Their knowledge of the terrain and the increasingly weaker guarded borders due to the diminished resources of the Confederate Army, offered little trouble to those familiar with the terrain making the trek.

Davis was now coming under serious criticism for the failure to prevent the siege of Atlanta. In addition to intelligence on military activities received from her network, Elizabeth also used her couriers to send information on conditions in Richmond and the public mood.

She sometimes sent clips from Richmond newspapers, such as the *Richmond Examiner* and *Richmond Whig* on their criticism of Davis. Both newspapers blamed him for losing Atlanta when he replaced Johnston with Hood. As noted in the *Richmond Examiner*:

Now, it is not cruelly hard, that the struggle of eight millions, who sacrifice their lives, sacrifice their money till the blood starts to sweat -should come to naught – should end in ruin of us all – in order that the predilections and antipathies, the pitiful personal feelings, of a single man be indulged?

Elizabeth Van Lew also provided information, passed on from Mary Bowser, concerning Jefferson Davis and his recent temperament. By now it was public information that Davis had rejected an overture by unofficial envoys proposing a plan for peace. When James Jacques and James Gilmore met with Davis and Judah Benjamin in Richmond, in late July under a "Flag of Truce," Davis rejected any talk of peace without meeting Confederate demands. He proclaimed:

> I desire peace as much as you do. I deplore bloodshed as much as you do; but I feel that not one drop of the bloodshed in this war is on my hands,—I can look up to my God and say this. I tried all in my power to avert this war...We are not fighting for slavery. We are fighting for Independence,—and that, or extermination, we will have.

Information received from Mary indicated that the Confederate President was planning to do another trip across the South in late September to rouse spirits and bolster continued support for the War. Yet, as Mary related, he was less careful in meetings at his home on a few recent occasions. One time she overheard Davis confide with his wife about his doubts and concerns regarding how much longer the Confederates could continue to fight.

Varina Davis, who had given birth to another child in June was increasingly concerned about the physical health of her husband. She too, had begun to have heart related ailments.

Mary also learned as she continued to try and listen in to private conversations between Davis and select military and political officials, that despite what he regarded as a great disappointment concerning the failed uprising in the Midwest, and, McClellan, a "War Democrat" winning the Democratic Nomination, they were still committed to new covert efforts targeting the North. Dashing hopes that the failed Midwest uprising would put an end to the Confederate guerilla war campaign, Mary's latest intelligence indicated that there was much more to come.

She heard part of a conversation between the Secretary of War, James Seddon, and a Congressman she did not know while they waited to meet with President Davis. They had to have seen her in the next room cleaning up, but spoke as if she wasn't there, or perhaps assumed she was incapable of grasping the significance of the discussion. Davis and his guests seemed to be less cautious. Not always speaking behind closed doors on sensitive war related matters. She wondered if it was a sign they were becoming more desperate.

Mary heard something about "the Doc," who had concluded his successful field work experiments and planned to travel around the Union blockade with a new type of "biological" weapon. She didn't hear the name of the doctor, what type of experiments he had conducted, or where he was travelling to or from. She heard the Congressman say, "The Doc believes this will prove devastating to Northern war efforts. I am of the opinion it could reverse recent setbacks."

When this was passed on by Van Lew, Sharpe immediately responded back asking for as much additional intelligence that could be gained, and to alert her network of spies to make finding out more a top priority.

Also top of mind for Sharpe was finding out as much as he could on Confederate plans concerning Early's cavalry threatening Washington and the battle front between Richmond and Petersburg. Would Early continue to move towards Washington, or would he be recalled to support Lee?

Before his planned trip across the South, Davis hosted a meeting with his top generals at the Executive Mansion. The staff had received no prior notice and had to scramble to prepare.

The meeting was held in the east parlor. After serving refreshments, this time the doors closed. The servants were instructed to only enter if requested. After several minutes the help was invited back in. Mary and Melissa served drinks. Gaby passed around finger food. All under the watchful eye of May, who occasionally pitched in, but mostly stood just outside the door providing serving recommendations to the other maids under her supervision. She presented these politely in front of the guests, more like suggestions than commands.

Mary's services were only needed in the beginning. May dismissed her after the first door closing. Gaby and Melissa could handle what amounted to mostly refills without her. Mary stepped into the kitchen. When asked, Sadie said she didn't need any additional help, either. Mary took her apron off, and poured herself a glass of water.

While Mary was in the kitchen, she could see Gaby and Melissa still serving in the parlor once the doors opened again. Sadie the cook with her back turned was washing dishes. The door to the basement was opposite the sink where Sadie was standing as she washed, back turned away from Mary and the basement entrance.

The men were talking loudly and passionately, but she could not get close enough with the other housemaids nearby. Then it occurred to her. Mary had noticed on other occasions that sometimes she could hear conversations from much of the first floor below in the basement. It might just be possible to hear exactly what they were discussing, if she could sneak down without being noticed. She would have to move fast. Before any of the other servants returned to the kitchen.

She pulled back the door, then closed it carefully behind her to not make any noise. Lighting a candle, she descended the steps. The basement had two entrances, one from the outside of the house and the one she just used from the kitchen. She didn't have access to the outside lock to open it in advance. She would have to exit the same way she entered, hopefully without anyone paying much attention.

The basement was mostly used for storing coal and nonperishable goods. The smell was musty and stale. As she moved deeper into the main storage area, she could hear the men quite clearly. The conversation was even more heated now.

"I can't hold the Valley much longer if I'm not given more men."

"With our weakening lines protecting Richmond, we need all the help we can get to protect our critical under belly between Richmond and Petersburg against Grant."

Mary believed that last argument came from Lee.

"I agree." Mary knew this was from Davis. "Jub, you do not return to the Valley. We need your help here to push back Grant. No more men, no more supplies can be spared."

She heard footsteps. It was Sadie with May behind her. Mary darted over to a box close by.

"What are you doing?" May snapped.

"I noticed when cleaning earlier today that I needed to replace candles in several rooms. Given you didn't need my help anymore, I decided to get them to put around tomorrow morning."

"Getting candles shouldn't take so long," May pointed out, looking very sternly at Mary in the glow of the candle she still held.

"Somebody must have moved them. Took me a while to find."

"They are in the box right in front of you, in the same place they always are."

Mary responded, trying not to sound defensive, "That's only because I moved them back." She pointed to a far corner. "Found them over there under other boxes. Somebody must have moved them."

"Why would somebody have done that?" May asked.

"Not sure, but the floor here is still very damp." She walked over to an exposed section of the wall and lowered the candle she was holding. Pointing to the dark wet spot that extended about two inches up from the crevice, she said, "Probably from the heavy rains we had last week. Often gets flooded here. Maybe somebody moved things to clean up the water and didn't put them back."

They could hear the men talking from the room upstairs. May did not look convinced.

"We all need to get back upstairs."

Mary reached into the box and grabbed a handful of candle sticks. She was the last to take the stairs. May was waiting for her at the top.

"I've warned you before, Mary. I'm afraid this time I just may have a talk with Mrs. Davis. Or maybe even Mr. Davis."

One of Elizabeth Van Lew's couriers brought the following news to Sharpe: "No supplies are being sent to General Early whatsoever. Early must fall back to support Lee or subsist by himself or starve."

Always worried that messages could be planted misinformation from the enemy, Sharpe was relieved when scouts confirmed that a division of General Kershaw's cavalry was moving back towards Lee. Another division of his cavalry had already been recalled.

Learning this before Early could leave the Valley as ordered to support Lee proved to be a huge coup for the Union. This also was a great relief for Lincoln who worried about Early advancing on Washington. Knowing he was weakened and could not depend on additional men or supplies, Grant ordered General Philip Sheridan and his cavalry, which vastly out-numbered Early, to attack in the Shenandoah Valley.

A prolonged assault by Sheridan's cavalry had pinned down Early and prevented his reinforcing Lee. Sheridan's men would also destroy provisions, livestock and railroads as they advanced. Estimates were that over 400 square miles were demolished and became uninhabitable. Locals referred to it as "The Burning."

George William Bagby, an American physician, renowned humorist and editorial writer for the *Southern Literary Messenger,* wrote that Sheridan's Shenandoah raid, "killed indiscriminately all the animals they could not carry off, even to the hens and chickens. Large families were left without a morsel to eat."

Mary Bowser knew that she had provided some useful information, but was discouraged that despite her best efforts, she could not find out more about the mysterious doctor and his devastating "new type of weapon."

With Davis leaving town, she knew she could no longer peer through sealed envelopes and try to read his mail. The recent, more frequent days when Davis was not home, May collected his mail and held it, as opposed to leaving on his desk. This added to her frustration. May obviously didn't trust her and this made any out of the ordinary actions by Mary significantly more dangerous. She could not get caught again.

One thing did please her. If May did talk to Varina, there was no sign of it. Varina was concerned about her husband and his health. Taking the extensive trip by rail across the South without Catherine the nurse to accompany him was cause of real concern.

Her husband needed a nurse to travel with him. They also needed a nurse for her new baby, as well as the other children. Jefferson Davis had been cool with Catherine since the accident. Mary and the other servants were convinced he still blamed her for the death of his beloved Joseph. Yet the other children, while seeming to prefer Mary, were still comfortable with Catherine.

Varina Davis was eager to find another good, reputable nurse to accompany her husband and his doctor for the upcoming trip. She finally found one, highly recommended and available. The nurse had to cancel out at the last minute when she received word that her husband, serving under General Early, had sustained serious injuries at the Battle of Opequon Creek in the Shenandoah Valley. He was one of over 3,000 Confederate causalities.

Varina still had no available nurse identified to care for her husband, just before he was supposed to leave. Mary was close by when she heard Varina asking Catherine if she could recommend someone else.

"I'm sorry, Mrs. Davis. Don't think so, but I could maybe check around. Talk to a few people who might know of someone."

"We don't have much time," a stressful Varina responded.

Mary was in the drawing room opening shutters. She stepped aside and crossed the narrow hall. She leaned in to the entrance of the piano room and knocked lightly on the side of the open of the door.

"Excuse me, Mrs. Davis, Catherine. I couldn't help but hear you mention something about needing a good nurse. I know one who might do. She's a slave girl like me, but she is a very good nurse. Everybody says so. She's supposed to start working at the Chimborazo Hospital, but hasn't started yet. Her name is Dolores Halsey."

With Libby Prison closed, Dolores had stayed on to take care of prisoners too sick or too seriously injured to be moved to Georgia. She had just been reassigned to the hospital for Confederate soldiers. Mary was aware of the help she had provided for prisoners at Libby and had gotten to know her very well at Church. Mary knew she was miserable having to go back there.

"But those poor sick and wounded soldiers need all the help they can get. What makes you think she could be spared?" Varina questioned.

"Well, ma'am. She's on loan to the government. She has been working in the hospital at Libby Prison. Maybe her start date could be pushed off a little."

Catherine chimed in. "Taking care of our President is very important, too."

"Any chance you could get her to come by today?" Varina asked. "If Dr. Garnett determines she is up to the task, I could have someone talk to the Hospital Chief of Staff."

Varina met with Dolores Halsey, as did Dr. Garnett, the family physician. They were both satisfied that she could provide nursing care for her husband while on his trip, along with the military physician. Mary asked for one thing. She wanted Dolores to keep her eyes and ears open for any information that could help the Union.

Davis and his entourage left on September 20 on a railroad trip through the Deep South. They stopped in Danville, Virginia, the Carolinas, Macon, Georgia, and Montgomery, Alabama.

At most stops he gave rousing speeches, praising citizens, encouraging them to keep up the fight and predicting that they would drive Sherman out of Georgia. He also told crowds to beware of "croakers," those who would distill poison and disaffection.

Dolores noticed that he wasn't his usual self on the day he was to speak in Macon, Georgia. She was surprised when the doctor travelling with them had given him a large dose of quinine to suppress a suspected bout with malaria. This had led to a severe headache.

His speech this time was decidedly harsh and allegoric. Davis admitted that it was a time of adversity. He told the crowd that if only the soldiers who went "AWOL" returned to the Army of Tennessee, they could defeat Sherman. He said:

> What, though misfortune has befallen our arms from Decatur to Jonesboro, our cause is not lost. Sherman cannot keep up his long line of communication, and retreat sooner or later, he must. And when that day comes, the fate that befell the army of the French Empire and its retreat from Moscow will be reacted. Our cavalry and our people will harass and destroy his army as did the Cossacks that of Napoleon, and the Yankee General, like him will escape with only a body guard.

The Macon Speech did little to improve morale. There was also no need for Dolores to relay intelligence related to plans to confront and reverse Sherman's assault in Georgia. Davis laid it out in his talk.

The *Macon Telegraph* and other Georgia newspapers printed his speech which disclosed information on the planned Confederate counteroffensive. They would attack Sherman's supply and communication lines. Without these lines in enemy territory, Sherman would be forced to retreat.

When Grant read the newspaper report, he noted, "Who is to furnish the snow for this Moscow retreat?"

Sensing Jefferson Davis had realized his speech fell flat, Georgia Governor Joseph Brown visited the Confederate President in his railroad car. Dolores heard the following.

"Jeff, I agree with you. We can send Sherman fleeing. Our Georgia Regiments have the advantage of knowing the landscape and we can launch a series of unexpected guerilla style attacks."

"Thanks Joe, I know we have had our differences. I appreciate the support."

"We still have Northern Copperhead support, too. I was talking with your Vice President, Alexander Stephens. We've known each other since the days he served in the Georgia Senate. He told me about Dr. Blackburn's work in Bermuda and the trunks he shipped to Halifax. You sure this is a good idea?"

"Let's talk about this later..."

Dolores remembered Mary telling her to be mindful of any information on the doctor. She now had the doctor's name and his itinerary. Also that he had trunks containing something mysterious and most probably dangerous.

Sherman persuaded Grant that efforts to protect his supply lines were futile. "By attempting to hold the roads we will lose a thousand men monthly," Sherman declared. However, he did not want to retreat as Davis had promised he would have to in his Macon speech. His plan was to march deeper into Georgia, all the way to the sea.

Henry Halleck, former Union General-Chief-of-Staff, who was now simply Chief-of-Staff reporting to Grant raised issues with Sherman's plan. Halleck, who helped persuade Lincoln to relieve Hooker before Gettysburg, was now primarily responsible for administrative duties for the entire army. He argued that by intentionally separating himself from his supplies lines, Sherman's actions could end in catastrophe. His army could end up many starving, captured, killed or deserting.

Grant disagreed. He knew and trusted Sherman. Lincoln had previously told Grant he was in charge and had the authority to do what he believed was best. Grant supported Sherman's plan. Lincoln approved it based on Grant's recommendation.

Like Lee's advance through the Shenandoah Valley into Pennsylvania before being stopped in Gettysburg, Sherman's Army would live off the land and confiscate provisions as they marched. Not being dependent and constricted by supply lines, Sherman hoped to move swiftly. His army would also destroy property along the way. For this, he would be vilified by Southerners.

General Hood attempted to impede progress by getting out in front, mining roads, blowing up bridges, and killing livestock. He also destroyed property. Sherman labeled these actions as examples of "barbarism." He retaliated by escalating his own previously planned scorched earth campaign as his army began to push through to Savannah.

Sherman rationalized his approach as follows:

> You cannot qualify war in harsher terms than I will. War is cruelty, and you cannot refine it; and those who brought war into our country deserve all the curses and maledictions a people can pour out. I know I had no hand in making this war, and I know I will make more sacrifices to-day than any of you to secure peace.

He would later coin the phrase, *"War is hell."*

In October, with the Presidential election a month away, Lee launched an aggressive campaign in an effort to drive Grant away from Richmond. Grant responded with a 40,000 man assault attempting to destroy the last railroad links between Petersburg and Richmond.

Robert E Lee recognized that with his depleted army, low on supplies, he could not defeat Grant, but he refused to give up. Grant, on the other hand, had turned his field headquarters at City Point, Virginia, a small port town at the confluence of the Appomattox and James Rivers into a thriving major hub for his army. With so much activity, it became one of the busiest seaports and a major supply base, with ships delivering food, clothing and ammunition to support Grant's troops.

Through a masterful display of military logistics, the Federals were able to supply over 100,000 Union troops, almost 40 percent larger than Lee's. Over 65,000 horses and mules were also fed by arriving Union vessels. At any given time, there were over 200 of these ships en route, coming and going on the river in support of Grant's Army.

A series of offenses and counter offenses ensued. Lee's ability to constantly mount fierce response to Grant's unending aggression could not be sustained. Eventually he was forced to move his defensive lines back, closer to the Confederate Capital.

A meeting in Montreal took place around this same time. The war momentum was clearly shifting to the Yankees. Early attempts to instill fear and increase discontent over the war with the northern civilian population had failed. This meeting was about ratcheting up guerilla activities and planning new terrorist events in the North.

Jacob Thompson and Clement Clay were there. Like Thompson, Clay was appointed by Davis to help run secret espionage operations in Canada. The other man at the October 1864 Montreal meeting was the popular American actor, John Wilkes Booth.

Chapter 20: Spreading Bermuda Fever

Soldiers reporting to Thompson crossed the Canadian border and raided banks in St. Albans, Vermont. This happened on October 19, 1864. They planned to burn buildings in the town using the Confederate developed Greek Fire, and divert federal troops to the northern border. The Greek Fire failed to ignite, but 200,000 in U.S. currency was stolen from several banks. When some villagers tried to resist, one was killed, two others wounded.

Canadian officials could no longer turn a blind eye with many in their own citizenry outraged by the St. Albans assault. With assistance from the United States Consul in Toronto, David Thurston, the raiders were captured. Like his counterpart John Potter in Montreal, Thurston was under instructions from the Lincoln administration to identify and monitor potential Confederate agitators.

In addition to protecting U.S. citizens abroad, and helping to facilitate trade and forge relationships with host country representatives, assigned consuls in foreign countries were expected to provide intelligence for the U.S. Government. They often had to do much of the legwork on their own, given limited budgets and staff. They became essential to the Lincoln Administration's intelligence gathering and counter espionage efforts.

Fourteen suspects were tried in a Canadian court, facing extradition. The court ruled, however, that they were Confederate soldiers acting upon military orders and Canada needed to remain neutral in the Civil War conflict between North and South.

Approximately 80,000 U.S. dollars were recovered. The "Greek Fire" used for the St. Albans Raid created only limited damage – not the undistinguishable conflagration as promised by the Confederate sponsored chemists. McCulloh and other scientists working at Nitre were continuing to work long hours trying to improve the combustible compound which worked only intermittently.

Just as he had with John Potter, the U.S. Consul in Montreal, even before the St. Albans Raid, Colonel George Sharpe had been in close contact with David Thurston regarding the rebel operations being conducted out of Toronto. It appeared that most of the rebel activity in Canada was being consolidated in Toronto.

Sharpe now surmised that the intent of the St. Albans Raid was to replenish the coffers of the Canadian team, after making substantial investments to support the failed Sons of Liberty uprising in the Midwest. He also concluded this could only be to support more surreptitious missions against the North.

He argued that the St. Albans Raid proved that the Rebels had no intention of suspending covert activities. It also demonstrated that all U.S. States, territories, as well as regions outside of U.S. control, were possible staging areas and potentially targets. He shared his concerns with the Lincoln Administration.

Sharpe soon learned it wasn't only eastern Canada they needed to monitor. As far away as the west coast of Canada, Allen Francis, U.S. Consul for the Vancouver Island Colony, and a close friend of the Lincoln's, was also busy observing suspicious activities. When he first arrived, Francis immediately noticed Confederate flags on many buildings and households.

One place in particular stood out. A local saloon named "The Confederate." Francis sent one of his agents who eventually worked his way in as a regular. The clientele must have assumed anyone frequenting the establishment had Confederate sympathies. Some of the customers were self-proclaimed Confederate raiders. They often bragged about what they knew and sometimes disclosed future plans where they claimed they would be an active participant. Some of these planned raids would take place as far away as San Francisco.

California became a State in 1850, and while it remained with the Union, there were many Californians who were sympathetic to the Confederate cause, as was the case in British Columbia. Soon Francis was learning about Confederate activities to steal gold shipments from British Columbia, and California. He provided frequent reports on his findings to the Secretary of State William Seward.

Based on his investigative work and developed sources, Francis reported to authorities of both the United States and Canadian governments on these attempted plots to steal gold. Most of these plots were ill conceived and fell apart on their own, or were abandoned.

Francis also learned in advance about a specific plan to commandeer the *U.S.S. Shubrick* for the Confederacy. The *Shubrick* was a side-wheel steamer ship fitted with five brass cannons, ammunition and additional supplies. Francis alerted the commander of the San Francisco Navy Yard, Captain Thomas Selfridge, in advance so he could take precautionary measures to prevent the attempted seizure.

On the opposite coast, 700 miles by sea from Wilmington, North Carolina, Bermuda had become a staging base for Confederate blockade runners. Sleeker, faster moving steamboats and other smaller crafts quickly replaced the slower, more traditional steamships. These were better equipped to slip past the Union imposed blockade, bringing cotton and other goods to Europe. They often returned with armaments. Bermuda had also become a valuable alternate route by sea to trade with Canada.

Charles Maxwell Allen was appointed as the United States Consul to Bermuda by Abraham Lincoln, in 1861, a few months after the start of the Civil War. Bermuda was critical for United States interests, given its easy access for Confederate blockade runners. Like Thurston and Potter in eastern Canada, Francis in Vancouver, Allen was highly regarded. He came from New England roots, but had moved his family to Amity, New York.

He was a staunch abolitionist who had provided assistance in settling runaway slaves who had escaped the South through the Underground Railroad. He was a founding member of the New York State Republican Party and became active in State politics with William Seward, before he became Secretary of State.

Seward suggested that Lincoln appoint Allen. He gladly accepted to help represent the United States interests in Bermuda. Allen made preparations to take care of his family while away and then sailed to the "Devils Isles."

Similar to Francis, Allen soon realized that he was in a hostile environment where Confederates and Confederate sympathizers dominated commerce in the trade hub of St. George, Bermuda. He quickly discovered that the British authorities, who claimed to be neutral, were complicit in helping many of the blockade runners.

As with the other consuls, he knew one of his most important responsibilities was to support the efforts of the United States Secret Service during the War. He had to do so alone, and with no budget. Allen began to send confidential correspondence to Colonel Sharpe on information he was able to gather on shipments of guns and ammunition from Europe, and the destination of these shipments in the South.

When Sharpe asked Allen to look into the activities of Doctor Luke Blackburn, and provide any information available, Blackburn had already left Bermuda for Canada. He had left three weeks before. Allen had been aware of Blackburn and had met him on several occasions.

A yellow fever epidemic had broken out in Bermuda. There was no known cure. There was a 30% fatality rate for those infected. Hundreds of Bermuda inhabitants were dying. Doctor Blackburn had come to Hamilton in Bermuda, offering his services voluntarily to help treat patients.

At first Allen thought this was commendable, particularly considering that Dr. Blackburn was putting his own life at risk by assisting infected patients. Not much was known at the time about what caused yellow fever, but it was proven to be highly contagious.

Major Norman S. Walker was the Confederate States of America Quartermaster agent in Bermuda. Walker's office helped coordinate trade provisions between the South and Europe. Allen reached out to one of the administrators in his office who he knew. They met in a local pub. The man was visibly uncomfortable talking to Allan. It took a few pints to ease his tension.

"This Doctor Blackburn was very strange," the man finally shared with Allan.

"How so?"

The man gulped another sip of beer. "Talk to the nurses who worked with him."

"Do you have a name?"

"Ummm, let me think. Dinah. Dinah somethin'. Oh yeah, Dinah Amery. Talk to her. Still at the Hamilton Hotel. I think."

"That's it? Nothing else?" Allen asked.

The man stared into his beer. Allen threw a couple coins on the table and began to get up.

"He was doing this on his own, so he said," the man was slurring his words. His voice raised, he added, "This God awful killer disease stirred him to want to come here and help those who were infected. That's what he told us."

"Driven by a charitable inclination?"

"Maybe, but, then, why were his expenses here being paid by the Confederate Treasury?"

"You sure about that?" Allen asked.

"Dead certain. Sorry, bad choice of words."

Allen left the pub and walked over to the Hamilton. The hotel was still being used as a hospital for yellow fever patients. He stepped into the main lobby. The stench was overbearing. Walking over to a desk where an administrator was sitting, he asked for Dinah Amery.

"Who are you, and may I ask what this is about?"

"My name is Charles Maxwell Allen. I'm the United States Consul for Bermuda. I'd like to speak with her about a U.S. citizen who worked as a physician here and recently left. Doctor Luke Pryor Blackburn. It is official state business."

"I see. Come with me."

The administrator, a tall, lean man with hollowed cheeks led him down a hall to a meeting room with a long wooden table surrounded by an assortment of mismatched chairs and benches. He was told to sit and wait.

The windows were open and he could hear someone crying, presumably from one of the rooms upstairs. It seemed quite a while before he finally heard footsteps approaching.

Two nurses entered the room. Allen stood to greet them.

"Mr. Allen, I'm Dinah Amery. They said you wanted to talk about Dr. Blackburn. I brought Frances Cameron who also worked with the doctor."

"Hello," Nurse Cameron said. Both women rattled off words with a British Cockney accent.

"Nice to meet both of you. Please ladies, have a seat."

Allen pulled out chairs and helped each of them take a seat. He crossed over and assumed a place on the opposite side of the table.

Before he could speak, Nurse Amery asked, "What is the nature of this inquiry about Doctor Blackburn?"

"Official United States business. We have reason to believe he may have been up to something, besides helping patients. Not sure what. I am interested in learning what your impressions were of Dr. Blackburn, and if you noticed anything out of the ordinary about his behavior."

The women looked at each other, both maintaining a stoic countenance. Nurse Amery spoke first.

"When Dr. Blackburn first got here, I was assisting a woman seriously sick with yellow fever. Wasn't very hot outside. The heat was more intense inside the patient rooms. Dr. Blackburn insisted I close the window and bring woolen blankets to cover this poor, desperately ill woman. I didn't think the women required any extra clothing, as she was sweating profusely at the time."

"Did you question him why he wanted to do this?"

"I did. He was dismissive. Told me I was only a nurse and he was the doctor. Reminded me that I was supposed to follow his orders. I also told him only a few clean blankets remained. The rest were contaminated, soaked with sweat and excrement from patients who had died."

"Did you get him the blankets?"

"I did. The few remaining clean ones. He wrapped them tightly around the patient. Dr. Blackburn said this was 'to prevent air from getting in'. I'd never heard of anything like this being done before for yellow fever victims."

Allen had pulled out a pad and was now taking notes. "Anything more with this patient?"

"Yes. When he left I took the heavy blankets off and opened the window. The woman seemed to improve from the slight breeze. Dr. Blackburn came back. He got very annoyed."

"What did he say?"

"He yelled at me." Nurse Amery was upset. Her whole body shook as she continued. "Asked me to follow him to his room. When we got there, he told me to help him lift down a trunk. He took out brand new shirts, trousers, coats - all woolen. Blackburn wrapped them tightly around the woman. By the next day, the woman was dead."

"What happened to these clothes?" Allen asked.

"I saw him gather them up. The clothing, as well as the soiled bedding. He packed them neatly back in one of his trunks, along with what appeared to be new clothes. I saw him do this with other patients, too."

"How many?"

"Hard to say. I'd say five or six."

Nurse Cameron added, "I saw an additional two. Did the same with me. He sent me out of the room. When I got back, the patient's clothes had always been removed and they were covered only in sheets."

"Was any of this reported?"

"I tried to," Nurse Amery said. "The head nurse told me that Doctor Blackburn had already complained about me. She told me if I wanted to keep my job, I should do what the doctor told me to do. She reminded me he was considered an expert in the treatment of yellow fever patients."

"What happened to the trunks?"

Miss Cameron spoke up first. "Dr. Blackburn took two or three with him back to Canada. The rest were delivered to an address Dr. Blackburn gave the driver."

"Do you know who the driver was?"

"I don't."

"Might be logged downstairs," said Nurse Amery.

Allen was able to get the name of the coachman and he remembered the address where he brought the trunks. Allen couldn't get over how a doctor, especially one with a reputation as a foremost expert in treating diseases such as yellow fever, could do this. Doctors, he thought to himself, take the "Hippocratic Oath," to help the sick and uphold high ethical standards. How could he?

When he knocked at the door, a man with a weathered, with a face of a heavy drinker, opened it part way. The door was chained.

"What do you want?" the man asked, overpowering Allan with a liquor soaked breath.

"I want information, and I am willing to pay for it."

The door shut. Allen knocked again. He heard the chain being released. The man invited him in.

His place was a mess. The man had to clear a chair filled with a pile of dirty clothes for Allan. The man sat down on his bed close by. Allen noticed a bottle of rum and a half-filled glass on the table next to the bed.

"What kind of information you want?"

"About some trunks you had delivered here a few weeks ago."

"They're no longer here."

"Where are they now?"

"First things first. I'm not saying I'm gonna tell ya, but how much you willing to pay?"

"How much you want?" Allen asked.

"If I were to tell you, I want 500 in British pounds."

"I can't pay that."

"Well, that's too bad. I'm gettin' paid handsomely to say nuttin'."

"How much?"

"They pay me 150 pounds per month, until these trunks are delivered where they supposed to go. Then they gonna pay me 500."

"Are the trunks still in Bermuda?"

"Aye."

"I take it that they're supposed be delivered to the States, correct?"

"Uh huh." The man reached for his half-full glass of rum and swallowed all of it.

"Well, that will never happen. We will be watching for them. Watching you, too. Mark my words, you could end up in jail for a very long time. There's good reason to believe that there is dangerous material in these trunks meant to kill innocent people."

Allan knew the odds of this were low, given the complicity of local authorities in helping the Confederates, and his lack of a staff to fully monitor all possible loading docks, or even keep an eye on this coachman, but it seemed to have the desired effect.

The man was holding his empty glass so tightly Allan thought he might break it.

"When are they scheduled to ship out?"

"Haven't been. Still working things out on the receiving end."

"I have a better idea. I'll pay you 200 pounds. All I can afford to pay. You tell me where they are and they don't need to know how we found them. May get another check or two before they realize what happened. But I guarantee you, you'll never see the 500. Might as well cut your losses."

Armed with the information he needed, Allen then went to the Health Officer in Saint George. Along with two other officers, they went to the house where the trunks were stored and demanded that they be turned over.

They learned that the plan was to have the trunks delivered to New York City and other northern cities in a few weeks, after arrangements on the delivery side were finalized. The contents were to be sold to clothing merchants, who would inadvertently help to spread yellow fever to their customers. Blackburn and his associates hoped to create an epidemic across industrial cities of the North.

Instead, the trunks were brought to a Quarantine Station where they were opened. They found wearing apparel and bedding, with dirty flannel drawers and shirts on the outside, clean apparel on the inside. Apparently the clean apparel was to be infected by the surrounding dirty items. All the contents were hosed down and soaked with soap.

While Allen was pleased he was able to stop this shipment, he still worried about the ones Blackburn took with him. Allen contacted his counterpart, the United States Consul for Toronto, David Thurston, to see what he could find out about Blackburn and the shipment that went to Canada.

Chapter 21: Insurrection Before Election: A Hoax?

THROUGHOUT MOST OF 1864, few believed President Lincoln could win a second term. Casualties continued to mount. The South refused to relinquish and continued to mount a vigorous fight. It didn't help that the Union Army, despite its advantages in numbers of soldiers, industrial output, and logistical support, seemed incapable of pounding the Confederates into submission. Advantage seemed to ebb and flow on both sides, with little progress made to end the conflict.

The North was divided. Many Democrats in northern states initially supported the war. That support peeled off after Lincoln's "Emancipation Proclamation." They did not like that the war was now positioned as a fight about the rights of slaves versus state rights. Radical Republicans believed Lincoln's efforts at emancipation were not nearly enough. They also argued that the President's proposed conditions to readmit the Confederate states were far too lenient. All this weighed heavy against Lincoln's prospects.

Late summer and early fall momentum began to swing to the Federals. While Grant remained pinned down near Petersburg, Sherman had captured Atlanta in September and was continuing to advance through Georgia. The Union Navy captured Mobile, Alabama. Sheridan had pushed Early back from Washington and by October his army had captured the Shenandoah Valley. Still most believed Lincoln could not win a second term.

Prior to Lincoln's reelection, Colonel Sharpe was concerned that other Confederate sponsored terrorist attacks were being developed. Sons of Liberty in collusion with the Confederates hiding in Canada had planned the Chicago attack during the Democratic Convention. What if they tried something around Election Day? If they did, what city, or cities, would they target? He wished they had someone embedded in the core Canadian team, as they had in the Sons of Liberty. Efforts to do this had failed.

There were suspicious editorials in Copperhead, anti-Lincoln newspapers across several cities. He was convinced there were coded messages in these articles, but they were impossible to decipher. He asked Elizabeth Van Lew if she could put her well-placed sources to work on it and try to find out all they could.

Intelligence from Joe Mills in the War Department had dried up. Elizabeth assumed it was because the Department was being more guarded in protecting its most sensitive information. Perhaps Joe Mills, afraid he was under suspicion, had decided he couldn't take additional risks for fear of being caught. When she last tried to reach out to him, he told her it was not a good time to exchange messages.

The health of Jefferson Davis began to improve as he resumed his regular schedule working from his downtown office. Almost all of his business was now being conducted there. Any papers he brought home were locked in his personal safe. No papers were left on his desk.

He was very polite with Mary Bowser. Always wishing her "good day" when he left home for his office. Varina, still seemed very appreciative of the little things Mary did around the house, and continued to encourage her interaction and devotion to the children. Although Mary didn't notice any discernible difference in the way she was treated by the Davis family, there was cause for concern. May was acting differently.

She had become increasingly suspicious. Conversation was more stilted. Her expression as she presented Mary her list of chores for the day was cold, distant. This wasn't simply her imagination. She couldn't help but wonder if May was still planning to say something to Jefferson Davis, or his wife, as she once warned. Was May looking to catch her one more time to remove any doubt? Maybe she already had shared her misgivings.

Mary asked Wayne to arrange another meeting with Elizabeth in the back of his store. This time Daniel was there as well.

"Recently, it has become much more difficult finding things out," Mary confided. "I do have something to share, but, I'm afraid it is not much, and what I do have is disturbing."

"I'm afraid to ask," Elizabeth remarked.

"I heard a few days ago that Jefferson Davis met with two French Diplomats."

"At the house?" Elizabeth asked.

"No, they never came to the house. I don't think the meeting went well. When Mr. Davis came home, he was not happy. Sadie, the family cook heard him say to Mrs. Davis it would have been a much different meeting if they had won at either Gettysburg or Vicksburg."

"That is good news, is it not?" Daniel questioned. "About the French. Could mean that they are not going to enter the war to help the Confederates."

"It could. This also might lead Jefferson Davis to conclude that they must try something more drastic on their own," Elizabeth suggested.

"That is what has me so anxious." Mary said. "I had not been there long, but I remember just before General Lee launched his attack into Pennsylvania, Jefferson Davis was leaving early for work and returning late. He's been doing it again, since the meeting with the French. He carries a haversack back and forth, filled with documents."

"Any possibility you might get a chance, at some point, to peek inside at the contents?"

"I doubt it, Miss Van Lew. Sorry to say. The haversack has a lock. I believe it was a gift from the French. Patterned cloth and fine leather. He must put it in the safe when he comes home. I have not seen it anywhere else in the house. No papers are left unattended on his desk, or anywhere else."

Daniel quickly asserted, "While he may not be suspicious of you in particular, Mary, it sure sounds like he's bein' very distrustful in general."

Elizabeth spoke next. "With May watching you very closely, and even if Jefferson Davis is not suspicious of you, yet, as you say, Mary, he is spending less time working from home, and more careful with what he does bring home. Maybe it is time we get you out. You've already done so much. Maybe I should ask Varina Davis to let you come back home to us."

"Please believe me, Miss Van Lew. I am most appreciative of your concern, but that is not why I am telling you this. Hopefully I can continue to be of value at some point by staying where I am, but gathering any additional intelligence these days has become close to impossible. I can't be replaced once I leave. You know that."

Daniel said "Miss Van Lew is right to be concerned about you safety. With Jefferson Davis more suspicious lately, you need to be extra careful, Mary. Whether May said something or not. He may be on to you."

"I've been thinking a lot about this and I don't think so, Daniel. He would have gotten rid of me already if he suspected me of spying."

Elizabeth wasn't convinced. "What makes you think it could change?"

"Davis and his visitors have become much more careful, but there is always a chance at some point they might get careless. A conversation that I overheard, or one of the other slaves could hear something important and share it with the rest of us. A letter left out. Also, the health of Jefferson Davis. He has had ongoing periodic bouts with his malaria infliction. When it gets real bad, at least in the past, it has forced him to work from home. That's when some of his papers can become more accessible."

Elizabeth continued to probe. "Even if this happens again, you are now being watched by May. Perhaps others. What makes you think you can do this without being caught?"

"That is always a possibility, of course, a horrible possibility I don't want to think about. But, I will be much more careful. I want to stay. The reason I am here is to let you know not to expect much from me right now. I am hopeful this will change. Shortly, I hope."

Elizabeth commented, "Yes, especially after you said you suspect they may be planning something big again."

"I might be wrong," Mary responded, "but I worry they may be planning another major attack. Maybe using some of those new weapons we know they've been testing on at the Nitre Mining Bureau. What if they are getting ready to do something terrible and we can't find out anything in time to stop it?"

A few moments of uncomfortable silence followed, before Daniel piped up.

"Walter," Daniel said, looking directly at Elizabeth.

"Walter?" Mary was perplexed. "Walter, who worked as a slave at Libby Prison?"

"The same. Daniel told me about Walter last night," Elizabeth responded.

"I know he was a huge help with prison escapes," Mary mentioned, still looking very confused.

"I heard yesterday Walter is now working, cleaning offices in the old Richmond Custom House on Bank Street," Daniel explained.

Mary immediately understood the significance. Jefferson Davis, as well as other members of his cabinet, had offices there. Confederate Cabinet meetings were also held there.

"Just might be another way to find things out," Daniel said.

Elizabeth added, "Daniel and I were discussing last night that there may be a way Walter could slip documents out at night and bring them back early the next day. Before regular working hours."

"Have you spoken with Walter?" Mary asked.

"No, not yet. A lot of things would need to be worked out. Even if he agreed to help us again," Daniel noted.

They decided Mary would leave the store room exit to the alley first. As Mary started to get up, she reached over and placed her hand on Elizabeth's.

"I understood from the beginning how dangerous this would be. You have always been very honest about this, Miss Van Lew," Mary said.

"Well, maybe not totally honest."

"Ma'am?"

"I once told you deceiving others does become easier over time. Pretending to be someone you are not. I think I was actually deceiving myself. I was trying desperately to believe this. I now know it doesn't. Never did I think the war would last this long. I find in some ways it has become even more difficult. Always wondering who may be suspicious, and if someone will turn you in. It was inconceivable to me that both you and I would still be doing this. And that you, Mary, so much more vulnerable, have to keep your guard up every moment within the nest of the viper."

"I hope you didn't think, Miss Van Lew, that this little talk would inspire me with vigor," Mary remarked. She then laughed.

"It's enough to say, Mary, what you are doing is remarkable. We are both very grateful," Daniel quickly added.

"That we are," Elizabeth said.

Mary walked to the door, turned and said, "Your grammar is much improved, Daniel."

"You should hear Harriett Anne. All thanks to Miss Van Lew."

"Stop it, both of you, now. You should go, Mary."

"First, let me make sure no one is in the alley," Daniel insisted.

Daniel and Elizabeth would wait before leaving themselves. Elizabeth would go through the store. Talk to Wayne. Purchase a few goods. Daniel would wait longer, and then leave through the back, same as Mary.

Elizabeth was walking home from Wayne's store by herself. She was about to cross 25th Street, a few short blocks from her home, when she heard someone call out.

"Hello Elizabeth, isn't it a little cold for taking a late afternoon stroll?"

There was a woman approaching her from the other side of the street. She was well dressed in a reddish-brown cape with a full fur collar wrapped tightly around a laced bonnet, making it difficult to see her face. That voice, she recognized the voice. Now, as the woman got closer, Elizabeth could also see the face.

"Nice to see you Phoebe. I could say the same about you."

"Oh, I was at St. John's practicing with Mr. Hastings. He is so gifted on the organ. Just a short walk home for me." Casting her eyes down at the package Elizabeth was carrying, she added, "You must have been shopping down town, and walking home with only a wrap to keep you warm. You could catch a frightful cold."

"Yes, I was shopping. I'm fine as well. The walk was very refreshing." Elizabeth was determined not to offer any explanation more than necessary.

"We haven't seen you, or your lovely mother at any of our recent social events."

"We are both very sorry about this, Phoebe. Mother has not been well of late. Frankly, it has been more than I can handle keeping up with things these days without having John around."

"I am so sorry for Eliza. Oh, and I did hear about your brother," Phoebe Reynolds acknowledged, in a slightly sardonic tone. "I wanted to mention something else to you, Elizabeth. The last time I was in the company of Varina Davis, she indicated that she has a slave girl maid named Mary Bowser. Varina told me she used to work for you. I don't remember a housemaid named Mary Bowser."

It was all Elizabeth could do to keep her composure. Mary was already under suspicion. This had the potential to make things even worse. She knew Phoebe armed with this information could spell doom for Mary.

Gathering herself, Elizabeth said, "Mary Richards was her maiden name when she worked as a slave for us. She is married now."

"Hmm. I still don't remember her."

"She was a scullery maid, most of the time she was with us. She cleaned dishes, floors, polished the brass and silver. I don't think we ever used her to serve during the parties you might have attended. I doubt you would have ever had reason to be around her. It is getting late. I must be getting along. Mother will be worried. Nice to see you, Phoebe."

"You as well, Elizabeth. Don't forget to extend my greetings to Eliza."

Daniel came in through the kitchen door shortly after Elizabeth had done the same. He knew immediately there was a problem. Harriett Anne did as well, leaving the room to give them privacy to talk.

After sharing her conversation with Phoebe, Elizabeth, still emotionally shook up, suggested, "Probably best to not tell her. Mary already has enough to worry about and she already knows she is being carefully watched."

"I'm not so sure about this, Miss Van Lew."

"What good would it do to tell her, Daniel? This will make her even more upset. I'm afraid that alone could impact her disposition. Making them even more suspicious."

"Miss Van Lew, I know you would want me to be honest with you."

"Yes, of course Daniel."

"I believe we need to get word to Mary about this..."

"Why do you think this?"

"In case anyone asks Mary about it. She needs to say the same as what you just told Phoebe Reynolds."

Elizabeth paused for a moment and then said, "You are so right, Daniel. I'm afraid my fears about Mary being exposed as a spy, and, to be honest, my strong feelings of guilt, having placed her in this situation, may be clouding my judgment. Preventing me from thinking clearly."

"Miss Van Lew, you are just trying to do the right thing. Still, Mary needs to know. If alright with you, I will talk with her. Then I'll go see Walter."

"Yes Daniel, please do." As he was about to leave the kitchen, Elizabeth called after him. "Daniel, thank you."

After Libby Prison closed, Walter was still owned by the head of the Tobacco Company that had been converted into Libby Prison. Like Dolores, he had been essentially leased to work for the Confederate Government.

He had a reputation for working hard. His denials when questioned about his possible involvement in the Libby escape were eventually accepted. For a while he had been doing odd jobs. When one of the owner's other slaves who had worked at the Custom House recently escaped North, the job was given to Walter.

Daniel immediately went to see Walter in his dilapidated boarding house room. As Daniel explained to him the importance of looking for information that could prove vital to defeating the Confederates, Walter stopped him.

"They don't leave anything out when they go home. All gets locked up at night. Even if they did, I can't read any. How would I know if it's important? Then what? You want me to sneak it out? They'd know for sure."

"What if you help me sneak in to have a look? Not real good at it yet, but I've been learning to read. Enough, I hope, so I could figure some of it out. At least, if it's important or not."

"Miss Van Lew teach ya?"

"Yeah, no one is supposed to know."

"But like I said, they don't leave nothin' out."

"Maybe we'll get lucky, Walter. We have to try."

The plan was for Daniel to disguise himself as a maintenance worker who had to be called in to fix rain damage from the roof of the Richmond Custom House. It was a few weeks before the election. The damage causing rain leakage had some help from Walter. He simply ripped out a previous patch on the roof from the last attempt to stop a recurring leak. This he followed up with by dumping a few buckets of water into the reopened hole.

He showed the wet ceiling and puddle in an upstairs meeting room to his boss.

"Probably worked its way down from a rain shower a few days ago," Walter noted.

He was told to get the fellow who worked on it last time to come fix it. If anyone asked, he would tell them the man was not available, so they sent Daniel instead.

Walter escorted Daniel up to the roof to repair the latest leak damage. It was midday. He left Daniel there and went back down to carry on with his assigned cleaning duties. Things seemed to work to plan. After a while, the few office workers who saw them come in appeared to forget there was someone, not a working regular, who had not left. Walter waited for cabinet officers and their staff to leave. After regular working hours, he would step out the main door, like he always did, with a guard locking it behind him. It was already pitch black.

He then walked around the corner to the back of the building. He made sure no one was watching and then knocked on the delivery door. Daniel released the inside bolt and the two men disappeared into the dark entrance, bolting the door behind them.

Daniel handed Walter the candle he was holding and followed him upstairs. Jefferson Davis had locked the door to his office.

"I can tell ya that even if it was open, everything inside would be locked up in a cabinet or his desk," Walter explained.

They next checked Secretary of State, Judah Benjamin's office. The door was open. Desk locked. They checked his secretary's desk. Also locked. No luck with Secretary of Treasury, George Trenholm, either.

Next they looked at the Secretary of War, James Seddon's office. His desk was locked. So was his secretary's desk, which was in an adjoining much smaller office space. Daniel immediately noticed that the secretary's work area was different.

There were scattered papers on the desk and in the trash basket. Daniel held the candle and looked closely over the contents on the desk. He flattened out the crumbled pages from the trash. Nothing of consequence.

"I tried to let you know. They're very careful. Leave nothin' important out for folks to see," Walter said again.

Daniel began to look around more closely at the secretary's office space.

"The others all much neater. Not this one. He's got to be more disorganized. Maybe forgetful too."

He walked over to the door and reached his hand over the upper door frame in a sweeping motion, finding only dust. As he slapped his hands together to knock off the dirt, he noticed the large potted plant in a corner of the room.

Daniel moved across the room, leaning the vase over with one hand. He slid his other hand underneath. "Clank." He touched a set of keys.

"Let's try the boss first," Daniel suggested.

He tried a couple of the keys. One finally opened Seddon's office. Another unlocked his desk. Daniel began to look through papers inside one of the drawers. There was a note from Robert E. Lee addressed to James Seddon. Daniel read it to himself:

> Sir: I beg leave to inquire whether there is any prospect of my obtaining any increase to this army. If not, it will be very difficult for us to maintain ourselves. The enemy's numerical superiority enable him to hold his lines with an adequate force, and extend on each flank with numbers so much greater than ours that we can only meet his corps, increased by recent recruits, with a division reduced by long and arduous service.

"Know what it says?" Walter asked.

Daniel nodded. "Think so. Most of it. Lee is telling Seddon he is outnumbered and can't continue like this much longer."

"Sounds like good news to me. Something we can take back."

"Let's see if we can find more," Daniel suggested.

Walter noted, "Shouldn't stay too much longer. A guard does a round, on all the floors, probably starting pretty soon."

Daniel then found in another drawer a long document Seddon was writing entitled "Report of the Secretary of War."

"Looks like he may be getting ready to do a speech." Daniel skimmed the document as best he could, and then started to snicker.

"What is it?" Walter inquired.

"Doesn't sound like they going to back down anytime soon. Making it sound like all is rosy." Daniel then said, "Listen to this:"

> We have resisted the mightiest of the efforts of our enemies; we have encountered and defeated his largest and best appointed armies; we have thwarted his best laid plans...

"You read better than you talk," Walter mused.

"Miss Van Lew says so too. She tells me I still need to work on it, but all in all, making good progress. So she says."

"Wish I could learn."

Daniel then spotted a note buried in the stack of papers he had pulled from the desk drawer. This was a memo addressed to Judah Benjamin. He must have passed it over to Seddon.

This one was labeled from "Napoleon," regarding "Atlantis." Daniel read aloud once again:

> I spoke with Governor who said that in the event of an insurrec-
> tion on Election Day that he would remain neutral.

"If this says what I think it says, a state governor up north is talking about an uprising on Election Day, and when it happens, he won't do nothing. I meant to say 'anything' about it. Walter, I'm thinking Atlantis must be code name for a city."

Walter responded, "Don't know nothin' 'bout Atlantis. Maybe New York City? It's on the Atlantic coast."

"Good guess. Maybe."

Daniel picked up a note with Confederate letterhead off the desk and pulled out a dip pen from its stand, also on the desk, and began to scribble notes. He knew from Mary that "Napoleon" was code for one of the leaders out of Canada, but he didn't remember whom.

"Write too?" Walter commented, sarcastically.

"Some, but I'm no Mary Bowser."

They heard a noise from downstairs. Someone was entering the building. Daniel pulled together the papers, shuffled them back together and pushed them back into the desk and locked it. As he put the pen back, Walter took the keys and placed them back under the vase. They took the backstairs up to the roof.

Walter waved his candle. An African American on the adjoining roof pulled up a ladder.

"Good thing I told Sammy to standby and be ready, just in case."

The man called Sammy, a big man, raised a long, narrow ladder near the edge of the opposite building where he was standing and lowered it down slowly over the alley below so Walter could grab the other end before it slammed against the rooftop where he and Daniel were standing. They took turns crossing as Sammy helped them kept the ladder steady, as best he could.

The information Daniel relayed to Elizabeth, and she passed to Sharpe, was also sent to David Thurston in Toronto. One of his agents had learned where the Confederate transplants were operating in Toronto, and where most of them lived in a subdivided house in downtown Toronto.

The agent was keeping tabs on their movement, which had picked up of late. He would follow them to the Toronto Train Station to determine their travel itinerary. He was ordered to simply watch and report, as the United States government was still adamant to not do anything that could lead to an international incident on Canadian soil.

He reported late October that at least five or six had boarded trains, travelling separately to New York. The Governor there was Horatio Seymour, a well-known Lincoln hater. New York City at the time was a diverse population, with many groups and individuals sympathetic to the South. Some citizens were fearful of losing jobs if slaves were freed. This was where the Draft Riots had broken out a year ago.

Several pieces of the puzzle were coming together. It had to be New York City. At first when Sharpe presented his concerns about New York being targeted for a terrorist attack, General John A. Dix, commander of the Eastern Department based in New York City was skeptical. He thought it was a hoax. So did John A. Kennedy, the Superintendent of Police. None of this dissuaded Sharpe. He knew exactly what needed to be done.

There were eight of them. The leader was a dashing Confederate Officer, Lieutenant Colonel Robert Maxwell Martin. He, like the others, had escaped from the Union prison for Confederate soldiers, Johnson Island in Lake Erie near the Ohio coast. They had joined Jacob Thompson's team to plan and execute terrorist acts against the U.S. Federal Government.

They arrived 10 days before the election to familiarize themselves with the city streets. The men booked rooms in separate New York City Hotels. When they first met together, one of them commented, "I saw the President caricatured in many ludicrous and ungainly pictures. The spirit of revolt is manifest. It only needs a start with a new leadership."

The men planned to burn each hotel where they were staying and create a huge panic on Election Day. They would use the latest design of the Confederate's Greek Fire weapon, with development instructions supplied to a New York City chemist with Confederate sympathies.

Lieutenant Martin told the group, "As I'm sure some of you heard, there were problems with the Greek Fire we tried to use in past. Since then the Nitre Bureau scientists have continued to experiment. I am told they have now perfected it so it should have a devastating impact when used. Virtually impossible to put out the flames from this latest version."

Twelve dozen bottles of the flammable mixture were distributed to the group. They were told that breaking one of the bottles would start a fire that would burn everything it touched.

They left, each with different assignments. Most of them to scope the targeted hotels. One of the conspirators, John Headley, was assigned to meet with the chemist. A few others would work on the plan to escape back to Canada. They met a few more times.

As planned, the men met one final time, early on Election Day. It was in a rented cottage at the edge of Central Park. They reviewed the final plans and waited for the order to head back to their assigned hotels and launch the attacks. Adrenaline was flowing. Martin believed if things went to plan they could expect close to 20,000 citizens to rise up and join in the rampage.

As John Headley tried to assure Martin, "The spirit of revolt in the City is manifest. The tangible prospects are best for an uprising." Another told Martin, "You can rely on us for bold and unflinching action when the hour arrives for crucial duty."

The order never came. Instead, they received word that General Benjamin Butler had marched into New York City with 10,000 troops. Gunboats moved into the Hudson and East Rivers surrounding Manhattan to support his troops.

Martin told his men to stand down. He explained that a conference of Confederate leaders had decided the operation needed to be postponed. The angry, disappointed men scattered to avoid being caught.

The day before the election, *The New York Times* had printed the following letter from Butler describing General Orders No. 1, "to preserve the peace and prevent Rebel incursions," stating the following::

> The armies of the United States are "ministers of good and not of evil." They are safeguards of constitutional liberty, which is FREEDOM TO DO RIGHT, NOT WRONG. They can be a terror to evil doers only, and those who fear them are accused by their own consciences. Let every citizen having a right to vote, as according to the inspiration of his own judgment, freely. He will be protected in that right by the whole power of the Government if it shall become necessary.

> Maj.-Gen. BENJ. F. BUTLER.

The skeptics may have felt vindicated when nothing happened on Election Day. Sharpe knew otherwise.

On Tuesday November 8, 1864, Lincoln defeated McClellan, his former general, to win his second term. Lincoln won 55 percent of the electoral votes. McClellan, the general who refused to engage as Lincoln wanted but remained popular with his men, won only 21 percent. A vast majority of McClellan's former Army of the Potomac voted for Lincoln as Commander-in-Chief over their former commander.

Elizabeth Van Lew invited Unionists friends and members of her spy ring for a low-key celebration at her home the following Saturday afternoon. The celebration was primarily about the election. It was also about what did not happen on Election Day.

This party at the Van Lew's was quite different from all previous gatherings. Before the guests arrived, Elizabeth made sure, with the help of Daniel, that all windows were covered with blankets, to keep nosey neighbors from snooping. Elizabeth and her visiting cousin did the cooking. They served boiled pork and bean soup, followed by molasses apple pie for dessert.

In addition to her visiting cousin, the guests around the dining table included Unionist friends and Van Lew servants. Sam Ruth, Thomas McNiven, William Rowley and Frederick Lohmann. Wayne Evans was also there. He would sit next to Elizabeth who was still busy in the kitchen.

Daniel and his wife Harriett Anne sat together across from Wayne. Isaac was seated next to McNiven. On his opposite side was Dolores, no longer needed in the services of Jefferson Davis. Elizabeth worked out an arrangement with the help of a well-placed friend inside the government. Dolores now lived with the Van Lew's, and was caring for Eliza, whose health was on the decline.

Eliza sat at the end of the table. Elizabeth's cousin would sit between Sam Ruth and Walter. His reluctance to enter Church Hill had subsided as he no longer worked at the prison where he feared he was not trusted.

When the two ladies who had prepared the meal finally sat down, Wayne rose to give a toast, holding up his glass of wine.

"First, let us celebrate the reelection of our President who has endured so much. I am convinced he and his new command will help us secure victory very soon."

After glasses clinked, Wayne continued, looking directly into Elizabeth's eyes, "To my right is the most amazing woman I have ever met. The best secret weapon of the Federal government. Her cooking, by the way, may not be up to Harriett Anne's standards, but is not half bad either..."

More clinking of glasses with plenty of laughter.

Elizabeth politely smiled, but didn't blush or appear flustered. She waited for the volume of noise to dissipate. She remained seated and placed her glass back on the table.

"Thank you one and all, but I have been just a small bit player in our efforts. Everyone in this room deserves credit for what each and every one of you has contributed in this fight for justice and what is right. We have all made great sacrifices, putting our lives in serious danger."

"But some more than others," McNiven commented, as several nodded in agreement.

Elizabeth shook her head in disagreement. "There's no one in this room who hasn't taken great risks to help right this wrong that surrounds us. Right here in Richmond! This is still hard for me to comprehend, but I do think it is appropriate to call attention to the following. Most recently Walter and Daniel were instrumental in providing critical intelligence that may have prevented the planned attack in New York City."

Ruth added, "No doubt in my mind, Elizabeth, their efforts were a big reason your friend General Butler and his Army arrived in New York City just before the election. Things could have gone real bad if they hadn't."

Rowley held up his glass. "You are so right Sam. There is still a lot of anti-Lincoln sentiment in New York. I heard McClellan nearly doubled the amount of votes that Lincoln received there. The agitators in New York could have riled them up to a frenzy, had they been successful." He concluded his remarks looking across as Walter and Daniel. "Yes, gentlemen, very well done."

Others raised their glasses. Neither Daniel nor Walter looked as if they appreciated the attention.

Elizabeth spoke again. "My only regret is that one of us who has risked so very much could not be here today. We all know who this is..."

"Let's drink to Mary," Wayne added.

"To Mary," echoed around the table.

"We also, must not forget," Elizabeth commented, "We cannot let up. There is still much we all need to do."

Chapter 22: Evacuation Day

Varina Davis dealt with personal demons. The devastating impact of losing a young child in a tragic accident, the war, and her husband's bad health, all weighed heavily. So did her family ties to the North which the prolonged war had fractured, perhaps irreparably.

Yet, she was generally kind to the help, and not overly demanding. They all knew there was one thing she detested. When guests tracked mud into her home she would get upset, especially if not cleaned immediately. It happened again.

When she called out to May about the foyer, there was no time to lose. May pulled Mary away from performing her current duties and asked her to wash down the entranceway and sitting room.

Mary gladly obliged. At first she was afraid Mrs. Davis was going to ask her something else. Had May spoken to her? She had also been warned about Phoebe Reynolds. Had this Richmond socialite with access to the First Lady of the Confederacy said something more? Perhaps Mrs. Davis had heard from both.

She was on her knees scrubbing the floor. May who had been watching, while barking orders, had moved into another location in the house. While she was busy cleaning up the dirt on the floor, she heard a knock. Rising to her feet, Mary waited a moment for Wilbur the doorman to respond. She called out to him. No answer. He must have been preoccupied with something else. She went over and opened it.

Mary recognized him immediately. It was General Thomas A. Harris. He had come to the house once before, with Judah Benjamin. She had talked to the soldier who came with them. While Harris met with President Davis, the soldier had told her about experimenting with cats.

Harris was also on the list with code names she saw, next to McCulloh, the scientist. She knew both McCulloh and the retired general were working at the Nitre Bureau. She remembered McCulloh's code name was "Richard," and for Harris it was "Alexander." Mary assumed the codes were used in the messages passed back and forth from Richmond to Canada.

"Good day, Harris said. Is President Davis in? Tell him General Harris is here."

"He is resting, and we were told he is not to be disturbed." Mary responded. "How can I help you, General?"

He held up the envelope he was holding. Mary noticed it had a Confederate wax seal. "Would you please give this to President Davis?"

"Yes, I will."

"Please make sure you give it to him as soon as he is available. This is very important."

"Yes, sir. I will."

He handed her the envelope, turned, walked down the front steps and disappeared down the street within moments, where Clay Street curved into Leigh Street. Mary watched from the stoop, then turned to re-enter the house. May was standing in the doorway.

"I'll take that," May said.

Mary handed the envelope over, hiding her deep feeling of disappointment. May took the envelope and placed it in her apron pocket.

"Now, get back to work before Mrs. Davis comes by," May ordered.

"Yes ma'am."

Mary dropped back down on her knees and continued to scrub. Harris had said it was something important. How could she get to see the contents of that letter? She decided her best chance to intercept the letter would be lunchtime. Assuming May didn't bring it to Jefferson Davis before that. She hoped he would stay sleeping and undisturbed.

The servants, including May, ate in one of the extension rooms built on to the back of the Executive Mansion, next to the kitchen. The maids and servants took off their aprons and hung them on hooks near the door while eating. Mary hoped she could swipe the letter, try to hold up to the light, as she had done in the past. She could then either place it back into May's apron if possible, or if not, leave it someplace on the floor, to make it look as if it may have fallen out from May's apron as she scurried about.

She finished cleaning the foyer and resumed her other duties. Time before lunch seemed to stand still. She decided to come late for lunch, hoping she could pull the letter from May's apron and place into hers without drawing attention.

May's apron was distinct from the rest of the help. Most were white. Hers was green. There it was. She stood in front of it as she undid her own apron tie around her back. With one hand holding her apron up, she reached into May's apron pocket. Nothing there. She tried the other pocket. Still nothing. She hung hers up, and joined the others for lunch.

"Where would it be?" she wondered. Did May already bring it to the office of President Davis? She didn't remember seeing her walk up the stairs. The President was still resting with the door closed and the instructions were that he was not to be disturbed while sleeping.

Mary surmised President Davis must be sick again. As she continued housecleaning after lunch, Mary looked in all the potential places in the house she thought it might be. Again, she came up empty.

Then another possibility occurred to her. Could May have brought it to her room? She often went there right before lunch. When Mary was able to slip away, she took the back staircase behind the kitchen, upstairs to the sleeping quarters where Edward, the steward, Sadie the cook, and May, the head housekeeper had their separate rooms.

The door to May's room was closed, but unlocked. She slipped into the room and began searching closets, the desk draws, a separate table with a basket of papers on top. No luck. Where else could it be, she wondered as she surveyed the room? Maybe under the bed? She bent over to look. There she found another box filled with papers. On top was the envelope.

The sun was bright, pouring through the curtains. Mary pulled them wide and took the envelope and held it up to the window. The envelope paper was too thick. She couldn't see any content inside. Exasperated, she placed the envelope inside her blouse and headed back to the main section of the mansion before she was missed.

President Davis ate dinner with his family and appeared to be feeling better. There was no sign that May had gone back for the letter to hand it over during the evening. Mary deduced that May would most probably look for the letter first thing in the morning to bring it to him.

After supper, Mary waited for Sadie the cook to check the back door through the kitchen, to make sure it was locked. When Sadie left, Mary went back into the kitchen and opened the lock, so she could sneak back later from her unattached bungalow, and reenter the main house.

She then left the house and joined Melissa and Gaby in their shared room. Gaby was fast asleep. Melissa was just getting into bed. "Good night Mary," she whispered as she rolled over facing the wall. As usual, Melissa fell asleep soon after hitting her pillow. Mary lay dressed on her bed for what she thought was a reasonable time, waiting for the others in the main residence to retire.

The Executive Mansion had over 10 coal fireplaces to warm almost all the rooms. She needed to get to one of the few running on the ground floor that evening, while the coals were still hot. Her best bet she decided was in the salon, where the President and his wife had spent the waning hours of the evening after dinner. It was also slightly more secluded than other rooms such as the parlor, kitchen, or dining room.

Mary slipped back into the main residence, careful not to make any noise. She picked up a kitchen knife and headed directly for the salon, squatting in front of the fireplace. The coals were still hot. Mary pulled the envelope from her pocket, along with the knife. She also took out one of her cleaning gloves from her pocket.

Mary heated the knife over the coals with her gloved hand, until she believed it was warm enough, but not too hot. She began to gently lift the wax seal, trying not to break or melt it. Carefully working the knife on the edges of the seal, she was able to gradually separate it from the envelope. This was a skill Thomas McNiven had shared with her before she first came to the Davis residence. It worked.

She pulled the letter from the opened envelope. A note from Professor McCulloh. She had the ability to read and grasp things quickly, but this was puzzling:

November 15, 1864
His Excellency Jefferson Davis

President Confederate States

Sir, I wish to inform you that you will see the improvements
made with our latest Greek Fire the day of the city evacuation.

Also, I would like to invite you and your cabinet to see another
demonstration of a weapon we are perfecting that produces
lethal gas.

I firmly believe that together, these newly perfected weapons
will demonstrate the viability of a final chemical solution. With
these weapons, we could potentially eliminate the necessity of
sending persons of military service into the enemy's country for
us to be victorious against our Union foes.

Professor Richard Sears McCulloh

Mary was mystified. Was it possible McCulloh was referring to the
failed New York plot? No, it was dated a week after the Election Day. Did
this mean that another terrorist attack against a city in the North was imminent? Would these toxic chemicals kill a large number of people, while
also forcing a mass evacuation?

She glanced once again at the note trying to make sense of it. She then
repeated the same process of heating the knife and gently wiping it against
the back of the seal so that it would stick back onto the envelope. Mary was
pleased that it worked so well. It looked as if it had never been tampered
with, or so she thought.

But how would she get the letter back where she found it? Mary began
to consider different possibilities as she passed from the salon back into the
kitchen.

She had an idea. There were four servants, including May, who had
rooms in the servant's quarters above the kitchen. There was also an unoccupied room. This room had once belonged to Henry who had escaped
North after starting the basement fire. Another servant had been using it
until President Davis, irritated at her apparent poor performance, had sold
her off.

Mary would stay there and wait for early morning. May was one of the earliest risers. As she went to the shared wash room, this would give Mary her opening to place the letter back under her bed.

The bed was unmade. There we no blankets. She was shivering from the cold. She assumed she could stay awake and be ready when she heard May leave her room. Eventually Mary did doze off. She woke, panicking, afraid she may have overslept and missed her chance. It was only a couple hours after midnight. She decided to sit against the bed board for the rest of the night to ensure she wouldn't miss her chance.

Finally, Mary could hear May stirring in the room across the hall. This part of the house, the kitchen with upstairs bedrooms for servants, was an extension to the mansion and not nearly as well constructed. The walls were planks of thin wood, nailed to foundational beams. She heard May open her door and walk down the hall to the wash room. As soon as she heard a second door close, Mary moved swiftly from her room into May's. She placed the envelope back in the box under the bed.

Her heart was pounding and she was now sweating, as she stepped out of the main house into the cold air and walked to her bungalow. Melissa was dressed, fixing her hair. Gaby had already left to assume her early morning chores.

"Who you stay with last night? I saw you comin' down the steps this mornin' from the main servants quarters."

"I really can't say," Mary answered.

"I am very surprised. Didn't think you were that kind of a girl, and you're a married woman."

Mary washed up, changed clothes and went to work. She was changing sheets in the children's room when she sensed someone was watching her. It was May, standing in the bedroom doorway.

"Good morning, ma'am," Mary said.

"Mornin', Mary," May said back, in her thick Irish brogue. "When you're done with all that, come see me downstairs," she added.

May met her at the bottom of the steps. She directed Mary to follow her into the small corner room where President Davis often entertained a small number of guests. She let Mary enter first, closing the door behind them.

"When I found the letter from General Harris missing from under my bed, I knew it had to be you," May whispered, but her tone was sharp, accusatory.

It felt as if her stomach had dropped. Mary realized she had been caught.

"What letter?" Mary, following May's example, was also whispering.

May was red-faced and her jaw clenched as she stared back at Mary for a moment before continuing.

"You surely know what I'm talkin' about. You know I've been keepin' an eye on you for some time, Miss Mary Bowser. I knew you were up to something."

Thoughts raced through Mary's head. What could she possibly conjure up as an excuse? Nothing came to mind. There were no excuses that could explain this away. Not this time.

"Ma'am..."

"Hear me out." May pulled the envelope from her apron, as if it had never left it. "I can tell you opened the seal. Very well done, I must say. One needs to look very closely, like I did, to notice it had been tinkered with. Did you sneak out last night? Did you bring it to someone who could read the content? A Unionist spy. Maybe?"

"No ma'am, I did not."

"You're lying to me."

"I am not," Mary insisted. There was a long uncomfortable pause, before Mary continued. "I read it myself."

"You read it?"

"Yes ma'am. I was schooled up North. A Quaker school."

"I'll be damned. A negro slave snooping around in the residence of the Confederate President. On top of that, one who can read. I thought you were up to no good for some time, but this..."

"I am sorry ma'am, but I was doing what I thought was right."

"What did it say? Did you copy the note?"

"Didn't have to. I have a very good memory. The letter was delivered by General Harris, but written by a Professor McCulloh. The subject concerned a demonstration of improved Greek Fire. Leading to a city evacuation. This first part, frankly was a little vague – at least I had trouble understanding."

For several seconds a bewildered May stared back at Mary before resuming her interrogation.

"Did it say what city?"

"No, it did not, ma'am. But, I suspect a city up north."

"What else did it say?"

"Ma'am, you caught me. I assume you will turn me in. Only I am to blame. No one else. You have my word. I have not shared this with anyone else."

"Well, maybe I wish you did."

"Ma'am?"

"What else did it say?"

"He mentioned Greek Fire and another weapon being perfected with a lethal gas. It then described how these weapons, and I quote, "Could potentially eliminate the necessity of sending persons of military service into the enemy's country for us to be victorious against our Union foes."

"You must have a very good memory," Miss Bowser. "Anything else?"

"Professor McCulloh offered to show a demonstration of the lethal gas weapon for President Davis and his cabinet."

"How lovely. That strange professor, with support of General Harris and high level Confederate officials is conducting hideous experiments with cats. I don't think President Davis is too thrilled about it. These people he has surrounded himself with, I'm convinced, have persuaded him to go along. Given recent Union gains, I guess they're all getting very desperate."

"I've heard about the cats."

"That's not the worst of it, as I assume you figured out. The experiments are being done so they can test it on these poor little creatures before they use it against the North. I didn't take it too seriously at first. I mean against innocent civilians. Thought it was just a crazy idea they liked to banter about. Killing cats was bad enough. Mary, do you know why I placed the letter under my bed instead of bringing it to President Davis right away?"

Mary shook her head.

"General Harris has been observing the work of Professor McCulloh at Nitre. Already know some of the terrible things they're up to. Soon as I saw him as the door, I wanted to open it and read it myself before I gave it to Mr. Davis. Perhaps, depending on what it said, never give it to him. When Mr. Davis is sick, he lets me open his mail for him. He trusts me. Never would have guessed I was taking advantage of that trust."

"I've noticed how much both he and Mrs. Davis trust you. We all have."

"Had to earn it. In the past, I always saw my role as working very hard and being loyal to the family I serve, but this business of building these terrible weapon, experimenting with cats, and then planning to attack cities up North where innocent civilian populations live. It's odd to be sharing all this with you. But, frankly I've been struggling with my conscience. An awful lot lately."

"I can understand," Mary said.

"The tipping point for me came when they decided to attack New York. I have family there. A brother and two sisters."

"We've all heard about the New York City scare. Everybody in the Church where I go knows about it. Guess it was written up in the Richmond newspapers, and word spread all over town."

"What did you hear?"

"About General Butler showing up and preventing a planned attack. An attack that could have led to riots on Election Day. Imagine if it had been carried through."

"I asked you before if the letter mentioned the city and you said no."

"Yes, it did not."

"The city is New York. The men who were sent there decided to stay."

Mary was stunned hearing this. "A second attack in New York?"

"Yes," May answered. "They plan to try again. I heard this. I am hoping you might be able to get word to your contact."

Mary stared back at May, hesitating before speaking. She couldn't help but wonder if this was staged to expose not only her, but also her "contact." She considered the consequences. Far worse, she reasoned, if this was her only chance to send word and try to help prevent it. She was still mindful that she would have to do all in her power to protect Elizabeth and the others.

"I can," finally she said. "You're sure about this, Ma'am?"

"I am. Secretary Seddon was playing cribbage with President Davis, right in this very room the other day, just before the President took sick. The Secretary told him several of the men had stayed behind in New York City and planned to try again. This was the word from Jacob Thompson who is running attacks on the North from Canada. Why are you smiling? This is terrible."

"Sorry ma'am. Yes, I agree. Terrible. I was just thinking that I wasn't the only one eavesdropping around here..."

"I was hoping Mr. Seddon would say what date they were planning for, but if he did, I didn't hear it. Sadly, by now General Butler may have already withdrawn his troops."

"This is very important information. I will get it to my contact. Probably should leave as soon as possible. Could you cover for me?"

"I'll do better than that. I'll give you the rest of the day off. The other girls can take care of your work. I'll tell Mrs. Davis you needed to spend the day with your husband."

"Thank you, Ma'am." Mary stood up and was about to exit the room.

"Mary, before you leave. You said the first part of the letter was difficult to understand. Why don't I open it and read for myself while you are here."

"I can tell you what it said. It was addressed to 'His Excellency Jefferson Davis, President Confederate States,' and read: Sir, I wish to inform you that you will see the improvements made with our latest Greek Fire the day of the city evacuation."

May broke the seal, saying "I planned to open it anyway, like I do with all his letters he receives at home." She began to read.

"You were verbatim, Mary. Extraordinary." She continued to stare down at the page. With her eyes still glued to the note, her head sprung up and she next stuck a pointed finger into the top part of the creased page. "That's it. That's the day."

"Sorry, Ma'am, I don't understand."

"Once when I visited my family in New York City we went to a parade that started where they lived, near Coopers Union and moved downtown. They called it the Evacuation Day Parade. Celebrating when the British left New York during the Revolutionary War. Irish immigrant families like mine loved to participate. Perhaps hoping one day our mother country could vacate the British, just like the Americans did."

"I think you just solved the mystery behind this. Do you remember what day it is celebrated?"

"No, but I think it was near the end of November, or early December."

The women gave each other a hug before leaving the room. Mary left for the Van Lew mansion, taking a circuitous route, in case it was a set up.

Chapter 23: New York's Finest on the Trail

Evacuation Day had been celebrated on November 25thfor over 80 years, commemorating the end of the British seven year occupation of New York City, in 1783. In the revised plan, the eight Confederate agents who stayed in New York City would set fire during the celebration to hotels, across Broadway in the downtown Business District.

It was not lost on the conspirators that Butler who had stayed to keep the peace after the election had withdrawn his troops the week before. As one of them said to the others, "The Bluecoats are gone. We've gotten rid of those among us who were weak. Now we have left the best, the bravest. Nothing will stand in our way of causing the greatest damage on Broadway, and creating a sensation in New York."

They took an oath that this time they would go through with it, regardless of a change in orders, the response of the enemy, or the consequences, including the threat of death. To avoid being apprehended red handed after the Election Day, the men had destroyed their Greek Fire flasks, as ordered. This meant Headley would need to visit the Chemist again.

Evacuation Day would be celebrated on the coming Friday. That Wednesday, Thomas J. Roche arrived early for work at Police Headquarters, 300 Mulberry Street. His boss, New York City Police Detective, John Young, had called a meeting.

Roche was a veteran who had been with the 11th New York Volunteer Infantry Regiment. He was wounded in the leg during the first Battle of Bull Run. He walked with a limp and carried a cane. He considered himself lucky. So many of his fellow soldiers lost limbs, pretty much the prescribed procedure when hit by enemy fire in the arms or legs, or to prevent the spread of infection.

STEPHEN ROMAINE

After they had gathered in the main meeting room, Young began to address the officers in attendance.

"We have good reason to believe that the same saboteurs who were here to create havoc on Election Day are still here and may be planning to attack this Friday during the Evacuation Day celebration."

"Where?" one of the detectives in the meeting asked, while another whispered to the policeman next to him, "Guess we'll be looking for them on every holiday now..."

"We are not sure where, how, or exactly what time of the day, but we believe they will be using what they call "Greek Fire." Very difficult to extinguish, if it works. So far, they have had mixed results. I suspect that they will be attempting to burn buildings with easy access. With many office buildings closed for the holiday, my guess is they may be looking at hotels to start these fires. Probably along the parade route."

A police officer asked, "What's this Greek Fire made from?"

"No one is real clear on that, some kind of special mixture. Supposedly some pretty bad stuff. Highly combustible, and very difficult, if not impossible to extinguish. From what I hear."

Roche took this very hard. He had been in a local Times Square pub, several blocks from his brownstone walk up apartment, just before Election Day. Roche noticed four or five men drinking heavily. They were dressed as civilians, but as they ordered more rounds, he noticed they began referring to each other by military titles, "Lieutenant, Colonel, Captain..." They also had southern accents.

Didn't think much about it at the time. He finished his whiskey and left. Not until the news broke on Election Day about a possible Copperhead plot. He told his boss, but nothing happened and he never saw them again. He now wondered if some of these same men were involved in planning the attack.

Young was still talking. He indicated that he had notified the Fire Department to be on alert.

"What I need from each of you is to be vigilant right up and through the holiday. We're each going to split up and cover hotels from midtown to downtown. Talk to the hotel management. We don't want them to create an unnecessary scare with guests or nearby pedestrians, but we do want them to watch for anyone engaged in activities that seem unusual."

A police sergeant in the back asked, "when do you want us to start?"

"Right away. Butler's troops are no longer here to help us, and to be perfectly honest, city officials think it's just another hoax. I hope they're right, but we can't afford to assume so. All up to us to stop and apprehend these conspirators, if we can. I'm counting on each of you to do your part."

Roche, Young's best detective, was given the major hotels close to the parade route. He started with his assigned downtown hotels, including the Metropolitan, the Lovejoys Hotel, the Astor House, and LaFarage. He spoke with management as ordered, flashed his badge, and walked around, looking for any telltale signs of foul play. He worked his way up to the Everett House on 17th Street, and the Saint James, a few blocks over. He also covered the Fifth Avenue Hotel, on 23rd Street.

While, for the most part, hotel management was deferential and polite, he didn't get a sense they would provide much assistance. At the Saint James, the manager displayed a sarcastic attitude.

"Why don't you go back to catching burglars and chasing vagrants out of the park, versus hunting down fictitious villains?"

Roche planned to cover additional hotels on his list in the midtown area the next day. Before going home, he decided to look for the strange group of men, who with their southern mannerisms and speech, looked completely out of place. He went back to the neighborhood pub where he had noticed them, just before Lincoln's reelection, but no luck. Roche walked the streets nearby, looking into bars and eateries. No sign of them.

Rising from bed early the next day, Roche decided to slightly change his plans. Before casing more hotels, he headed to the center of Times Square where he stood on the street corner, lit a cigar and watched as people began pouring into the street. It was mild weather for late November.

The odds were low, but he rationalized that if some of these men were staying close by where he first saw them, there was a slim chance he might spot one of them. Roche doubted, as much as they might try, that any of these men he had seen could easily blend in as New Yorkers. There was a chance he might see at least one of them.

Rush hour passed. Again, no luck. Roche decided to stay a little longer than he originally planned. At least an hour passed. He lit another cigar.

He noticed him right away as he walked up 7th Avenue to where it crossed with Broadway. He would have been hard to miss. Carrying a large suitcase. Appeared empty, as it swung in and out easily, colliding against his legs as he moved along.

This was the one the others called "Lieutenant." Beady-eyed, a round head with a stocky chest anchored by short legs; he was wearing a long gray woolen coat that looked second hand, tattered and worn. Also donning a working man's' cap, too big for his crown, with locks of dark brown hair hanging down to his neckline. He would be easy to tail, or so Roche was thinking.

The man was a block away. Roche realized he was directly in front of a regular street car stop on Broadway. A horse drawn street car running on the rails immediately pulled up. Roche tried to move as fast as he could to reach the carriage, dragging his injured leg, slowing his stride.

He was too late, the driver started to pull away. Roche needed to act fast. As the street car approached, Roche stepped into the middle of the street rails waving his cane. The driver pulled back the reins on his horses. The horses jerked back, attempting to rear up.

The driver yelled, "Watch where you're goin', fella."

"My apologies Sir, can't move that fast with this bum leg."

It looked like four or five people were sitting in the car. At rush hour all 12 seats would have been filled, with passengers standing, packed together as well. The so called Lieutenant was in a middle seat.

As Roche climbed into the carriage and paid his fare, the driver asked, "war injury?"

"Nah, got it working at the Cornell Iron Works. Downtown."

Roche would have preferred not calling attention to himself. As if his disability wasn't enough of a problem, trying to follow a suspect without detection. The man didn't seem to be paying much attention to him as he moved to the back of the car. He was busy instead positioning his large suit-case in the space next to him in the outside seat.

They travelled south on Broadway. When a lady sitting in the front seat closest to the driver got off at Union Square, the man grabbed his empty suitcase and moved up to the vacant front seat. This time he placed the suit-case on the floor next to him.

The street car always stopped at Prince Street to allow pedestrians to cross. As the street car began to pull away, the man tossed his suitcase out of the carriage proceeded to jump while the street car was still moving, falling on his side and rolling over. He immediately collected himself and stood up.

The driver "Hey, what the hell you doing?"

The man ignored him. Picked up the case, heading east across the street.

"Damn," Roche thought to himself. He must have figured out he was being followed. Maybe he recognized him from the pub. Roche moved up to the front seat, announced he was a police officer, while showing his badge. He asked the driver to pull over right away. Ironically, he was within minutes from his desk at police headquarters.

He hopped off the street car just before Spring Street and headed back to Prince. Prince Street was mostly a residential, cast iron architecture, combined with stone and brick structures. Also a few store fronts. His fear was that the suspect was headed to the Bowery, just south of Coopers Square.

If so, finding him could be very difficult. Cheap rooming houses, broth-els, pawn shops, beer gardens and low-brow theatres, packed closely togeth-er. Should the suspect disappear in the Bowery, he figured he might be able to get help from the 13th Precinct on Delancey to expand the search. This was the same precinct that had been called in to break up last year's New York City Draft Riots. He knew the station commander there, Cap-tain Thomas Steers. Colonel Sharpe had met with earlier when investigat-ing Richard McCulloh's activities before moving to Richmond.

Roche worried. By now he might be too late to find the man with the suitcase. He reached the corner of Prince, just in time to see the man turn up a side street heading back north, towards Houston Street. By the time he got to Crosby, the side street, the man had disappeared. Roche walked the street, up to Houston. No sign of his suspect. Standing at the corner of Houston, he looked both ways.

There was a street merchant on the opposite corner. Roche walked up to him and asked if he had seen the tall man with the big suitcase.

"No, sir."

There was a man sitting in a small passenger carriage, probably taking a break. There was a luxury hotel nearby, the St. Nicholas, Broadway and Spring. Another detective had been assigned to check the St. Nicholas.

Roche thought to himself that odds were high that this driver's next large tip paying clients would be staying there. The driver was looking at him. He must have overheard the conversation between Roche and the merchant.

"Hey Mister, if he had a big suitcase, I would have seen 'em."

Roche knew it had to be Crosby, between Houston and Spring. There was a combination of factories, store fronts, single homes and a few multi-family dwellings.

Walking slowly back down the street he studied each and every building structure along the way. Roche noticed a man working to fix a broken front door stoop.

"You see where the man who came by here with a suitcase went?"

"Who is asking?" The worker never looked up as he continued his repair.

"Police."

Now he looked back at Roche. "No. Can't help you. Sorry."

As Roche continued to move down Crosby, he came to a vacant lot. Most probably a former residence recently cleared for a new business establishment. The former residential neighborhood was turning commercial.

There were two ladies standing in front of the lot, watching their children play. Roche crossed the street and approached them. One of the little boys saw him and ran towards his mother. The other boy followed.

"Pardon me, ladies. Did either of you see where a man carrying a suitcase? And if so, where he went? I'm with the police." Roche pulled his badge out of his pocket and flashed it.

"He went in there," the first little boy said, pointing at one of the multifamily buildings.

The ladies looked at each other and smiled.

One of the ladies said, "Maybe Jimmy will be a policeman one day. He's right. We thought it was a little strange seeing him walk by."

"Definitely not from the neighborhood," the other woman said.

Roche climbed the stoop, favoring his bad leg, and went through the main door which was open. Drawing his colt army revolver, as he stepped into the house. He immediately noticed a bad odor. Smelled like rotten eggs. There was an upstairs and ground floor apartment. The smell was from the ground floor.

The door was locked. Putting his head against the door it sounded as if someone was cleaning dishes. Roche knocked. It got quiet. He knocked again. Still no sound. Nothing.

"This is the police, open the door. *NOW.* Or we'll break it down."

He heard the lock turn. The door opened a crack. Roche pushed it wider. There was an old man behind the other side holding the edge of the door. His knuckles were white from squeezing. Roche pushed him back, with the barrel of his gun, stepped into the flat and closed the door behind.

It was that rancid dead egg smell. Much worse now. He knew immediately he was in the right place. The old timer standing in front of him took a step back. Roche could see the kitchen behind him. It looked like a chemistry lab. There must have been close to 20 capped bottles lined up, on the kitchen counter, most of them filled with a liquid mixture of some kind. Maybe four or five were empty.

His gun still pointed out, Roche sternly asked, "Where is he?"

"Who?" The old man responded. Followed by, "Not here. He left."

"Sit down in that chair over there," Roche commanded.

The man followed the instructions as requested.

"What's your name?"

"Joseph Tyler."

Roche noticed the empty suitcase. There was also a table with flasks, each containing different ingredients.

"Stay right there," Roche said.

He walked around, checking the small, adjacent rooms, including the bedroom in the back, making sure there was no one else there. There was a backdoor near the bedroom with a chain lock in place. He looked out, but could only see the backyard of another residence. Roche came back and stood in front of the old man.

"Is that sulfur I smell?"

"Yes."

Pointing over at the to the kitchen counter at the filled bottles, he asked, "What else is in those?" The man who called himself Tyler shook his head and stared down at his shoes. Roche started to walk into the kitchen. He noticed a piece of paper with instructions on the table. There was also an unsigned cover letter with the name "Nitre and Mining Bureau" on the letterhead. Roche started to pick up one of the bottles.

"Be careful. You don't want to set any of them off."

"If they are going to go off, better here than some populated place you and your friends are planning to attack."

"They're not my friends."

"Who are they?"

"Copperheads, I guess. They wouldn't tell me."

He picked up the instructions instead and walked back and stood in front of the old man. Roche looked down at the paper and said, so this is what your composing?" He continued, "Yup, says right here, *sulfur.* Also, *naphtha gum, bitumen.* Just lovely."

"They threatened me if I didn't."

"I don't believe you. I've been outside here since he arrived. Never saw him leave."

"He went out the back."

Roche folded the paper with instructions and placed it in his pocket, as he said, "Don't think you'll be needing this any longer."

"Guess not," Tyler responded.

"How can you be doing something so despicable? Making Greek Fire to kill innocent people." Tyler looked surprised that he knew about it. Roche continued, "By the looks of it, you're going to be complicit in the attempted killing of hundreds, if not thousands." Roche glanced at the bottles lined up in the kitchen, pointing towards them with his gun.

Tyler kept staring at the ground. Probably in his mid-50s Roche surmised. Short and scraggly. The little hair he had left along the sides of his crown was tousled and dirty. Tyler was wearing a blotched sleeveless undershirt with britches, held up by half a suspender. The other had fallen and was now draped around his butt. He was sweating and his glasses were fogged up. He took a handkerchief from his back pocket and began to wipe them.

"Where were they planning on using these bombs?" Roche asked.

"They never told me. Didn't want me to know," Tyler stammered.

"What did they tell you?"

Dead silence.

"You better start talking, or I'll do some things you won't like. Believe me, I'll make you talk. I don't care how old you are..."

"He'll do worse. He'll kill me."

"Not if you help me catch him. You don't have a choice. You'll tell me what I need to know, or I'll make things so painful you'll wish you were dead, and if I have to...", Roche said, as he cocked the trigger of his revolver.

"He's coming back."

"When?"

"About an hour or so. I told him I wasn't done. Suggested that he go find a place to get a cup of coffee and come back later."

"What place? Did you suggest a place? Did he tell you were he was going?"

"No. There are plenty of places in the area, but I think he may have changed his mind. He may have decided to go get others to come back with him. I told him I didn't think one person could carry all this."

Roche was silent for a few moments as he mulled over his options.

"Here's what you are going to do. You're going to start destroying this mixture here."

"This whole place could blow up if they are exposed to air, or you try to destroy it in any conventional way, as you say. The dangerous part of the composition is already in place in most of these bottles. It can't be extracted."

"There must be something you can do. Unless you want to spend the rest of your life in jail."

Tyler stayed silent for a few moments. "There may be something I could do. I could try to water it down. When the finished mixture is exposed to air, it will even burn on water, but by diluting the composition in its current state, before it is exposed to the air. It just might work. I'm not sure how effective this would be, but it might render it inflammable."

"Alright. Get started."

Tyler went into the kitchen. There were several large jugs of water on the floor near the corner. He picked one up and placed it on the counter next to one of the sealed bottles. Tyler then took a bowl, which looked like it contained flour and starting making a mix with water.

"What's that?" Roche asked.

"Plaster of Paris, to reseal the bottle."

Roche watched as he inserted a tube with a control nozzle into the jug of water. After making sure all the air was removed from the tube, he carefully poked it through the closed seal and added water.

"You understand. Not sure this will work."

Neither was Roche. He wasn't even sure he could trust the chemist. Roche was at a loss to know if what Tyler was doing would neutralize the bombs. He could only hope. Roche continued to think about his limited options.

"They will find me and will kill me, you know."

"Don't worry. You will be safe in prison. I'm more worried about the people you're trying to kill. Pour, and make sure you pour it into all of these bottles."

As Tyler began to pour, Roche called out to him again. "You just keep working on it, Mr. Tyler. I'm going to step outside and look around. Don't try anything stupid."

Roche had decided he would go to his Mulberry Street station house for backup. It was only a five-minute walk away. He didn't tell this to Tyler, or he might decide to try and flee.

He exited from the back door to size up the perimeter of the house and to be less conspicuous, in case anyone was watching from the street. He stepped into an alleyway separating the next door house. He looked both ways before stepping out onto Crosby and heading north to the station.

Roche would never remember exactly what happened, but somewhere along the way, he felt a sharp instrument plunge into his back. Then everything went dark.

Chapter 24: Fires, Thirteen NYC Hotels

There were crowds of pedestrians in the street, just thinner than recent years. Pounding rain and a cold, gusty wind kept many Evacuation Day parade spectators and planned festivity goers away. Some watched the parade from residential buildings or their hotel rooms overlooking Broadway. Wealthy elites watched the parade from the covered balconies of their opulent homes.

The New York City police put in double shifts along the parade route. Police officers and plain clothes detectives canvassed local hotels, making their presence highly visible.

Thomas Roche was missing from the protection detail. He was in the hospital in a coma. The doctor told his boss, Detective Young, it was caused by a combination of loss of blood from the stab wound in his back, and from a head injury. Most probably, caused when Roche fell and hit the pavement.

Young was pretty confident it must have been related to the planned attack. The day he was assaulted, Roche was supposed to be uptown checking with hotel managers, asking about suspicious occupants, looking around. He was found close to headquarters. Was he coming to the office with useful intelligence? If only Roche could talk.

The parade started at Cooper Union and ended at the downtown Battery, where artillery, back when New York was a Dutch Settlement, protected the city. As the parade ended, and spectators began to disperse, some New York officials assumed the threat was once again a hoax.

One of the premier events of the day was an evening performance by the famous Booth brothers, Edwin, Julius, and John Wilkes at the Winter Garden Theatre. This was the first time they appeared together in a play. The brothers had their differences, including politics.

When Edwin told his brother that he voted for Lincoln, John was outraged. He believed despite being reelected, Lincoln was an illegitimate leader. For John Wilkes Booth, Lincoln was a scheming, power-hungry politician who appealed to sectional zealots. Lincoln, he declared, was "made the tool of the North to crush out, or try to crush out slavery."

The Booth brothers performed together that evening in Shakespeare's tragedy, *Julius Caesar*, about the assassination of the popular emperor. Proceeds would go to the building of a bronze Shakespeare statue in Central Park. Ironically, a few months later, Edwin Booth would save the life of Lincoln's son, Richard Todd Lincoln, when he fell in front of an oncoming train in New Jersey.

Police were stationed both inside and outside, surrounding the theatre. Even after the parade had ended, there were still police at some of the potential hotels, near the parade route, that were potential targets. Was the threat over? Was there ever a real threat?

At approximately nine o'clock in the evening, a guest at the Saint James Hotel on 23rd Street reported smoke from another guest room. A policeman downstairs was summoned. He broke down the locked door. There was a small fire. Apparently started from a pile of clothes, drapes and newspapers. A hotel employee behind him had a bucket of water. He threw the water, easily extinguishing the fire. The room was otherwise completely empty, except for a cracked bottle and satchel.

Within minutes, another fire was reported at the United States Hotel, also easily extinguished. Fires were spotted at the New England Hotel, and then the Lovejoy, followed by the Everett. Now it was obvious that fires were started around the same time in multiple hotels. Fire brigades raced through the city in response to the alarms.

Guests and staff easily extinguished a fire at the Lafarge House, and also one at the adjoining Winter Garden. Edwin Booth and a police inspector tried to calm the theatre crowd. Fires were also reported at the Howard and the Hanford.

At ten o'clock in the evening, more fires, as the arsonists moved, undetected, to other hotels. This time it was the Belmont Hotel, the Metropolitan, and the Fifth Avenue Hotel. At eleven o'clock, it was the New England House and Tammany. Fire alarms sounded for hours. Frightened people poured out of their hotel rooms onto the streets.

All told, the fires were started in 13 hotels, a theatre, and the Barnum Animal Museum. They were all easily put out. As police, firemen, and hotel staffs focused on the fires, the culprits who started them slipped away. Hay barges in the harbor were also set ablaze, but the fire department put those out, as well, with little difficulty.

Four days after Evacuation Day, Chief Detective John Young received good news. Thomas Roche was no longer in a coma. He had been unconscious for a little over a week. Young left his office immediately to walk over to the New York Hospital on Broadway and Worth Streets.

"How you feeling?" Young asked.

"I've been better."

"You had us really worried. They weren't sure you were going to make it."

"Neither was I. The nurses told me they did set fires on Evacuation Day, but none of them caused much damage."

"That's true. We were on top of it. Fire department also did great work."

"Catch 'em?"

"We figure there were six or seven of them who attempted to set the fires. Several Copperheads who may have had a hand in assisting them have been rounded up. Sorry to say, we think the actual arsonists got away, but let's get back to you. Any idea what happened?"

"Felt like it was a bad dream. I think I'm starting to piece it together. Don't remember much about getting stabbed."

"What do you remember?"

Roche gazed up at the ceiling and then back at his boss. He took Young through as best as he could what he remembered, following the man with the suitcase, and entering the building on Crosby where he discovered Tyler, the chemist. Roche told him how the chemist agreed to dilute the compound, and how he seemed to be doing this, but he couldn't be sure he continued after he left to get help.

"Funny." Young was smiling.

"How so?"

"There's been a lot of speculation that the arsonists must have been inept. I don't think they were inept."

"Doesn't sound like they were inept getting away. Reminds me. Check my jacket pocket over there."

His jacket was hanging near the door. Young got up and checked the pockets.

"Nothing here."

"Damn. They must have swiped it after stabbing me."

"Your wallet and badge are still here," Young noted.

Roche said, "Definitely had to be one of them."

"What was it they took?" Young asked.

"Meticulous instructions on how to make Greek Fire. My guess they would have received similar instructions on how to detonate it, too."

"That's why I was smiling before. Not to take away from the rest of the fellows, but you lying in a coma here the day of the attacks, did more to stop it than any of the others."

"Guess we'll never know for sure."

"I brought something for you to read. The *New York Times,* from the other day," Young said, looking down at the paper, he added, "November 27, 1864, to be exact."

"Not sure, I can read it just yet, Chief. My head is still spinning."

Young read the following out loud for Roche from Page 1:

> The diabolical plot to burn the City of New-York, published yesterday morning, proves to be far more extensive than was at first supposed. It was evidently the intention of the conspirators to fire the city, at a given moment, at a great many different points, each as far remote from the other as possible, except through Broadway, and this thoroughfare they wished to see in a complete blaze, from one end to the other.

Looking up from the newspaper, Young provided his own commentary. "We now think it was even bigger than this. One of the Confederate sympathizers that we arrested was aware of the plot. He told us the fires were meant to divert our attention as other Rebels rose up to capture the Treasury and release the prisoners at Fort Lafayette. Of course, none of that happened when the fires didn't take hold."

He continued reading:

> Had all these hotels, hay barges, theatres, been set on fire at the same moment, and each fire well kindled, the Fire Department would not have been strong enough to extinguish them all…the best portion of the city would have been laid in ashes. But fortunately, thanks to the Police, Fire Department, and the bungling manner in which the plan was executed by the conspirators, it proved a complete and miserable failure.

"I hope you're not thinking about correcting the record by suggesting the weapons may have been tampered with. Better to let everyone think the Rebels are inept. Surely, one of them would have gotten it right."

"Well, the other side of that Thomas, is that we don't take them seriously enough and miss the next one." He handed the newspaper over to Roche. "You can read the rest later when you're feeling better. I have to go, but I'll be back tomorrow. Give me the address and any additional information about the chemist residence on Crosby. You get better, now."

After taking down the house address on a notepad, Young started for the door of the hospital room. Roche glanced down at the newspaper on his blanket covered lap and called out, "Hey Chief, they commend you in the article by name."

"Wish they hadn't. I also don't like that the editors mentioned that we had advance warning and these actions were 'anticipated.' Did not need to let them know that we have a well-placed informant."

"Says you and your detective corps 'were constantly at work, day and night. Told proprietors of hotels to double the watch in halls."

"Thought you said it hurt your head when you tried to read. Get some rest. Get better, and get back to work."

Both men laughed.

When the police showed up at Tyler the chemist's place, they learned from the neighbor upstairs that he had been gone since Evacuation Day.

"Good riddance, too," the neighbor said. "Got rid of him and that awful stink, too."

Before the early November election, Colonel Sharpe had agents monitoring the Toronto train station and the Lake Ontario seaport with easy access to Buffalo, New York by way of Queenston. In addition to alerting U.S. officials of suspicious individuals headed to New York City, the same agent spotted two men travelling together to Boston. At least it was their original destination.

One looked like Dr. Luke Blackburn, based on a description received from David Thurston, U.S. Consul in Toronto. Thurston had received this from his counterpart in Bermuda. Receding white hair, piercing gray eyes, long ears with hanging lobes, as if pinned to his head, heavy set, not very tall, always dressed immaculately.

The other traveler was unknown. The agent was convinced the names they were travelling under, J.W. Harris and Lenny Green, were false. He alerted Thurston who in turn notified Boston officials.

Like New York City, there were no major terrorist incidents or riots in Boston on Election Day. A few days later, the man travelling under the name J.W. Harris was spotted after arriving from a train back to Toronto, travelling alone. A woman who may have been his wife greeted him at the station.

The agent walked towards the couple, attempting to look preoccupied at the posted train schedule nearby. The man had dropped his suitcases to embrace the woman. They were talking loud, to hear each other over the surrounding noise from trains and passengers, coming and going.

"How did it go?" the woman asked.

"Not exactly to plan."

"Did he pay you yet, like he said he would? Been rough lately, especially with you gone and all..."

"I know it has, dear. Says he will when he gets back."

"What if he doesn't come back?"

"Oh, he will. Trust me. I'll make sure he pays me as soon as he does."

The agent followed the couple. They were staying in a boarding house on Carlton Street. He took note of the address.

Early the next morning the agent went back. He brought David Thurston with him. They stood at the corner street and struck up what appeared to be a spontaneous conversation about Canadian football.

"That's him," the agent said, using his eyes to direct Thurston's attention.

They watched Harris leave his apartment house and stroll a street block to the local butcher. He was dressed in a suit.

"Don't need you anymore, Phil. I can handle it from here," Thurston said.

"I'm sure you can. I'll just stay here. Just in case."

Thurston waited until the man came out of the butcher shop, crossing the street to intercept him before he reentered his flat. He was carrying a piece of meat covered in paper.

"Mr. Harris, or whatever your name is, I'd like to talk to you."

"Who the hell are you, and what makes you think I want to talk?"

"You can help me, and maybe I can help you."

"Help me? Haaa! Don't need your help, Mister, whoever the hell you are."

"Thurston, David Thurston. United Stated Consul to Toronto. Willing to pay you for some information."

"I got nothin' to say to you. Now, gotta go." Holding up the slab of meat, he added, "Got to get this back to the missus, and then get back to work. Late already."

"Who you working for? Dr. Luke Blackburn?" The man was taken back. "Yes. We are well aware of his treasonous actions against the U.S. government. You can go down with him, or we can strike up a financial arrangement where you can redeem yourself from these diabolical and highly criminal activities."

The man stared back at Thurston, before saying, "Don't know what you are talking about. I have to go." He turned and began to walk into the doorway of his residence.

Thurston called after him, "Think about it."

The door slammed shut.

Chapter 25: More Civilian Attacks to Come, Plus "The Big One"

On December 18, 1864 the Thirteenth Amendment to the Constitution

A bolishing slavery passes the U.S. House of Representatives. The vote was 119 to 56. It would now go to the states where it required ratification by two-thirds of those states.

Shortly after the reelection of Lincoln, Sherman began his infamous March to the Sea. As he advanced from Atlanta through Georgia, he left it to General George Thomas to confront Hood. After much prodding from Grant, frustrated that Thomas was spending too much time preparing, as did McClellan, Thomas took the initiative. His army broke through Hood's lines, causing a chaotic Rebel retreat to Tennessee.

Troops under the command of General Thomas gave chase and routed Hood in the Battle of Nashville. There were almost 23,000 causalities from Hood's initial army of 38,000. Hood had no choice but to retreat further, to Mississippi. This led to more criticism of Jefferson Davis, urging him to reinstate Johnston.

After leading about 60,000 soldiers for 285 miles from Atlanta, on December 21st, Sherman's troops captured Savannah. This became a "scorched earth" campaign, where both military and civilian property was demolished along the way. Transportation networks were destroyed. It was also estimated that the army seized 10,000 horses, 13,000 heads of cattle, millions of pounds of corn and fodder.

The next day, Sherman telegraphed Lincoln, "I beg to present you as a Christmas gift the City of Savannah, with 150 guns and plenty of ammunition, also about 25,000 bales of cotton."

Sherman would now move north through the Carolinas and Virginia to help Grant increase his vise grip against Lee. Outnumbered, poorly supplied and with increased desertions, Lee pleaded with Davis for help. His besieged Army of Northern Virginia was now facing insurmountable odds.

Pinned down between Petersburg and Richmond, Lee needed reinforcements. His army was attempting to defend thirty miles of Union entrenchments. What would have been unthinkable for most Confederate leaders was now being discussed. Enlisting slaves in the army to fight the Union was gaining some support.

Another somber Christmas Season arrived. The war was extending into a fourth year. Even for Unionists, like the Van Lew's, who believed the tide had turned and defeat of the Confederate States of America was inevitable, conditions were abysmal.

Citizens of Richmond had endured food rationing, undernourishment, conscription, martial law, devaluation of currency, reduced family assets, and steep decline in income. A barrel of flour cost 1,000 in Confederate dollars. It was estimated that close to one quarter of the male population was dead. The city had been overwhelmed for most of the war with sick and wounded soldiers in makeshift hospitals and wayside homes.

In addition to stepped up efforts to find out about new potential plots, Elizabeth also believed her Unionist network needed to provide as much detailed information on Rebel war plans, troop position and movement to Union commanders as possible. Expediting an end to the war could reduce the carnage on the battlefield. This might also prevent horrific acts of terror across the North. Initial attempts may have been unsuccessful. No telling if given enough time what might happen the next time.

Elizabeth Van Lew's secret communication network had now established an effective relay method, using five Unionist homes as stations along the way, where couriers could hand off cipher messages. These messages went back and forth between Van Lew and Grant's command headquarters at City Point on a more frequent basis.

Flowers were no longer in season, but the messages sent to Grant were wrapped in the Richmond morning paper, often from the same day. The papers provided additional insight into the political discussion, public sentiment, and the latest on Richmond economic conditions.

Sam Ruth continued to provide a second wing of the clandestine network, using his railroad and Unionist connections north of Richmond to dispatch communications across the Potomac. Between the two networks, detailed information was provided upon request on military positions in North Carolina and southern Virginia. Slaves and former slaves, updated Daniel regularly at the African Baptist Church.

There was one setback in what had been otherwise a string of Union successes.

Despite having detailed information on number of Confederate troops surrounding Wilmington, and the Cape Fear River, a Federal assault on Fort Fisher, protecting the seaport, was pushed back. General Butler was in command of another failed mission.

Christmas dinner at the Van Lew's consisted of what had become rare delicacies for Richmond. Harriett Anne prepared turkey, beef, mince pie and plum pudding. John Minor Botts had procured the services of fellow Unionist, Frederick Lohmann, to deliver a bounty of food as a Christmas gift to the Van Lew's. As he said in the note delivered with the food, "for all your family and help have done to restore our great country." Only hoarders in town, or perhaps the Davis family, would eat as well.

Elizabeth and her mother lamented that John was not with them. He was still in Philadelphia. Neither was Mary Bowser. Daniel was there. So were Dolores and Isaac. Two additional servants who had worked the farm had recently escaped north, with Daniels help and Elizabeth blessing, as conditions further deteriorated in Richmond.

After dinner, Elizabeth and her mother decided to give U.S. greenbacks as gifts – the few they had left in the family safe. Their generosity, providing funding for runaway slaves, bribing prison guards to help Union soldiers escape, and providing legal support for accused Unionists had brought them to the verge of bankruptcy.

"Hopefully, these will be good to use again very soon," Elizabeth said as she passed out envelopes with the financial presents. "In the meantime, don't try to use them. Keep this hidden."

Daniel and Harriet Anne waited for the others to leave. They then invited Elizabeth to join them in the kitchen.

Harriet Anne spoke first. "We have a very special gift for you this year, Miss Van Lew, but it doesn't actually come from us," Daniel noted. "We are just doing the delivery."

He reached under the table and pulled out a large, leather valise.

"Oh, this is beautiful," Elizabeth said.

"That's not the half of it. Open it up," Harriett Anne suggested.

Elizabeth unfastened the buckle and pulled out a folded flag of the United States of America.

There was an encrypted note inside.

"I'll be right back."

Elizabeth stormed up the stairs to her room. Daniel and Harriett Anne smiled at each other as they could hear Elizabeth scurrying back down the stairs and into the kitchen with her folded cipher letter translation chart in hand, along with a blank page of paper and her quill pen. She pulled her reading spectacles from her pocket. She began to reassemble the letters.

She smiled as she came to the end.

"Read it aloud," Harriett Anne said.

Elizabeth read:

Dear Miss Van Lew,

I wish you and your family a very happy and blessed Christmas. Please accept this gift from me. My hope is that you will raise it up as I march into Richmond.

I am very respectfully, your obedient servant,

Ulysses S. Grant

Commanding General of the United States Army

At breakfast for the servants, Mary Bowser could tell May was upset. She assumed it was about the holidays, being away from her family. When she tried to console her later, May wanted no part of it.

"Do your chores, Mary, and mind your own business."

Later that day, Mary was outside beating carpets with a rod to free the dust and caked in dirt. May came out to see her. It was cold. Mary was wearing a beat up overcoat. May had none.

"Sorry Mary, I wasn't in the mood to talk earlier."

Mary turned and lowered the rod she was holding to her side. She could see May was shivering already from the cold.

"No need to be sorry, Ma'am. You need to get back inside before you catch cold."

"Come by my room after supper."

When Mary knocked on her door, May invited her in and asked her to close the door. Mary sat on the one lone chair and watched as May pulled another letter from under her bed.

"I overheard a conversation between Mr. and Mrs. Davis about Jacob Thompson while they were having breakfast. President Davis told her that Judah Benjamin was stopping by to talk about him."

"I saw Mr. Benjamin when he came by. Met behind closed doors, of course. Does Mrs. Davis know about the activities in Canada?"

"Not sure. She knew Mr. Thompson and probably that he was operating up North, but she might not have known about what he was up to." "I see."

"Mr. Davis told his wife he had made up his mind to remove Thompson."

Mary looked up at May. She said, "This is very good news, is it not?

"So I thought." May went on to explain, as she reached for a crumbled up note on her side table. "I found this when straightenin' things up this afternoon. After Mr. Benjamin left," May said, with her pitched brogue rising. "Sometimes Mr. Davis can act impulsively. He must have tossed this into the waste basket. He can be a little less careful when upset."

She gave it to Mary to read and sat down on the edge of the bed, close to the chair where Mary sat.

As we discussed, I drafted the letter to Napoleon relieving him of command and requesting that that he transfer to the gentleman who will arrive, carrying my letter, all information that he had obtained, and release to him all funds. I also instructed him to return to the Confederacy.

With very great regard,

Judah Benjamin

Secretary of State

Mary looked up at May. She said, "Jacob Thompson is being replaced?"

"At first I figured they were closing down the Canadian operation. I thought this meant no more plots to attack innocent people."

"Any idea who will replace him?"

"No, but Mr. Davis did mention something else to his wife. He said Mr. Benjamin was bringing a report written by Jacob Thompson and smuggled through the blockade by one of their spies. He then told her that Judah read it and thought it was written as an attempt to blame others and justify his failed efforts."

"I take it you don't know who this new person is replacing Thompson."

"No, but we may just have a way of finding out what some of the dirty tricks they may still be planning might be."

"How so?" Mary asked.

May got up from the bed and walked to the door. She opened it and looked around, before closing it again. She remained standing.

"They met in the office upstairs. Behind closed doors for almost an hour. When Mr. Davis walked Mr. Benjamin down and to the door, I noticed the document was left on his desk." May paused.

"Did you get a chance to look at it?"

"Only the cover," May responded. "From 'Napoleon', it said. I didn't have time to look into it, but on the cover it said report on 1864 activities and plans for 1865. I didn't think much of it at the time. I had already heard Mr. Davis say to his wife he was going to sack him and, like I said, I assumed the worst was over."

"Did Mr. Davis take it with him when he left in the afternoon for his office?"

"No," May said.

"Then it must be in his safe."

"It is."

Mary shrugged her shoulders. "We won't be able to see it unless President Davis leaves it out, and I doubt that would ever happen."

"You are so right, Mary. He might get careless with a note that upsets him, but not with detailed confidential documents. However, there may be another way to get a look at it."

"But how?" Mary inquired.

"Only he and Mrs. Davis are supposed to have the combination for the safe in his office. In case of an emergency, she also has access."

"I don't see how that helps us," Mary confided.

"Once when he was sick in bed, suffering from a bout of malaria, and Mrs. Davis wasn't home, he wrote the safe combination down on a slip of paper and asked me to get some papers for him. He told me once I was done, to rip the paper up."

"You still have it?"

"No, I did as he said, but first I wrote it down on a separate paper. Not sure why I did it at the time, but now I'm glad I did. Tomorrow after Mr. Davis leaves for his office downtown, and when Mrs. Davis and the others are not around...we can try to have a look."

"God bless you, May."

Mary happened to be walking by as Jefferson Davis came down the stairs the next morning to leave for his Bank Street office. He looked upset. He said nothing as he passed by.

Mary called out, "Good day, Mr. Davis."

He said nothing as he went straight to the entrance where Wilbur opened the door then closed it behind him. Wilbur looked back at Mary and shrugged his shoulders.

"Wondering what's botherin' him," Wilbur pondered aloud.

Mary then checked to make sure all was clear. Mrs. Davis was in the piano room reading the newspaper, she and Elizabeth Van Lew, thanks to her friend Wayne Evans, were part of the very few residents of Richmond still sipping tea. She went back to the foot of the stairs. May was upstairs leaning against the rail. She signaled to Mary that it was safe upstairs as well.

The nurse was with the children and the door was shut, as it often was in the morning after breakfast, so the children would not disturb the adults.

Mary took the stairs and joined May in the master bedroom, walking over to the side room office entrance. May handed her the slip of paper with the combination. Mary looked at it and handed it back.

"You sure you don't need this. The numbers, the amount of turns, whether to the left or right? May asked.

"I have it, thanks."

May kept watch as Mary entered the Confederate President's home office room and went straight to the safe. May left the door open a crack.

First try it didn't work. Then she tried again, and this time it opened. There it was. A thick document on top of other papers. The document had a cover note from "Napoleon," just as May had described.

She quickly sifted through to look at the ones below. Mostly correspondence. Nothing that caught her attention. She focused her complete attention on the thick report.

The first part was about the reasons for his teams' actions. Dahlgren was mentioned. Also the ruthless Sheridan campaign in the Shenandoah Valley. Followed by Sherman's siege of Atlanta and his March to the Sea, pillaging and destroying everything his army could along the way. The claim was made that there was ample justification for the Confederacy covert operations under his command. The document argued that this mission, under his direction, was the only option left that could turn the tide of the war.

Next, the failed plots in Chicago and New York City were presented. Speculating that the lack of success may have been caused by someone within the highest levels of the Confederate Government who was a spy, the document advanced the question: how else could one explain how the enemy anticipated so many of our clandestine plans in advance? This made Mary cringe, fearful that even if Jefferson Davis didn't suspect her before, he might now.

Local city police and fire were surely tipped off. There was also the suggestion that the chemist used to develop the incendiary devices for the New York Hotel fires may have also betrayed them by purposely tampering with the compound mixture.

Also, cited was the lack of backbone on the part of Copperheads. They had backed out when they were needed the most. Many of these individuals had pledged their help to escalate fear and panic by rioting, damaging Federal property, and disrupting conventions and other events. They seemed to talk much and always got 'cold feet' at the very last moment.

He went on to say that he was now working with a much smaller group and could attest to their loyalty. This would improve future planned attacks, adding the ones planned for next year would require less resources. They could still inflict maximum impact on the enemy, leading to victory, and the end of hostilities, and ensuring the complete independence for the Confederacy.

Mary moved to the section on plans for next year. The objectives had not changed. To commit acts of terror that would scare the general population of the North and pressure the government to end the war.

She just started to review it, when May pushed the door further open and stepped into the room.

"The children's room door just opened," she whispered. "I'm going to close this office door."

Mary could hear May's voice, followed by the nurse.

"Good morning children. Be careful on the stairs. Hello Catherine."

"Hello ma'am. Got them all bundled up. Going to take them into the backyard. Don't think they will want to be out very long. Little nippy."

Mary waited until it was quiet again.

She opened the section on 1865 planned activities. Mary stared down at a list of items in disbelief.

1. A bomb factory is being built in Toronto to weaponize guerilla raids across the border.
2. We are still working on a plan to poison the New York City water supply for the Croton, New York City reservoir. The 'Doctor' is spearheading this effort.
3. We have identified potential places in Chicago, Boston and New York City to launch the new weapon perfected by Richard and his team.
4. We continue to move forward with the plan to kidnap Target 1,

and negotiate for concessions, despite previous failed attempt. If this didn't work, the Doctor's 'Big One' could also be launched. If both of these failed, a third plan was ready to be executed.

Mary had first overheard a conversation about a "Doc" with trunks that contained something deadly. She later heard from Dolores after her trip with President Davis that his name was Luke Blackburn. She guessed the reference to 'Doctor' was probably him. Then the reference to the "Big One." What additional horrors were they planning?

She couldn't understand how a physician who was supposed to treat patients could be doing things this terrible. Mary also remembered Richard was the code name of Professor McCulloh. She needed to get this information back to Elizabeth Van Lew as soon as possible.

She heard May say, "You need to close it up before somebody comes. Hurry up."

Later in the day, when Mary and May were alone in the antechamber to the parlor, Mary asked to have a word. They moved into one of the storage rooms down the hall and closed the door.

"May, I was wondering. Did you speak with Mrs. Davis about me after the time you confronted me in the basement?"

"Yes, I did. I had concerns about you, Mary, before then, as you know, and I didn't think I could ignore them anymore. Finally, I did tell Mrs. Davis that I thought you might be trying to listen in to private conversations that were none of your business. Mary, you know I am very sorry about doing this now, but..."

"What did Mrs. Davis say?" Mary inquired.

May replied, "She asked me if these were family matters, or her husband's private business affairs."

"What did you say?"

"I told her I thought it was mostly meetings Mr. Davis was having related to military activities. Then what Mrs. Davis said was very curious. She indicated it was understandable that I would be suspicious, and this was a good quality for a head housekeeper. She then asked me if I was absolutely sure you were trying to pry into sensitive military matters."

"I don't fault you for doing this, Mary. Not back then."

"I told her I wasn't absolutely sure. Simply that I thought there was a strong possibility that you might be..."

"Isn't it strange that she never confronted me about this?"

"That to me is why I found this entire exchange, and the lack of anything to come from it so peculiar. Mrs. Davis simply thanked me for bringing it to her attention. She suggested I let her know if it happened again and walked away. That seemed to be the last of it."

On the first of the New Year, a loud blast could be heard from Richmond. It came from the James River. After almost a half year of digging, Union soldiers completed the "Dutch Gap" Canal. Meant to help them bypass the deep and dangerous downriver loop, they had set off six tons of gunpowder. Most of the discharged earth fell back into the wide cut of land.

This too was under Butler's command. Lincoln decided it was time to replace him, since he was a politically appointed general. He had been popular with Radical Republicans, and had been the first Union commander to establish communications with Elizabeth Van Lew. However in military effectiveness, his record was less than stellar. He was replaced with a military trained officer, Brigadier General Alfred Terry.

Butler gave a moving speech to the men in his Department of Virginia and North Carolina. He closed with a special commendation for the "Colored Troops of the Army of the James," many of whom were recruited from the tent city at Freedom Fortress:

> In this Army you have been treated not as laborers but as soldiers. You have shown yourselves worthy of the uniform you wear. The best officers of the Union seek to command you. Your bravery has won the admiration even of those who would be your masters. Your patriotism, fidelity, and courage have illustrated the best qualities of manhood. With the bayonet you have unlocked the iron-barred gates of prejudice, opening new fields of freedom, liberty, and equality of right to yourselves and your race forever. Comrades of the Army of the James, I bid you farewell! farewell!

Benj. F. Butler, Maj. Gen'l. Comd'g.

January 8, 1865

Two weeks later, now under the command of General Terry, the Yankees captured Fort Fisher, protecting Wilmington. They had captured the last Confederate seaport on the Atlantic. With this loss, Lee no longer had an available avenue for receiving supplies by sea. A promotion from Davis, received February 1, to "General-in-Chief" for all the armies of the Confederate State was little consolation for General Lee who knew he was running out of options.

Just several days later, a brokered peace conference was held on the River Queen steamship, near Fort Monroe in Hampton Roads, Virginia. Representing the North was President Lincoln and his Secretary of State, William Seward. The South was represented by Vice President Alexander H. Stephens, Assistant Secretary of War John A. Campbell, and Senator Robert M.T. Hunter.

Lincoln insisted that the Rebel states had to pledge to rejoin the United States as one nation, and to agree to the end of slavery. The Confederate commissioners were bound by Jefferson Davis to accept nothing less than independence as a condition for negotiation. Ending with no agreement, Davis soon after gave a speech blaming the North for refusing to compromise.

Chapter 26: Making of a Double Agent

It was with a heavy heart Elizabeth sat in front of the blush pink credenza in her bedroom where under lock and key she kept her coder for encrypted messages. She pulled out the notes she had taken from her last meeting with Mary and began to transcribe with cipher symbols and letters.

Success in executing anyone of these plots could have devastating repercussions to innocent people. Any one of these could prolong the war, or, in a worst case scenario, alter the outcome. How could they all be stopped? Would it not be virtually impossible to monitor or infiltrate what had been described as a smaller, more tightly knit group? From the little she knew, these were Confederate men who had fought together in the past.

Perhaps whoever was taking over for Thompson might shut down all or most of these planned activities. What if he didn't? What if even more audacious plots were being conceived?

Elizabeth ended her note with an encrypted plea to Union Command at City Point: "My sincere hope is that you will understand from this message the increased urgency that you move swiftly to defeat the enemy and take Richmond. The timing of this campaign is most critical."

She also added a postscript:

With regard to your last request for information on which roads into Richmond are mined with torpedoes, please note the enemy has planted torpedoes on all roads leading to the city.

The Confederacy was falling apart. The economy had tanked. The general public was living in abject poverty, and many were starving. Railroads and shipping channels had been cut off. Armies were demoralized, staggering to defend their land. Malnutrition was rampant. Desertions were skyrocketing. Some deserters were now preying on local citizens to steal food, supplies, or other valuables.

Lee became a decisive voice in gaining support for the argument to consider purchasing slaves to help defend the Rebel government. Finally, in February 1865, Davis wrote to John Forsyth, the editor of the *Mobile Advertiser and Register*, and a proponent of using slaves to fight for the South:

> It is now becoming daily more evident to all reflecting persons that we are reduced to choosing whether the negroes shall fight for or against us, and that all arguments as to the positive advantages or disadvantages of employing them are beside the question, which is simply one of *relative* advantage between having their fighting element in our ranks or in those of our enemy.

Davis would attempt to convince Congress to pass legislation to purchase slaves to fight the Union. There was still stiff opposition and misgivings from politicians and the Richmond press. As noted in the *Richmond Daily Dispatch*:

> The measures passed by Congress during the present session of recruiting the army are considered by the President inefficient; and it is said that the results of the law authorizing the employment of slaves as soldiers will be less than anticipated, in consequence of the dilatory action of Congress in adopting the measure. That a law so radical in its character, so repugnant to the prejudices of our people, and so intimately affecting the organism of society, should encounter opposition, and receive a tardy sanction, ought not to excite surprise...

When Van Lew's note was shared with Colonel Sharpe, he pinpointed the Target 1 kidnapping threat and the contamination of the Croton water supply as the most imminent threats.

Target 1, he presumed, had to be President Lincoln. Others agreed. He sent word to Lincoln's security detail to increase protection, be less specific about Lincoln travel plans in advance, and avoid using the same travel itinerary, taking different, less predictable routes to scheduled events.

Authorities in New York were notified of the potential threat against the Croton Reservoir. However, even with additional resources assigned and staff put on high alert, given the vast expanse of the distribution system, feeding the reservoir, officials knew protecting it from acts of sabotage, with only minimal information supplied, would be close to impossible.

The reservoir itself measured 1,826 feet long and 836 feet wide. Five million gallons flowed 41 miles daily from the Croton Dam in Westchester County. Croton was New York City's main source of water supply. It was first built because other water resources had become inadequate with the increased population and the pollution that came with it. Given the vast expanse of the reservoir and its aqueduct system, the potential target of attack would be almost impossible to pinpoint. Sharpe was summoned to try to find more information to help them prevent the possible threat.

In Toronto, U.S. spy agents took turns monitoring the coming and goings of the man they believed was working for Dr. Luke Blackburn. "Dr. Black Vomit," they nicknamed him. The man didn't have a regular job. To date, he had not led them to the doctor.

One morning, one of the spies followed him and his assumed wife to the Toronto seaport. The man was carrying baggage. They were online for ferry tickets. The woman handed her purse to the man and left the line, presumably to use the nearby powder room.

Approaching the man, the spy asked, "Is this where you get tickets for Queenston?"

"Yeah, just like the sign over there says," the man responded as he pointed in that direction, while projecting an incredulous sneer.

"Thanks, I don't know. Little too cold for a boat ride."

"I agree, but my wife wanted to see the Falls before we leave."

Looking at the bag of luggage, the spy inquired, "Take it you're not coming back today."

"No, we have a room at the Clifton Hotel."

"Well, I guess you finally got paid by Dr. Blackburn."

"None of your business, mister."

The agent could see the woman from a distance walking back to join her husband in the line which had moved up slightly while the two men were talking. He pulled a card from his pocket and handed it to the man.

"David Thurston from the U.S. Consul Office would still like to have a word with you." Pointing to the card in the man's hand, the agent added, "That's his address. We can still make it worth your while."

He had been a lumber dealer in Massachusetts before becoming a consular agent in Toronto, eventually appointed to the lead consul role. He was "well and favorably" known in the department, and considered a "true, earnest and energetic officer." Secretary of State, William Henry Seward, dubbed Thurston as one of his top "trouble-shooting consuls," along with Charles Maxwell Allen, working in Bermuda, John Potter in Montreal, and Allen Francis in Vancouver. Thurston's secretary, a young man, also from New England, leaned into his office. "Someone here asking to see you, but he won't give me his name."

"Show him in, Philip, and then please close the door."

It was the man he hoped would one day show up, before it was too late. Thurston came around his desk to shake hands.

"Thanks for coming in. Please have a seat." As the man sat facing the desk, Thurston reclaimed his seat as well, walking back behind his thick, beaten up walnut desk. "Your name isn't really Harris, is it?"

"Not important what my name is. What is important is that I have something you want. I have very important information."

"What kind of information?"

"Information worth lots of money."

"How do I know this? I'm not going pay you if I don't know what I'm buying, and certainly not going to buy it from a man who won't even tell me his real name."

"Hyams. Godfrey Joseph Hyams."

"Hmmm, Mr. Hyams, and you were working with a Doctor Luke Blackburn, if I'm not mistaken."

"Yeah. I still am, sort of."

"What do you mean?" Thurston asked.

"I have been working for him, but we haven't been seeing eye to eye lately. I'm probably going to leave before he gives me the boot."

"About the money he owed you? I heard you took a nice trip lately. Figured you were finally squared away. Probably here to see if you can get a few more bucks out of it from me."

"No, not exactly."

"More than just about the money. What he wants me to do. Well, I have some misgivings."

"Is it about those trunks Blackburn brought back from Bermuda?"

"How do you know about that?"

"I know more than you think," Thurston said.

"I'm not sharing anything until we strike a deal."

Thurston replied, "I'm not striking any kind of deal until you convince me that you have useful information. Besides, we're in Canada. I can't have you arrested here, even though I might like to. So tell me something about the trunks."

"First off, I had no idea what it was all about. Just did what Blackburn told me to do."

"Off to a bad start. I don't believe you. You've got to do better than that."

"I had those trunks shipped to Boston in late summer. Sold one at an auction, then shipped one to a clothing store in New York, and others to Philadelphia and New Bern, North Carolina."

"What was in them?"

"I found out later. New clothes exposed and contaminated by clothes worn by patients who died of yellow fever. Supposed to cause an outbreak of the epidemic. Blackburn told me it would kill people at a 60 mile distance."

"You didn't have any misgivings about that?"

"Like I said, didn't know at the time. I mean I knew it was something bad. I was born in England but moved to the South. We were at war and I was doing my part to help my new country. Besides, I heard later they think only one or two people actually died from the clothes."

"You were paid for it."

Hyams looked mad. "Blackburn agreed to pay me 100,000 in U.S. dollars. He only paid me 26 pieces of gold, so far."

"Why not Confederate dollars?" Thurston cracked.

"Very funny. You know as well as I do, it's close to worthless," Hyams responded.

"You don't expect me to pay you for information on something this awful you did that already transpired?"

"He also gave me a valise with clothes carefully wrapped up inside. He asked me to bring it to people he knew in Washington that would have it delivered to the White House. For President Lincoln.

"Is this what is referred to as "the Big One?"

"Yes. You do know a lot, don't you?"

Ignoring the question, Thurston asked, "Where is it now?"

"Blackburn wanted it delivered so it would be opened when the weather was warm. He was mad when I told him I didn't do it last year. Couldn't bring myself to do it. Part of the reason he got mad. Had me put it in a secure site for storage until the weather would be better in Washington."

"Is it here, in Toronto?"

"Yes. It's to be delivered in May this year."

"Who has access to it?"

"Blackburn and me. We both have keys. Anyway, I've been thinking about this. Blackburn tells me I'll get my money when I finally take the valise to his contact in Washington. I don't believe him."

"For good reason. He doesn't sound like a very ethical doctor."

"Besides, my wife and I want to go back home to Arkansas. He'll just get someone else to do it. But, before I go, I could replace the valise with a double bought from the same store. Make it look similar. They'd never know. No one familiar with the scheme would dare to try and open it up. I'll destroy the original. All you just have to do is pay me 100,000 in greenbacks, and not a nickel less. Oh, and aaah, as part of the deal, you make sure when I leave Canada for home, I never get prosecuted."

"You must know, I don't have that kind of money, and on possible arrest once you leave here, that's not for me to decide either."

"The U.S. Government can. They have the money, too. How much is keeping Lincoln alive worth to your government?"

"This is a pretty outlandish story. They may not believe me."

"Well somebody's been feeding you and them information, and you and your government seemed real interested in getting to me."

"If I'm going to get this kind of money, they will need to know they can trust you. Won't care if I do. Listen, I know you've been working with Blackburn, and other Confederates here in Toronto on plots against the U.S."

You answer a few more questions first, so they know you can be trusted, and then I'll do what I can to get you the money. But I can't guarantee this, but if you cooperate, I can maybe persuade them to not come after you.

"Alright, I'll try, but may not be able to answer all of them."

"What can you tell me about Blackburn's plan to poison the Croton Reservoir water supply?"

"He was sending messages back and forth with a peculiar scientist in Richmond. Don't know his name. Blackburn went there recently, to Croton. He's been travelling in disguise lately. Decided after going there it couldn't be done. Plan now is to blow up the dam upstate."

"When?"

"Don't know."

"What happened when you and Blackburn went to Boston?"

"Nothing. Supposed to be a coordinated effort with other cities on Election Day. Once New York City fires started, we were supposed to work with local Copperheads to start a riot that same day in Boston. Similar plans were made for Chicago. We ended up standing down. I came back here. Blackburn went to Croton."

"Where's the bomb factory in Toronto?"

"Don't know. They've been very secretive about the location. I suspect it maybe one of those old manufacturing buildings near Wellington Street."

"Can you try to find out more?"

"I will, assuming you pay me the 100,000."

"Do you know anything about a new weapon to be used in northeast cities?"

"I heard they were testing something that would suffocate thousands of people, but don't know if it's ready yet. Think it's that same scientist I mentioned before. I can maybe find out more about that too."

"Assuming I can get the money, we'll have to arrange it so I am certain you do actually destroy your little gift for President Lincoln. What I don't understand, the Confederacy is reeling. Just a matter of time before it's defeated by the Union. Why are they still continuing to carry on?"

"The boys here in Toronto have pledged to each other to fight on. They think we can still win this, and they are the last best hope to do so. Another reason I'm leaving. I agree with you. I think it's over."

Thurston mockingly noted, "Maybe another reason you're here talking to me now. Switching sides to be with the victor. I think we both know it's more about the money."

"I couldn't live with myself if had a hand in assassinating President Lincoln."

"Others, regular folks are OK, huh? Not going to try to understand your values. I also heard Thompson is being replaced. Know anything about this?"

"Yeah. He is."

"Who is replacing him?"

Hyams broke out a wide grin. "Another Lee," he said.

"You mean Robert E. Lee's uncle, Cassius Lee? I know he's already in Canada..."

"No. Another General Lee. Brigadier General Edwin Lee. Second cousin to Robert E. He just got here to replace Jacob Thompson. He said he was here to 'help us boys up here carry on.'"

A week passed before Thurston could make arrangements. He sent word to Hyams. In the future he might be asked to testify against Blackburn and others, but he would not be prosecuted. Hyams was even more pleased to hear he would be paid.

Arrangements were set. He would meet with Thurston at a designated pier on the Toronto waterfront on the north end. He was to replace the valise as discussed with Thurston and bring the toxic, weaponized valise to the pier.

Thurston got there first. He waited a long time, seemed like an hour, before he spotted Hyams climbing up to the walkway to the pier and moving out towards him. The valise was strapped to his shoulder.

"Sorry, I'm late," Hyams said, speaking out of breath. "I had to make sure no one was following me. I see you have your own valise." Reaching his hands out, he then said, "let me see the money."

Thurston pulled back. "Alright, I'll show it to you. You can have it after you dispose of what you're carrying."

Thurston unfastened his folded canvas bag and flipped up the top, exposing a quick glimpse at the greenbacks inside.

"100,000, right?" Hyams asked.

"Yes."

Hyams grinned. "Oh, by the way, he said, I have the address of the bomb factory for you. An added bonus." He handed a piece of paper to Thurston.

"Looks like it's in a house."

"Yes it is. They are making the bombs look like lumps of coal so they can be mixed with real coal."

"To blow up boilers, I guess," Thurston suggested.

"Yes. Boilers or furnaces. Better tell whoever goes looking for them they will find the bombs stored under the floor boards on the first floor. Trample lightly..."

"Let's get on with it," Thurston said.

Hyams pulled the valise he was carrying off his shoulder, swung it by the strap in a circular motion with both hands, and flung it out into the bay.

They stood side by side and watched it sink. Thurston then handed Hyams the bag. Opening it and digging through with his free hand, Hyam's jaw immediately dropped.

"What in hell is this?"

"There's a 100,000 dollars in there, just like I said. I could only get 1,000 U.S. dollars in time. The rest are Confederate."

"They're worthless."

"Well, as you said, you did your part for your Confederate government. That included playing an important role in a heinous plot to try and kill innocent people. You should be grateful you're getting anything at all from my government."

Hyams closed the bag, and said something under his breath as he turned and walked back off the end of the pier.

Thurston notified the local police. They found the bombs, just as Hyams had told him.

Later, with more credible, specific information from Toronto, security around the Croton Dam in Northern Westchester County, the City's first artificial water supply, was immediately increased.

It was learned that previously an engineer from Montreal had recently visited the dam, claiming to be conducting an official inspection. He told workers at the dam that he was under contract from the State of New York. Turned out no such contract was in place. After authorities extended additional resources to protect Croton Dam, there were no further unusual incidents.

There were several failed attempts to kidnap Lincoln. The first attempt was to snatch Lincoln as he travelled from the White House to the Old Soldiers' Home, just outside Washington, where the Lincoln's had a residence for retreat.

In the past, Lincoln made frequent trips, always using the same route, and frequently unescorted. Walt Whitman lived along the route, working as a hospital volunteer in Washington, D.C., tending to wounded Union soldiers. Two years earlier he wrote the following to his mother:

> Mr. Lincoln passes here (14th St.) every evening on his way out (to the Soldiers' Home)...he was alone yesterday... I really think it would be safer for him just now to stop at the White House, but I expect he is too proud to abandon the former custom.

Now, with a Union cavalry unit assigned to accompany Lincoln on all future trips to the Soldiers' Home, the kidnap plan was scrapped. Walt Whitman would write his mother again:

> He always has a company of 25 or 30 cavalry, with sabers drawn and held upright over their shoulders. They say this guard was against his personal wish, but he lets his counselors have their way...

An alternate plan to kidnap Lincoln was hatched. This time the conspirators included John Wilkes Booth and two accomplices. Booth had met with Jacob Thompson and other expatriate Confederates in Montreal in late 1864. This plot also failed when there were last minute changes to the President's itinerary.

Six men, including Booth, were sent as part of a team for a third effort to kidnap Abraham Lincoln. One the day of the third attempt, Lincoln was to visit a Washington Hospital and later a play. His plans were changed, and he did neither. Lincoln's team was mixing up his schedule with last minute adjustments and never taking the same route for regular meetings and events. Unannounced cavalry escorts were periodically also used for longer trips.

Mary Bowser's regular day off was Sunday. She asked to have Saturday off as well. Her husband Wilson had family in town. She enjoyed his relatives and had a lovely time, as well as getting some much needed rest and relaxation.

That Sunday evening when Mary returned late to her shared room behind the Executive Mansion, Gaby had just finished washing up. She was as unfriendly as ever, as Mary said hello, only nodding without looking up as she continued to dry herself off. Melissa had begun to warm up again to Mary. She had been much more reserved since the morning she saw her sneaking back from the main house, assuming she had slept with one of the other servants.

"Good evening, Mary," Melissa said, adding "May asked that you go to see her as soon as you came in."

"Now? This late?"

"Yes."

Dropping off her things, Mary put her coat back on and headed over to the servant quarters above the kitchen. May heard her on the back steps and was standing in front of the door to her room. She looked upset as she ushered Mary into her room and closed the door. They both sat on the bed where they could converse softly, avoiding others listening in.

What's the matter May? Mary asked. "You look grim."

May began to explain. "Waldo Porter Johnson was here Saturday morning to see Mr. Davis. Confederate Congressman from Missouri. He was here once before with another congressman, Williamson Simpson Oldham from Texas."

"I remember that," Mary noted.

May nodded. "They met behind closed doors. No idea what it was about at the time."

"All I remember was that the two men seemed very somber when they left," Mary remarked.

"This time, when he first arrived, I heard the congressman say, 'I have some very good news. Something we haven't had much of lately.' Mr. Davis said, 'come in, come in. I can definitely use some of that.'"

"I'm almost afraid to hear anymore."

"That was all I heard before they crossed into the west parlor and into the side room Mr. Davis likes to use for smaller gatherings."

"The cribbage room."

"Yes. Or, as Melissa likes to call it, 'the Robert E. Lee Mud Room'. I desperately wanted to find out what the meeting was about, but most of the family was downstairs. Mrs. Davis was reading a magazine in the east parlor where the sun was shining brightly through the windows. Gaby was doing your usual morning chores. I couldn't take the risk."

"Of course not."

May sat quiet for a minute, apparently experiencing this moment again in her thoughts.

"Then it occurred to me. Even before I suspected you of using the basement to hear conversations in meeting rooms, I had already noticed that this could be done. I wasn't sure it would work from the cribbage room, but I decided to try."

"You went looking for candles."

May smiled. "I did."

"Could you hear anything?"

"Yes. The congressman was doing all the talking in the beginning. At some point he mentioned that Williamson Oldham was sorry he couldn't join them. He was traveling this weekend. He went on to say that he and Williamson Oldham had gone to see the latest experiment at Nitre. He said it was very successful."

"With cats?"

"Yes. Waldo Johnson then talked about Richard McCulloh. He told Mr. Davis how that fiend chemist McCulloh pulled out a vial filled with a colorless fluid gas. He told the audience 'if thrown from the gallery of the

House of Representatives in Washington, it would kill every member in five minutes.'"

"My God. Then what?"

"Johnson described in detail how from a window they watched as Mc-Culloh wearing special clothing and a mask, placed a handkerchief on the mantle, shook the vial and released it. He said the gas had immediate effect, killing all the cats. He concluded saying, 'the experiment was completely satisfactory.'"

"Satisfactory, how awful," Mary remarked.

"The congressman then told Mr. Davis that he and Oldham had answers to the questions the President had asked last time they met concerning the newly reconstituted mixture of Greek Fire." Before Mary could respond, May added, "he said Congressman Oldham, knowing he couldn't meet with the rest of them, had written a response to the questions in a letter. 'More eloquent than I could present them now,' he said, handing the letter to Mr. Davis. It then got quiet for a while as he read."

"Was any of it read or commented on aloud?" Mary inquired.

"Unfortunately no, not while I was listening. If only." May looked down, despairingly. "Decided I was there too long and better get back to my duties."

"Well this is very important and useful information, May."

"There's more. After going upstairs, I was close by when Mr. Davis walked him to the door. He was still holding the letter, and I hoped he might put it down somewhere, but he didn't. As soon as the congressman left, Mr. Davis went to his room. At first he sat at his desk, but very briefly. Then, I could hear him opening his safe."

"Well, perhaps..."

May cut Mary off before she could finish. "I was desperate to see the contents of that letter. I decided the best time to try and open the safe was when the family was at Sunday Service. So I did. Brought it back to my room and began to write notes, verbatim."

"You took a big risk doing this all on your own."

"I was a fool. Don't get me wrong, there is even more disturbing things in the letter, as you will see. The problem is that Mrs. Davis came home unexpectedly. She told Gaby she wasn't feeling well. Gaby thought she looked upset, like she had another argument with Mr. Davis. She has been in her room all day. I couldn't get to the adjoining office and put the letter back."

"I can help you do it tomorrow."

"Yes, thank you, Mary. Hopefully Mrs. Davis will be feeling better."

She pulled her box out from under the bed and grasped the letter on top. "You might as well read the original."

Mary skimmed the letter addressed to "His Excellency, Jefferson Davis, President, C.S.A." The letter started out referring to the previous meeting with the congressmen and Davis.

> I was not fully prepared to answer, but which upon subsequent conference with parties proposing the enterprise, I find cannot apply as objections to the scheme.

It went on to list two points:

1. These new highly combustible materials would not expose the parties using them to danger of detection
2. No necessity to send military into the enemy's country. It could be done by agent or even individuals ignorant of the facts

The letter concluded with the following:

> I have seen enough of the effects that can be produced to satisfy me that in most cases without any danger to the parties engaged, and in others very slight, we can: 1. Burn every vessel that leaves a foreign port of the United States. 2. We can burn every vessel transport that leaves the harbor of New York or other Northern port with supplies for the armies of the enemy in the South; 3. Burn every transport and gunboat on the Mississippi River, as well as devastate the country of the enemy, and fill his people with terror and consternation.

> I am respectfully, your obedient servant.

> W.S. Oldham

There was a hand scribbled note in the handwriting of Davis below Oldham's signature, *"Secretary Benjamin to contact General Harris about overcoming the difficulty heretofore experienced."*

Mary commented, "Now it appears they have two secret weapons. Greek Fire, which this seems to be about, and some kind of terrible lethal gas. It seems pretty clear that the Union must move even faster to end this war before many more people get killed. Why don't you give me the copy you made? Let's plan getting this back in the safe first thing tomorrow."

Nothing seemed out of the ordinary Monday morning. Jefferson Davis had left for his office. When the timing was right, May would stand lookout as Mary opened the safe to put the letter back. Just like the last time. Mary then planned to make a trip in the afternoon to Wayne's store to pass on the latest information.

Mary was doing her regular morning chores when May came up and pulled her aside. They stepped into the unoccupied Alabama Room and closed the door.

"He knows. I'm in big trouble, Mary."

"How does he know?"

"Melissa told me. Poor girl, she was conflicted about it. I assume it was her sense of loyalty to the Davis family that weighed against whether she should share it with me, her boss."

"What did she say?"

"Melissa overheard him saying goodbye to his wife this morning at the door. They didn't realize she was nearby. He told her there were only two people who could open the safe. His wife and me. She heard him say that I must have never destroyed the combination he once gave me as I asked her to do."

"Oh, no."

"Surprising to me, Melissa heard Mrs. Davis asked if he suspected her. Mr. Davis said, no, explaining that while they have their differences, he knows he can always count on her loyalty to him. Melissa then heard him say, he first suspected something like this a while ago, but couldn't be sure. He now thinks it may not have been the first time."

"I thought for sure the time I opened it I left his papers the same way I found them," Mary commented.

"You probably did. I think Mr. Davis is growing increasingly more paranoid, imagining things, but not this time."

"I guess it is possible he left a partial toothpick or something I didn't notice leaning against the hinge, but why wouldn't he have done something before?"

"From what Melissa said, it sounded like he has suspected me for some time. He may have been just waiting to try and catch me in the act. Doesn't really matter at this point. As Melissa relayed it, he told Mrs. Davis this morning a letter he had just placed there was missing. Had to be me, he said, according to Melissa. He couldn't deal with it right now. They had an important cabinet meeting first thing this morning. Told his wife not to breathe a word of it and act as if she heard nothing. He would take care of it when he got home. Melissa said Mrs. Davis looked very upset."

Mary thought for a few seconds. "Do you think it is possible that Mrs. Davis has also opened the safe in the past, without telling her husband? Perhaps she may have wanted to find out more about the activities run out of Canada? Plots against northern civilians?"

"There does seem to have been quite a bit of tension between Mr. and Mrs. Davis lately. Nah, but I don't think so," May responded.

"Highly unlikely," Mary agreed. "I think we still put it back when we can. He is bound to think he simply overlooked it, or maybe he inadvertently shuffled it behind other papers. If he did lean something on the hinge, I'll look for it and set it back. If he left the combination lock-dial on a specific number after closing the safe. I will make sure I do the same when I close it."

"No Mary, there is too much risk for me, and maybe for you, too. Besides, since we found out about the planned bombings in New York City, I'm not comfortable working for him anymore. I've given this plenty of thought. I need to leave, before Mr. Davis gets back, and I know you and your contacts can help me. Hopefully they may assume it was only me involved in spying. Maybe Mrs. Davis will think I tried to blame you to protect myself. I need to go. It is best all around. This is the only plausible alternative."

Mary reached over and hugged May who was holding back tears.

"Alright, don't worry. You'll be fine. I'm sure arrangements can be made to help you go North. I was planning to go the Dry Goods Store. You would be safe there. I can go earlier. I will let you know exactly when. You sneak out the back and meet me at the corner of Broad and 11 Street. Wear something over your head so as not to be recognized. In the meantime, get your things together."

When Mary later asked Mrs. Davis for permission to leave for Wayne's store, she told her not to go today.

"I need you to stay here in the house."

As soon as she could, Mary pulled May aside and explained.

"May, you will need to go on your own. You know Wayne Evans' store."

"Yes, I do. Ask to speak alone, about a delicate matter. Try to do this when no one else is in the store. Tell him I sent you. He will know what to do. Give him the letter and tell him all you told me. Now go, as soon as you think you can get away without being seen."

"I never thought I'd say this, but I will miss you, dear. You are truly an exceptional young lady. Thank you so very much." She leaned over and kissed Mary on the cheek.

As Mary walked away, a thought occurred, sending her into a heightened state of anxiety. What if it was she being set up and May was in on it? Wasn't this what Elizabeth had warned her about? Not to trust anyone else.

She had also been reminded before entering the Davis household how as a child her spontaneous inclinations once got her into trouble. A young slave girl going into town with no adult supervision and without a permission slip resulted in spending an afternoon in a jail. Was she not thinking things properly through on this? Could her impulsive decision to assist May expose the entire spy network?

She loved Elizabeth Van Lew and had always taken her advice to heart. Yet, if she had not trusted her instincts and relied on first Henry, the Davis family Butler, and then May to help her, she would not have been nearly as successful uncovering the valuable intelligence she was able to deliver.

Mary played back in her head the recent conversation and events. Why did May not turn her in earlier? Was it possible she agreed to set Mary up after being caught yesterday, while opening the safe? Back and forth she went, considering various scenarios before drawing a final conclusion. May, she was convinced, seemed completely sincere. She was definitely not pretending to be scared. Mary decided to continue to go with her instinct.

Mary would later hear from Daniel that May made it safely to her relatives in New York City.

"I am delighted to hear this," Mary declared. "You can't help becoming highly suspicious of everyone, and second guessing every action, when doing this kind of thing."

The Davis family never quite got over the disappearance of their head housemaid. This was far more devastating for Jefferson Davis than when Henry left. He concluded that May had been spying for some time, but he wasn't about to tell anyone else besides his wife.

Chapter 27: Grant Takes Richmond

For 10 months, the undermanned Army of Northern Virginia had fended off the Union assault, holding their ground between Petersburg and Richmond. With ever increasing numbers of desertions, lack of supplies, and his troops exhausted and undernourished, Lee was running out of options. He had to find a way to dramatically change things, surprise the enemy. Lee considered options where he could once again, as he had done so many times before, take the initiative and attempt to turn things around.

He decided to attack Union controlled Fort Stedman. The fort was lightly fortified and used as a depot for union supplies. Also, it was in close proximity to Confederate lines. If he could surprise the enemy with a sizable force, and take Fort Stedman, the Rebels would then be positioned to next attack City Point, Grant's supply base and headquarters, only 10 miles away.

Lee's fortunes had turned. Elizabeth Van Lew's confidante, Sam Ruth, learned about the planned attack from a Rebel engineer coordinating early logistics. He sent word that Lee would attack when the ground was dry enough to move artillery. He also made his railroad virtually inoperable for Lee in the early months of 1865, slowing down shipments, also shutting down operations at critical times.

The March 25 attack was a complete failure for the Confederates. A counter offensive by Grant, pushed the Rebels back. The Confederates suffered 4,000 causalities, with close to 1,900 soldiers captured, compared to about 1,000 causalities for the Federals.

The Army of Northern Virginia was pummeled for several days with Union artillery, the heaviest bombardment of the war. The ground shook all the way to Richmond. Grant attacked Lee's right flank, severing the last of his supply lines. Shortly after, Sheridan's Union Army broke through Confederate defensive lines at Five Forks, southwest of Petersburg.

While Grant was exploiting the weak Confederate defenses, Sherman was advancing north to join Grant in Virginia. At first, with no lines of communication, neither the Federals nor the Confederates knew what approach Sherman would take. Whether he would swing east, west or come up straight through the middle of the Carolinas. Just that he was coming to join forces with Grant. General Johnston had been reinstated to active duty to pursue Sherman and stop his advance. Johnston's efforts to catch and impede Sherman's progress once again proved inadequate.

From the beginning, Lee felt constrained, forced to take a defensive position protecting Richmond with limited options. He now recognized that his army could no longer defend the Confederate capital.

Lee believed he had only one viable response. By moving his army out, away from Richmond, he believed it could potentially lure Grant to give chase and save the Confederate capital, at least temporarily. Even if the bulk of Grant's Army gave pursuit, Lee still realized, an unprotected Richmond, could not sustain itself much longer.

Not being tied down on defense, able to move and adjust as needed in familiar territory gave Lee more of a chance to evade powerful Union forces and postpone what now seemed inevitable.

Calling his subordinate officers to a war council, Lee told them that he believed they could prolong the war, fighting on Virginia soil, for another two years. He argued that it was easier for his army to change position and move more quickly than the larger Union Army. Familiarity with the Virginia terrain was also an advantage to help extend the war.

"What is the point?" one of them asked, "Knowing that there is no hope we can ever win on the battlefield."

Undeterred, Lee also shared his views with Davis. He recommended that the Army of Northern Virginia should fight on, even as Richmond fell. He knew that the Confederate President held similar convictions. Davis had told his Congress at the end of 1864:

> Not the fall of Richmond, nor Savannah, nor Mobile, nor all combined, can save the enemy from the constant and exhaustive

drain of blood and treasure which must continue until he shall discover that no peace is attainable unless based on the recognition of our indefeasible rights.

Lee's message to Davis also warned that there might only be a few precious days left before Richmond could fall. Lee advised that Davis and his cabinet should prepare to take flight. Against her will, on March 30, 1865, Varina and the Davis children said goodbye to their husband and father, boarding a train for Charlotte, North Carolina. Only Catherine the family nurse went with them.

On April 1, Sadie the cook called Mary, who was close by. She could see smoke from the kitchen window. Mary, with Sadie trailing behind, stepped out of the kitchen door.

There was Jefferson Davis standing in front of a large metal can. What looked like a bonfire was kicking up flames and smoke from the receptacle. Davis had boxes filled with his papers nearby, and was tossing them into the can, one pile at a time.

Davis must have heard the door and looked back. He and Mary stared at each other, while Sadie tried to duck behind Mary. Determined not to be the first to look away, Mary and the beleaguered Confederate President continued to stare at each other for several uncomfortable moments. Davis finally turned and continued to destroy his papers.

"What will you do?" Sadie asked after they were back inside, "When this is over?"

"Don't know yet," Mary answered. "How about you?"

"Try to find my family. They also slaves. Scattered all over."

The Union Army launched another massive attack, encircling Petersburg on Sunday morning, April 2. Lee telegraphed the War Department that Richmond must be abandoned.

While attending Sunday Service at St. Paul's Episcopal Church, Jefferson Davis received the bad news. He left the church immediately and assembled the last meeting of his cabinet in Richmond. They all left on an early evening train for Danville, Virginia, about 140 miles southwest from Richmond. This was the last train out.

Late that same night, to provide cover for his withdrawal, Lee skillfully executed a defensive plan, with units positioned to protect the rest of his forces as they retreated. His army moved approximately 40 miles west, to Amelia Court House. They expected to find railroad cars filled with provisions, but they were not there. His troops had to scavenge the surrounding countryside for food.

The plan was then to move south to North Carolina and combine forces with General Joe Johnston's Army, close to the Danville railroad line. Grant had anticipated that Lee would at some point abandon Richmond and move south. Before Lee's soldiers could find nourishment and regroup, the Bluecoats had moved west, cutting off Lee's advance south of Amelia Court House, preventing those remaining in the decimated ranks of the Army of Northern Virginia from reaching Danville.

Throughout most of the war, as he promoted and then sacked one commanding general after another, Lincoln had insisted that they bear in mind that the primary objective was to destroy Lee's Army, not the capture of Richmond. Now there was complete agreement between Lincoln and Grant. It was Richmond. The sooner the better.

On the morning of April 3, the Federals entered the Rebel capital which was enveloped in clouds of smoke. Among the first to arrive were African Americans as part of 25th Corps of the Army of the James.

In the early evening, long after Colonel Parker and his men had left, Elizabeth had Daniel retrieve several bottles of wine she had been saving from the cellar. Family and friends drank with the Van Lew servants. Tears of joy filled the room.

Elizabeth turned to Isaac. "I have often wondered what I would have done if it was me that answered the door that night for the escaped soldiers, with our neighbors, so devoted to protecting the Confederacy, carefully watching."

"Miss Van Lew...," Isaac had just started to say before Elizabeth interjected.

"You did the right thing Isaac. No question in my mind about that, but I'm still not sure I could have been so strong. Surely, if I did invite them in, we all would have been sent to prison, along with those poor men."

At some point, Chloe reached under the table and placed the quilt she had made for Elizabeth on her lap.

"You can now reclaim your gift, Miss Van Lew. As you can plainly see, a little worn from the weather. Don't think we'll need to put it to work anymore."

"This still looks beautiful to me, Chloe, and I will keep it always. I am so glad it was useful during our darkest hours. Hopefully, the worse is behind us and things will be much better from now on. For all of us."

Daniel spoke next. "I have one other piece of news, Miss Van Lew. I saw Walter, when Wayne and I were helping to put out the fires downtown. So was Walter."

"Did you invite him to come by the house?"

"I did, but he said he couldn't make it. Walter told me he was going to Alexandria to live with his cousins and had a few things he needed to take care of first. Told me he would stop by before leaving. He also told me he has now taken a last name. 'Freeman,' he said."

Elizabeth smiled. "A distinguished name for a distinguished man who did so much. It is a shame other people will never know. That is true for you as well, Daniel."

"At least some of those people might not like what we did. Better they never find out. No telling what they might try to do."

"Sadly, you are probably right, Daniel. Please send word to Mr. Walter Freeman that we insist he must pay us a visit before he leaves."

"Yes ma'am. I will."

Here she was, days later sitting on her front porch with the Commanding General of the Union Army, Ulysses S. Grant. They had been in direct communication since he set up camp at City Point, Virginia, about 30 miles from Richmond. It was as if they knew each other intimately before they ever met.

"General, would you like a little more tea?"

Grant was not one to linger when he had pressing business concerns of an urgent matter he, and he alone, needed to address. Yet, he was both charmed and fascinated by this woman who had provided so much help to the Union cause, despite putting herself in great peril by her many clandestine activities as a spy leader, defying the Confederate government.

He looked down at the cup of fine china that he was nursing on his lap and smiled. "Yes, I would, Miss Van Lew, if it is not too much trouble."

"I'll ask Harriett Anne to heat another pot. Excuse me for a moment. I'll be right back."

When she returned she caught the general deep in his own thoughts. "It will be just a few minutes," she said.

"Miss Van Lew, I do have a question, if you kindly don't mind. The individual who provided critical intelligence from the Confederate White House..."

"You know?"

"Yes. We know this person was one of your best highly placed sources. Colonel Sharpe has known for some time, but not the identity of the spy. This has been a carefully guarded secret by you and the others who knew. We don't even know if it was a slave or a free servant, or perhaps a close acquaintance of the family."

"I can tell you it was a servant."

"I realize whomever it was might be concerned about what could happen if their activities were ever exposed. On my word, I would never tell anyone else in keeping with this individual's desire. However, I would like to personally thank this person for the exceptional effort in helping the Union."

"Very thoughtful of you, General Grant, but in keeping with the promise I made to never divulge this information to anyone, I really can't. Certainly, I hope you can understand this."

Just as Elizabeth finished speaking, Mary Bowser stepped onto the porch, carrying a tray with a teapot, cream and sugar. Grant immediately noticed Elizabeth's surprised reaction as he stood facing Mary. There was no indication if Mary had heard the conversation. She appeared unaffected, as she placed the tray on a small serving table across from Elizabeth.

"Harriett Anne is busy cooking. She asked me to serve, Miss Van Lew."

Elizabeth spoke next. "Mary, glad to see you. I was looking for you earlier to introduce you to the General."

"Oh, sorry Miss Van Lew. I went into town to take care of a few errands," Mary responded.

"General Grant, may I present Mary Bowser," Elizabeth pronounced, somewhat awkwardly in her delivery.

They both politely bowed.

Grant spoke first. "Very nice to meet you, Miss Bowser."

"A true pleasure meeting you, General Grant," Mary replied.

"It's Mrs. Bowser," Elizabeth noted. "Her husband, Wilson, had been assisting as a volunteer scout during their advance on Richmond."

"He entered the city with the 25th Corps, as they marched up Osborne Turnpike," Mary proudly shared.

"Excellent," Grant said.

"I believe the 25th was organized by General Benjamin Butler," Elizabeth added.

"Yes, you are correct, Miss Van Lew. The 25th Corps is part of General Godfrey Weitzel's 1st Division, aptly named. They were the first division to enter and occupy Richmond. Many were former slaves who fled to Fortress Freedom, as it was then called after General Butler made his stand on the 'contraband of war,'" Grant said.

"And refused to return them as runaway slaves," Elizabeth added.

"Absolutely correct. General's Butler and Weitzel, Butler's chief engineer at the time, helped make the 25th a very effective fighting unit. Please thank your husband Wilson for me, Mrs. Bowser," Grant said.

"I most certainly will," Mary said, adding "He should be coming by in a little while."

"Well, maybe the General could thank him personally, if time allows," Elizabeth mentioned. After a few seconds of uncomfortable awkwardness, she continued. "Mary and Wilson have been staying with us. Poor dears, their place was in one of the hardest hit areas from the downtown fires."

Mary looked directly at Elizabeth. "While I was in town today I stopped by to get a few things from our apartment."

"Sorry to hear about your home," Grant said.

"Thank you, General."

Mary began to move away as Grant returned to his seat, Elizabeth reached over and lifted the pot and began to pour into the general's cup. She looked back at Mary who was about to step through the door back into the house.

"Mary, there is plenty of tea here. Why don't you get a cup for yourself and join us. That is if the general doesn't mind." Elizabeth pointed to the empty chair across from where she and Grant sat.

After stopping, turning around, Mary now looked slightly baffled by the suggestion, as she studied Elizabeth's countenance, attempting to grasp any indication of the underlying intent behind this unusual suggestion. Elizabeth had agreed not to say anything to anyone. Had she decided for some reason to reveal her role spying on the Davis family, without her consent?

"I'd welcome it," Grant said.

"Yes ma'am, I'll get another cup. Thank you," she whispered as she left, still uncomfortable as to where this might lead.

Elizabeth finished pouring into the general's cup and added slightly more to her own, still half full cup.

"Mary is a lovely young lady," she said. "She volunteers her time with children at her church. Her husband, Wilson, is also an exceptional young person. He became a free man just before the war began."

"I can see how she would be very good with children. Was Mary free during the war as well?

"Rather complicated to get into. She went north when she was much younger, before the secession started. Met Wilson in Philadelphia. They decided to come back to Virginia. Mary ended up as a slave again."

Grant took another sip of coffee. "I see."

"Is there any chance you could stay for dinner, General?" Elizabeth inquired. "Harriett Anne is cooking one of her specialty meals. Baked mutton with gravy, with black eye peas and mashed potatoes."

"Thank you Miss Van Lew, perhaps another time. I must get back to town in a short while. Unfortunately, the war is still not over. Not yet."

Mary Bowser joined them with a cup in hand. She placed it on the table and Elizabeth poured.

"Thank you, ma'am," she said. Her eyes caste down upon her cup. She picked it up and moved over to the empty seat.

"Was there significant damage to your home?" Grant asked.

"We were actually quite lucky," Mary answered. "No fire damage, just the awful smell of smoke, and soot everywhere. It will be awhile I'm afraid before we can get rid of the smell, but we should eventually be able to move back. Frankly, of more importance, life in Richmond should be much better for all of us, going forward."

"We certainly hope so," Grant responded.

Changing the subject, Elizabeth asserted, "As we were discussing earlier, General, you made the point that the war continues. You must, I would assume, feel confident that with the Union's recent success, the Confederates could not possibly hold out very much longer."

"Jefferson Davis, is now in Danville, which they are calling the new Confederate Capital. He is urging that all Confederates continue fighting, even with Richmond now lost. He defiantly proclaimed the South should never consent to allowing one foot of enemy soil passing over to the Union."

"He must be delusional," Elizabeth suggested.

"Perhaps," Grant responded. "Luckily, we have now cut off most of their communication channels, so I don't think this message from Davis carried very far. Yet, we should not underestimate the determination of the enemy to continue to fight."

Mary noted, "Very surprising to me when I went into town. There were people on the street, sharing stories and expressing their feelings. I heard several voicing their anger and criticism of the Confederates. Something one never would have heard before."

Elizabeth added, "I have also spoken to several acquaintances, long time secessionists. Some have had an apparent change of heart. One told me he felt betrayed by the Confederate leaders who started this war. Especially now, how they slithered off under the cover of darkness, leaving our city in a pile of rubble."

"Truly a shame," Grant asserted.

"Before the war, you might never have suspected it today, General. Richmond was a thriving community of almost 40,000 inhabitants. Second only to New Orleans in the South."

"I wish I could have seen the city back then," Grant said.

Elizabeth continued. "There was international influence in Richmond. Foreign dignitaries, writers, artists and actors, visiting often. We had five consulates representing other nations. Some of the largest flour mills in the world, paper mills too, and as I'm sure you were well aware, a huge tobacco industry which contributed to a very prosperous economy."

Grant nodded, "Yes, of course. But even though, perhaps not as dependent as in the Deep South, it was an economy where slavery and the trading of slaves was an important part."

"Very true," Mary said. Elizabeth nodded before continuing.

"During the war it all changed. Commercial enterprises were replaced by factories supplying military weapons for the war. Cannons, guns, ammunition, bomb making facilities, and of course military prisons. Just as you suggested, General, still dependent on the use of slaves for preserving what they referred to as "the Cause." A disgraceful turn of events in so many ways. Look at us now. As if we are being punished."

"The prisons were horrible," Mary commented.

"Yes," Elizabeth said. "Bad for army prisoners, but, here again, always worse for the slaves in Richmond's jails."

"I know that you and your connections with the Underground Railroad helped many of our imprisoned soldiers escape. I am most grateful for all of this, and so are the men and their families you helped. This will not be forgotten."

"I will never forget them," Elizabeth said.

Grant continued. "Many of the slaves who escaped across enemy lines provided valuable intelligence. Some we know were working for you and your network. In some cases, to our astonishment, they would return to the enemy side, to help even more."

"They were willing to give up their own freedom to continue working for the freedom of all," Elizabeth pointed out.

"Truly remarkable," Grant said. "It was also not lost on us that when slaves began leaving the South in great numbers, they not only were escaping the bondage of slavery, but were also helping reduce the number of Confederate workers available to perform critical nonmilitary functions. This really hurt the enemy."

"As I mentioned before, General, there are many who contributed. Some in extraordinary ways." Elizabeth never shifted her gaze from Grant. She could sense the turn in the conversation was making Mary uncomfortable again.

"I understand your position on this, Miss Van Lew. Well, this has been very pleasant and a much needed diversion from my usual activities. Now, if you wonderful ladies don't mind, it's about time I get moving along. I would like, however, to first freshen up."

"Mary, why don't you show General Grant to the wash room, and in the meantime, let me see how Harriett Anne is doing in the kitchen."

When Elizabeth and Mary came back to the porch, Grant was already there, standing against the porch rail, looking out to the street.

"Thank you again, ladies, I had a very nice time."

"So did we, General."

"Good day, Miss Van Lew. Mrs. Bowser. Oh, and Mrs. Bowser, please don't forget to thank your husband on my behalf."

Both women curtsied as Grant placed a hand to his chest and bowed, this time very gracefully.

As he stepped from the porch, "Please come visit us again," Elizabeth called from behind.

"I will," he said as he walked along the stone walkway leading from the main entrance of the Van Lew estate to the road, saluting as he passed the flag, and waving back to the ladies.

They both stood and watched as the General stepped onto the street where there was a carriage waiting. It had been further away in a shady area, away from the Van Lew home while the General visited. The driver noticed Grant before he left the property and had begun moving the horse drawn carriage up towards the Van Lew entrance.

As Mary reached down to pick up the tray she found a folded note. She called it to Elizabeth's attention. Elizabeth looked over Mary's should as she unfolded it.

Dear Mrs. Bowser,

It was indeed a pleasure making your acquaintance and I am humbled by your service to our country. If ever I can be of assistance, please share this note with one of my staff, and they will arrange for us to meet privately.

Very Respectfully Yours,

U.S. Grant

Before Mary could say anything, Elizabeth interjected. "I never breathed a word."

"Then how did he know?"

"He's a smart man. Smarter than some folks ever suspected, I believe. After all, he outsmarted Robert E. Lee."

Epilogue

With Richmond now in shambles, the fate of the Confederacy was considerably bleaker. Davis and his generals already knew they could not win by traditional methods. They must have concluded their only hope was continuing clandestine operations targeting Northern leaders and more expansive terrorist acts aimed at the general population in northern cities. The string of battlefield victories in the early part of the war were a distant memory.

They also must have realized they needed to buy time. None of their unconventional war methods to date had inflicted the necessary blow to shock the North into turning against the war and giving up the fight. Almost all had failed miserably. Perhaps now with new leadership in Canada operations would be more effective. It was up to Robert E. Lee to fight on and extend the timeline of the war. This would give his cousin's team a chance to strike the necessary blow.

After leaving defensive positions in Richmond, and finding no provisions as expected at Amelia Court House, Robert E. Lee's Army of Northern Virginia now planned to march to the new Confederate Capital in Danville. With Lee on the move, and the taking of Richmond not ending the conflict, Grant had no choice but to pursue his nemesis until he could corner the Army of Northern Virginia and force him to surrender.

This didn't take long, Sheridan's cavalry and two infantry corps surrounded and successfully bottled up Lee's Army of Northern at Sailor's Creek on April 6. Close to 8,000 Confederates, including generals, were captured. This represented about one quarter of Lee's forces. The next day Grant sent a message to Lee asking for his surrender.

At dawn, April 9, in a last attempt to break out, Confederate forces attempted to push back the Union cavalry and take the high ground near Appomattox Court House, only to find two Union infantry corps on the opposite side of the ridge. There would be no escape this time.

Grant offered what he believed were generous terms. The Confederate soldiers would not be prosecuted for treason, for example. Lee asked Grant to also provide rations for his starving troops and allow them to retain their horses. He explained to Grant that his men owned their own horses, unlike the Union. Horses would be essential for planting season once they returned to their farms. Grant acquiesced to the request and Lee accepted the terms for surrender.

Crowds in northern cities took to the streets and sang patriotic songs. Cannons fired 500 gun salutes. Not all Confederate armies would stop fighting after Lee's formal surrender at Appomattox, April 12, but the end of the war was in close reach.

On the evening of April 14, the Christian Holy Day of Good Friday, President Abraham Lincoln was assassinated at Ford's Theatre. His wife, Mary Todd Lincoln, was with him but was physically unharmed. Lincoln was shot in the back of the head by John Wilkes Booth. After shooting Lincoln, Booth allegedly declared, "*Sic semper tyrannis*," a Latin phrase meaning "thus always to tyrants." This quote was often attributed to Brutus after killing Julius Caesar. Shakespeare's *Julius Caesar* was the play Booth performed with his brothers in New York City on Evacuation Day. He then jumped from the Lincoln's upper box seat to the stage, breaking his leg. He still managed to escape through a rear alley.

Lincoln died the next morning in a boarding house close by. Upon hearing the news, Secretary of War Edwin Stanton said, "Now he belongs to the ages." The nation was in shock. The death of her husband led to his wife, Mary Todd descending into a deep depression. This was compounded a few years later by the death of her youngest child, Thomas.

It was established immediately that Booth had not acted alone. He was part of a larger planned conspiracy. Lincoln was not the only target. At the same time, the same evening when Lincoln was shot, an associate of Booth's, Lewis Powell, assaulted Secretary of State William Seward at his home. Seward was in bed at the time, recuperating from a fall from a horse drawn carriage.

Claiming to be delivering medicine to the butler, Powell forced his way into Seward's bedroom. Powell's gun jammed when confronted by a bodyguard. Using his gun barrel as a weapon, and also pulling out a knife, he injured the bodyguard and several of Seward's children. Powell then forced himself onto the Secretary in his bed, attempting to stab him three times in the throat with his knife. It was believed a metal splint Seward was wearing after breaking his jaw saved his life.

Later it was learned that a third member of the Lincoln Administration was also targeted for assassination that same evening, Vice President Andrew Johnson. Another conspirator working with Booth, George Atzerodt, lost his nerve and decided not to go through with the plan.

Grant, who declined an invitation for his wife and he to join Lincoln that evening at Ford's Theatre, was convinced from the start it was a Confederate conspiracy. Grant suggested that the Mayor of Richmond and the City Council be rounded up. He wanted them placed in Libby Prison. He later rescinded the order for fear it might lead to riots and additional hostilities.

Hundreds of people were interviewed and arrested in the following days. John Wilkes Booth and David Herold, who had conspired with Booth earlier in one of the kidnapping plots, were tracked by Federal troops to a barn in Port Royal, Virginia. Herold complied with the demand to give himself up. Booth refused. The barn was set on fire. Booth was killed by a shot fired into the burning barn.

Eight conspirators were convicted by a military tribunal. Herold, Powell, Atzerodt and Mary Surratt were hanged. Surrat owned the boarding house used to devise the plot. Four others were convicted as charged for their part in the assassination by a military tribunal. Three received life imprisonment. One a six year jail term. Mary Surrat's son, John Surratt, another conspirator, escaped to Canada.

Elizabeth Van Lew's feelings of relief that the worse was finally over, were abruptly upended. She, like other Richmond Unionists, was devastated by Lincoln's assassination. African Americans were heartbroken. They worried the Federal Government that they had hoped would now protect them, might not carry through with Lincoln's plans. Their concerns were well founded.

Andrew Johnson, the Democratic Vice President under Lincoln, who escaped potential assassination, became the 17th President of the United States. Johnson favored a quick restoration of the Confederate States. President Johnson did not believe in giving special protection to former slaves, setting the stage for a bitter confrontation with Congressional Republicans, and emboldening former Confederates.

As part of what became known as the "Presidential Reconstruction," state legislatures in the South moved quickly to pass "black codes" to control the behavior of African Americans, including jobs and voting. Johnston rejected Secretary of War Edwin Stanton's proposal for military occupation to enforce Federal law and establish order. The new President moved to fire Stanton without "the advice and consent of the Senate." The House of Representatives then moved to impeach Johnson. He was acquitted in the Senate by one vote.

"Radical Reconstruction," started after northern Republicans seized control of the congressional elections in November, 1866 and continued into the election of President Grant in 1869. This gave newly enfranchised blacks a voice in government for the first time. There was, however, a new dangerous backlash, with long term implications. Racism, with calls for "white supremacy" took hold in the South and to a lesser degree in other regions. This included the formation of the Ku Klux Klan.

"Separate but equal" was enshrined in 1896 by the Supreme Court in "Plessy v. Ferguson." State enacted Jim Crow laws spread throughout the South enforcing racial discrimination and suppression. Mob violence against African Americans, was frequent, often in response to minor infractions, or simply because of unsubstantiated accusations. Based on the research begun by Monroe Nathan Work at the Tuskegee Institute, there were 4,743 lynchings between 1882 and 1968. Approximately 3,446 were African American, and 73 percent of these were in Southern States.

Elizabeth Van Lew had used most of her inheritance to provide assistance to runaway slaves and Union escaped prisoners. Ulysses S. Grant authorized a payment of $2,000 for her family, but it did little to offset the Van Lew financial predicament. Elizabeth was scorned by many of her neighbors and former friends for the assistance she provided the Federal Government during the war.

In addition to Grant, who indicated Van Lew provided the most valuable intelligence received by the Union from Richmond during the war, Colonel Sharpe, who headed the Federal Bureau of Military Information as weighed in. He wrote:

> From the beginning, the family, with all its influences, took a strong position against the Rebel movement, and never ceased fighting it until our armies entered Richmond. Their position, character and charities gave them a commanding influence over many families of plain people, who were decided and encouraged by them to remain true to the flag... For a long, long time, she represented all that was left of the power of the U.S. Government in the city of Richmond.

> They sent emissaries to our lines; when no one else could for the moment be found, they sent their own servants. They employed counsel for union people on trial – they had clerks in the Rebel war and navy departments in their confidences; and soon after our arrival at City Point, Miss Van Lew mastered a system of correspondence in cipher by which specific information asked for by the General was obtained.

When Grant became President, he named Elizabeth Van Lew postmaster for Richmond. Appointing a women to this coveted role was uncommon at the time. Van Lew served as postmaster from 1869 to 1877. She passed away on September 25, 1900, still detested by many of her fellow citizens in Richmond, and throughout the South.

The Revere family helped pay for her burial and shipped a massive boulder for her gravestone from Boston to Shockoe Hill Cemetery. It would eventually be desecrated by locals who hated her. The Revere's from Boston were thankful for the comfort and aid Elizabeth Van Lew provided Paul Joseph Revere, while he was a prisoner at Libby Prison. The grandson of the Revolutionary War hero, Paul Joseph Revere who had died at Gettysburg.

After the war, Mary Bowser joined the Christian Commission, working with the Union army to provide education for freed slaves. She also worked with the Baptist Missionary Society, teaching 200 African American children. She changed her name back to Richards, perhaps after divorcing Wilson Bowser.

She eventually went north to give speeches on her experiences during the war and living in the antebellum South, also highly unusual for women in the early days of the suffrage movement, particularly for woman of color. She continued teaching African American children. At some point she may have married again. There are no records after she was last known to be teaching at a school in St. Mary's, Georgia.

As best they could, Samuel Ruth, Thomas McNiven, the Lohmann brothers, and other Union spies and scouts who had worked with Elizabeth, tried to reassemble their former lives. Not much exists in the public record after the war, except that some of them were also compensated, between $200-500, for their help to the Federal Government during the war. In some cases, Elizabeth Van Lew interceded for them through her government contacts. No doubt, these individuals did not want to amplify their efforts during the war, abetting the Union, which continued to be vilified by many of their neighbors and business associates.

John Minor Botts presided over a Unionist convention, in May 1866, and also attended the midyear Southern Loyalist Convention in Philadelphia for the midterm elections. He unsuccessfully tried to win support of the Southern Union Republican Party to adopt more radical elements of the National Republican Party that promoted both black suffrage and the disfranchisement of all former Confederates. Botts' position had evolved from the days he supported the Union, but was against freeing the slaves. His new views were aligned with the winning Republican majority.

Jefferson Davis was heartsick after Lee surrendered, refusing to accept defeat. He wanted to flee to Europe, and was considering the idea to set up a government in exile, but was captured in Irwinville, Georgia with his wife and children. It was reported that he was apprehended wearing his wife's shawl to avoid detection. The Northern press roundly ridiculed him as a coward.

Davis was transported to Fort Monroe where he was held as a military prisoner for two years. He was indicted for treason but never brought to trial. There were those who wanted to prosecute him for the assassination of Lincoln, but when no evidence of a connection surfaced during the assassination trials, it was assumed by government officials there was no connection, or at least no proof of a connection. Jefferson Davis was released from prison two years later. He lost most of his wealth and his U.S. citizenship. He refused to request a pardon or restoration of his citizenship.

Varina Davis was restricted from travel while her husband was incarcerated. She and the Davis children reunited with Jefferson Davis after he was released. They travelled outside the United States to Europe and Canada, where Jefferson Davis hoped to rebuild his fortunes and reputation. Varina and her husband would live apart for long intervals, suggesting ongoing marital difficulties. After her husband died of acute bronchitis and complications from malaria, Varina Davis moved to New York City.

Robert E. Lee was not arrested after the war. He did lose the right to vote and his property in northern Virginia was confiscated. His family mansion, the "Curtis-Lee" Estate, which had been seized by Union forces during the war, was converted into Arlington National Cemetery. Equated with legendary status, and generally considered most representative of the gallantry and heroism of the fabled "Lost Cause," Lee was associated with a romanticized view of the South, held by many who fought on the losing side. Much of Lee's actions and beliefs have been recast and embedded in revisionist myth. While he racked up exceptional military accomplishments while facing considerable disadvantage, he also suffered devastating defeats.

After the war, Lee did become an advocate for intersectional reconciliation, and also emancipation of slaves, but he believed the enslaved should be freed in a slow, gradual process, not immediately as abolitionists demanded. The Lee family did own slaves, and while they were eventually freed, this was in accordance with the will of Lee's father-in-law, when he and his wife inherited them. The will stipulated that the slaves should be freed after five years.

In a letter to his wife in 1856, prior to the Civil War, Robert E. Lee wrote, "In this enlightened age, there are few I believe, but what will acknowledge that slavery as an institution, is a moral and political evil in any Country." Yet, in the same letter, Lee indicated that he believed slavery was "a greater evil to the white man than to the black race," and also that, "The painful discipline they are undergoing is necessary for their instruction as a race." Some have argued that Lee's views on the subject evolved since the letter was written, yet there is little in the public record to support this.

Near the end of the war, when conditions were desperate for the South, only then did Lee recommend slaves be deployed as soldiers to help fight for the Confederacy. It was clear to most by this time the war was all about slavery. Lee may have been unaware that slaves and former slaves were covertly assisting the Union, passing intelligence across enemy lines, and helping Union prisoners escape, who also at times brought sensitive information on the Confederates. However, he most certainly knew that the high number of slaves, fleeing north and abandoning their non-military activities critical for supporting his army had a devastating effect over time on his ability to prosecute war against the Union. Robert E. Lee died in 1870 at the age of 63, only five years after the Civil War ended.

Lee's second cousin, Brigadier General Edwin Gray Lee, in bad health, took over the Canadian covert operations from Jacob Thompson in the beginning of 1865. One of his first decisions was to move operations from Toronto to Montreal. His group of agents in Canada were still prepared to conduct guerilla warfare for Confederate independence. As Edwin Lee said upon hearing about his cousin, Robert E. Lee, conceding defeat and accepting Grant's terms at Appomattox Court House:

> I cannot and will not believe that because General Lee was compelled
> to surrender 22,000 men, we therefore have and can wage war no more.

Lee's cousin met with John Surrat, part of the Lincoln assassination plot, in Montreal, a month after Lincoln was assassinated. Surrat had a letter from Judah Benjamin, Confederate Secretary of State. This included a warrant for $1,500 in gold from "the Confederate Secret Service account." While in Canada Edwin Gray Lee helped move Surrat from one safe house to another. He also helped him gain safe passage by ship to Europe. In letters, he talked about being treated by his new personal physician, Doctor Luke Blackburn.

Upon the request of U.S. Secretary of State, William Seward, Colonel Sharpe agreed to leave the country and track down John Surratt. He followed Surratt's trail from England to Italy. Eventually Sharpe captured the suspected assassin conspirator in Egypt. Surratt was brought back to the United States where he was tried in a civilian court. After a hung jury was declared, Surratt was set free, never to be prosecuted again.

With his health failing, Edwin Gray Lee was charged with handling Lincoln conspirator and fugitive, John Surratt. He decided to stay in Canada until 1866. Edwin would travel home, his sickness becoming increasingly debilitating. Edwin Lee would die in his sleep at Yellow Sulphur Springs, Virginia in 1869. Robert E. Lee, praised his second cousin, "He was a true man, and, if health had permitted, would have been an ornament as well as a benefit to his race."

Benjamin Butler, the politically appointed Union general, was despised by Confederates and criticized by his superiors for his military failures. His contraband of war argument cleverly devised for not returning slaves who escaped from the enemy defied the Fugitive Slave Act which was still accepted law across the North and U.S. territories. Thousands of slaves from Virginia, many of whom had been forced to work in non-military roles for the Rebel Army, fled to Fort Monroe as a result. His contraband of war rationale influenced Lincoln's Emancipation Proclamation. Butler established a secret communication channel with Elizabeth Van Lew in early 1864. He, and later General Grant, would receive encrypted messages on Confederate military plans, disposition of troops, fortifications and movement of supplies. Butler commanded African American soldiers during the war. He created the Butler Medal to honor African American soldiers for acts of bravery.

"Connecting the dots," it is highly likely that information passed from Van Lew to Butler prevented a terrorist plot from being carried out in New York City on Election Day during the Civil War. On November 8, 1864, Confederate funded operatives based in Canada planned to set fire to New York City Hotels. The Governor of New York, Horatio Seymour hated

Lincoln. He assured Jacob Thompson, leader of the terrorist group, in the event of an uprising he would remain neutral. New York City officials were notified in advance but shrugged it off, believing it was a hoax. Butler and his Army showed up just before the day of election forcing the Confederates to call off their insurrection plan. A second attempt after Butler's Army left town was also thwarted when the detonation of a re-engineered Greek Fire weapon failed to properly ignite in 13 hotels on November 25.

Elected to Congress as a Radical Republican after the war, Butler supported aggressive emancipation of slaves and military intervention to ensure it was implemented across the South. He played a leading role in the impeachment trial of Andrew Johnson. He would also serve as Governor of Massachusetts. Butler died in 1893.

Jacob Thompson, who preceded Edwin Gray Lee, as head of the Canadian operation, fled to England. He returned to Mississippi in 1868 after amnesty was granted.

As the cross-border operation began to fall apart, other members also elected to stay in Canada longer, for fear they might be apprehended. Dr. Blackburn believed that he had successfully kept his involvement secret and that his reputation, as a respectable physician, had not been tarnished. He had made plans to go home when word of Lee's surrender reached Canada. On May 19, he was arrested in Montreal.

Godfrey Joseph Hyams testified against him on how he had distributed trunks for Blackburn. The purpose of which was to incubate epidemics in select U.S. northern cities. Blackburn was also accused of devising a plan and offering to pay Hymans to send a potentially lethal valise filled with contaminated dress shirts to the White House. Despite damaging evidence against him, Blackburn was found not guilty of violating the Canadian neutrality act. Blackburn would eventually move back to the United States in 1867. He did not face prosecution in the United States. Blackburn was inaugurated Governor of Kentucky in 1879.

One of the trunks was shipped to New Bern, North Carolina, where 800 soldiers died from yellow fever. Near the Outer Banks, New Bern had fallen into Federal control in 1862, and remained this way throughout the war. It was highly unlikely, however, that the yellow fever outbreak was caused by the contents from Blackburn's trunk. It wasn't until 1902 that Walter Reed discovered that yellow fever was primarily transmitted by mosquitoes – rarely person to person contact, nor by articles of clothing being exposed to victims.

Richard Sears McCulloh experimented with at least two types of weapons while working at the Nitre Bureau, often using stray cats for testing. One was Greek Fire, the other a lethal gas. The Greek Fire weapon proved ineffective. In the case of Evacuation Day, November 25, 1864, where it was set off in 13 New York City Hotels, Barnum Animal Museum and the Winter Garden Theatre, each fire was easily put out, or extinguished by itself shortly after igniting.

There has been debate ever since whether the device itself was defective, whether it was improperly ignited in each case, or had been tampered with to prevent it from working. The original Winter Garden Theatre burned to the ground in 1867. The new Broadway theatre opened in 1911. Ironically, *Cats* became the longest running show, staged from 1982 to September 10, 2000.

The lethal gas weapon, comprised of a colorless liquid, was exhibited to a select group of Confederate congressmen in February, 1865. McCulloh reportedly released the gas in a secure room with cats for demonstration purposes. Richmond fell before the lethal gas could be used.

When a letter to Jefferson Davis from Congressman Williamson Simpson Oldham was recovered, describing how one of his weapons could potentially be used to destroy Union vessels, devastate the country of the enemy, and "fill his (*presumably Lincoln's*) people with fear and consternation," a warrant was issued for McCulloh's arrest.

McCulloh was captured on a boat off the coast of southern Florida, trying to escape the Confederacy in May,1865. He was tried, convicted and sentenced to prison. McCulloh was released in 1866.

Undercover agent Felix Stidger testified in court against members of the Sons of Liberty. The Sons of Liberty conspired to lead an uprising to destroy military assets, invade military prisons and release captured Confederates during the time of the 1864 Democratic Convention in Chicago.

Harrison Dodd, Dr. William A. Bowles, and four other co-conspirators were convicted of treason for attempting to steal weapons, and planning to invade military prisons. This became known as the Northwestern

Conspiracy. The case was appealed and went to the Supreme Court in 1866. The court ruled that because the co-conspirators were first tried in front of a military commission, they were denied constitutional protections. The convictions were overruled.

Clement Vallandigham, was implicated as the "Supreme Commander" of the Sons of Liberty in the trial and appeals. Vallandigham testified in April, 1865 at a separate conspiracy trial in Cincinnati, Ohio. There he admitted to meeting and conversing with Jacob Thompson, the operational leader of Confederate agents in Canada.

As an Ohio politician, Vallandigham had been convicted early in the Lincoln administration for displaying "sympathies with those in arms against the Government of the United States." He was banished to the Confederacy, managed to travel to Canada, and eventually returned before the Chicago Convention. Lincoln decided not to arrest him, avoiding the provocation Vallandigham and some his supporters desired. He returned to Ohio, without further prosecution.

William Seward's consuls, in Bermuda, Toronto, Montreal, and Vancouver, played critical roles in exposing Confederate plots, in addition to performing their regular consul duties. Each continued to serve with distinction. After reporting on Rebel blockade runners and preventing the shipment of Blackburn's trunks from Bermuda, Charles Maxwell Allen continued to work in Bermuda for the Federal government. His family joined him after the war. He was considered one of his country's' most able and longest serving diplomats. He stayed in Bermuda after retiring. Allen passed away in 1888, buried in his beloved Bermuda.

The Consul in Toronto, David Thurston, was recognized in 1865 by the State Department Consular Bureau. It was noted that he was "well and favorably known" in the department, as a "true, earnest and energetic officer." In addition to turning Hyams, in October, 1864, Thurston played an important role when Confederate soldiers from Canada crossed the border to successfully rob banks in St. Albans, Vermont to expand the Confederate Secret Service war chest. He worked with Canadian authorities to help identify and capture the raiders, although they were subsequently released by the Canadian court. Thurston did persuade Canadian officials to call up 2,000 militia volunteers to police the border against future Confederate raids from Canada into the United States.

Like Allen in Bermuda, Thurston elected to stay in Toronto after leaving his post. In 1866, John Potter left his post in Montreal and returned to East Troy, Wisconsin. There is little in the public record about Consul to Vancouver, Allen Francis, after he retired from his post.

Only one of the core team of conspirators to burn New York City Hotels was caught soon after. Confederate Captain Robert C. Kennedy, who had escaped to Canada with his co-conspirators, returned to the United States and was apprehended in Cleveland, Ohio in December 1864. He was tried and convicted. Kennedy was hung on March 25, 1865.

Another conspirator, John William Headley, would write a book about *Confederate Operations in Canada and New York,* published in 1906. He unabashedly bragged about the efforts to destroy New York City Hotels. In his book, Headley also argued that there had to have been an informant embedded in the Canadian team that exposed the New York City plot and other exploits. He suggested it was most probably Godfrey Joseph Hyams, who testified against Dr. Luke Blackburn, and went missing at critical times before various other plans were executed.

Other important characters in the book, Daniel Gates, Dolores Halsey, Wayne Evans, and Walter were fictional. The activities Daniel took part in, and to a lesser extent other characters, exploiting the routes of the underground railroad to help runaway slaves and Union prisoners escape, risking their lives to send military intelligence to the Federals, were indicative of the slaves, former slaves, white abolitionists and Unionists that actually did this.

When General Edmund Kirby Smith, commander of forces west of the Mississippi[1], the last Confederate Army still fighting, surrendered on June 2, 1865, the bloodiest four years in U.S. history finally ended. The unprecedented level of violence in the Civil War was appalling.

New technology deployed for combat combined with traditional military tactics, in large part consistent with those still in use since the Napoleonic period, exponentially increased the carnage. The Civil War became one of the most gruesome and bloodiest of conflicts. It pitted

1.   https://www.history.com/topics/us-states/mississippi

brothers against brothers, fathers against sons. More men died in captivity than in the entire Vietnam War. Thousands died of disease. An estimated 620,000 men died during the fighting, almost 2% of the entire population. One in four soldiers never returned home.

Over 180,000 African Americans volunteered to fight for the Union Army, roughly 10% of all soldiers. An unknown number of them, free men and women, slaves and escaped slaves, helped by spying, scouting, and as couriers transporting information as well as helping escaped Union prisoners move through enemy territory and safely across Union lines, at their own peril. At the conclusion of the Civil War, 4,000,000 slaves were eventually freed.

There is no question that over time the North with its superior manufacturing and numbers of soldiers, and its considerable advantages in its ability to equip and supply them, would eventually gain an insurmountable advantage.

The bloodshed, as horrific as it became, could have been worse. There is no telling how many additional soldiers and civilians would also have died if not for the intelligence provided by African Americans and White Unionists, Mary Bowser, Elizabeth Van Lew, and the many others who risked their lives working behind enemy lines.

It would take much longer than Elizabeth Van Lew realized at the time when the Union Army was advancing into Richmond, set ablaze by the fleeing Confederates, for the country to heal and correct the gross injustices imposed on a such large percentage of people. The healing continues to this day. Yet she and her secret army were an important catalyst for helping to bring the country back together, leading to the subsequent freedom for millions of people from the bondage of slavery.

> Civilization advanced a century. Justice, truth, humanity were vindicated. Labor was now without manacles, honored and respected. No wonder that the walls of our houses were swaying; the heart of our city a flaming altar...

Elizabeth Van Lew

April 2, 1865

Afterword

The underlying premise of this story is that Mary Bowser and Elizabeth Van Lew became highly effective spies, learning by doing, and without any formal training. It is inconceivable to this author that almost all of the Confederate plots of insurrection in northern cities following the military defeats at Vicksburg and Gettysburg were foiled separately without intelligence procured from sources with access to the highest levels of power in Confederate Richmond.

For their own personal safety, at risk long after the Civil War ended, it is reasonable to assume Union spies in Richmond might have chosen not to disclose the extent of their clandestine activities. Also, that much of the evidence on both sides would be destroyed. Also, it is reasonable to assume that the Davis family and Confederate leadership would deny that effective spying occurred within the Confederate Executive Mansion, which they did. If for no other reason, it would have been admitting to an embarrassing breach that may have impacted events to the detriment of Confederate strategic objectives.

Working together, Mary Bowser and Elizabeth Van Lew became proficient in both the gathering and dissemination of intelligence on the Confederates that was passed on to senior Union military officials. They became the cornerstone of a spy network that included people from all walks of life, including slaves, who filled essential roles. Leading double lives, these exceptional women created unassuming outward personas that provided cover and helped them deceive those around them. Both may have been suspected at various times. We do know based on public record that Elizabeth was being closely watched. We can assume that by necessity she must have become adept at using the defense of "plausible deniability," long before the term was coined during the Cold War period of the 1960's. Perhaps, Mary Bowser did as well.

The Richmond network of spies, where Elizabeth Van Lew and Mary Bowser were leading figures, was so successful in concealing their efforts that their contribution to the outcome of the war has been largely overlooked.

Bibliography

S ources of Civil War Research

"1ST COMPANY RICHMOND Howitzers," *The Civil War in the East.*

http://civilwarintheeast.com/confederate-regiments/virginia/1st-company-richmond-howitzers/

"1862: Civil War," *Civil War Trust.*
https://www.civilwar.org/learn/videos/1862-civil-war

"A Look Back … George Washington: America's First Military Intelligence Director," *Central Intelligence Agency,* 2007.

https://www.cia.gov/news-information/featured-story-archive/2007-featured-story-archive/george-washington.html

"Abraham Lincoln's First Inaugural Address March 4, 1861," *Civil War Trust.*

http://www.civilwar.org/education/history/primarysources/lincolninaugural1.html

"Academic Freedom and Treason at Columbia: The Strange Case of Professor R.S. McCulloh," New York Historical Society, November 25, 2015.

http://blog.nyhistory.org/academic-freedom-and-treason-at-columbia-the-strange-case-of-professor-r-s-mcculloh/

"Appearance of General Ulysses S. Grant, October 23, 1863," *Progressive Involvement.*

https://www.progressiveinvolvement.com/progressive_involvement/2010/06/appearance-of-general-ulysses-s-grant-october-23-1863.html

Agonito, Rosemary. *Miss Lizzie's War The Double Life of Southern Bell Spy Elizabeth Van Lew.* Guilford: Globe Pequot, 2012.

"Albert J. Myer," *Wikipedia.*
https://en.wikipedia.org/wiki/Albert_J._Myer

Allen, Charles Maxwell. Wiche, Glen N., Editor. *Dispatches from Bermuda.* Kent: Kent State University Press, 2008.

"Ambrose Burnside," *Wikipedia.*
https://en.wikipedia.org/wiki/Ambrose_Burnside

"American Civil War End, *History.net.*

https://www.history.com/this-day-in-[1]
history/american-civil-war-ends[2]

"American Civil War: Invading the North," *Military History Encyclopedia.* http://www.historyofwar.org/articles/wars_american_civil_war05_invading_north.html

American Civil War Census Data. The Civil War Home Page.
http://www.civil-war.net/census.asp?census=Total

"American Civil War January 1864,"

History Learning Site.

1. https://www.history.com/this-day-in-history/american-civil-war-ends
2. https://www.history.com/this-day-in-history/american-civil-war-ends

https://www.historylearningsite.co.uk/the-american-civil-war/american-civil-war-january-1864/

"America's Civil War: The Fall of Richmond, *History.net*, September 1, 2006.
http://www.historynet.com/americas-civil-war-the-fall-of-richmond.htm

"Anaconda Plan," *Civil War Academy*.
https://www.civilwaracademy.com/anaconda-plan

"Andersonville," *History.com, A&E Networks*, November 9, 2009.
https://www.history.com/topics/american-civil-war/andersonville
"Andrew Johnson," *Wikipedia*.

https://en.wikipedia.org/wiki/Andrew_[3]
Johnson[4]

"Antique Office Safes," *Early Office Museum*.

https://www.officemuseum.com/filing_[5]
equipment_safes.htm[6]

"Alexander H. Stephen Speech Before the Virginia Secession Convention," *Confederate Truths*.

http://www.confederatepastpresent.org/

Applebaum, Stanley, Editor. Selected Poems Walt Whitman. New York: Dover Publications, Inc., 1991.

Arenson, Adam, Graybill, Andrew R., eds. *Civil War Wests*. Oakland: University of California Press, 2015.

3. https://en.wikipedia.org/wiki/Andrew_Johnson

4. https://en.wikipedia.org/wiki/Andrew_Johnson

5. https://www.officemuseum.com/filing_equipment_safes.htm

6. https://www.officemuseum.com/filing_equipment_safes.htm

"Atlanta Campaign," *Wikipedia*.
https://en.wikipedia.org/wiki/Atlanta_Campaign

"Attempt to Escape Castle Thunder," *Richmond Daily Dispatch*, June 18, 1864, Page 1.

https://chroniclingamerica.loc.gov/

"August Conspiracy," *Mr. Lincoln and New York, Lehrman Institute*.

http://www.mrlincolnandnewyork.org/new-york-politics/august-conspiracy/

"Ball's Bluff Harrison's Island," *Civil War Trust*.
https://www.civilwar.org/learn/civil-war/battles/balls-bluff

"Baltimore Riots of 1861," *Wikipedia*.

https://en.wikipedia.org/wiki/Baltimore_[7]
riot_of_1861[8]

Barbauld, Anna Letitia. Pereira, Lucas, Editor. *Lessons for Children*. Rio de Janeiro: Eternity Ebooks, 2014.

"A Batch of Errors," *Richmond Enquirer*, February 8, 1861, Page 1.
http://chroniclingamerica.loc.gov/

"Battle Of Antietam," *HistoryNet*.
http://www.historynet.com/battle-of-antietam

"Battle of Appomattox Court House," *Wikipedia*.
https://en.wikipedia.org/wiki/Battle_of_[9]

---

7. https://en.wikipedia.org/wiki/Baltimore_riot_of_1861

8. https://en.wikipedia.org/wiki/Baltimore_riot_of_1861

Appomattox_Court_House[10]

"Battle of Atlanta," *Wikipedia.*

https://en.wikipedia.org/wiki/Battle_of_[11]
Atlanta[12]

"Battles of Bull Run," *Encyclopedia Britannica.* 15th ed., Chicago: *Encyclopedia Britannica, 2008 Ultimate DVD.*

https://www.britannica.com

"Battle of Chancellorsville," *National Park Service.*
https://www.nps.gov/frsp/learn/historyculture/chist.htm

"Battle of Chickamauga," *Wikipedia.*

https://en.wikipedia.org/wiki/Battle_of_[13]
Chickamauga[14]

"Battle of Dranesville," *Wikipedia.*
https://en.wikipedia.org/wiki/Battle_of_Dranesville

"Battle of Fredericksburg," *History.com, A&E Networks.*
http://www.history.com/topics/american-civil-war/battle-of-fredericksburg

"Battle of Gettysburg," *Wikipedia.*

http://www.shenandoahatwar.org/lees-[15]

9. https://en.wikipedia.org/wiki/Battle_of_Appomattox_Court_House

10. https://en.wikipedia.org/wiki/Battle_of_Appomattox_Court_House

11. https://en.wikipedia.org/wiki/Battle_of_Atlanta

12. https://en.wikipedia.org/wiki/Battle_of_Atlanta

13. https://en.wikipedia.org/wiki/Battle_of_Chickamauga

14. https://en.wikipedia.org/wiki/Battle_of_Chickamauga

15. http://www.shenandoahatwar.org/lees-1863-gettysburg-campaign/

1863-gettysburg-campaign/[16]

"Battle of Kennesaw Mountain," *Wikipedia.*

https://en.wikipedia.org/wiki/Battle_of_[17] Kennesaw_Mountain[18]

"Battle of Malvern Hill," *Wikipedia.*
https://en.wikipedia.org/wiki/Battle_of_Malvern_Hill

"Battle of Petersburg Facts & Summary," *American Battlefield Trust.* https://www.battlefields.org/learn/civil-war/battles/petersburg

"Battle of the Wilderness," HistoryNet.
https://www.history.com/topics/american-civil-war/battle-of-[19]
the-wilderness[20]

"Battle of the Wilderness," Wikipedia.

https://en.wikipedia.org/wiki/Battle_of_[21]
the_Wilderness[22]

Beatie, Daniel J. "A Clash of Sabres," Civil War Trust.
https://www.civilwar.org/learn/[23]
articles/clash-sabres[24]

16. http://www.shenandoahatwar.org/lees-1863-gettysburg-campaign/

17. https://en.wikipedia.org/wiki/Battle_of_Kennesaw_Mountain

18. https://en.wikipedia.org/wiki/Battle_of_Kennesaw_Mountain

19. https://www.history.com/topics/american-civil-war/battle-of-the-wilderness

20. https://www.history.com/topics/american-civil-war/battle-of-the-wilderness

21. https://en.wikipedia.org/wiki/Battle_of_the_Wilderness

22. https://en.wikipedia.org/wiki/Battle_of_the_Wilderness

23. https://www.civilwar.org/learn/articles/clash-sabres

Beard, Rick. "Fire in the Rear," *The New York Times,* May 8, 2013.

https://opinionator.blogs.nytimes.com/[25]
2013/05/08/the-fire-in-the-rear/[26]

Beard, Rick. "The Great Civil War Escape," *The New York Times,* February 11, 2014.

https://opinionator.blogs.nytimes.com/2014/02/11/the-great-civil-war-escape/

"Before the Pentagon, Where Were the Military Headquarters?" *Virginia Places.*

http://www.virginiaplaces.org/[27]

military/beforethepentagon.html[28]

"Benjamin J. Butler," ," *Civil War Trust.*
https://www.civilwar.org/learn/biographies/benjamin-f-butler

"Bermuda and the Blockade Runners,"
Bernews, November 18, 2010.
http://bernews.com/2010/11/[29]
history-bermuda-and-the-blockade-runners/[30]

"The Bermuda Hundred Campaign,"
Civil War Talk.
https://civilwartalk.com/threads/[31]

24. https://www.civilwar.org/learn/articles/clash-sabres

25. https://opinionator.blogs.nytimes.com/2013/05/08/the-fire-in-the-rear/

26. https://opinionator.blogs.nytimes.com/2013/05/08/the-fire-in-the-rear/

27. http://www.virginiaplaces.org/military/beforethepentagon.html

28. http://www.virginiaplaces.org/military/beforethepentagon.html

29. http://bernews.com/2010/11/history-bermuda-and-the-blockade-runners/

30. http://bernews.com/2010/11/history-bermuda-and-the-blockade-runners/

31. https://civilwartalk.com/threads/the-bermuda-hundred-campaign.16128/

the-bermuda-hundred-campaign.16128/[32]

"Bermuda Hundred Campaign," *Wikipedia.*

https://en.wikipedia.org/wiki/[33]
Bermuda_Hundred_Campaign[34]

Berry, Thomas S. "The Rise of Flour Milling in Richmond," *The Virginia Magazine of History and Biography,* October, 1970.

http://bordergroves.com/canal_lives/omeka/files/original/95912066695c9a8813b6709ffe8b82c2.pdf

Beymer, William Gilmore. "Miss Van Lew," *Civil War Richmond (reprinted). Harpers Monthly Magazine,* June 1911, PPS 86-89.

http://www.civilwarrichmond.com/written-accounts/other-sources/4666-1911-06-harper-s-monthly-magazine-pp-86-99-beymer-william-gilmore-miss-van-lew

Bibble, Nicholas, Editor. *The Journals of the Expedition Under the Command of Capts. Lewis & Clark.* New York: Heritage Press, 1962.

Blackwell, Sarah Ellen. *A Military Genius; Life of Anna Ella Carroll, of Maryland.* Lincolnshire: Classic Reprint Series, 2012.

"Bleeding Kansas," *Wikipedia.*

https://en.wikipedia.org/wiki/[35]
Bleeding_Kansas[36]

32. https://civilwartalk.com/threads/the-bermuda-hundred-campaign.16128/
33. https://en.wikipedia.org/wiki/Bermuda_Hundred_Campaign
34. https://en.wikipedia.org/wiki/Bermuda_Hundred_Campaign
35. https://en.wikipedia.org/wiki/Bleeding_Kansas
36. https://en.wikipedia.org/wiki/Bleeding_Kansas

Book of Common Prayer. Philadelphia: J.B. Lippincott & Co., 1843.
Blount Jr., Roy. *Robert E. Lee: A Life.* New York: Penguin Books, 2003.

"Botts and Helper Stand Together," *Richmond Enquirer.* January 21, 1860. Library of Virginia.

http://virginiachronicle.com/cgi-bin/virginia?a=d&d=RE18600124.1.2#[37]

"Bowery," *Wikipedia.*
https://en.wikipedia.org/wiki/Bowery

Brooks, Rebecca Beatrice. 'Paul Revere's Grandsons in the Civil War," *Civil War Saga.* April 16, 2012.

http://civilwarsaga.com/paul-reveres-grandsons-fought-in-the-civil-war/

Brown, R. J., editor. "Use of Greek Fire in the Civil War," *Civil War Talk*, May 26, 2013.

https://civilwartalk.com/threads/[38]

use-of-greek-fire-in-the-civil-war.84611/[39]

Bryant, William. "The Dahlgren Affair and the Lincoln Assassination," Christopher Wren Association, August 23, 2017.

https://www.wm.edu/sites/cwa/course-info/classnotes/fall2017/BryantDAHLGRENAFFAIR.pdf

"'Boyle would have been hung', the scapegoat for Butler's failed raid," *To the Sounds of the Guns*

37. http://virginiachronicle.com/cgi-bin/virginia?a=d&d=RE18600124.1.2

38. https://civilwartalk.com/threads/use-of-greek-fire-in-the-civil-war.84611/

39. https://civilwartalk.com/threads/use-of-greek-fire-in-the-civil-war.84611/

https://markerhunter.wordpress.com/2014/02/08/butlers-scapegoat/

Brooks, Rebecca Beatrice, "Why Did Edwin Booth Vote for Abraham Lincoln," *Civil War Saga,* April 2, 2013.

http://civilwarsaga.com/edwin-booth[40]

-voted-for-abraham-lincoln/[41]

"Bull Run Casualties during the Battle Of Bull Run of the American Civil War," *HistoryNet.*

http://www.historynet.com/bull-run-casualties

"Burnside's North Carolina Expedition," *Wikipedia.* https://en.wikipedia.org/wiki/Burnside%27s_North_Carolina_Expedition

Butler, Benjamin, F. *Correspondence of Gen. Benjamin F. Butler.* Vols. 1-5. Big Byte Books. 2017. Privately Issued 1917.

Butler Medal, *Wikipedia.* https://en.wikipedia.org/wiki/Butler_Medal

Calkins, Chris. "Petersburg: The Wearing Down of Lee's Army," American Battlefield Trust.

https://www.battlefields.org/learn/articles/petersburg-wearing-down-lees-army

Careless, James Maurice Stockford. "Toronto," *The Canadian Encyclopedia.* March 17, 2013.

https://www.thecanadianencyclopedia.ca/en/article/toronto

40. http://civilwarsaga.com/edwin-booth-voted-for-abraham-lincoln/
41. http://civilwarsaga.com/edwin-booth-voted-for-abraham-lincoln/

"Cassius Lee's summer home found itself at center of war," *Alexandria Times,* April 19 2012. https://www.alexandria-va.gov/uploadedFiles/historic/info/attic/2012/Attic20120419Menokin.pdf

Casstevens, Frances H. *George W. Alexander and Castle Thunder A Confederate Prison and Its Commandant.* Jefferson: MacFarland and Company, Inc. 2004.

Castle, Albert. "Samuel Ruth: Union Spy," *Civil War Times. Illustrated.* Gettysburg: Historical Times, Inc., February, 1976, Pages 36-44.

"Cavalry in the American Civil War," *Wikipedia.*

https://en.wikipedia.org/wiki/Cavalry_in_the_American_Civil_War

"Chancellorsville," *Civil War Trust.* https://www.civilwar.org/learn/civil-war/battles/chancellorsville

Charleston in the American Civil War. *Wikipedia.* https://en.wikipedia.org/wiki/[42] Charleston_in_the_American_Civil_War[43]

Charleston, Siege of (1863-1865)[44], *South Carolina Encyclopedia.* http://www.scencyclopedia.org/sce/entries/charleston-siege-of-1863-1865/

---

42. https://en.wikipedia.org/wiki/Charleston_in_the_American_Civil_War
43. https://en.wikipedia.org/wiki/Charleston_in_the_American_Civil_War
44. http://www.scencyclopedia.org/sce/entries/charleston-siege-of-1863-1865/

Charisse, Marc. "Roads North: Learn about Lee's invasion of Pa.," The Evening Sun, April 21, 2016.

https://www.eveningsun.com/story/archives/2016/04/21/roads-north-general-robert-lee-invasion-pennsylvania-battle-gettysburg/83279378/

"Chattanooga Campaign," Wikipedia.

https://en.wikipedia.org/[45]
wiki/Chattanooga_Campaign[46]

From Chicago.; "The Democratic Convention Immense Gathering Vallandigham and his Admirers Probable Character of the Platform," The New York Times, August 30, 1864, Page 1.

https://www.nytimes.com/1864/08/30/archives/from-chicago-the-democratic-convention-immense-gathering.html

"Children of Jefferson Davis," CivilWarTalk, January 25, 2011. https://civilwartalk.com/threads/children-of-jefferson-davis.21573/

"They Choose a Name for Themselves' - Surnames In Slavery and Freedom," This Cruel War, March 31, 2016.

http://www.thiscruelwar.com/they-choose-a-name-for-themselves-surnames-in-slavery-and-freedom/

"The Civil War in America April 1862–November 1862," Library of Congress.

https://www.loc.gov/exhibits/civil-war-in-america/april-1862-november-1862.html

45. https://en.wikipedia.org/wiki/Chattanooga_Campaign
46. https://en.wikipedia.org/wiki/Chattanooga_Campaign

"Civil War Causalities," *American Battlefield Trust.* https://www.battlefields.org/learn/[47] articles/civil-war-casualties[48]

"The Civil War and emancipation," *PBS.org.*

http://www.pbs.org/wgbh/aia/[49] part4/4p2967.html[50]

Civil War City Point: 1864-1865 Period of Significance Landscape Documentation, *National Park Service, U. S. Department of Interior,* July 2009.

https://www.nps.gov/parkhistory/online_books/pete/ city_point_landscape.pdf

"Civil War: The execution of a Union spy," *rvanews,* September 25, 2013. https://rvanews.com/features/[51] civil-war-execution-union-spy/102938[52]

"Civil War Timeline / Chronology," *Georgia's Blue and Gray Trail Presents American Civil War.*

http://blueandgraytrail.com/year/186312

Clancy, Paul. "Escape to Fort Monroe, beginning of slavery's end," *African American Today.*

47. https://www.battlefields.org/learn/articles/civil-war-casualties

48. https://www.battlefields.org/learn/articles/civil-war-casualties

49. http://www.pbs.org/wgbh/aia/part4/4p2967.html

50. http://www.pbs.org/wgbh/aia/part4/4p2967.html

51. https://rvanews.com/features/civil-war-execution-union-spy/102938

52. https://rvanews.com/features/civil-war-execution-union-spy/102938

STEPHEN ROMAINE

http://pilotonline.com/guides/african-american-today/escape-to-fort-monroe-beginning-of-slavery-send/article_2da62a63-b5fa-544d-b8d0-93186793071a.html

"Clement Vallandigham," *Wikipedia.*

https://en.wikipedia.org/[53]

wiki/Clement_Vallandigham[54]

Cohen, Spencer. "History of Street: Crosby Street in Soho," *Untapped Cities.*

https://untappedcities.com/2014/03/03/history-of-streets-crosby-street-in-soho/

Cole, David, Survey of the U.S. Army Uniforms, Weapons and Accoutrements," November, 2007.

https://history.army.mil/html/[55]

museums/uniforms/survey_uwa.pdf[56]

"Col. Hill's Official Report," *Richmond Daily Dispatch*, June 15, 1861. http://chroniclingamerica.loc.gov/lccn/sn84024738/

"Confederate capital of Richmond is captured," *History.com.*

https://www.history.com/this-day-in-history/confederate-capital-of-richmond-is-captured

"Confederate Draft," *Atlas Editions;*
Civil War Cards

53. https://en.wikipedia.org/wiki/Clement_Vallandigham
54. https://en.wikipedia.org/wiki/Clement_Vallandigham
55. https://history.army.mil/html/museums/uniforms/survey_uwa.pdf
56. https://history.army.mil/html/museums/uniforms/survey_uwa.pdf

http://www.wtv[57]
-zone.com/civilwar/condraft.html[58]

"Confederate Newspapers in Virginia during the Civil War," *Encyclopedia Virginia*, Virginia Foundation for the Humanities in Partnership Library of Virginia.

http://www.encyclopediavirginia.org/Newspapers_in_Virginia_During_the_Civil_War_Confederate#start_entry

"Confederate Privateer," *Wikipedia.*
https://en.wikipedia.org/wiki/Confederate_privateer

"Confederate States of America," *Wikipedia.*
https://en.wikipedia.org/wiki/Confederate_States_of_America

"Confederate White," *Wikipedia.*
https://en.wikipedia.org/wiki/White_House_of_the_Confederacy

Conradt, Stacy. "John Wilkes Booth's Three Plots Against Lincoln," *Mental Floss,*

April 14, 2017.

http://mentalfloss.com/article/62568/john-wilkes-booths-three-plots-against-lincoln

"Consul (representative)," *Wikipedia.*

https://en.wikipedia.org/wiki/Consul_(representative)

"The Convention Opening Day," *Chicago Tribune,* August 30, 1864, Page 1. https://chroniclingamerica.loc.gov

57. http://www.wtv-zone.com/civilwar/condraft.html
58. http://www.wtv-zone.com/civilwar/condraft.html

Coon, Dean. "Time Travel: Why did Sherman spare Savannah?" *Savannah Morning News,* May 23, 2014.

https://www.savannahnow.com/column-accent/2014-05-23/time-travel-why-did-sherman-spare-savannah

"Cornell Iron Works," https://glassian.org/Prism/Cornell/index.html

"The Croton Aqueduct," *New-York Historical Society.* https://www.nyhistory.org/seneca/croton.html

"Croton Aqueduct," *Wikipedia.* https://en.wikipedia.org/wiki/Croton_Aqueduct

"Culpeper, Virginia, *Wikipedia.* https://en.wikipedia.org/wiki/Culpeper,_Virginia

Cumming, Carman. Devil's Game: *The Civil War Intrigues of Charles A. Dunham.* Chicago: University of Illinois Press, 2004.

Current, Richard N. "Lincoln's Plan for Reconstruction," *American Heritage,* Volume 6, Issue 4, June 1955.

https://www.americanheritage.com/content/lincoln's-plan-re-construction[59]

"Dahlgren," *Richmond Daily Dispatch,* March 11, 1864, Page1. https://chroniclingamerica.loc.gov/lccn/sn84024738/1864-03-11/ed-1/seq-2/#[60]

"The Dahlgren Affair," *Naked History.* http://www.historynaked.com/the-dahlgren-affair/

"The Dahlgren Affair," *Wikipedia.*

59. https://www.americanheritage.com/content/lincoln's-plan-reconstruction
60. https://chroniclingamerica.loc.gov/lccn/sn84024738/1864-03-11/ed-1/seq-2/

https://en.wikipedia.org/wiki/Dahlgren_affair

Daniel, John M. *The Richmond Examiner During the War.* New York: Forgotten Books, 2012.

"Davis declares Butler a felon," *History.com.* http://www.history.com/this-day-in-history/davis-declares-butler-a-felon

Davis, Jefferson. "Jefferson Davis' Message to the Fourth Session of the First Confederate Congress," WIKISOURCE.

https://en.wikisource.org/wiki/Jefferson_Davis%27_Message_to_the_FourthSession_of_the_First_Confederate_Congress

Davis, Jefferson. Crist, Lynda Lasswell, Dix, Mary Seaton, Editors. *The Papers of Jefferson Davis. Volume 7, 1861.* Baton Rouge: Louisiana State University Press, 1992.

DeAngelis, James Alexander. "Richmond's reaction to Abraham Lincoln: from November 1860 - March 1881," *University of Richmond Scholarship Repository*, 1965.

http://scholarship.richmond.edu/cgi/viewcontent.cgi?article=1235&context=masters-theses

DeCredico, Mary. "Richmond Bread Riot," *Encyclopedia Virginia*. Virginia Foundation for the Humanities in Partnership Library of Virginia.

https://www.encyclopediavirginia.org/Bread_Riot_Richmond#start_entry

DeCredico, Mary. Martinez, Jaime Amanda. "Richmond during the Civil War," *Encyclopedia Virginia.* Virginia Foundation for the Humanities in Partnership Library of Virginia. June 12, 2009

https://www.encyclopediavirginia.org/Richmond_During_the_Civil_War#contrib

"Defending the James River in the Civil War," *Virginia Places.*
http://www.virginiaplaces.org/military/[61]
defendthejames.html[62]

"Democratic Party Platform," *Sons of the South.*

http://www.sonofthesouth.net/union-generals/mcclellan/democratic-platform-1864.htm

"Donne, George. *"Lee vs. Hooker The Utility of Intelligence in the Gettysburg Campaign,"* Gettysburg Magazine, Number 58, January, 2018.

https://muse.jhu.edu/article/682817

"Dismal Swamp Canal," *Wikipedia.*
https://en.wikipedia.org/wiki/Dismal_Swamp_Canal

"Dismal Swamp Canal The Battle of South Mills," *City of Chesapeake, Virginia.*

http://www.cityofchesapeake.net/Assets/documents/boards_commissions/historic_preservation_commission/civilwartrails/DismalSwamp.pdf

"Direct Trade with the South," *Richmond Daily Dispatch*, August 12, 1861, Page 1.

---

61. http://www.virginiaplaces.org/military/defendthejames.html

62. http://www.virginiaplaces.org/military/defendthejames.html

http://chroniclingamerica.loc.gov/lccn/sn84024738/

"1864 Democratic National Convention, *Wikipedia.*
https://en.wikipedia.org/wiki/1864_Democratic_National_Convention

"1864 October 15: Treason in Indiana—The Trial of H. H.
Dodd," The Civil war and Northwest Wisconsin, October 18,
2014

https://thecivilwarandnorthwestwisconsin.wordpress.com/
2014/10/18/1864-october-15-treason-in-indiana-the-trial-of-
h-h-dodd/

"Elizabeth Van Lew," *American Civil
War Story.*
http://www.americancivilwarstory.com/[63]
elizabeth-van-lew.html[64]

Encyclopedia Britannica. 15th ed.,
Chicago: Encyclopedia Britannica, 1974.

Encyclopedia Virginia. Virginia Foundation for the Humanities
in Partnership Library of Virginia.

http://www.encyclopediavirginia.org/[65]

Erickson, Doug. "The Persistence of the Lewis and Clark Story
in American Literature," Discovering Lewis & Clark, 1998.

http://www.lewis-clark.org/article/3028

63. http://www.americancivilwarstory.com/elizabeth-van-lew.html
64. http://www.americancivilwarstory.com/elizabeth-van-lew.html
65. http://www.encyclopediavirginia.org/Letcher_John_1813-1884#start_entry

Erickson, Mark., "Black troops from Hampton Roads among the first Union forces to occupy Richmond," *Daily Press,* April 2, 2015.

https://www.dailypress.com/features/history/dp-nws-civil-war-fall-of-richmond-20150402-story.html

"The Escape from Libby Prison," *Harpers Weekly,* March 5, 1864, Page 151. Son of the South, Lee Foundation.

http://www.sonofthesouth.net/leefoundation/civil-war/1864/march/libey-prison-escape.htm

Etcheson, Nicole, "The War Democrats' Big Night, *The New York Times,* October 18, 2012.

https://opinionator.blogs.nytimes.com/2012/10/18/the-war-democrats-big-night/

11th New York Infantry, *Wikipedia.*
https://en.wikipedia.org/wiki/[66]
11th_New_York_Infantry[67]

"Evacuation Day (New York)," *Wikipedia.*
https://en.wikipedia.org/wiki/Evacuation_Day_(New_York)
"Fall of Richmond," CIVILWARACADEMY.COM

https://www.civilwaracademy.com/[68]
fall-of-richmond[69]

"Fall of Richmond and Petersburg, Appomattox Campaign; Surrenders of Lee and Johnston; Lincoln Assassinated: April 1865," *Iron Brigadier,* March 31, 2015.

66. https://en.wikipedia.org/wiki/11th_New_York_Infantry

67. https://en.wikipedia.org/wiki/11th_New_York_Infantry

68. https://www.civilwaracademy.com/fall-of-richmond

69. https://www.civilwaracademy.com/fall-of-richmond

https://ironbrigader.com/2015/03/31/fall-richmond-peters-burg-appomattox-campaign-surrenders-lee-johnston-lincoln-assassinated-april-1865/

Fazio, John C. "Confederate Complicity in the Assassination of Abraham Lincoln. *The Cleveland Civil War Roundtable,* Part 1, 2008.

http://clevelandcivilwarroundtable.com/articles/lincoln/con-federate_complicity1.htm

"Fighting on the Border," *Crossroads of War, Maryland and the Border in the Civil War.*

http://www.crossroadsofwar.org/discover-the-story/fighting-on-the-border/fighting-on-the-border/

Fesler, Mayo. *Secret Political Societies in the North during the Civil War.* Indiana Magazine of History. Sep 1, 1918. Vol 14, Number 3.

https://scholarworks.iu.edu/journals/index.php/imh/article/view/6096

Fishel, Edwin C., "Military Intelligence 1861-63 Part II, *Central Intelligence Agency.*

https://www.cia.gov/library/center-for-the-study-of-intelligence/kent-csi/vol10no4/html/v10i4a06p_0001.htm

"Franklin Stearns," *Wikipedia.*
https://en.wikipedia.org/wiki/Franklin_Stearns

"First African Baptist Church (Richmond, VA), *Wikipedia.*

https://en.wikipedia.org/wiki/First_African_Bap-tist_Church_(Richmond,_Virginia)

"First Battle of Bull Run, *Wikipedia.* https://en.wikipedia.org/wiki/First_Battle_of_Bull_Run

Flood, Charles Bracelen, Lee The Last Years. New York: Houghton Mifflin Company, 1981.

"Fort Monroe, *Wikipedia.*
https://en.m.wikipedia.org/wiki/Fort_Monroe

"Fort Stedman," American Battlefield Trust.

https://www.battlefields.org/learn/[70]
civil-war/battles/fort-stedman[71]

"Fort Stedman," *Wikipedia.*

https://en.wikipedia.org/wiki/Battle_[72]
of_Fort_Stedman[73]

"Fort Sumter," *History.com.*
http://www.history.com/topics/american-civil-war/fort-sumter

Fortin, Jacey. "What Robert E. Lee Wrote the The Times About Slavery in 1858," *The New York Times*, April 18, 2017.

https://www.nytimes.com/2017/08/18/us/robert-e-lee-slaves.html

"Forty-rod, Blue Ruin & Oh Be Joyful: Civil War Alcohol Abuse," WAREFARE HISTORY NETWORK, October , 2018

---

70. https://www.battlefields.org/learn/civil-war/battles/fort-stedman

71. https://www.battlefields.org/learn/civil-war/battles/fort-stedman

72. https://en.wikipedia.org/wiki/Battle_of_Fort_Stedman

73. https://en.wikipedia.org/wiki/Battle_of_Fort_Stedman

https://www.encyclopediavirginia.org/Hook-er_Joseph_1814-1879#start_entry

Glatthaar, Joseph. "Army of Northern Virginia," *Encyclopedia Virginia*. Virginia Foundation for the Humanities in Partnership Library of Virginia.

https://www.encyclopediavirginia.org/Army_of_Northern_Virginia#start_entry

Glymph, Thavolia. "Noncombatant Military in the Civil War," *OAH Magazine of History*, April, 2012.

https://academic.oup.com/maghis/article-pdf/26/2/25/3212155/oas007.pdf

"Go Down Moses," *Wikipedia*.

https://en.wikipedia.org/wiki/[77]
Go_Down_Moses[78]

Golden, Alan Lawrence. "Castle under : The Confederate Provost Marshal's prison, 1862-1865," *University of Richmond UR Scholarship Repository,* September 25, 1980.

https://scholarship.richmond.edu/cgi/viewcontent.cgi?referer=https://www.google.com/&httpsredir=1&article=1444&context=masters-theses

Googheart, Adam, "The Future of 'Freedom's Fortress, Fort Monroe," *The New York Times,* August 18, 2011,

https://opinionator.blogs.nytimes.com/2011/08/18/the-future-of-freedoms-fortress/

77. https://en.wikipedia.org/wiki/Go_Down_Moses
78. https://en.wikipedia.org/wiki/Go_Down_Moses

Goodheart, Adam. 'How Slavery Really Ended in America," *The New York Times.* April 1, 2011.

http://www.nytimes.com/2011/04/03/magazine/mag-03CivilWar-t.html

Gorton, Gary. "Ante Bellum Transportation Indices," *The Warton School, University of Pennsylvania,* PA, 1989.

"Grant & Lee: Masters of War,"
The Sentinel, National Park Service.
https://www.nps.gov/frsp/learn/news/[79]
upload/Overland-Sentinel-FINAL.pdf[80]

"Great March.; Review of Gen Sherman's Georgia Campaign. *The New York Times.*

December 24, 1864, Page 3.

https://www.nytimes.com/1864/12/20/archives/the-great-march-review-of-gen-shermans-georgia-campaign-from.html

"Greek Fire," *Wikipedia.*
https://en.wikipedia.org/wiki/Greek_fire

Greene, A. Wilson. *A Campaign of Giants The Battle for Petersburg.* Chapel Hill: University of North Carolina Press, 2018.

"Grenville M. Dodge and George H. Sharpe: Grant's Intelligence Chiefs in West and East," *Signal Corps. Association (1860 to 1865).*

http://www.civilwarsignals.org/pages/[81]

79. https://www.nps.gov/frsp/learn/news/upload/Overland-Sentinel-FINAL.pdf

80. https://www.nps.gov/frsp/learn/news/upload/Overland-Sentinel-FINAL.pdf

81. http://www.civilwarsignals.org/pages/spy/pages/grantintel.html

spy/pages/grantintel.html[82]

Griffin, Martin, "How Whitman Remembered Lincoln," *The New York Times*, May 4, 2015.

https://opinionator.blogs.nytimes.com/2015/05/04/how-whitman-remembered-lincoln/

Guelzo, Allen C. "Robert E. Lee and Slavery," *Encyclopedia Virginia*. Virginia Foundation for the Humanities in Partnership Library of Virginia.

https://www.encyclopediavirginia.org/[83]

Lee_Robert_E_and_Slavery[84]

"Hampton Roads Conference," *Wikipedia*.
https://en.wikipedia.org/wiki/Hampton_Roads_Conference

Hanchett, William. *The Lincoln Murder Conspiracies*. Champaign: Illini Books, 1986.

"The Harper's Ferry Invasion as Party Capital," *Richmond Enquirer*, October 25, 1859, http://history.furman.edu/benson/docs/varejb59a25a.htm

"Harrisburg, Pennsylvania," *Wikipedia*.
https://en.wikipedia.org/wiki/Harrisburg,_Pennsylvania

Hartwig, D. Scott. "The Army of Northern Virginia and the Gettysburg Campaign," *2010 Gettysburg Seminar*.

http://npshistory.com/series/symposia/gettysburg_seminars/13/essay3.pdf

82. http://www.civilwarsignals.org/pages/spy/pages/grantintel.html

83. https://www.encyclopediavirginia.org/Lee_Robert_E_and_Slavery

84. https://www.encyclopediavirginia.org/Lee_Robert_E_and_Slavery

Hartwig, D. Scott. "Gettysburg Campaign," *Encyclopedia Virginia*.
https://www.encyclopediavirginia.org/Gettysburg_Campaign

Hasegawa, Guy. R. *Villainous Compounds Chemical Weapons & The American Civil War.* Carbondale: Southern Illinois University Press, 2015

Hays, J.E.S., Ed. "Back In My Time: A Writer's Guide to the 19th Century," August 5, 2012. Previously published: Weekly Wisconsin Patriot, February 9, 1861.

http://backinmytime.blogspot.com/[85]

2012/08/the-general-store.html[86]

Headley, John W. *Confederate Operations in Canada and New York.* New York: The Neal Publishing Company, 1906. Kindle Digitized Version.

Headley, John W. "The Secret Service of the Confederacy," *Signal Corps. Association (1860 to 1865).*

http://www.civilwarsignals.org/[87]

pages/spy/confedsecret/confedsecret.html[88]

Helin, Don. "'Capture It': Tour Some of the Lesser Known Sites along the Gettysburg/Harrisburg Campaign, Burg News, May 24, 2013

https://theburgnews.com/sports-health/614
"Henry Halleck," *Wikipedia*.

85. http://backinmytime.blogspot.com/2012/08/the-general-store.html
86. http://backinmytime.blogspot.com/2012/08/the-general-store.html
87. http://www.civilwarsignals.org/pages/spy/confedsecret/confedsecret.html
88. http://www.civilwarsignals.org/pages/spy/confedsecret/confedsecret.html

https://en.wikipedia.org/wiki/Henry_Halleck

"Henry A. Wise (1806-1876), John Brown's Holy War," *PBS American Experience.*

http://www.pbs.org/wgbh/amex/brown/peopleevents/pande05.html

"Henry Heth," *Wikipedia.*
https://en.wikipedia.org/wiki/Henry_Heth

"How Bee and Bartow Died," *Richmond Enquirer*, August 9, 1861, Page 2.
http://chroniclingamerica.loc.gov/

"Henry S. Foote," *Wikipedia.*
https://en.wikipedia.org/wiki/Henry_S._Foote

"History of Policing in the City of New York,"

WordPress.

http://nypdhistory.com/whats-the-deal-with-the-rich-history-of-the-nypds-lost-13th-precinct-station-houses-in-todays-nypd-7th-precinct/

Hood, John Bell, *Wikipedia.*

https://en.wikipedia.org/wiki/[89]
John_Bell_Hood[90]

"How Did Slaves Support the Confederacy?," *Virginia Museum of History & Culture.*

---

89. https://en.wikipedia.org/wiki/John_Bell_Hood

90. https://en.wikipedia.org/wiki/John_Bell_Hood

https://www.virginiahistory.org/collections-and-resources/virginia-history-explorer/american-turning-point-civil-war-virginia-1/how

Fane, Alec. "How do I open a wax seal letter?" *Quora,* July 8, 2016. https://www.quora.com/[91] How-do-I-open-a-wax-seal-letter[92]

Hubbard, Charles M., Editor. *Lincoln, the Law, and Presidential Leadership.* Carbondale: Southern Illinois University Press, 2015.

Huhn, Wilson, "Jefferson Davis' Speech of September 23, 1864 at Macon, Georgia: Worst Speech Ever?" *Akron Beacon Journal,* April 18, 2012.

https://www.ohio.com/akron/pages/jefferson-davis-speech-of-september-23-1864-at-macon-georgia-worst-speech-ever

"I Will Send a Barrel of This Wonderful Whiskey to Every General in the Army," *WordPress*

https://quoteinvestigator.com/2013/02/18/[93]

barrel-of-whiskey/[94]

"Immigrants Rush To Join the Union Army—Why?," *CivilWarTalk.*

https://civilwartalk.com/threads/immigrants-rush-to-join-the-union-army—why.24607/[95]

91. https://www.quora.com/How-do-I-open-a-wax-seal-letter
92. https://www.quora.com/How-do-I-open-a-wax-seal-letter
93. https://quoteinvestigator.com/2013/02/18/barrel-of-whiskey/
94. https://quoteinvestigator.com/2013/02/18/barrel-of-whiskey/
95. https://civilwartalk.com/threads/immigrants-rush-to-join-the-union-army_*why.24607/

"In the Richmond Slave Market," *History Matters.*
http://historymatters.gmu.edu/d/6762/

"Industry and Economy during the Civil War," *National Park Service.*
https://www.nps.gov/resources/story.htm%3Fid%3D251

"Intelligence in the Civil War," *Central Intelligence Agency Library*, August 23, 2016.

https://www.cia.gov/library/publications/intelligence-history/civil-war/Intel_in_the_CW1.pdf

"Iron-clad Ships," *Richmond Enquirer,* March 25, 1862, Page 4.
http://chroniclingamerica.loc.gov/

"Ironclad Warship, *Wikipedia.*
https://en.wikipedia.org/wiki/Ironclad_warship

Ives, Sarah, "Did Quilts Hold Codes to the Underground Railroad?" *National Geographic News,* February 5, 2004, http://news.nationalgeographic.com/news/2004/02/0205_040205_slavequilts.html

Jameson, Heath B., "A Critical Analysis of Robert E. Lee's Campaign Plan for a Second Northern Invasion," Marine Corps University, April 2010.

www.dtic.mil/get-tr-doc/pdf?AD=ADA603264[96]

Janney, Caroline E. "The Lost Cause," *Encyclopedia Virginia.* Virginia Foundation for the Humanities in Partnership Library of Virginia.

https://www.encyclopediavirginia.org/[97]

96. http://www.dtic.mil/get-tr-doc/pdf?AD=ADA603264
97. https://www.encyclopediavirginia.org/lost_cause_the#start_entry

lost_cause_the#start_entry[98]

"J. E. B. Stuart," *Wikipedia.*
https://en.wikipedia.org/wiki/J._E._B._Stuart

"Jefferson Davis Captured," *History.com*

https://www.history.com/[99]
this-day-in-history/jefferson-davis-captured[100]

"Jefferson Davis' Infamous Proclamation," *Civil War Emancipation*, December 26, 2012. https://cwemancipation.wordpress.com/2012/12/26/jefferson-davis-infamous-proclamation/

"Jefferson Davis to John Forsyth," *Rice University: The Papers of Jefferson Davis*, February 21, 1865.

https://jeffersondavis.rice.edu/archives/documents/jefferson-davis-john-forsyth

"Jefferson Davis on Nullification Opposition, in his own words," *Tenth Amendment Center.*

http://tenthamendmentcenter.com/2014/03/18/jefferson-davis-confederate-president-vs-nullification/

"Jefferson Davis' Second Inaugural Address," Rice University: The Papers of Jefferson Davis

https://jeffersondavis.rice.edu/archives/documents/jefferson-davis-second-inaugural-address

98. https://www.encyclopediavirginia.org/lost_cause_the#start_entry
99. https://www.history.com/this-day-in-history/jefferson-davis-captured
100. https://www.history.com/this-day-in-history/jefferson-davis-captured

"Jefferson Davis's Wife and Children Flee Richmond," *Vermont Humanities Civil War Book of Days,* March 27, 2015.

https://civilwarbookofdays.org/2015/03/27/jefferson-daviss-wife-and-children-flee-richmond/

"John A. Dahlgren," *Wikipedia.*

https://en.wikipedia.org/wiki/[101] John_A._Dahlgren[102]

"John Buford," *Wikipedia.*
https://en.wikipedia.org/wiki/John_Buford

"John B. Magruder," *Wikipedia.*
https://en.wikipedia.org/wiki/John_B._Magruder

"John Brown's Soul," *National Parks Conservation Association,* 2005. https://www.npca.org/articles/925-john-brown-s-soul

"John Ellis Wool," *Wikipedia.*
https://en.wikipedia.org/wiki/John_E._Wool

John F. Potter, *Wikipedia.*
https://en.wikipedia.org/wiki/John_F._Potter

John H. Winder, *Encyclopedia Virginia.* Virginia Foundation for the Humanities in Partnership Library of Virginia.

https://www.encyclopediavirginia.org/ Winder_John_H_1800-1865

"John Minor Botts," *Education @ Library*

of Virginia.

101. https://en.wikipedia.org/wiki/John_A._Dahlgren

102. https://en.wikipedia.org/wiki/John_A._Dahlgren

http://edu.lva.virginia.gov/online_classroom/union_or_seces-sion/people/john_botts

"John Minor Botts Civil War Peace Offers," *Teachinghisotry.org.*

http://teachinghistory.org/category/keywords/john-minor-botts

"John Minor Botts in the Field – He Denounces the Disunionists," *Richmond Enquirer,* October 5, 1860

http://chroniclingamerica.loc.gov/

Jones, Francis I.W., "This Fraudulent Trade: Confederate Blockade-Running from Halifax During the American Civil War," *The Northern Mariner.*

https://www.cnrs-scrn.org/northern_mariner/vol09/nm_9_4_35-46.pdf

Jones, Howard, *Union in Peril. Crisis Over British Intervention in the Civil War.* Lincoln: University of Nebraska Press, 1992.

Jones, J. William. "The Kilpatrick-Dahlgren Raid Against Richmond." *Southern Historical Society Papers*, Vol. 13, 1889.

Jones, William, J. *The Davis memorial volume.* Richmond: Published by Authority of Mrs. Davis, B.F. Johnson & Co., 1890. (Digitized by Googlebooks)

"Joseph Hooker," *History.com.* https://www.history.com/topics/american-civil-war/joseph-hooker

"Joseph Hooker," *Wikipedia.* https://en.wikipedia.org/wiki/Joseph_Hooker

"Joseph E. Johnston," *Wikipedia.*

https://en.wikipedia.org/wiki/[103]
Joseph_E._Johnston[104]

"Kane, T, Harnett, "Elizabeth 'Crazy Bet' Van Lew, *Spies For The Blue And Gray.* New York: Doubleday, 1954.

http://www.civilwarhome.com/crazybet.html

Keegan, John. *The American Civil War.*
New York: Alfred A. Knopf, 2009.

"Kentucky in the American Civil War," *Wikipedia.*
https://en.wikipedia.org/wiki/Kentucky_in_the_American_Civil_War

Khederian, Robert "How Christmas decorations evolved through the 1800s," *Curbed,* December 9, 2016

http://www.curbed.com/2016/12/9/13898774/christmas-decorations-history-holiday

"Kilpatrick-Dahlgren raid begins," *This Day in History, February 28, 1864, History.com.*

https://www.history.com/this-day-in-history/[105]

kilpatrick-dahlgren-raid-begins[106]

Kingseed, Wyatt. "The Fire in the Rear: Clement Vallandigham and the Copperheads," *HistoryNet,* April 11, 2016.

---

103. https://en.wikipedia.org/wiki/Joseph_E._Johnston

104. https://en.wikipedia.org/wiki/Joseph_E._Johnston

105. https://www.history.com/this-day-in-history/kilpatrick-dahlgren-raid-begins

106. https://www.history.com/this-day-in-history/kilpatrick-dahlgren-raid-begins

http://www.historynet.com/the-fire-in-the-rear-clement-val-landigham-and-the-copperheads.htm

Klein, Christopher. "7 Ways the Battle of Antietam Changed America," *History.com,*

August 31, 2018.

https://www.history.com/news/7-ways-the-battle-of-antietam-changed-america

Klein, Gil, "Slavery, Freedom, and Fort Monroe," *Advisory Council on Historic Preservation*[107].

http://www.achp.gov/fort_monroe_final_story.pdf

Koenig, Louis, W. "The Most Unpopular Man in the North," *American Heritage,* February 1964.

https://www.americanheritage.com/content/most-unpopular-man-north"

Kotar, S.L. & Gessler, J.E. *Ballooning A History 1782-1900.* Jefferson: McFarland & Company, Inc., 2001.

Kwok, Gordon, "Revere Brothers," *Olde Colony Civil War Round Table.* https://sites.google.com/site/oldecolonycwrt/Home/revere-brothers

Lane, Helena. "History of St. John's Church Richmond, Virginia," *Henrico County, Virginia Genealogy and History.*

---

107. http://www.google.com/url?sa=t&rct=j&q=&esrc=s&source=web&cd=1&cad=rja&uact=8&ved=0ahUKEwio4Pu71LnX-AhVG_4MKHUpMB5wQFggmMAA&url=http%3A%2F%2Fwww.achp.gov%2F&usg=AOvVaw1XIc88qXRJTwkGs7OFEztK

http://genealogytrails.com/vir/henrico/st_johns_church_history.html

Lankford, Nelson D. "Virginia Convention of 1861," *Encyclopedia Virginia,* Virginia Foundation for the Humanities in Partnership Library of Virginia, June 20, 2014.

http://www.encyclopediavirginia.org/Virginia_Constitutional_Convention_of_1861#start_entry

"The Last Terrible Agonies," *Richmond Daily Dispatch,* March 10, 1862, Page 2.

http://chroniclingamerica.loc.gov/

"Latest Manifesto of Governor Wise, The Virginia State Convention," *New York Herald*, March 12, 1861.

http://chroniclingamerica.loc.gov/

"The legendary police headquarters at 300 Mulberry Street, Bowery Boys New York City History

http://www.boweryboyshistory.com/2011/07/legendary-police-headquarters-at-300.html

Leigh, Phil, "Who Burned Atlanta?" *The New York Times,* November 13, 2014.
https://opinionator.blogs.nytimes.com/2014/11/13/who-burned-atlanta/

"Lee Resigns from U.S. Army," *This Day in History,* April 20, 1861, History.com.

http://www.history.com/this-day-in-history/lee-resigns-from-u-s-army

Lee, Robert E. "Letter to His Wife on Slavery, Selections, December 27, 1856," *Fair Use Repository.*

http://fair-use.org/robert-e-lee/letter-to-his-wife-on-slavery

Lee, Robert E. "Robert E. Lee to James B. Seddon, 1864 October 4," *Lee Family Digital Archive.*

https://leefamilyarchive.org/family-papers/letters/letters-1864/9-family-papers/1758-robert-e-lee-to-james-b-seddon-1864-october-4

Lee, Susanna Michele. "Free Blacks during the Civil War," *Encyclopedia Virginia*, Virginia Foundation for the Humanities in Partnership Library of Virginia, 2009. http://www.encyclopediavirginia.org/Free_Blacks_During_the_Civil_War

"Lee's 1863 Gettysburg Campaign,"
Shenandoah at War, June 11, 2015.
http://www.shenandoahatwar.org/[108]
lees-1863-gettysburg-campaign/[109]

"Letter to General Grant, April 30, 1864," *Lincoln as the Great Communicator.*

https://lincolnasgreatcommunicator.wordpress.com/public-letters/letter-to-general-grant-april-30-1864/

"A Letter for the Submissionists," *Richmond Enquirer*, December 14, 1860.
http://chroniclingamerica.loc.gov/

Leveen, Lois. "Mary Richards Bowser," *Encyclopedia Virginia*, Virginia Foundation for the Humanities in Partnership Library of Virginia, 2009.

108. http://www.shenandoahatwar.org/lees-1863-gettysburg-campaign/

109. http://www.shenandoahatwar.org/lees-1863-gettysburg-campaign/

https://www.encyclopediavirginia.org/

Leveen, Lois. *The Secrets of Mary Bowser.* New York: William Morrow, 2012.

"Lewis and Clark Quotes," *Lewis-and-Clark-Expedition.org.* http://www.lewis-and-clark-expedition.org/lewis-clark-quotes.htm

"Libby Prison," *Encyclopedia Virginia*, Virginia Foundation for the Humanities in Partnership Library of Virginia.

https://www.encyclopediavirginia.org/Libby_Prison

"Libby Prison Escape," *Big Family Tree.*

https://bigfamilytree.weebly.com/[110] libby-prison-escape.html#escapees[111]

"Libby Prison of War Camp." The American Civil War. https://www.mycivilwar.com/pow/va-libby.html

"Lincoln Arrives in Washington," *This Day in History,* February 23, 1861, History.com.

http://www.history.com/this-day-in-history/lincoln-arrives-in-washington

"Lincoln's Inaugural," *Western Sentinel*, March 15, 1861, Page 2. http://chroniclingamerica.loc.gov/

"Lincoln issues Proclamation of Amnesty and Reconstruction," *HISTORY.com.*

---

110. https://bigfamilytree.weebly.com/libby-prison-escape.html#escapees
111. https://bigfamilytree.weebly.com/libby-prison-escape.html#escapees

https://www.history.com/this-day-in-history/lincoln-issues-proclamation-of-amnesty-and-reconstruction

"Lincoln Reelected," *HISTORY.com.*

https://www.history.com/[112]
this-day-in-history/lincoln-reelected[113]

"Lincoln's Nomination of Grant," *National Archives.*
https://www.archives.gov/legislative/features/grant

"Lincoln's Visit to Richmond,"
National Park Service.
https://www.nps.gov/rich/learn/[114]
historyculture/lincvisit.htm[115]

Linder, Douglas O. "John Wilkes Booth,"
Famous Trials.

http://famous-trials.com/lincoln/2146-booth

Lineberry, Cate. "Elizabeth Van Lew: An Unlikely Union Spy,"
Smithsonian.com, 2011.

http://www.smithsonianmag.com/history/elizabeth-van-lew-an-unlikely-union-spy-158755584/?no-ist

Link, William A. *Roots of Secession: Slavery and Politics in Antebellum Virginia.* Chapel Hill: The University of North Carolina Press, 2003.

112. https://www.history.com/this-day-in-history/lincoln-reelected

113. https://www.history.com/this-day-in-history/lincoln-reelected

114. https://www.nps.gov/rich/learn/historyculture/lincvisit.htm

115. https://www.nps.gov/rich/learn/historyculture/lincvisit.htm

Lipman, Don. "April 1861: The War Between the States begins— what was the weather like?" *The Washington Post,* April 11, 2011.

https://www.washingtonpost.com/blogs/capital-weather-gang/post/april-1861-the-war-between-the-states-begins-what-was-the-weather-like/2011/04/11/ AFU3DxKD_blog.html?utm_term=.6c64effe87ed

"Lipsky, Seth. *The Citizen's Constitution An Annotated Guide.* New York: Basic Books, 2011.

"List of Revolvers," *Wikipedia.*

https://en.wikipedia.org/[116] wiki/List_of_revolvers[117]

Lively, Mathew. W. "Yellow Fever Plot of 1864 Targeted Lincoln, U.S. cities. Civil War Profiles.

http://www.civilwarprofiles.com/yellow-fever-plot-of-1864-targeted-lincoln-u-s-cities/

Longfellow, Henry Wadsworth. "Paul Revere's Ride," *The Atlantic Online,* January, 1861.

https://www.theatlantic.com/magazine/archive/1861/01/ paul-revere-s-ride/308349/

"Louisiana Purchase," *HISTORY.com.*

http://www.history.com/[118] topics/louisiana-purchase[119]

116. https://en.wikipedia.org/wiki/List_of_revolvers

117. https://en.wikipedia.org/wiki/List_of_revolvers

118. http://www.history.com/topics/louisiana-purchase

119. http://www.history.com/topics/louisiana-purchase

Luebke, Peter, C. "Army of the James," *Encyclopedia Virginia.* Virginia Foundation for the Humanities in Partnership Library of Virginia.

https://www.encyclopediavirginia.org/[120]

Army_of_the_James#start_entry[121]

Luebke, Peter, C. "Battle of Seven Pines–Fair Oaks," *Encyclopedia Virginia.* Virginia Foundation for the Humanities in Partnership Library of Virginia.

https://www.encyclopediavirginia.org/Seven_Pines_Battle_of#start_entry

Luebke, Peter, C. "Kilpatrick-Dahlgren Raid," *Encyclopedia Virginia.* Virginia Foundation for the Humanities in Partnership Library of Virginia.

https://www.encyclopediavirginia.org/Kilpatrick-Dahlgren_Raid

"Luke P. Blackburn," *Wikipedia.*

https://en.wikipedia.org/[122]
wiki/Luke_P._Blackburn[123]

Lynching in the United States, *Wikipedia.*
https://en.wikipedia.org/wiki/Lynching_in_the_United_States

Maass, John, "Battle of Chickamauga September 19-20, 1863," *U.S. Army Center of Military History,* September 2015.

120. https://www.encyclopediavirginia.org/Army_of_the_James#start_entry

121. https://www.encyclopediavirginia.org/Army_of_the_James#start_entry

122. https://en.wikipedia.org/wiki/Luke_P._Blackburn

123. https://en.wikipedia.org/wiki/Luke_P._Blackburn

https://history.army.mil/news/[124]

2015/150900a_chickamauga.html[125]

MacLean, Maggie. "The First Lady of the Confederate States of America," *Civil War Women*. June 26, 2010.

https://www.civilwarwomenblog.com/varina-davis/

MacLean, Maggie. "Wife of Union Spy Timothy Webster," *Civil War Women*. January 1, 2016.

https://www.civilwarwomenblog.com/charlotte-sprowles-webster/

MacLean, Maggie. "Women and Girls in the Browns Island Explosion," *Civil War Women*. January 4, 2008.

https://www.civilwarwomenblog.com/women-and-girls-in-the-browns-island-explosion/

"Mail Service and the Civil War," *about.usps.com, Library of Congress.*

https://about.usps.com/news/national-releases/2012/pr12_civil-war-mail-history.pdf

"Major-General Halleck, Commander-in-Chief," *Harpers Weekly,* August 9, 1862.

http://www.sonofthesouth.net/leefoundation/civil-war/1862/august/general-halleck.htm

---

124. https://history.army.mil/news/2015/150900a_chickamauga.html
125. https://history.army.mil/news/2015/150900a_chickamauga.html

"Manassas Gap Railroad during the Civil War," *Encyclopedia Virginia*. Virginia Foundation for the Humanities in Partnership Library of Virginia.

https://www.encyclopediavirginia.org

Markle, Donald E. *Spies & Spymasters of the Civil War.* New York: Hippocrene Books, 2004.

"Martial Law in Richmond," *Richmond Enquirer.* March 4, 1862, Page 4.
http://chroniclingamerica.loc.gov/

Marvel, William, "Battle of Balls Bluff, *HistoryNet,* August, 2011.
http://www.historynet.com/battle-of-balls-bluff-2.htm

Mayers, Adams. "Confederacy's Canadian Mission: Spies Across the Border,"

HistoryNet, June 12, 2006. Reprinted from *Civil War Times Magazine,* June 2001. http://www.historynet.com/confederacys-canadian-mission-spies-across-the-border.htm

Midtown campus. *Wikipedia.*
http://www.wikicu.com/Midtown_campus

McPherson, James M. "A Brief Overview of the American Civil War," American Battlefield Trust.

https://www.battlefields.org/learn/articles/brief-overview-american-civil-war

McPherson, James M. *Embattled Rebel Jefferson Davis and The Confederate Civil War.* New York: Penguin Books, 2015.

McPherson, James M. *Tried by War Abraham Lincoln as Commander and Chief.* New York: Penguin Books, 2008.

"McRae, Jr., Bernie. "Lest We Forget," The Black Confederate Brigade in the Civil War.

http://lestweforget.hamptonu.edu/page.cfm?uuid=9FEC2DC4-9AC2-AAF9-E9F170DF7240A9CD

"Miracle on 21st Street Transformation Revalidates Shockoe Bottom," *Style Weekly,* August 24, 2011.

http://www.styleweekly.com/richmond/miracle-on-21st-street/Content?oid=1602954

Monroe Work Today Dataset Compilation, Tuskegee University Archives Repository http://192.203.127.197/archive/handle/123456789/984

Moore, Glenn. "A Civil War Feud: Jefferson Davis vs. Joseph E. Johnston," Auburn University, 1993.

https://archives.columbusstate.edu/[126]

gah/1993/72-81.pdf[127]

"My Days Have Been So Wonderous Free," *Song Of America.* https://songofamerica.net/song/my-days-have-been-so-wondrous-free/

Nash, Jay Robert. *Spies: A Narrative Encyclopedia of Dirty Tricks and Double Dealing from Biblical Times to Today.* New York: M. Evans and Company, Inc. 1997.

---

126. https://archives.columbusstate.edu/gah/1993/72-81.pdf
127. https://archives.columbusstate.edu/gah/1993/72-81.pdf

"National Troubles," *The New York Times,* January 30, 1891, Page 2.

http://www.nytimes.com/1861/01/30/news/national-troubles-important-washington-more-troops-wanted-protect-capital.html?pagewanted=2

"National Register of Historic Places," *U.S. Department of the Interior.*

http://www.dhr.virginia.gov/registers/Cities/Richmond/127-0057_Executive_Mansion_1988_Final_Nomination.pdf

Nevins, Allan. *The War for the Nation.*
New York: Scribner, 1959.
"News of the Day," *Alexandria Gazette,* August 10, 1860,
http://chroniclingamerica.loc.gov/lccn/sn84024728/

Newsome, Hampton, *Richmond Must Fall.* Kent: Kent State University, 2013.

"New York City in the American Civil War," *Wikipedia.*

https://en.wikipedia.org/wiki/[128]
New_York_City_in_the_American_Civil_War[129]

O'Connell, Daniel F., "Bermuda Hundred Campaign," *Essential Civil War Curriculum*

http://essentialcivilwarcurriculum.com/[130]

the-bermuda-hundred-campaign.html[131]

---

128. https://en.wikipedia.org/wiki/New_York_City_in_the_American_Civil_War
129. https://en.wikipedia.org/wiki/New_York_City_in_the_American_Civil_War
130. http://essentialcivilwarcurriculum.com/the-bermuda-hundred-campaign.html
131. http://essentialcivilwarcurriculum.com/the-bermuda-hundred-campaign.html

"Old City Hall (Richmond, Virginia),"
Wikipedia.
https://en.wikipedia.org/wiki/[132]
Old_City_Hall_(Richmond,_Virginia)[133]

O'Reilly, Bill, & Dugard, Martin. *Killing Lincoln.* New York: Henry Holt & Company, LLC., 2011.

"150 Years Later Tensions Echo Between Va. And U.S.," *Richmond Daily Dispatch.* April 17, 2011.

http://www.richmond.com/news/years-later-tensions-echo-be-tween-va-and-u-s/article_385d11f7-e373-583f-a6c8-064ea16ae2e1.html

"150 years ago: Jefferson Davis visits Charleston," *Wordpress.com*

https://markerhunter.wordpress.com/2013/11/02/davis-visits-charleston/

Osterman, Cody. The Day New York Forgot: The Legacy of Trauma in Collective Memory Through a Study of Evacuation Day," Bowling Green: Bowling Green State University, December, 2016.

https://etd.ohiolink.edu/!etd.send_file?accession=bg-su1471431771&disposition=inline

Onion, Rebecca. "Lincoln's Promise: We'll Take an Eye for an Eye to Protect Our Black Troops," *Slate.com*

http://www.slate.com/blogs/the_vault/2013/08/06/abra-ham_lincoln_the_president_s_general_order_to_pro-tect_black_pows_from.html

---

132. https://en.wikipedia.org/wiki/Old_City_Hall_(Richmond,_Virginia)

133. https://en.wikipedia.org/wiki/Old_City_Hall_(Richmond,_Virginia)

"Opequon or Third Winchester (19 September 1864)," *National Park Service.*
https://www.nps.gov/abpp/[134]
shenandoah/svs3-12.html[135]

Owens, Mackubin T., "Lee's Invasion of Pennsylvania," July, 2007. Ashbrook Ashland University.

http://ashbrook.org/publications/oped-owens-07-gettysburg/

"Pacha's Rams," *Richmond Enquirer.*
October 28, 1863. Page 1.

https://chroniclingamerica.loc.gov/

"Paris Declaration Respecting Maritime Law," *Wikipedia.*
https://en.wikipedia.org/wiki/Paris_Declaration_Respecting_Maritime_Law

"Pathways to Freedom: Maryland & the Underground Railroad," *Maryland Public Television,* 2018.

http://pathways.thinkport.org/[136]

secrets/music2.cfm[137]

"Patrick Cleburne," *Wikipedia.*

https://en.wikipedia.org/[138]
wiki/Patrick_Cleburne[139]

---

134. https://www.nps.gov/abpp/shenandoah/svs3-12.html

135. https://www.nps.gov/abpp/shenandoah/svs3-12.html

136. http://pathways.thinkport.org/secrets/music2.cfm

137. http://pathways.thinkport.org/secrets/music2.cfm

138. https://en.wikipedia.org/wiki/Patrick_Cleburne

139. https://en.wikipedia.org/wiki/Patrick_Cleburne

"Pauline Cushman," *Biography*, A&E Television Networks, April 20, 2016. https://www.biography.com/people/pauline-cushman

Peace Prospects South, The New York Times, August 16, 1864. https://www.nytimes.com/1864/08/18/archives/peace-prospects-south-interesting-narrative-of-the-mission-of.html

"Peach Conference of 1861," *Wikipedia*, March 8, 2017, https://en.wikipedia.org/wiki/Peace_Conference_of_1861

"The Peninsula Campaign From Hampton Roads to Seven Pines," *Civil War Trust*. https://www.civilwar.org/learn/articles/peninsula-campaign-0

Pearlman, Michael D. The Union at Risk: How Lincoln and Grant Nearly Lost the War in 1864," *HistoryNet*.

http://www.historynet.com/the-union-at-risk-how-lincoln-and-grant-nearly-lost-the-war-in-1864.htm

"To the People of the Confederate States of America," *Rice University: The Papers of Jefferson Davis*, April 4, 1865.

https://jeffersondavis.rice.edu/archives/documents/people-confederate-states-america

"Philadelphia Female Anti-Slavery Society Historical Marker." *ExplorePAhistory.com*,

http://explorepahistory.com/hmarker.php?markerId=1-A-105

"Philip Sheridan," *Wikipedia*.

https://en.wikipedia.org/[140]

140. https://en.wikipedia.org/wiki/Philip_Sheridan

wiki/Philip_Sheridan[141]

"The Pinkertons," Today in History - August 25, *Library of Congress, Digital Collection,*

https://www.loc.gov/item/today-in-history/august-25

"The Plot," *The New York Times,*

November 27, 1864, Page 1.

https://timesmachine.nytimes.com/timesmachine/1864/11/27/78734827.html?pageNumber=1

Poore, Devin, "Ironclad Fever," The New York Times, January 20, 2013.
https://opinionator.blogs.nytimes.com/2013/01/20/ironclad-fever/

Pogue, Dennis J. & Sanford, Douglas. "Slave Housing in Virginia," *Encyclopedia Virginia.* Virginia Foundation for the Humanities in Partnership Library of Virginia.

https://www.encyclopediavirginia.org/Slave_Housing_in_Virginia#start_entry

"Preliminary Emancipation Proclamation, 1862," *American Originals*, National Archives & Records Administration. https://www.archives.gov/exhibits/american_originals_iv/sections/preliminary_emancipation_proclamation.html

"Private Conant and the First Bull Run Prisoners," *The New York Times.* July 22, 2011, https://opinionator.blogs.nytimes.com/2011/07/22/private-conant-and-the-first-bull-run-prisoners/

141. https://en.wikipedia.org/wiki/Philip_Sheridan

"The Proclamation of Amnesty and Reconstruction," *Freedom & Southern Society Project.*

http://www.freedmen.umd.edu/procamn.htm

"Proclamation by the Confederate President," *Freedmen & Southern Society Project.*

http://www.freedmen.umd.edu/[142]

pow.htm[143]

"The Prospect Before Us," *Richmond Enquirer,* May 22, 1860, Page 1.
http://chroniclingamerica.loc.gov/

Quarters 1 (Fort Monroe), *Wikipedia.*

https://en.wikipedia.org/[144]
wiki/Quarters_1_(Fort_Monroe)[145]

Quatman, G. William, "The Engineer Who Captured Richmond,"

https://samenews.org/the-engineer-who-captured-richmond/

"Question of Privateering," *The New York Times,* May 22, 1861.

http://www.nytimes.com/1861/05/22/news/the-question-of-privateering.html?pagewanted=all&mcubz=1

"Rapped over Knucks," *Richmond Daily Dispatch,* July 31, 1861, Page 2.

142. http://www.freedmen.umd.edu/pow.htm

143. http://www.freedmen.umd.edu/pow.htm

144. https://en.wikipedia.org/wiki/Quarters_1_(Fort_Monroe)

145. https://en.wikipedia.org/wiki/Quarters_1_(Fort_Monroe)

http://chroniclingamerica.loc.gov/lccn/sn84024738/

Rachleff, Peter, J., *Black Labor in Richmond*. Champaign: University of Illinois Press, 1989.

"Reconstruction," *History.net.*

https://www.history.com/topics/[146]
american-civil-war/reconstruction[147]

"Reaction to the Fall of Richmond," *American Battlefield Trust*

https://www.battlefields.org/[148]
learn/articles/reaction-fall-richmond[149]

"Rebel with a Union Cause,"
Washington Times, November 9, 2002.
https://www.washingtontimes.com/[150]
news/2002/nov/9/20021109-100425-7355r/[151]

Recko, Corey. *A Spy for the Union The Life and Execution of Timothy Webster.* Jefferson: McFarland & Company, Inc., 2013.

"Recruiting African American soldiers for the Union Army," *Frederick Douglass Heritage.*

http://www.frederick-douglass-[152]

heritage.org/african-american-civil-war/[153]

---

146. https://www.history.com/topics/american-civil-war/reconstruction

147. https://www.history.com/topics/american-civil-war/reconstruction

148. https://www.battlefields.org/learn/articles/reaction-fall-richmond

149. https://www.battlefields.org/learn/articles/reaction-fall-richmond

150. https://www.washingtontimes.com/news/2002/nov/9/20021109-100425-7355r/

151. https://www.washingtontimes.com/news/2002/nov/9/20021109-100425-7355r/

152. http://www.frederick-douglass-heritage.org/african-american-civil-war/

153. http://www.frederick-douglass-heritage.org/african-american-civil-war/

Reiner, Karl. *Remembering Fairfax County, Virginia.* Charleston: The History Press, 2006.

"Report of the Senate Committee on President Davis's Late Message," *Richmond Daily Dispatch*, March 20, 1865, Page 1.

https://chroniclingamerica.loc.gov

"Retaliation in Treatment of Prisoners," *The New York Times*, November 19, 1861

http://www.nytimes.com/1861/11/19/news/retaliation-in-treatment-of-prisoners.html

"Revolution in the North," Evansville Daily Journal, August 24, 1864, Page 2.

https://chroniclingamerica.loc.gov

Reynolds, Donald E., *Editors Make War.* Carbondale: Southern Illinois University Press, 2006.

Richmond Daily Dispatch, 1850-1884. *Library of Congress.* http://chroniclingamerica.loc.gov/lccn/sn84024738/ 1856-08-16/ed-1/

"Richard Sears McCulloh," *Wikipedia.*

https://en.wikipedia.org/[154] wiki/Richard_Sears_McCulloh[155]

"Richard S. Ewell," *Wikipedia.*

https://en.wikipedia.org/[156]

---

154. https://en.wikipedia.org/wiki/Richard_Sears_McCulloh

155. https://en.wikipedia.org/wiki/Richard_Sears_McCulloh

156. https://en.wikipedia.org/wiki/Richard_S._Ewell

wiki/Richard_S._Ewell[157]

Ringelsletter, Matt. "Walt Whitman And President Lincoln," *President Lincoln's Cottage,* September 28, 2007.

https://www.lincolncottage.org/walt-whitman-and-president-lincoln/

"Robert E. Lee," *Wikipedia.* https://en.wikipedia.org/wiki/Robert_E._Lee

Robertson, James. *After the Civil War.* Washington, D.C. National Geographic Society, 2015.

Robertson, William Glenn. *The First Battle for Petersburg.* El Dorado Hills: Savas Beatie LLC, 2015.

Robertson, William Glenn. The First Battle for Petersburg: The Attack and Defense of the Cockade City, June 9, 1864 (Kindle Location 8). Savas Beatie. Kindle Edition.

Roth, Jeffrey B. "Dead Cattle and Greek Fire," *The New York Times,* March 25, 2014

https://opinionator.blogs.nytimes.com/2014/03/25/dead-cattle-and-greek-fire/

Roueche, Michael. "Castle Thunder: Visiting the Southern Bastille," http://www.michaeljroueche.com/2013/10/castle-thunder-the-southern-bastille/

Ruane, Michael E. "War's End, While Union forces corner Robert E. Lee, the Confederacy's capital goes up in flames, *The Washington Post,* March 27, 2015.

157. https://en.wikipedia.org/wiki/Richard_S._Ewell

https://www.washingtonpost.com/sf/style/2015/03/27/wars-end/?utm_term=.3e31d4160c8f

Ruckman, Jr., P.S. and Kincaid, David. "Inside Lincoln's Clemency Decision Making," *Presidential Studies Quarterly.* Vol. 29, No. 1, March, 1999), PPS 84-99.

https://www.jstor.org/journal/presstudq

Ryan, David D., Ed. *A Yankee Spy in Richmond the Civil War Diary of "Crazy Bet" Van Lew.* Mechanicsburg: Stackpole Books, 2001.

Ryan, Joe. "The Gettysburg Letterbook of General Robert E Lee Army of Northern Virginia," AmericanCivilWar.com

https://americancivilwar.com/authors/Joseph_Ryan/Articles/Lee-Historical-Documents/Army-of-Northern-Virginia-Documents.html

Ryan, Thomas, J. *Spies, Scouts, and Secrets in the Gettysburg Campaign.* El Dorado Hills: Savas Beatie LLC, 2015.

"Sailor's Creek Sayler's Creek,"
American Battlefield Trust.
https://www.battlefields.org/[158]
learn/civil-war/battles/sailors-creek[159]

"The Savannah Privateers," Richmond Enquirer, October 11, 1861. Rep. from New York Evening Post.

http://chroniclingamerica.loc.gov/

Scheel, Eugene. "Underground Railroad - Journey to Freedom Was Risky for Slaves and Guides," *The History of Loudoun Coun-*

---

158. https://www.battlefields.org/learn/civil-war/battles/sailors-creek

159. https://www.battlefields.org/learn/civil-war/battles/sailors-creek

ty, Virginia. http://www.loudounhistory.org/history/underground-railroad.htm

Schroeder, Patrick A. "Joseph Hooker (1814-1879)," *Encyclopedia Virginia.* Virginia Foundation for the Humanities in Partnership Library of Virginia.

https://www.encyclopediavirginia.org/Hooker_Joseph_1814-1879#start_entry

Schultz, Duane. *The Dahlgren Affair.* New York: W.W. Norton & Company, 1998.

Scott, Phil, "American History: 1864 Attack on New York," *HistoryNet.* Originally published *American History Magazine,* January 2002.

http://www.historynet.com/[160]

american-history-1864-attack-on-new-york.htm[161]

"Second Battle of Winchester," *Wikipedia.*

https://en.wikipedia.org/wiki/[162]
Second_Battle_of_Winchester[163]

"Second Battle of Charleston Harbor," *Wikipedia.*

https://en.wikipedia.org/[164]
wiki/Second_Battle_of_Charleston_Harbor[165]

160. http://www.historynet.com/american-history-1864-attack-on-new-york.htm

161. http://www.historynet.com/american-history-1864-attack-on-new-york.htm

162. https://en.wikipedia.org/wiki/Second_Battle_of_Winchester

163. https://en.wikipedia.org/wiki/Second_Battle_of_Winchester

164. https://en.wikipedia.org/wiki/Second_Battle_of_Charleston_Harbor

165. https://en.wikipedia.org/wiki/Second_Battle_of_Charleston_Harbor

Seddon, James. "Report of the Secretary of War," *War Department, Confederate States of America.* Richmond: November 3, 1864.

https://babel.hathitrust.org/cgi/pt?id=dul1.ark:/13960/t6j10vv5q;view=1up;seq=1

Selcer, Richard. "South's Feuding Generals – November '99 America's Civil War Feature," *HistoryNet.*

http://www.historynet.com/souths-feuding-generals-november-99-americas-civil-war-feature.htm

"Servants and Slaves in the White House of the Confederacy[166]," (Embedded Video) *The American Civil War Museum.*

https://acwm.org/learn-and-do/online-resources/video-resources/video-servants-and-slaves-white-house-confederacy

Shaara, Jeff. *Gods and Generals.* New York: Ballantine Books, 1996.

Shaara, Jeff. *The Last Full Measure.* New York: Ballantine Books, 1998.

Shaara, Michael. *The Killer Angels.* New York: Ballantine Books, 1974.

"Sherman's March to the Sea," *History.com,*

February 22, 2010.
https://www.history.com/[167]
topics/american-civil-war/shermans-march[168]

---

166. https://www.youtube.com/watch?v=CYmOiHURZeQ

167. https://www.history.com/topics/american-civil-war/shermans-march

168. https://www.history.com/topics/american-civil-war/shermans-march

"Siege of Petersburg," *Wikipedia.*

https://en.wikipedia.org/wiki/[169]
Siege_of_Petersburg[170]

17th Street Farmers' Market," *Richmond, Virginia.*

http://www.richmondgov.com/[171]
FarmersMarket/History.aspx[172]

Seward, William H., "Appeal to a Higher Law," *Classic Senate Speeches,* March 11, 1850. https://www.senate.gov/artandhistory/history/common/generic/Speeches_Seward_NewTerritories.htm

Seward, William H., "Irreconcilable Conflict Speech," *The World's Famous Orations,* Bartleby.com, October 25, 1858.

http://www.bartleby.com/268/9/16.html

"Sherman's March to the Sea, *Wikipedia.*

https://en.wikipedia.org/wiki/[173]
Sherman%27s_March_to_the_Sea[174]

"Siege of Vicksburg," *Wikipedia.*
https://en.wikipedia.org/wiki/Siege_of_Vicksburg

"Siege of Yorktown (1862)," *Wikipedia.*
https://en.wikipedia.org/wiki/Siege_of_Yorktown_(1862)

169. https://en.wikipedia.org/wiki/Siege_of_Petersburg

170. https://en.wikipedia.org/wiki/Siege_of_Petersburg

171. http://www.richmondgov.com/FarmersMarket/History.aspx

172. http://www.richmondgov.com/FarmersMarket/History.aspx

173. https://en.wikipedia.org/wiki/Sherman%27s_March_to_the_Sea

174. https://en.wikipedia.org/wiki/Sherman%27s_March_to_the_Sea

Simpson, Brooks, D. "Jefferson Davis Rejects Peace With Re-union, 1864," *Crossroads.*

https://cwcrossroads.wordpress.com/2013/03/03/jefferson-davis-rejects-peace-with-reunion-1864/

Singer, Jane. *The Confederate Dirty War.* Jefferson: McFarland & Company, Inc., 2005.

Singer, Jane. "The Fiend in Gray," *The Washington Post,* June 1, 2003

https://www.washingtonpost.com/archive/lifestyle/magazine/2003/06/01/the-fiend-in-gray/818f9565-ca66-4ccc-b70d-c5023229966a/?noredirect=on&utm_term=.04ed36188438

"Sir James Steuart on the Managed Market," *Economic Thought And Political Theory.* ed. Kluwer Academic Publishers, 1994.

"The Situation," *New York Herald,.*

October 31, 1863, Page 6.

https://chroniclingamerica.loc.gov
"The Situation," *New York Herald,*
November 28, 1863, Page 6.
https://chroniclingamerica.loc.gov
"The Situation, *New York Herald.* December 14, 1863, Page 4.
https://chroniclingamerica.loc.gov

Siebert, Wilbur. *The Underground Railroad, a Comprehensive History.* Waxkeep Publishing, 2015; First published New York: The MacMillan Company, 1898.

Smith, Andrew F. Smith. "Did Hunger Defeat the Confederacy?" *North and South,* May 2011, Vol 13, Number 1.

http://andrewfsmith.com/wp-content/themes/wooden-man-nequin/pdf/HungerArticle.pdf

Smith, Michael Thomas. "Benjamin F. Butler (1818–1893)," *Encyclopedia Virginia*. Virginia Foundation for the Humanities in Partnership Library of Virginia.

https://www.encyclopediavirginia.org/Butler_Benjamin_F_1818-1893#start_entry

Solensky, Richard, Author. Bellows, Alan, Ed. "The Confederacy's Secret Agent," *Damn Interesting*.

https://www.damninteresting.com/the-confederacys-special-agent/

"The Sons of Liberty in Court Trial of H.H. Dodd.; TESTIMONY OF FELIX G. STIDGER. MILITARY CHARACTER OF THE ORDER. THE COMMITTEE OF THIRTEEN, *The New York Times,* October 2, 1864.

https://www.nytimes.com/1864/10/02/archives/the-sons-of-liberty-in-court-trial-of-hh-dodd-testimony-of-felix-g.html

Soodalter, Ron. "The Plot to Burn New York City," *The New York Times*, November 5, 2014.

https://opinionator.blogs.nytimes.com/2014/11/05/the-plot-to-burn-new-york-city/

"Southern Bread Riots, *Wikipedia*.
https://en.wikipedia.org/wiki/Southern_bread_riots

Smith, Stephen Trent. "The Great Libby Prison Breakout," Historynet.
http://www.historynet.com/[175]

---

175. http://www.historynet.com/great-libby-prison-breakout.htm

great-libby-prison-breakout.htm[176]

"Southern Women with Northern Sympathies," *Richmond Examiner*, July 29, Page 3.

http://www.civilwarrichmond.com/written-accounts/newspapers/richmond-examiner/10-7-29-1861-condemnation-of-two-ladies-living-on-church-hill-who-are-attending-the-yankee-wounded-elizabeth-van-lew-and-her-mother

"Speech of John Preston to the Virginia Convention," *Causes of the Civil War*, April 4, 2015.

http://www.civilwarcauses.org/preston.htm

Speer, Lonnie R. *War of Vengeance Actos of Retaliation Civil War POWs*. Mechanicsburg: Stackpole Books, 2002.

"Spencer Kellogg to be executed at Camp Lee today for spying, *Richmond Daily Dispatch*, September 25, 1863, Page 1.

http://chroniclingamerica.loc.gov/

"Spying in the Civil War," *History.com*, 2011.
http://www.history.com/topics/american-civil-war/civil-war-spies

"St. Albans Raid," *Wikipedia*.

https://en.wikipedia.org/[177]
wiki/St._Albans_Raid[178]

"St. John's Episcopal Church & Churchyard," *Architecture Richmond*.

---

176. http://www.historynet.com/great-libby-prison-breakout.htm

177. https://en.wikipedia.org/wiki/St._Albans_Raid

178. https://en.wikipedia.org/wiki/St._Albans_Raid

http://architecturerichmond.com/inventory/st-johns-episco-pal-church-and-churchyard-5/

"St. Paul's Episcopal Church,"
Architecture Richmond.
https://architecturerichmond.com/[179]
inventory/st-pauls-episcopal-church/[180]

"Star of the West is Fired Upon, this Day in History January 9, 1861, *History.com,* 2009.

http://www.history.com/this-day-in-history/star-of-the-west-is-fired-upon

"State of Opinion in the North," *Richmond Daily Dispatch,* July 24, 1862, Page 2

https://chroniclingamerica.loc.gov

Stauffer, John. "Yes, There Were Black Confederates. Here's Why," *The Root, January 20, 2015.*

https://www.theroot.com/yes-there-were-black-confederates-here-s-why-1790858546

Steers, Edward, Jr. "A Rebel plot and germ warfare," Washington Times, November 10, 2001.

https://www.washingtontimes.com/news/2001/nov/10/20011110-031019-5285r/

Stidger, Felix Grundy. *Treason history of the Order of the sons of Liberty.* Chicago: Printed by Author, Felix Grundy Stidger, 1903. Digitized and reprinted by University of California Libraries.

179. https://architecturerichmond.com/inventory/st-pauls-episcopal-church/
180. https://architecturerichmond.com/inventory/st-pauls-episcopal-church/

Still, William. *The Underground Railroad.* New York: Dover Publications, Inc. 2007; First published, Philadelphia: Porter & Coates, 1872.

"Stonewall Jackson," *Wikipedia.*

https://en.wikipedia.org/[181]
wiki/Stonewall_Jackson[182]

Stuart, Meriwether. "Samuel Ruth and General R. E. Lee: Disloyalty and the Line of Supply to Fredericksburg,1862-1863," *The Virginia Magazine of History and Biography, Vol. 71, No. 1, Part One,* January, 1963.

https://www.jstor.org/stable/4246915

"Suspension Of The Writ Of Habeas Corpus," *Civil War Authority.com.*
https://civilwarauthority.com/writ-of-habeas-corpus/

Sutherland, Daniel E. "Culpeper County during the Civil War," *Encyclopedia Virginia.* Virginia Foundation for the Humanities in Partnership Library of Virginia.

https://www.encyclopediavirginia.org/Culpeper_County_During_the_Civil_War#start_entry

Swick, Gerald D. "Virginia's Great Divorce," America's Civil War Magazine. *HistoryNet,* March 5, 2013

http://www.historynet.com/virginias-great-divorce.htm

Synder, Anna. "Playbill: John Wilkes Booth Performed at the Ford's Theatre Before Assassinating Lincoln at Ford's," *Ford's Theatre.*

https://www.fords.org/blog/post/playbills-john-wilkes-booth-performed-at-fords-before-assassinating-lincoln-at-fords/

Tapp, Bruce. "The Joint Committee on the Conduct of the War," *Essential Civil War Curriculum.*

http://www.essentialcivilwarcurriculum.com/the-joint-committee-on-the-conduct-of-the-war.html

"Ten Facts About Harpers Ferry," *Civil War Trust.*

http://www.civilwar.org/battlefields/harpersferry/harpers-ferry-history-articles/ten-facts-about-harpers-ferry.html

"10 Facts: Malvern Hill," *Civil War Trust.*
https://www.civilwar.org/learn/articles/10-facts-malvern-hill

"Theatrical," *Richmond Daily Dispatch.*
September 14, 1863, Page 2.

Third Battle of Winchester, *Wikipedia.*
https://en.wikipedia.org/wiki/Third_Battle_of_Winchester

"Ten Facts The Petersburg Campaign,"
American Battlefield Trust.
https://www.battlefields.org/[183]
learn/articles/10-facts-petersburg-campaign[184]

"Terrorist Conspiracy: Hotel Bombings," *"The Lehrman Institute Presents: Mr. Lincoln & New York."*

http://www.mrlincolnandnewyork.org/new-york-politics/terrorist-conspiracy-hotel-bombings/

---

183. https://www.battlefields.org/learn/articles/10-facts-petersburg-campaign
184. https://www.battlefields.org/learn/articles/10-facts-petersburg-campaign

Thad Tate, "Henry, Patrick," American National Biography Online[185], February 2000.

"To Patriots of All Parties,"
Richmond Enquirer, August 10, 1860.

http://chroniclingamerica.loc.gov/
"Thomas Hines," *Wikipedia.*
https://en.wikipedia.org/wiki/Thomas_Hines

"Thurston, David," *Dictionary of
Canadian Biography.*
http://www.biographi.ca/[186]
en/bio/thurston_david_11E.html[187]

"The Trip of the President's Suite," *New York Herald,* February 24, 1861, Page 1.

http://chroniclingamerica.loc.gov/

"Thrilling Narrative. Escape from Richmond," *Chicago Tribune,* February 24, 1864, Page 1.

https://chroniclingamerica.loc.gov/

Tidwell, William A. *Confederate Covert
Action in the American Civil War.*

Kent: Kent State University Press, 1995.

"GENERAL ORDERS NO. 1. Troops Detailed to Preserve the Peace and Prevent Rebel Incursions, *The New York Times,* November 7, 1864, Page 1

185. https://en.wikipedia.org/wiki/American_National_Biography_Online

186. http://www.biographi.ca/en/bio/thurston_david_11E.html

187. http://www.biographi.ca/en/bio/thurston_david_11E.html

https://www.nytimes.com/1864/11/07/archives/tomorrows-election-gen-butler-in-command-in-the-state-of-newyork.html

Towne, Stephen E. Surveillance and Spies in the Civil War. Athens: Ohio University Press, 2015.

"Troop engagements of the American Civil War, 1862," *Wikipedia.*

https://en.wikipedia.org/wiki/Troop_engagements_of_the_American_Civil_War,_1862

Tsouras, Peter G. *Major General H. Sharpe.* Oxford: Casemate Publishers, 2181.

Tucker, Spencer. American Civil War: *The Definitive Encyclopedia and Document Collection.* Santa Barbara: ABC-CLIO, LLC. 2013.

"Turning Point of the American Civil War," *Wikipedia.*
https://en.wikipedia.org/[188]
wiki/Turning_point_of_the_American_Civil_War[189]

"2 Yankee officers at Libby to be hanged in retaliation for E. Tennessee murders. To draw straws," *Richmond Daily Dispatch,* May 19,1863, Page 1.

http://chroniclingamerica.loc.gov/

"Ulysses S. Grant," *Biography.com*
https://www.biography.com/people/ulysses-s-grant-9318285

"Ulysses S. Grant," *Wikipedia.*

---

188. https://en.wikipedia.org/wiki/Turning_point_of_the_American_Civil_War
189. https://en.wikipedia.org/wiki/Turning_point_of_the_American_Civil_War

https://en.wikipedia.org/[190]
wiki/Ulysses_S._Grant[191]

Ulysses S. Grant and the American Civil War," *Wikipedia.*

https://en.wikipedia.org/wiki/
Ulysses_S._Grant_and_the_American_Civil_War

"Union or Secession," *Magazine of the Library of Virginia,* Winter, 2011.
https://www.lva.virginia.gov/news/broadside/2011-Winter.pdf

"Unionism in Virginia during the Civil War " *Encyclopedia Virginia.* Virginia Foundation for the Humanities in Partnership Library of Virginia.

http://www.encyclopediavirginia.org/[192]

"Ulric Dahlgren," *Wikipedia.*
https://en.wikipedia.org/wiki/Ulric_Dahlgren

"Varina Davis," *Wikipedia.*
https://en.wikipedia.org/wiki/Varina_Davis

Varhola, Michael, J. *Everyday Life During the Civil War.* Cincinnati: Writer's Digest Books, 1999.

"Varina Howell Davis (1826–1906)," *Encyclopedia Virginia.* Virginia Foundation for the Humanities in Partnership Library of Virginia.

http://www.encyclopediavirginia.org/[193]

190. https://en.wikipedia.org/wiki/Ulysses_S._Grant

191. https://en.wikipedia.org/wiki/Ulysses_S._Grant

192. http://www.encyclopediavirginia.org/Letcher_John_1813-1884#start_entry

193. http://www.encyclopediavirginia.org/Letcher_John_1813-1884#start_entry

Varon, Elizabeth R. *Southern Lady, Yankee Spy: The True Story of Elizabeth Van Lew, a Union Agent in the Heart of the Confederacy.* New York: Oxford Press, 2003.

"Vicksburg Campaign," *HistoryNet.* http://www.history.com/topics/american-civil-war/vicksburg-campaign

"Virginia Convention of 1861," *Encyclopedia Virginia.* Virginia Foundation for the Humanities in Partnership Library of Virginia.

http://www.encyclopediavirginia.org/[194]

"Virginia Governor's Mansion," *National Park Service, U.S. Department of the Interior.* https://www.nps.gov/nr/travel/richmond/GovernorsMansion.html;

"Virginia's Reactions to John Brown's Raid on Harper's Ferry, October 16-18, 1859," *University of Richmond UR Scholarship Repository,* 1972. http://scholarship.richmond.edu/cgi/viewcontent.cgi?article=1585&context=honors-theses

"Virginia and Tennessee Railroad," *Wikipedia.*

https://en.wikipedia.org/[195] wiki/Virginia_and_Tennessee_Railroad[196]

Walls, Dr. Bryan. "Henry "Box" Brown," *Freedom Market: Courage & Creativity* , adapted from PBS Series, Public Broadcasting Service (PBS), 2012.

http://www.pbs.org/black-culture/shows/list/underground-railroad/stories-freedom/henry-box-brown/

---

194. http://www.encyclopediavirginia.org/Letcher_John_1813-1884#start_entry

195. https://en.wikipedia.org/wiki/Virginia_and_Tennessee_Railroad

196. https://en.wikipedia.org/wiki/Virginia_and_Tennessee_Railroad

Wagner, Margaret, E., Gallagher, Gary W., Finkelman, Editors. *Library of Congress Civil War Desk Reference.* New York: Simon & Shuster, 2002.

Wagner, Margaret E. *Library of Congress Illustrated Timeline of the Civil War.* New York: Hachette Book Group, 2011.

"War News, The Battle of Bethel Church," *Lancaster Ledger.* June 19, 1861, Page 2.

http://chroniclingamerica.loc.gov/lccn/sn84026900/1861-06-19/ed-1/seq-1/

Weitzel, Godfrey. Manarin, Louis H., Ed. . *Richmond Occupied Entry of the United States Forces into Richmond, VA. April 3, 1865.* Library of Congress. https://www.civilwarrichmond.com/images/pdf/occupied.pdf

"What would have happened if Robert E. Lee attacked Philadelphia," *Quora.*

https://www.quora.com/What-would-have-happened-if-Robert-E-Lee-attacked-Philadelphia

Wheelan, Joseph. *Libby Prison Breakout: The Daring Escape from the Notorious Civil War Prison.* Philadelphia: Public Affairs, Perseus Books Group, 2010.

"Which side had the more effective cavalry during the Civil War?" YoExpert
http://american-history.yoexpert.com/civil-war/expert/18382.html

"While Union forces corner Robert E. Lee, the Confederacy's capital goes up in flames" *The Washington Post.* March 27, 2015. http://www.washingtonpost.com/sf/style/2015/03/27/wars-end/?utm_term=.4afbbe23a55c

"White House of the Confederacy," *Wikipedia.*
https://en.wikipedia.org/wiki/White_House_of_the_Confederacy

"White House of the Confederacy, Part 1," (Embedded Video), *C-Span.*
https://www.c-span.org/video/?306591-1/white-house-confederacy-part-1

"Why did the South invade the North,"
Historynet.
http://www.historynet.com/[197]
why-did-the-south-invade-the-north.htm[198]

William Averell's Cavalry Raid on the Virginia & Tennessee Railroad," Historynet.

http://www.historynet.com/william-averells-cavalry-raid-on-the-virginia-tennessee-railroad.htm

William Tecumseh Sherman, *Wikipedia.*

https://en.wikipedia.org/[199]
wiki/William_Tecumseh_Sherman[200]

Williams, T. Harry. *Lincoln and His Generals.* New York: 1952: Alfred A. Knopf, Jr. 1952.

Wolfe, Brendan. "Chancellorsville Campaign," *Encyclopedia Virginia*, Virginia Foundation for the Humanities in Partnership Library of Virginia.

197. http://www.historynet.com/why-did-the-south-invade-the-north.htm

198. http://www.historynet.com/why-did-the-south-invade-the-north.htm

199. https://en.wikipedia.org/wiki/William_Tecumseh_Sherman

200. https://en.wikipedia.org/wiki/William_Tecumseh_Sherman

https://www.encyclopediavirginia.org/chancellorsville_campaign

Wyss, Johann David. *Swiss Family Robinson*. London: Godwin's Juvenile Library, 1814.

"Yellow Fever Plot," *The New York Times*, May 24, 1865, Page 5. (Reprinted from *Toronto Globe*, May 22, 1865.)

https://timesmachine.nytimes.com/timesmachine/1865/05/24/issue.html?action=click&contentCollection=Archives&module=LedeAsset&region=Archive-Body&pgtype=article

Zombek, Angela M. "Belle Island Prison," *Encyclopedia Virginia*. https://www.encyclopediavirginia.org/[201] Belle_Isle_Prison#start_entry[202]

Zombek, Angela M. "Castle Thunder Prison," *Encyclopedia Virginia*. https://www.encyclopediavirginia.org/[203] Castle_Thunder_Prison[204]

201. https://www.encyclopediavirginia.org/Belle_Isle_Prison#start_entry
202. https://www.encyclopediavirginia.org/Belle_Isle_Prison#start_entry
203. https://www.encyclopediavirginia.org/Castle_Thunder_Prison
204. https://www.encyclopediavirginia.org/Castle_Thunder_Prison

Made in the
USA
Columbia, SC